THE HOLLAND FAMILY S...

# Part II

# UNDYING LOVE

## by

## CLEVER BLACK

I first would like to thank God above for blessing with the ability to tell a story. From him, my talent flows. As we move forward with this Saga, a lot of things are going through my mind, namely the nervousness of releasing this sophomore installment to the Holland Family Saga. It is my every intention to deliver a solid, cohesive story filled with characters that will provoke emotions from my readers, be it good or bad. May you like, love and yes, hate some of them as you delve deeper into the Saga.

Speaking of readers, I would like to thank everybody that purchased, downloaded for free, or borrowed Part One. Whatever your opinion, I thank you all for taking the time to read my first novel. Moving forward, I would like to thank all of the Book Clubs and their readers for supporting the Saga. A special thanks goes out to Black Faithful Sister and Brothers Book Club and its members.

Carla Towns, thanks for your enthusiasm. Gabrielle GotemHatin Dotson, thanks for adding me to the group. Dama Cargle and Arabia D, y'all crazy, brer. Well, family, here we go! Happy Reading!

Clever Black.

ISBN: 978-0-9853509-6-3

This is strictly a work of fiction. Any references to actual events, real people, living or dead, or actual localities, is to enhance the realism of the story. Events within the novel that coincide with actual events is purely coincidental.

All material copy-written and filed on site at the Library of Congress.

# The Holland Family Saga Part Two

# The Holland Family Saga Part Two

# CHAPTER 1

## A LETTER HOME

### September, 1944

*My dearest love, Veronica Jenkins,*

*Words can't began to express how much I love and miss you, my dear. Being far away from home in this foreign country of enemies has indeed gained me greater appreciation for the things we have back in America. Much work still needs to be done, but the atrocities I've seen here can't compare to the troubles we as a race of people face back home. War, in my eyes, is hell on Earth. There's no other way to describe it, lover. As you already know, every other day I sit in my P-51 Mustang and guard those flying coffins that rain down death on occupied Germany. Flying coffins, I call the big bombers that name because so many of the men aboard those crafts never make it home. I often hear the agonizing screams of men, some I know, as they are in their final seconds of life, hurdling towards a fiery crash. What gets the bombers are the countless little black clouds of smoke that seem harmless—until one explodes right beside one of the planes. The black clouds, they call it flak, is relentless and indiscriminate towards the metal and flesh that lie in its seething, white-hot path. Going down inside one of those bombers has to be one of the worst ways for a man to die, Veronica. Pure hell. But us fighter pilots don't have it any easier as you've already learned. I've decided to name my new plane 'Henrietta', after this newborn baby who opened my eyes and unknowingly showed me just how serious this war really is, and what it means to people like her and her surviving family.*

*When I was shot down in June over the Black Alps, this nurse, who lived in a small village of sheepherders and farmers, helped save my life by hiding me inside a wall deep in the village church's basement. She gave me her baby to hold and told me her name just before she and the rest of her congregation went and approached a squadron of German Soldiers who were looking for downed American pilots.*

*The soldiers those people encountered weren't just German ground troops, they were Waffen SS—and for the Waffen—if you weren't German—then you were a part of the problem. They killed them all, Veronica. Defenseless civilians they killed. At least two dozen. They lined them all up in front of the church and gunned them down simultaneously. It was only by the grace of God the SS didn't set the church afire as many Waffen SS troops were known to do.*

*I held this baby in my arms for two days and she didn't cry one time. The Germans were plundering the village, raping women, and shooting old men, women and children at random while trying to get them to tell them if there were any Americans hiding in their village. Those who knew, kept silent, even in the face of death. Brave people they were. I remained hidden with this baby for what felt like an eternity; and all we had was this tin kettle that I would let fill with dew at night and drink in the morning to carry us through. I knew we were in danger, and it was as if this little girl knew we were both being hunted and it was in her best interest to remain still and quiet. She's a survivor.*

*On the third day, French Troops along with members of the 86th Infantry Division fought off the small platoon of Germans that had occupied the village and rescued us both. I turned the baby over to the French Troops, and when they asked me her name, I said, 'Henrietta'. Her last name was Boudreax. I pointed out her mother's corpse as troops were lining bodies up to be identified and walked away wondering. I wonder what will become of Henrietta Boudreax, only weeks old. I may not have the answer, but from what I've seen, it tells me that if we don't win this war, children like Henrietta will perish. I will do my part to give her a chance at life. It is my duty to not let her fate become that of her parents, and countless other civilians entrenched in this war of attrition. After seeing the corpse of that child's mother and the other citizens of this tranquil village, bodies which lay stiff and decaying outside the church for over two days, I know why we fight, Veronica. That little girl now flies with me everyday. I fly and fight for people like Henrietta.*

*I can't wait until my tour is done and I'm able to return stateside. We have so much to look forward to, Veronica. Kids. Grandchildren. I want a family for us. Tell the rest of the ladies at the sewing factory to keep up the good work, and let the congregation know that the boys are fighting the good fight with optimism and victory in sight. Many of our men need those jackets and rubber masks that you all are putting together for us and shipping over here to Italy and we are very appreciative.*

*I have to be honest, Veronica, it's not very nice over here because if the racism, but through it all, the white bomber crews know very well that the Tuskegee Airmen are the best support they could ever have in defending them against the Luftwaffe. This war seems endless, and it's getting worse by the day. I don't know when I'll be home exactly, all I can say is that my time is close; but don't count the days, please, don't count the days. I am unafraid, and I expect the same from my wife. This chapter we will finish and start anew stateside.*

*I miss your smile, Veronica, your beautiful eyes, and the warmth of your body next to mines. I love you, Misses Jenkins. Keep me in your prayers and thoughts, and I'll do the same for you.*

*Love Always, Benjamin.*

Twenty seven year-old Benjamin Jenkins sat on his cot stuffing the letter he'd just written to his wife, on a clear starry night in September of 1944, into an envelope to get it ready to send home. Benjamin Jenkins was Captain of a squadron of African American fighter pilots that were known as The Red Tails. The squadron of all black fighter pilots ran missions from bases in Ramitelli, Italy, across the Adriatic Sea, into occupied Yugoslavia and Poland. Benjamin and his squadron's job was to provide air support to the heavy B-17 and B-24 bombers that pounded Germany and surrounding areas during the violent air campaign taking place in 1944. The bombers had the task of destroying the oil refineries in occupied Poland and other countries, a strategic assignment that was extremely crucial to wiping out the German Luftwaffe.

Benjamin had been overseas for two years fighting the Axis Powers. The man looked forward to returning to the United States to be rejoined with his junior high school sweet heart, and now wife, Veronica Jenkins. He placed a picture of himself standing beside his newly named plane, *Henrietta*, into the envelope and sealed it, and walked briskly to the mail center to mail his letter. Along the way, he ran into his wing man, another pilot by the name of Wilbur Hughes, who accompanied him to the mail center.

Benjamin and Wilbur met during training in Tuskegee, Alabama in January of 1942 and had been friends ever since. Assigned to the 332 Fighter Squadron of the Army Airforce, both men had become aces within three months of actual combat, meaning they each had shot down no less than five enemy aircraft. Wilbur often talked to Benjamin about his family back in Philadelphia; and Benjamin would relate stories about how his wife had taken it upon herself to aide in the war effort by volunteering to work at a sewing factory back home in New Orleans, Louisiana shortly after he enlisted into the Army.

The two men walked out of the mail room and lit cigars as they walked in front of a long row of silver P-51 Mustang fighter planes that were parked beside a long dirt runway. The night air was cold and crisp, only a dim light from headquarters, a rickety tan canvas tent, which contained the mail room, could be seen; but it soon went out so as not to give away the American position from the air.

"It won't be too long now Captain." Wilbur said as he puffed on his cigar. "The boys on the ground got the Germans' backs against the wall in the Black Alps. Command say they may make a stand on the Austrian border."

"There's a lot of oil fields there. Don't be surprised if we get called up to aide the big bombers tonight." Benjamin replied as he paused in front of Henrietta.

"I can't wait. We have a good chance of depleting the German Luftwaffe with their ground forces retreating. We got 'em on the run, my friend." Wilbur remarked.

Benjamin laughed in the darkness.

"What's funny?" Wilbur asked.

"I never thought I'd meet someone who loves being in the air more than me."

Wilbur laughed as his tall lanky frame swayed side to side. He shoved Ben playfully and said, "I signed up because they told me I couldn't fly. I wanted to prove them wrong. That's the very reason you signed up, man. And now, they can't get rid of us. Flying is addictive."

Benjamin spoke lowly, stating that he agreed, just as a loud siren was heard, letting the pilots know it was time for an airstrike. The two men ran towards their headquarters and met up with several dozen other pilots and were soon greeted by their commanding officers. The two Generals walked up to the airmen and they parted in order to let the two middle-aged white men through. The two Generals paused midway down the parted group of Negro airmen and saluted the men before they walked into the command center. The pilots all followed and took seats inside the medium-sized canvas tent with a dirt floor and waited in silence.

One of the Generals pulled down a map of Europe with red lines marking a flight path.

"Gentleman!" the General spoke loudly. "Tonight we hit the oil refineries in the city of Blechammer, Poland. You will be providing support for B-17s in the Fifth Bombardment Wing. These synthetic oil refineries are a main fueling center for the Luftwaffe and they will do all they can to defend this location. You men know your jobs—so do it well! We take to the air at twenty-four hundred hours." the General ended.

Several hours later, just as the sun began to break the horizon, three-hundred and nineteen B-17 bombers from the Fifth Bombardment Wing were closing their bomb bay doors to turn and head back to friendly airspace. They had encountered relentless flak during their bombing campaign; but they still accomplished their goal by completely demolishing the oil refineries; although ten bomber planes and crews, one hundred men in total, were lost in the heavy flak as they approached their target.

The German Luftwaffe was now closing in to finish off the remaining bombers, which could not make evasive maneuvers as they were too big and slow. They had no choice but to hold formation and ward off the German fighters with the .50 caliber machine guns aboard their planes. The morning sky was soon full of tracer bullets and exploding aircraft as the dogfight got underway. Many of the bombers were calling out for help. "Little friend", a term often used by bomber pilots in distress to get the Tuskegee fighters' attention, was being yelled repeatedly.

Benjamin and Wilbur were trailing a German plane that had a bead on a beloved B-17 bomber's tail. The tail gunner had been shot and killed and the plane was being torn to shreds from the rear and in danger of being shot down.

"Captain, I'm going below deck." Wilbur radioed to Benjamin. "I'm going to swing in underneath that son-of-bitch and get him to pull off our boys. You attack him from the top once I distract him."

Benjamin looked down towards the ground and could see numerous flak clouds. "There's heavy flak down below, Wilbur. They're expecting that maneuver. The Nazis are setting some of the flak at low altitude to hit the fighters." he radioed back.

"Darnell and the boys are in trouble! I'm not leavin' them, Captain!"

Benjamin yelled aloud again for Wilbur to remain at his current altitude but Wilbur descended anyway—right into the flak.

Benjamin opened fire on the German fighter trailing the bomber and his plane exploded in mid-air. "I got 'em! I got 'em! Wilbur you can pull up now!"

It was then that Benjamin heard Wilbur scream aloud, "I'm hit! I'm hit!"

Through the chaos and smoke, Benjamin spotted Wilbur's plane going down in flames. He watched Wilbur's plane fall towards the ground as he listened to his friend's terrifying screams emanating from the radio. Wilbur called out to God and asked for the forgiveness of his family repeatedly until his radio began to emit static. He'd just slammed into the Earth.

Benjamin had just lost his best friend; but he had no time to mourn. A German ME-109 was heavy on his tail. Benjamin didn't realize he was being targeted at the out-set. He kept feeling small pings hitting the exterior of his plane, vibrating the metal bird slightly, and he began looking around. He quickly caught sight of the German fighter to his rear and realized that the pings were bullets coming from the German plane's machine guns. Smoke began pouring from the left wing of the plane.

"Not again! Henrietta! Keep daddy in the air!" Benjamin said aloud.

Benjamin knew if he turned sharply either way, the Me-109, which had a sharper turning radius than the P-51, would turn inwards and have a clear line of fire. To dive below deck meant the severe possibility of facing Wilbur's fate. Benjamin was facing a serious dilemma, but opportunity lay just ahead. Just to Benjamin's right about a half mile ahead was the B-17 bomber plane that Wilbur had been trying to protect, a B-17 bomber plane named *Murderous Rowe*.

*Murderous Rowe* was a crew of ten white men; all from Benjamin's home state of Louisiana. What made the plane special was the fact that it had a white bomber pilot that always spoke highly of the Tuskegee Airmen and requested their services during every bombing run, an act which created an affinity towards the plane from many of the Tuskegee Airmen, including Benjamin. *Murderous Rowe* was an experienced and brave crew; as were all the Airmen. The bomber crew had flown into enemy territory with Benjamin's squadron countless numbers of times; and each time, Benjamin, and Wilbur had made it a point to protect the plane.

The pilot of the bomber plane, 1st Lieutenant Darnell Rowe, was from New Orleans, Benjamin's hometown. The two had a good rapport in the air. Darnell always sought out Benjamin after a bombing run and would tip his wing, a way of saluting Benjamin, the man he always said was "the best damn fighter pilot the Army Airforce has ever seen". The two admired one another's abilities in the air, even though they had never met in person on the ground as the white bomber crews and black fighter pilots were always segregated. Darnell's gunners weren't slouches either; they had racked up more German fighter kills than any other B-17 bomber crew in their bombardment wing.

"Murderous Rowe," Benjamin radioed, "I have an ME that I can't shake. How's your left gunner?"

"Krauts is everywhere! Left gunner down! Tail gunner out of commission! Engineer blown to pieces!" Darnell replied just as another cloud of flak exploded beside the plane. "Son-of-a bitch!"

"I'm whizzing by on the right then! Get your right gunner to spray this Nazi on my tail and I'll cover you the rest of the way!"

"If ya' comin' ya' better come soon, Jenkins! We gettin' ate up over here!"

Benjamin made a slight turn to the right, but not enough to give the German fighter a clear shot. He flew towards the right side of *Murderous Rowe* and the right gunner opened fire, aiming at Benjamin's plane. That tactic was on purpose, as the right gunner knew by the time his bullets reached Benjamin's plane, he would be clear and the German fighter would absorb the bullets.

When Benjamin passed the big bomber, the .50 caliber bullets shattered the canopy on the ME-109, decapitating the German pilot's skull. The plane twirled violently and dropped out of sight.

"Another Nazi headed to hell," the right gunner radioed proudly through his oxygen mask.

"Thanks boys! I got your asses covered from here on out!" Benjamin radioed back.

Benjamin, with one good wing on Henrietta, shot down two more German ME-109s that were trying to attack *Murderous Rowe* and had saved the lives of seven men aboard the plane. During this battle, over Blechammer, Poland, Benjamin had attained the status of Double Ace. He'd shot down ten enemy aircraft up until this point. Five kills was a rarity—ten was unheard of. Benjamin Jenkins had become a legend within the ranks of the Tuskegee Airmen on this day in September of 1944.

Returning to his base in Italy, and after debriefing the Generals and informing them of Wilbur's death, Benjamin returned to his bunk and sat on his cot and cried in silence as he stared at Wilbur's empty cot. The mirror beside the downed pilot's bed contained pictures of his wife and two young sons. Benjamin could only imagine the heartache that Wilbur's family was due to face. He got up and walked over to his friend's cot and began to pack his belongings to have them shipped back to America.

The following morning, Benjamin was back at the mail center with Wilbur's possessions and a handwritten letter to his family.

"Better write two," the mail clerk said.

Benjamin looked at the clerk with a puzzled look as he was handed a telegraph. He opened the telegraph and read the first two sentences: *You have been relegated to ground duty for the next week as you await transfer back to London. Your tour of duty has expired. Great job!*

It was a bittersweet announcement for Benjamin; but good news all-the-more. The mail clerk then gave him a telegraph addressed to Wilbur and Benjamin knew right away that it was identical to his. Benjamin had finished his tour of duty, Wilbur, however, fell short by one mission. The somber Captain kept Wilbur's telegraph in his possession. He couldn't bring himself to put the message in with Wilbur's belongings as he believed it would only add more grief to Wilbur's family if they were to know that he was scheduled to return stateside the day he was killed. Benjamin knew it was selfish, but he wanted to spare Wilbur's family unnecessary heartache and not prolong their grief.

After mailing Wilbur's things back to America, Benjamin went and sat inside *Henrietta* and wrote one last time and wrote one last letter home to his wife, stating that he would call her the moment he landed back on American soil and let her know the date of his arrival back to the city of New Orleans. The man had served his country and was now looking forward to spending the rest of his life with his beloved wife. Benjamin arrived home in early November of 1944, having fought for over two years. His wife eagerly greeted him at the small airport on New Orleans' Lakefront.

Veronica Jenkins, a light-skinned, 5' 9" one-hundred and forty-five pound, grey eyed woman ran into the arms of her husband and shed tears on his shoulder. She had missed the man dearly the two years he was away fighting the war and it felt so good just to touch him.

"Hey lover," Veronica then said in a loving tone towards Benjamin as she stood before him wearing a pink dress and white three inch heeled shoes. A white head scarf covered her shoulder length, wavy brown hair; but Veronica's most precious asset, her gorgeous grey eyes, which were teeming with joy, were hidden from Benjamin's sight by a pair of huge, dark sunglasses.

"Hey lover," Benjamin responded as he placed his duffel bag on the ground and removed his wife's sunshades to stare into her eyes.

Veronica batted her eyes as she adjusted to the sunlight and Benjamin couldn't help but to exhale and smile in delight. His wife's eyes were the prettiest pair eyes ever created to him. The man removed his beret and pulled his woman into his six-foot two-hundred pound frame and planted a passionate kiss on her lips. They remained embraced, rocking to and fro, eyes closed, smiling gently and stroking one another's back, repeatedly professing their love and stating how much they missed one another. Veronica could have remained right there in her husband's arms, but she was awakened from her trance when she heard Benjamin whistle towards a taxi. He ushered his wife inside and the two were whisked away.

The taxi pulled up to their cozy, three bedroom home which was located on Flood Street in New Orleans' Lower Ninth Ward section. All was quiet as the two approached the front door. When Veronica unlocked the door and entered the home, she hurriedly turned on the lights. When she did, a huge crowd of people yelled, "Welcome Home Benjamin!"

Benjamin was surprised to see his living room full of members of his church cheering and congratulating him. The war veteran was nearly moved to tears as people in the crowd hugged him one by one and welcomed him home from the war.

Veronica had decided to throw a huge party for her husband's return stateside. She prepared a dinner fit for an army battalion: spaghetti and meatballs, garlic bread, green peas, fried chicken and baked macaroni and cheese and string beans and dinner rolls. She also made an apple pie from scratch, and placed an American flag on top of a homemade chocolate cake in celebration of America's seemingly inevitable defeat of the Axis Powers.

Jazz music was popular during the forties, and Veronica had amassed a huge record collection consisting of Louis "Satchmo" Armstrong, Dizzy Gillespie, and a young, up and coming crooner by the name of Nat King Cole. The group partied into the wee hours of the morning doing the various swing and tap dances that held sway over the country. It was a festive mood to say the least.

"I'd like to propose a toast!" Veronica yelled aloud over the music and the dancing crowd as she tapped a fork against her champagne glass, "I'd like to congratulate my beloved husband!" she said as the music was lowered and the crowd quieted. "I would like to toast Captain Benjamin Jenkins! They said a Negro couldn't fly a plane! My husband, and many more men like him, in color and spirit, proved just how wrong they were! I love you, baby! Welcome home!"

The crowd erupted into cheers and the party continued on into the early morning hours.

Later, after all the party goers had gone to their respective homes, Benjamin and Veronica were inside their kitchen stacking dishes in the sink. They were sincerely trying to tidy up their place but they just couldn't keep their hands off one another. They blushed at one another and constantly and purposely brushed up against each other's body. Benjamin placed the cake dish into the sink and as he did so, he pressed his loins against Veronica's derriere.

"Mister Jenkins!" Veronica gasped playfully.

Benjamin grabbed his wife and turned her around to face him. Veronica's mouth was agape, a slight smile on her face and her grey eyes were full of want.

"Are you going to take me here? Take me now? An impatient man you are, Mister Jenkins! We have to clean up our home!" Veronica remarked in mocked concern over cleaning the home.

"I haven't seen you in over two years, Veronica. Everyday I dreamt of you while I was away, baby. I fought hard to return to you, woman. Veronica, you, you are my world. My everything, and my reason for being. Nothing else matters. I missed you, baby." Benjamin said as he gripped Veronica tightly as kissed her lips.

Veronica dropped the champagne glasses she held in either hand and let them crash to the floor as she cried aloud through gasps of air as she kissed her husband, "Benjamin! Your, your home! I missed you! I missed you!" she exclaimed as she began to cry and kiss her husband passionately.

The two kissed one another hungrily as they wrestled with one another towards their bedroom. Benjamin's uniform, shoes and head gear, left a trial from the kitchen to the bedroom. Veronica's pink corsage, white pumps and ultimately the pink dress she wore was left in the hallway as well.

Veronica fell back onto the bed, resting upon her elbows as Benjamin now hovered above her and slowly pressed his body flat upon hers. They lay back and locked hands and kissed passionately as Benjamin penetrated his wife, an act which emanated a moan of delight and relief from both lovers who'd been hungering for one another for over two years. Cries of pleasure were soon emanating from both lovers and within a few short minutes, they climaxed together.

As they lay side by side in all their nudity, body hairs matted, and their flesh sticky with drying sweat, Veronica asked, "Where do we go from here, lover?" as she lay with her head on her husband's broad chest.

"Baby, I would love for us to travel. Let's take a trip cross the country. Just the two of us."

"I thought you wanted kids. You talked of us having kids in your letters. I want kids, too. Don't you want to have a family?" Veronica asked contentedly as she nuzzled against her husband with her eyes closed and a tranquil smile on her face.

"I want a family, Veronica—but I want to enjoy us. Can it just be you and I for a while? And then we can have kids. Let's travel first."

"Okay, lover. But how can we travel? We don't even own a car."

"I can buy us a car to get around town, but I'm talking about really traveling. Let's take a long train ride."

"A train ride across country? Sounds, romantic, my love."

"It will be, baby. It will be." Benjamin replied as he ran his hands through his wife's hair and kissed her once more.

Over the next few months, Veronica and Benjamin lived a peaceful and humble life. The two would attend church regularly and enjoy each other's company at home and the few public places Negroes were allowed to patronize.

Early in March of 1945, Benjamin had purchased his first automobile—a used 1942 black four door Cadillac from a black woman whose husband was killed during the attack on

Okinawa in the Pacific Theater. The car was well-kept and in mint condition. It had a nice paint job and tan interior which was covered with plastic. It also sported thick white wall tires and chrome bumpers.

Benjamin and Veronica loved taking long drives on Sunday afternoons. Louisiana had a lot to see in all its diversity, including pretty sugar cane fields, rolling pastures and mystic swamps.

Benjamin had also saved enough money in order for he and his wife to take that trip they'd discussed several months back. He mentioned it to Veronica as they were riding pass a lush green pasture spotted with numerous grazing cows.

After seeing what a beautiful state Louisiana was, Veronica herself had become eager to take the cross country trip with her husband. The pair set out a month later, taking the train cross country. They visited the Grand Canyon, Hollywood, and took in a ball game at Wrigley Field. They visited numerous historical landmarks throughout the country via railroad, including Mount Rushmore, and the Washington Monument. They topped it off with a trip to New York City where they visited the Statue of Liberty and enjoyed a play on Broadway. The icing on the cake was when the couple visited *Minton's Playhouse* in Harlem and got to see Dizzy Gillespie hold a live jazz session for over four hours with Bud Powell and Al Tinney at his side.

The tour was a refreshing and true blessing for the couple; although it took much longer than expected. Benjamin had church members tend to his home and car while he and his wife were away on a railroad expedition across the country that had taken them almost two years. When they returned home in February 1947, Benjamin and Veronica decided to bring kids into the world. In May of 1948, Benjamin and Veronica Jenkins became parents to Henrietta Jenkins. Benjamin had named his first born daughter after the child he'd rescued, and the very plane that had protected him and enabled him to return home to the United States to start life anew with his wife.

Nine years later, in August of 1957, Veronica gave birth to a little girl whom she and Benjamin named Gabriella Jenkins.

And it is here, with the birth of Gabriella Jenkins in the year of 1957, that part of the foundation to the Holland Family's Saga had been laid.

## CHAPTER 2

## THE ADVOCATE

### January 2005

Twenty-three year-old Katrina McMillan had just stepped off an American Airlines flight onto the gateway at Logan International Airport in Boston, Massachusetts. As she walked through the airport's gateway, Katrina listened to R&B singer Leela James' song titled *When You Love Somebody*, playing in her MP-3 player.

Katrina thought hard about the battle she was undertaking as she walked through the crowded airport listening to the song and its deep, thought-provoking lyrics that somewhat defined her current life's situation. *"Is it worth it? Or am I wasting my time?"* she asked herself.

Katrina had flown from Phoenix, Arizona to Boston against the wishes of her husband, Timothy, to meet with a lawyer on behalf of her life-long friend, Ben Holland. Katrina had been fighting hard since the year 2002, almost three years, to earn an appeal for Ben. She had taken on this endeavor when she first visited Ben in Florence, Colorado back in 2001, after recovering from the gunshot wound she had received in 1999, and getting her life in order down in Phoenix, Arizona.

Now it is January of 2005 and Ben Holland's chances of coming home were looking slim and next to naught in Katrina's eyes. In May of 2004, after his second appeal was rejected by the Colorado State Court of Appeals, Katrina had begun to run out of resources. Her letters to various court judges in Colorado were no longer getting responses. Her husband of three-plus years was of no comfort or support to Katrina at that time and had even encouraged Katrina to give up the appeals process. Something inside of Katrina, however, forced her to continue on, so she decided to hire a lawyer and take Ben's case to the Tenth Circuit Court of Appeals.

Katrina knew she could not hire just any lawyer. The young woman knew if she got Ben Holland a new day in court, the lawyer she hired would have to be the best lawyer to represent Ben because that lawyer would have only one shot at earning Ben Holland his freedom. If the Tenth Circuit, the next court of judges to rule on Ben's appeal, ruled against Ben, Katrina knew the next step would be the U. S. Supreme Court and that battle could take years if it ever was granted a hearing to begin with.

Katrina thought about those things as she walked through the airport, sincerely hoping the lawyer she had found was the right man for the job and up to the task. She was fighting hard for Ben; but she also had problems of her own that she had to deal with back home. Katrina's husband, Timothy McMillan, was a philandering NBA player worth millions, but he paid her little or no attention. Katrina had met the young man at college in Tempe, Arizona during one of her visits to the college campus. She took care of Timothy while they were in college together with two-hundred and fifty thousand dollars that Ben had given her just days before the shootout occurred back in 1999.

Katrina, after a protracted and arduous pregnancy, gave birth to Timothy's child in November of 2000 and they married in June of 2001 while they were still in college. Katrina, during that time, also began looking for an idea to put her money to work shortly after she was married as she had grown accustomed to the freedoms and opportunities that wealth could provide a person. She wanted to open an eatery since her associates in college often complemented her on her New Orleans style cooking ability, a skill she had picked up from her deceased friend Oscar Henderson.

Katrina practiced cooking red-beans and rice, Cajunblackened steak, gumbo, crawfish ettoufe`, spicy stuffed crabs, and numerous other New Orleans-styled entrees. Her colleagues, and a great majority of professors all loved her dishes. People on the campus loved Katrina's cooking so much so, that on weekends, she was compelled to sell dinner plates of food right out of her and Timothy's apartment which was nearby Arizona State's campus. Katrina could easily make a thousand dollars or more over the two day weekend selling deep-fried catfish plates with sides of baked macaroni and cheese and potato salad, and red beans and rice with fried-chicken and homemade Mexican cornbread. The money being made from selling dinner plates, coupled with the money Ben Holland had given her early on, was getting her and Timothy through college and supporting the baby.

Once she felt confident that her products would sell inside of an established place of business, Katrina decided to go through with her idea. In December of 2001, she bought a medium-sized, dilapidated building in downtown Phoenix for a little over one-hundred thousand dollars. She opened the doors to her restaurant in the spring of 2002 and the restaurant had quickly become a hit in the city thanks to the clientele Katrina had created at Arizona State University. Within a few month's time, *The New Orleans Café* had become *thee* place to eat in downtown Phoenix. Katrina's restaurant, which also featured a catering service, was often at the top of lists for various parties, weddings, power meetings, and the like. *The New Orleans Café* had become the talk of the town by the fall of 2002.

Katrina's husband, Timothy McMillan, was drafted by the Phoenix Suns in the first round of the NBA draft in June of 2003 and had signed an NBA contract worth millions of dollars in endorsement deals. Soon after, he bought him and Katrina a luxurious two-story seven bedroom mansion in Mesa, Arizona.

Katrina earned a degree in business management in the fall of 2003 and soon opened another restaurant in the town of Mesa, Arizona shortly thereafter. By the end of 2004, Katrina had made a couple of million dollars of her own from her two successful restaurants and catering firm.

All was good in the beginning for the newly married

couple, but after spending a little time in the NBA, Katrina's husband became an egotistical jerk. After all she had done for him in the past, Timothy, or Tim as he's often called, once he got rich, acted as if Katrina was now beneath him. He turned the tables on Katrina, acting as if he always took care of her and she had never done anything for him in her life. That attitude, coupled with his numerous on-going affairs and mistreatment of his wife had begun to cause serious rifts in the marriage.

Not even two years into her marriage, Katrina found herself constantly thinking hard about divorcing her husband; but for her son Timothy Jr's sake, Katrina chose to stay. Tim would go on the road for a week or two, even during the NBA's off season, and party with dozens of women. He had a woman or two in just about every city that the NBA had a team and Katrina knew it.

She caught on after she began to find condoms in Tim's travel bags when he returned home from road games and "meetings"; not to mention the text messages Katrina often read on Tim's Blackberry whenever he left his phone on the bed when he took a shower. Katrina said nothing. She tolerated the philandering. Besides, she was too occupied with her business endeavors and her overwhelming desire to free Ben Holland. It would be over a period of time, from the year 2003, shortly after her husband joined the NBA, up until the present day in January of 2005 that Katrina's feelings for Ben Holland had grown proportionately.

It wasn't too long after saying a long, heartfelt prayer and crying alone as she sat in her '04 convertible Bentley atop a hill overlooking the city in December of 2004, that Katrina had come to fully understand the reasons she was so downtrodden most times. She had come to realize that after all the time that had passed while she worked on her friend's appeal, she had come to have deep feelings for Ben Holland and he wasn't "home".

Katrina returned home on that warm December night in 2004 and entered her gym and turned on CNN news. She sat down on the soft carpet and ate a grilled-chicken salad as she watched television, thinking of a way to get Ben Holland back into court. As she was being consumed with her thoughts, Katrina saw a twenty second profile on an attorney by the name of Dante` O'Malley on the national news. Katrina did a search on-line for Dante` O'Malley that night and she contacted him by phone the next day.

Katrina and O'Malley had a conversation over the phone, where Katrina learned that O'Malley was a criminal defense attorney of long-standing Irish descent. He'd been married for over twenty-five years, a sign of stability to Katrina, and had entered his career in law over thirty-three years ago. That meant the man was experienced in the world of litigation in Katrina's eyes. Katrina also learned that O'Malley had once turned the tables on the prosecution in an extortion trial up in Boston, Massachusetts which led to the arrest and prosecution of several police officers who falsely arrested his uncle, a reputed Irish mobster, and had gotten the man out of jail.

O'Malley had also recently succeeded in getting a notorious drug dealer from Miami, Florida a get-out-of-jail free-card after it was discovered that three of the arresting DEA agents were taking bribes from the drug dealer. Katrina quickly understood that O'Malley was proficient in the realm of criminal law and was highly successful at getting his defendants off the hook. She agreed right then and there to hire Dante` on behalf of Ben Holland.

Dante` and Katrina talked nearly everyday throughout the month of December and the lawyer had come to know the Ben Holland case fully. When Katrina told him about a newspaper article she had in her possession, Dante` requested a face-to-face meeting the following month. Katrina was over-joyed having found Dante`. She believed finding this particular lawyer was indeed a blessing, and the right fit for Ben.

Katrina walked at a slow pace through the airport searching for Dante`. When she reached the designated rendezvous location, she looked around and pulled back the sleeves of her dark-brown mink coat and matching business suit and checked the time on her diamond crusted Tag Hauer watch, a gift from Ben Holland from back in the day. Katrina's flight was thirty minutes late because of the snowy weather and she hoped Dante` didn't have leave for another scheduled meeting.

She walked into the waiting area where she was scheduled to meet Dante` and looked around but didn't see the man. She placed her hand on her round hips and looked into the mirror at her 5' 7" frame. She then turned to the side and removed her coat in order to get a better view of her plump derriere. She weighed one-hundred and sixty pounds now, a far cry from her high school days when her friends often stated that she resembled actress Kellie Shanygne Williams, who played a character named Laura on a TV sitcom titled *Family Matters*.

Katrina now had a motherly appeal. She was proud of that, but she decided she would work a little harder inside the custom-built gym she had in her mansion back in Mesa, Arizona instead of just eating a salad while watching the news. As she looked at herself in the mirror, Katrina couldn't help but to think that she looked every bit like her mother, Faye Sanders. Her eyes began to water as thoughts of the terrible things her mother had put her through before she was rescued resurfaced.

Katrina wiped her watery eyes as she continued to look at herself in the mirror, all the while wishing her mother had made different choices in life early on. "*Maybe we would still be mother and daughter,*" Katrina thought to herself as she turned and faced the mirror head on. "*I hope she's not real fat in her old age; if she's even still alive. Otherwise I'll look like her when I get older.*" Katrina said to herself as she turned to the side once more and stared at her plump rear end again.

"I know," a voice said softly, "my wife asks me all the time if her behind's too big and I always answer correctly by saying, 'you look the same today as you were the day we married'."

Katrina whipped her neck around having been shaken from her past thoughts by the voice. Her dark-brown eyes grew low and she cracked a smile when she saw fifty-eight year-old Dante O'Malley standing behind her in what she knew to be a custom tailored light grey silk Calvin Klein suit and black matching shoes. The Rolex watch on his wrist was worth at least seventy-five thousand dollars. The black wool trench coat the attorney wore was exquisite and the black felt fedora O'Malley had on gave the six-foot-four tall counselor a distinguished appeal. Katrina was immediately impressed.

Dante` removed his hat and his full head of peppered hair came into view; further impressing Katrina, as she believed O'Malley's peppered hair was a symbol that he was a wise man. O'Malley and Katrina shook hands and the attorney ordered a French vanilla cappuccino for Katrina as he'd learned via phone conversations that Katrina loved French vanilla cappuccinos. The two conversed as they waited for Katrina's drink, and after tipping the waitress, the two headed for the exit.

"Let me hold the package if you don't mind." Dante` requested as the two walked through the crowded airport.

Katrina opened her briefcase and pulled out a manila envelope, which was wrapped neatly in plastic.

"I can't wait to examine this piece." O'Malley said as he grabbed the package and escorted Katrina out the front door into the falling snow towards his waiting limousine.

The two then rode to Dante's exclusive downtown Boston Agency that overlooked Boston Harbor and sat inside his lavish mahogany and leather-filled office behind closed doors. O'Malley pulled out a magnified lens, put on a pair of rubber gloves and gently flipped open the envelope and pulled out a blood-stained newspaper article dating back to March of 1999.

"Hmm," he said, "it looks like it's in fairly good shape. We may have something here, Misses McMillan," he said as he scanned the article with the magnifying lens.

"Please, call me Miss Sanders."

"Ohh, you finally went ahead with the divorce? In only a month's time? I told you to call me. I would've gotten my wife to do that for free."

"No, I'm still married. I just use my maiden name now."

"You still married to that guy? Jesus, Katrina. How can you put up with that guy?"

"I have a son."

"From what I've come to know about your personal life over this short period of time, Katrina, is the fact that you have a very successful business that'll support you and give you and your son the same lifestyle you have now—*without Timothy!*" Dante` said as he continued to look over the newspaper, never looking up at Katrina.

"Let's not talk about Timothy. I can deal with that on my own. I'm here for Ben."

O'Malley looked up at Katrina and reached out and patted her hand. He looked her square in the eyes and said, "I'm sorry. I'm sorry for saying that, Katrina. I just care about your happiness. That was not a lawyer talking. I said that as a concerned friend. Misses O'Malley is an excellent practitioner of family and estate law, you need anything you let us know, okay?"

"Okay. Thank you, Mister O'Malley."

"Call me Dante`. My friends call me Dante`." The lawyer stated as he placed the magnifying lens back before the news article, bringing a smile to Katrina's face.

Dante` wasn't reading the article; he was scanning it for evidence. Katrina had gotten the article when she made a trip back to New Orleans a couple of months ago and visited her friend Kantrell. Kantrell owned a beauty shop in the Ninth Ward, Katrina's old neighborhood and she was the one who had received the article, which originated in Memphis, Tennessee. Kantrell held on to the article, picking it up during all the chaos that transpired after the shootout in 1999. Ben dropped the article when he hopped into his Mercedes with Jason and Oscar in order to follow Katrina's ambulance to the hospital that fateful day. The article described the slaying of three individuals in Memphis, Tennessee and Katrina believed it could be instrumental in her endeavors towards earning Ben Holland his freedom.

"Have you gotten your story together? I mean, can we trust that the witnesses that you believe in and trust completely will testify on Ben's behalf and help me put this case in a different light? Are these people reliable, Katrina?" O'Malley asked.

"They're very reliable, Dante`. They're my friends."

Dante leaned back in his chair and ran his right index finger across his chin as he stared at his client. "We're taking a huge risk here, Katrina," he said as he leaned forward and intertwined his fingers. "You know that, right? If this thing backfires, if the prosecution is able to shred your witnesses, this entire case will blow up in everybody's face."

"My friends will do just fine, Dante`. You don't know them like I do. I wouldn't risk it if I didn't have faith in them."

Dante` knew he was taking a huge risk by taking on this case; but it was a compelling one to say the least. Not to mention it paid well. Still, the lawyer was unsure of the people Katrina was giving him to fight with on Ben's behalf. "If I go in front the judge with this story we're gonna tell and the prosecution produces a witness that can contradict what we say, we are sunk! You hear me? *Sunk!*" Dante` stated.

Katrina was keenly aware of Dante's apprehension; but she also knew he was the right man for the job. She also knew that Dante` knew just as well as she did that Ben was guilty; but there was an angle that could be used to get him out of jail and Dante` knew how to work it. He had done it before and Katrina knew it all-too-well. She wanted this lawyer to fight for Ben like he had done for so many of his clients in the past. Katrina thought about those things as she spoke confidently, "Carmella Lapiente` was the only person able contradict what we are bringing forth, Dante`. She died in an ambush—killed by rival drug dealers south of Brownsville, Texas. It will work because Carmella is out of the picture. Not to mention Sherman is dead. And you can work around those tapes. That's what you do. And you do it so very well." Katrina remarked.

Dante` leaned back in his chair and chuckled. Katrina's attempt at flattery only garnered small percentage points; the man knew he was a first-class lawyer, he just hated to lose a case. "Your patronizing me won't get you far, young lady. But I like it! This case is by far one of the most difficult cases I've ever encountered. We have to be dead on solid in all that we do and say. Are you sure about your friends? And if there are any witnesses that you know of that the prosecution may produce, you have to tell me."

Katrina was getting antsy. She wanted Dante` to commit fully on this day. She spoke again, this time hoping she would get her point across fully concerning possible witnesses for the prosecution, "All the people that either knew of, or even cared that Carmella was Damenga's sister are dead and gone now. The rival cartel that took out Carmella killed Damenga's remaining soldiers during that hit and took over his entire operation. No one gives a damn about the Lapiente` family, Mister, excuse me, Dante`. No one cares about the Lapiente` family so you need not worry about those people. They—are—history! Understand? History! Furthermore, I'm willing to take the stand and testify myself about the events that took place. So if you go down, I go down with you! My ma—Ben doesn't have anything to lose in this matter."

"How long have you loved him?" O'Malley asked, recognizing that Katrina had almost called Ben her "man".

"Ever since the first day I met him," Katrina responded before she sipped her cappuccino and leaned back into the soft leather chair situated in front of O'Malley's huge marble desk.

"I know you have loved Ben since you were a young child," O'Malley stated as he looked Katrina directly in the eyes. "What I'm asking now is, how long have you had feelings towards him like I have towards my wife, Olivia?"

"I don't know Dante`. Maybe they have always been there, but it really grew over the last two years or so, you know?"

"Careful not to let your heart get involved, Katrina. If we're not successful, it can only lead to more disappointment."

"I know Mister O'Malley, but this love for Ben that I have inside of my heart? I can't turn it off, man." Katrina responded as she wiped tears from her eyes. "I just can't turn it off." she ended in a somber tone of voice.

Dante` eyed Katrina as she stared at the floor. Whatever it was compelling this young woman to fight for Ben Holland, it was now beginning to hold sway over his psyche.

"Okay," O'Malley stated, deciding to press further, "we've been going over this case for a month or so, and with this here evidence we have here, we may have a stake in this fight—*if* the evidence corroborates with the things we have gone over. A quick question though—why did it take so long for your friend Kantrell to produce this article?"

Katrina looked up and smiled.

"Mister O'Malley," she said, "where I'm from, people go to jail all the time and they are quickly forgotten about. It's like out of sight out of mind. Kantrell didn't produce that article, I found it. Kantrell only held onto that article because she was a part of some drama that took place back in the day. She picked it up when Ben dropped it and she just happened to keep it. She kept it in this envelope in a drawer behind her chair in her salon—she said it was a part of Black History." Katrina said as she chuckled and continued conversing with Dante`. "I was shocked myself when she showed it to me. But with all the new technology and what not, I figured this article could be the very thing we need to get Ben a new day in court. Especially when I saw the blood stains on it. That has to be worth something, Dante`. For this article to survive for over five years it could be nothing but a blessing."

"You're right Katrina. I've just decided to commit fully to this case. Now, I know how we're going to approach the court, but you haven't told me Ben's connection to Memphis, Tennessee. You told me about Sherman Davis and we can make that story work; but I have to know *Ben's* connection to Sherman, *and* the city of Memphis. I need for you to tell me what happened when Ben Holland went there in 1999."

"I did O'Malley. You know all about Sherman and Ben's affiliation."

"I know Sherman Davis was killed. I know about the guns he supposedly held for Ben—but what else happened? Did Ben Holland really travel to Memphis and murder three people like Sherman stated to the police?"

Katrina was reluctant to tell O'Malley what she knew to be

the truth about the night Ben Holland and his boys went to Memphis, Tennessee in March of 1999; but she also knew that Dante` had to be fully equipped to go in front of a jury. She took a sip of her cappuccino, sighed, and said, "Sherman set the whole thing up and Ben laid out the plan and pulled off the heist, Dante`, but Ben is not like that anymore. You have to believe that."

"It doesn't matter Katrina. I still have to know what happened. Look, I've represented some of the *worst* criminals in society, okay? Including members of my own family. So it's not much I haven't heard or seen."

"This here is different Dante`. Ben, Ben and his crew did some horrible things to people. I don't want you to become opinionated against him. Some of the things he and his boys did that night in Memphis will probably turn your skin pale."

"In order to fight, Katrina, I have to know this case inside and out, up and down and sideways. I'm only trying to help. I've never lost a case, but I will lose this one if you send me into that court room with a gun half-cocked."

"Okay Dante`," Katrina said lowly as she leaned forward and rested her elbows on the desk top. "Here's what I know about that night in Memphis, but don't say I didn't warn you…"

*******

Katrina leaned back and stared at Dante` after relating the details of the night Ben and his crew traveled to Memphis, Tennessee, and just as she had stated moments earlier, Dante`s face had grown pale.

Dante` turned around in his leather executive-style swivel chair and looked out the window of his corner office on the eighteenth floor of the building and just stared blankly at the falling snow. He was thinking about his uncle and some of the stories he'd heard early on. Dante's uncle was a hit-man for the Boston and Philly Irish mafia families during the late sixties and throughout the seventies. He'd heard stories of his uncle having shot people in the back of the head and blowing up rival mafioso in cars. Dante` knew his uncle was brutal; but his uncle was affiliated with the Irish mafia—that was their style.

Ben Holland and his gang's brand of violence was exceedingly brutal and rare for a criminal not affiliated with any nationally known criminal organization, if Dante` had to tell it.

"Are you okay, Dante`?" Katrina asked, shaking Dante` from his thoughts.

Dante` turned back and faced Katrina. "I'm sorry for my rudeness. I was just digesting the things you told me. I'm not opinionated against your friend. I was just thinking that criminal enterprises haven't changed much since the old days. So, Carmella Lapiente` was the woman inside of the house?" Dante` asked Katrina as he got up to pour himself a shot of dry Scotch.

"Yeah. Oscar shot her two times in the head with a .357 magnum and she survived. Ben told me she had to have heard him call out Manny's name and she remembered it."

Dante` motioned towards his bar, offering Katrina drink. When she declined, he continued with his assessment of the situation in Memphis. "So, Ben Holland made a connection with Damenga Lapiente` shortly after the home invasion and Carmella, when she came through a couple of months later, told her brothers that a man named Manny attacked her. And this guy Manny, via an unfortunate twist of fate, happened to be a member of Ben Holland's crew. Correct?"

"Yes. But Damenga didn't kill Manny. Manny was killed over a fight—a simple fight with this dude named Rico who I used to fu—this dude I was dating. Damenga was still trying to find out who pulled the hit and he was cool with everybody at the start, but when Sherman got busted in Memphis with crack cocaine he tried to cut a deal to keep from going to jail by turning state's evidence. He told the feds that he knew about a triple murder in North Memphis, only he didn't know he was ratting to people that were working for Damenga and Carmella. Damenga's people killed Sherman after Sherman gave up Ben 'nem and then they went after Ben and his crew. Damenga` had it in for any and everybody affiliated with Ben after Sherman gave up the goods. Damenga's people killed my friend Lamont and then shot up his funeral. That was the day Anna died. They even blasted me in the stomach when they were trying to kill

Ben. It was a big mess, Dante`. Ben killed Damenga` in retaliation for what he did to me and Anna that day—not to cover his tracks. That's why I believe the story we put together will go over well with the jury." Katrina stated.

"Did Ben Holland ever harm any children?"

"Why you ask me that, Dante`?" Katrina asked with a confused look on her face.

"You told me about the little girl that was killed along with Sherman. That was hideous. I may represent criminals—I may not be opinionated against my clients— but I am sternly biased against anyone who harms a child. I don't represent those kinds of criminals no matter how winnable the case is."

"Dante`, please! Ben and his boys may have been ruthless —but they were in the game. You know yourself what goes down in the life. Ben didn't seek out nor harm those not affiliated with the game. Ben and Manny 'nem saved me from a life of desolation. My mother sold my body for sex when I was a little girl. Manny killed the man that raped me and he and Ben brought me into their life completely not too long after that. They fed me, bought me clothes and kept me in school and out of trouble—most of the time. I owe a lot to Ben and Manny, may he rest in peace. Believe me, Dante`, Ben Holland would never harm a child."

"I heard that story from you before. I'm sorry about your childhood, Katrina."

"We, we all grew up hard no doubt, Dante`. We had the attitude like, 'we from that nine and we don't mind dying'. Like we didn't give a damn. But when it got down to it, we all gave a damn. For a lot of us, it's too late, but for the ones that's still alive, we all making changes for the good."

"I believe you Katrina. Okay now," Dante` stated as he sat back down at his desk and placed the newspaper article back into a plastic bag, "it may take a couple of months for the data to come back on this piece of evidence; and that of the gun I found down in Memphis as well," O'Malley stated, "but my people are the best, they won't miss anything. If the evidence is here to coincide with the story we're going to sell—your friend will definitely have to go back before the judge. And if we can sell this story, which I firmly believe we will be able to do, Ben Holland will walk free, I promise." he ended as he leaned back in his chair and crossed his legs.

"What about the drug trafficking charge? The money laundering and racketeering charges as well?"

"I can get a dismissal on the money laundering since Ben didn't make any money from the airport hangar he leased. At least there is no paper work to document that he did. That'll work in his favor. The drug trafficking charge I can have thrown out since no drugs were ever found and that in itself will clear up the racketeering conviction. The right charge would have been conspiracy to run a criminal enterprise. Ben got lucky on that because conspiracy is hard to disprove. The public defender Mister Holland had really helped the government stick-it-to 'em; but he kept him from getting a conspiracy charge. Looks like he did one thing right. He left the door open for us, Katrina; but I still have to clean up that guy's mess before I can begin my battle. No need to worry about those things though. What we will have to worry about is the taped confession from Sherman Davis on the three murders in Memphis, and the footage of Ben murdering Damenga` and Alphonso inside the airport down in New Orleans. The prosecution will use those tapes to convince the jury that Ben killed Damenga` and his brother Alphonso to cover his tracks based on Sherman's statements. I'll file a motion to examine the tapes myself. My plan is to use those tapes to convince the jury that Ben acted in blind rage. If we sell this story and persuade the jury that he didn't murder anyone in Memphis, he will walk free." O'Malley said, smiling at Katrina.

Katrina smiled back as she reached into her pocketbook and handed O'Malley a check for three-hundred and fifty-three thousand dollars.

"I only needed twenty percent upfront." O'Malley stated in a surprised manner before he got on the phone and requested that his secretary have his chauffeur bring his wife and car around to the front of the building.

"I believe this will be the first and last time we have to sit here in your office like this. There will be no need to regroup, Dante`. The first time we go to court, they'll set a date for his release. It's been too long, and I believe God is thinking the same thing." Katrina replied.

"You're a woman of strong conviction, Miss Sanders. If the world had half the faith as you, we'd all live a more fulfilling life on this planet." Dante` stated as he got up and walked over and grabbed he and Katrina's coats from the coat rack.

"I don't think I have the power change the world, Dante`, but when you love somebody, you do what you can to change their life for the better." Katrina replied as Dante` helped her place her coat back on before she gathered her belongings.

Katrina and Dante` exited his office and rode the elevator down to the first floor and walked briskly through the blowing snow towards his limousine which was double parked in front of the building with its flashers blinking in the snowfall. They entered the limousine and Katrina was immediately greeted by Mr. O'Malley's wife, Olivia, who was waiting patiently inside the limousine, enjoying the soft sounds of saxophonist Kenny G's song, titled *Songbird*. Katrina greeted the woman with a handshake and the trio headed towards *Bull and Finch,* the original restaurant that was featured in the comedy show *Cheers* at Dante`s request.

Katrina tried her best to get her name engraved onto the pub's wall of fame by eating the *Norm Burger*, which is a giant double cheeseburger, but she just couldn't finish the sandwich.

The trio took doggy bags and headed to the O'Malley's home in Bainbridge where Katrina rested until her return flight was ready. She awoke a couple of hours later and the O'Malley's took her to the airport. As she rode with the O'Malley's, Katrina wondered what Ben Holland, the charismatic, light-skinned, 6' 2" gangster was doing in Florence, Colorado, hundreds of miles away, across two time zones.

## CHAPTER 3

## THE VISITOR

### January, 2005

I was lying in my bed listening to the radio when my cell door unlocked and in walked Yiska. I got up and greeted the Indian as he handed me a cup of coffee—black no sugar. "This kind of potent Yiska. Ain't much to do but sleep around this joint on a cold day like today. Why you tryin' to keep me woke? You need help taking down that young buck?"

Yiska had just come from the warden's office after having a fight with another inmate who made a comment about the seventy year-old man wearing his snow-white hair in pigtails. Yiska, although his name was of Navajo Indian descent, was a member of the Shoshone (show-sha-knee) Indian tribe that resided in the Snake River Valley in the state of Idaho. His name means "the night has passed". Yiska was serving a life sentence for murder and conspiracy against the U.S. government after he tried to rob the U.S. Mint in Denver, Colorado back in the seventies.

"I don't need your help to take down a fuckin' wanna-be gangster, Benjamin." He replied in his raspy, slow-pitched voice. "I gave you that coffee to keep you awake because I have a very strong feeling that a journey into a new chapter of your life is about to begin. You have a visitor, Ben. And I believe you are about to hear some good news. Someone has a story to tell you." Yiska stated to me in a low tone and continued, "I know from past conversations that you do not like this person, but the knowledge this person possesses may free you of the nightmares that you have been having."

Yiska had now aroused my curiosity. For almost two years I have been plagued by nightmares of my parents' homicide. I often dreamed of that terrible night. In my nightmare, I could see a blazing fire and my mother with her blood-covered face running towards me. My father would be silent but I could see him lying on the ground on his stomach. I would see a hand lifting something off the ground and an object fly through the air into the fiery inferno that was once our motel room. At that moment, my mother would fall a few feet away from me and I would awaken in a cold sweat crying to myself.

I quickly stood up and followed Yiska down the corridors into the visiting room, all the while intrigued by this new visitor as Yiska walked past me and turned around and stared at me. I could tell by the look on his face that he knew I would possibly be angry by what he was about to show me; but I also had the feeling that he knew that all the forgotten memories and unanswered questions about my parents' life lay just on the other side of the double doors that were on the opposite side of the room.

"Okay! He's ready now!" Yiska yelled.

One of the double doors slowly opened and there before my eyes stood my aunt, Henrietta Jenkins. Henrietta had thrown me out of a house in March of 1989 that was supposedly purchased for me in 1984 shortly after my parents were killed. It wasn't too long after my eviction that I turned to a life of crime. From that point forth, I secretly blamed Henrietta for my lot in life. I felt as if she had forced me to become a person I had no intention on becoming. Through her, I was able to justify my actions.

After a while though, with Yiska's help, I was able to forgive Henrietta—and myself; but I could never forget the way she rejected me and forced me out onto the streets. I slept in a homeless shelter for a few days until I met Anna and then I met a young man named Manuel 'Manny' Lawson Taylor Jr. shortly thereafter. The rest, as they say, is history.

I stared impassively at Henrietta, thinking back to the day she had thrown me out of that house. I needed money for clothes at the time and Henrietta had refused to give me a portion of my parents' insurance that was left for me. We were in the den of the home arguing…

New Orleans

March 1989

…"Etta, I need my money! I ain't had nothing new since Christmas! It's fucking March!"

"I don't care what month it is, Benjamin! I'm barely making it as it is. I feed you and you have a bed to sleep in. That's good enough for now until things get better. You have clothes in there from last spring and summer anyway, don't you? I know you want new items right now, but I simply can't afford it. I'm sorry." Henrietta replied as she sat at her dining room table with a calculator, never even bothering to look up at me.

"That's my mutherfuckin' money," I yelled. "You been stealing from me from day one! You ain't mean my momma and daddy no good from the get go!"

Henrietta removed her eyeglasses and stared at me with wide eyes, I knew she was dismayed by manner in which I was talking to her, but I didn't care because at the time I felt like she was fucking me and my parents over by misusing the funds. "How could you talk to me in that manner, Benjamin? And then you bring Gabriella and Samson into this discussion?" she said to me as she rested her hand against her chest and eyed me with a heartbroken look on her face. "I'm the only family member alive now that's willing and able to take care of you. I'm all you have left in this world and I'm doing the best that I can for you, son."

"Fuck you, brer!" I snapped as he walked out of the dining room.

"That's it!" Henrietta yelled aloud as she slammed her fists onto the table. She then stood up in frustration as tears began to flow down her cheeks. Henrietta, through her tears stared at me and said, "Every day you find a way to disrespect me,

Benjamin and I'm sick and tired of it! We both lost Gabriella! She was my *heart*! My baby sister! My *only* sister! How do you think I feel?"

"I don't care how you feel! All I know is ever since my momma and daddy died, you been—"

"Let them be! Let *her* be! God I can't take anymore!" Henrietta yelled aloud as she franticly waved her arms in the air and stormed past me. She opened the front door to the house and said, "Get the hell out!"

"This my house!" I yelled back.

"No, it's not!" Henrietta cried as she ran into the dining room and grabbed the deed to the house off the table and showed it to me. "This is *my name* on the deed! *I* own it! It ain't yours! So you get the hell out of here! I don't *have* any more money and I'm tired of you talking to me like I'm some trash off the street! And then you constantly, constantly throw Gabriella and Samson in my face every God-forsaken day of my life! Get the hell out of my house!"

*******

I had a stoic look on my face as I stared passively at Henrietta as she stood on the opposite side of the medium-sized visiting room. I could see Henrietta had aged well. She didn't look too much different than the last time I saw her back in March of 1989; although she wore thicker glasses and had added maybe about fifteen pounds to her 5' 7" tan-skinned frame. I guess she weighed around one-hundred and fifty pounds. She still had that beautiful tan skin and long brown hair that I could remember as a teenager as well. She looked at me in an apologetic and loving manner as she slowly walked in my direction, her face covered in tears and her arms slightly spread as if she was prepared to embrace me.

In spite of the turbulent, troubled past we both shared, this woman, my *mother's* sister, had the story of my family's history and I so desperately wanted to know that story. Yiska nudged me forward and I walked towards the aging woman and wrapped my arms around her. I could hear her exhale as she gripped my back and apologized again and again and cried on my shoulder. She had found me. The last link to my biological family had searched for, and found her only living relative. Henrietta looked up and told me she had a story to tell. I knew at that moment that I had to learn all over again who I was and where it was that I had come from.

The three of us, Henrietta, Yiska, and I sat down at a table in the corner of the room as Henrietta wiped her tears with a handkerchief. The woman could barely keep her composure as she looked into my eyes and told me that she had breast cancer and didn't know if she would survive for much longer. She also said she was visiting me in order to make amends. The emotional wounds that Henrietta inflicted on me still cut deep, but she was my blood. I forgave her in secret at this moment; but I also knew the two of us had so much to modify— Henrietta more than I as I felt that I was only a child at the time.

Fair or not, it was how I felt about the situation. Henrietta could have been stronger, but maybe she was being as strong as she could have been at the time given the circumstances. Either way, after nearly sixteen years of not speaking to me, Henrietta grabbed my hand tightly and looked at Yiska cautiously and then looked back at me. I told her that Yiska was family and it was okay for the Indian to listen to the things she was about to tell me as I made small circles on the table top with my finger tips, an act in which I noticed had brought an immediate smile to Henrietta's face.

"You have to know about your grandparents. We, we never talked about them after your parents passed away. Do you remember their last name?"

"No. I never knew my grandparents. I only know us as being Hollands. I thought that was all to it."

"No Ben, it's more, much more. We are Jenkins'. Your mother's last name was Jenkins in the beginning. Let me tell you a story about your grandfather that you must hear though, Ben."

\*\*\*\*\*\*\*

I listened as Henrietta told me of my grandfather's days as a fighter pilot during World War Two and the events leading up to the birth of she and my mother.

"Do I resemble my family?" I asked after hearing Henrietta's story.

"You are a mixture of them all, Ben. I see a little bit of each of them in you, especially, your mother. You have your grandfather's eyes, just like me. You have your father's physique. But my God, you look every bit like your mother. You have your mother's complexion and hair, her insatiable smile, and you have a habit of making little circles with your finger tips whenever you're anxious about a matter. That comes from your grandmother."

"My mother named me after my grandfather, right?"

"Yes. You were named after your grandfather, Benjamin Jenkins."

"And you were named after the plane he once flew, right?"

"Yes. The protector. That's what your grandfather called me, 'the protector'. Your mother, Gabriella? That was his 'little angel'. We had a wonderful life at the out-set."

I leaned forward and clasped Henrietta's hands tightly, "My grandmother, Veronica, what was she like?" I asked.

Henrietta chuckled and leaned back in her chair.

"My God! She, she was wonderful! My mother, my mother was—*to me?* The greatest! She was the strongest, most bravest woman I have *ever* known, Ben!" Henrietta stated proudly. "Let me tell you about her."

"Before you do that, let me ask you something, Henrietta."

"What, Ben?" Henrietta asked as she donned an anxious look.

I knew right away that Henrietta was thinking that I was going to ask her why she put me out of her home in 1989 and I have to admit, it felt good to see her sweat a little. I knew my

Aunt regretted what she had done though; the look on her face when she first laid eyes on me had spoken volumes. Henrietta was growing ever more worried, I believe she was holding her breath. I was smiling inside, but I decided not to make Henrietta dread what was coming any longer. I looked her in the eyes and asked with a smile, "How old are you now?"

Henrietta exhaled, patted her chest, then smiled and looked away briefly before she looked me in the eyes and said, "I'm fifty-six, Ben. I make fifty-seven on May tenth of this year. That day is very special to me as you will come to learn."

"You look years younger, Henrietta. And you have a lot of history behind you."

"Thank you, Ben. I do have history behind me, and I want to share that history with you. Can I?" Henrietta asked me in a meek tone.

I nodded calmly to say yes.

"Thank you, Ben. Just to let you know, this, this is going to be hard for me to relive some of these things. I've carried these memories with me all my life. After Gabriella died, *I* wanted to die. My sister was my everything. Your mother," Henrietta paused and began to cry, "she was my heart, Ben."

I watched as my Aunt broke down and cried openly. Yiska got up to get Henrietta a glass of water and she thanked him as she pulled out a bottle of pills. I'm guessing they're anti-depressants. She took two pills before she began fanning herself, "I'm sorry. From, from time to time, the memories come back on me real heavy. It seems like it was just yesterday when your mother was alive and healthy. I, I can't remove Gabriella's life from my mind. And I miss her so much, Ben."

I got up and walked around the table and pulled a chair up beside Henrietta and hugged her tightly as she leaned into my chest and cried aloud. She hadn't spoken a word about my mother's life but she was already breaking down. I have only four years or so of memories of my mother's life and no memories of my grandparents' life; but Henrietta knew everything. The memories she had, and the emotions she carried within were emotions I wanted to feel—love and joy, I mean—I already felt the tragedy, having lost my parents early on, and some of my closest friends years later, along with my freedom.

Henrietta looked at me with tear-filled eyes and exhaled, "Okay, I'm ready, Ben. Let me, let me tell you about our family."

As Henrietta began to speak, I closed my eyes and she began to reveal my family's history to me. I sunk into my chair and imaged in my mind what life was like for my grandparents, whom I've never seen or known, and also my parents as Henrietta began to bring to life chapters of my family's history that took place a long time ago, during an era that was forgotten all too soon.

## CHAPTER 4

## THE EARLY YEARS

"Mommy, it's nine 'o' clock! Put the song on for daddy!" Nine-year old Henrietta Jenkins yelled aloud to her mother.

Henrietta was residing with her mother, father and four month old baby sister Gabriella in a cozy, three bedroom home on Flood Street in the Lower Ninth Ward section, a predominately Black neighborhood on the outskirts of the city of New Orleans, Louisiana in December of 1957. It was a cold Friday night, just ten days before Christmas and Henrietta Jenkins, a skinny tan-skinned little girl with long brown hair and thick glasses, sat perched on the large window sill in the living room anxiously awaiting the return of her father, Benjamin Jenkins.

Benjamin now worked a couple of hour's drive away in Hattiesburg, Mississippi as a mid-shift supervisor for a large lumber mill. Rather than make the long drive twice daily to and from Hattiesburg, Benjamin would sleep in a trailer that was on the lumber yard's premises during the work week. Benjamin and Veronica had discussed the situation over eight months ago when Benjamin first agreed to take the new position. Veronica expressed her concerns about her husband's welfare; but Benjamin assured Veronica that he was protected on the premises at all times. Benjamin had been working at the lumber mill for nearly seven years and he always carried a .38 revolver to ward off any potential threats from the Ku Klux Klan or anyone else. The man was willing to risk his own safety in order to support his family as jobs for Black men were hard to come by in the late fifties. Although Veronica feared for her husband's safety, as racism was alive and flourishing throughout the south, especially in Mississippi, they both knew that the new position Benjamin was offered paid well; and with two small children, one a soon-to-be new born, Veronica knew she and Benjamin needed the income the job provided in order to support their two daughters.

Veronica held onto Gabriella tightly as she strolled from the kitchen and took the baby's hand and waved it towards Henrietta. Henrietta enthusiastically waved back at her little sister and mother.

"Mommy, it's time for daddy's song!" Henrietta stated again.

Veronica placed the four-month old child into a play pen and happily went to the record player in her living room and placed the needle onto the album and cranked the phonograph. When the music began to play, Veronica began to rock slowly to the music, her medium-built frame gyrating to Sam Cooke's song, *You Send Me*.

"Henrietta, get off that window sill! I told you you're going to knock over my flower arrangement someday! Here," Veronica added as she stretched out her hand, "come and dance with your mother."

"Here comes daddy!" Henrietta yelled as she leapt from the window sill, leaving her mother to dance alone.

Henrietta always looked forward to her father returning home on Fridays. Fridays were special to Henrietta because she got to stay up late whilst waiting for her father to return home. Benjamin would get off work at 7 P.M. and arrive home at exactly 9 P.M. Veronica would fix a huge dinner, usually pot roast with scalloped potatoes, candied yams, collard greens, fried chicken, cornbread, and homemade strawberry shortcake. Henrietta also knew that her father would always have a special gift for her. Benjamin would usually have a new baby doll, roller skates, or a new dress for his oldest daughter. Whatever he bought, Henrietta would always be pleased.

On this night, however, Henrietta knew that Christmas was only ten days away and she eagerly anticipated her father returning with the gift that Santa Claus had given her father to give to her. Henrietta rushed out of the door and ran and jumped into her father's arms. Benjamin had to drop the two boxes he held in order to grab his little girl. The man fell back against his '55 Thunderbird, laughing loudly as his daughter hugged his neck tightly. He cradled her in his arms as he walked towards his wife who was standing in the cold night air. Veronica wiped her hands on her apron, shifted her dress and brushed her long brown hair from her face and welcomed her husband with a hug and a soft kiss on his cheek. They stared into one another's eyes and made soft cooing sounds, telling each other how much they missed one another. After bringing in the two boxes, Benjamin walked over to the playpen and picked up his youngest daughter, Gabriella, and the baby started crying.

"Your hands are cold, Benjamin," Veronica said, as she grabbed the baby from her husband's hands and lovingly ordered him to warm them with hot water.

Benjamin warmed his hands and returned and held his precious daughter close to his heart while dancing to Sam Cooke's song *That's Heaven To Me.* Sam Cooke's lyrics created a soft serenity throughout the Jenkins home. "This is my little angel right here!" The man said as he stared into Gabriella's beautiful grey eyes and sung the lyrics to the song.

With tranquility, Gabriella stared into the eyes of her father. Her mouth was open and she smiled at the man who held her close to his heart. She was obviously comfortable in the arms of the towering figure who cradled her so lovingly and securely. Benjamin then looked over to Henrietta, who was dancing with her mother and announced that he had the most beautiful family in the world. Henrietta walked up to her father cheerily as he sat down on the sofa. As she shifted her eye glasses, Henrietta asked her father if he'd seen Santa.

"Well, I sure did my little protector. I sure did," he answered, "and he said he was so busy that he would have to bring your gifts personally on Christmas Eve!" Benjamin said as he placed his fedora on Henrietta's head.

"Did you tell him about the bike and the baby doll house?" Henrietta asked excitedly as she held on to the hat.

"Of course I did, Henrietta. He said he has those two items on hold especially for you!"

"I love you, daddy!" Henrietta said as she sat down next to her father and rested her head on his shoulder as she grasped her little sister's hand.

Sam Cooke continued to play as Veronica finished setting the table for dinner. When she returned to the living room twenty minutes later, she saw that all three were sleeping, nuzzled up against one another. Veronica awoke Henrietta and Benjamin, took Gabriella and laid the baby in the crib in Henrietta's bedroom, and the three ate dinner together.

Weekends went by fast in the Jenkins' household. Benjamin would spend every waking hour with his wife and two children. They would play board games, cards, and go for long drives on Saturdays. Sunday morning was spent in church and Benjamin would then take his family out for lunch. They would return home and relax the remainder of the evening as Veronica prepared dinner. During this time, Benjamin would review Henrietta's school work from the previous week and play his albums. The man loved to sing and he had an angelic voice. Henrietta would sometimes join him and the two would have the best of times as Veronica listened, and Gabriella rocked to and fro in her rocker.

When Henrietta would awaken on Monday morning, her father would be up, having fixed breakfast. This time was for Benjamin and his oldest daughter to be alone. Henrietta enjoyed these moments because her father would entertain her and pique her curiosity with various questions about the things she learned at her elementary school since he had last seen her. Henrietta would also ask her father questions about the rest of her world during those times. Benjamin had the hardest time explaining to Henrietta why the family had to drink from a different water fountain than white people whenever they were out in public and why they had to use the back entrance to some of the restaurants they visited. Henrietta also noticed that the white students who attended the segregated schools had new text books while hers and that of the other black students in her school were falling apart and/or missing pages. She asked her father why those things were.

"It's not always the tools that you have Henrietta, but it's what you do with the tools you are given." Benjamin said confidently to his daughter.

"I know daddy, but if I'm missing pages, I can't fully understand what the teacher is asking. And the teacher won't let us Negro students look in her book to see the missing pages because she said niggers aren't allowed to use the new text books and should just be happy with what we already have."

*"You are not a nigger!"* Benjamin said angrily, slamming his fists onto the table, frightening Henrietta.

Benjamin had to tolerate racial slurs, even though he was a supervisor at his job, and it hurt the man to hear that his daughter was being called a *nigger* by a teacher at her school. "I'm sorry for frightening you, Henrietta. It's, what's going on now just doesn't maker sense. I long for the day when people in this country can get past the color of a person's skin and take a person for what he or she is worth," he said to his daughter in a sincere tone of voice.

"Daddy, this math teacher said my grandmother had sex with a white man and that's how me, Gabriella and momma get our light skin. Is that true?"

"That white woman doesn't know anything about our family, Henrietta. Look at your father. I'm a tan-skinned black man with black curly hair. Your mother is a beautiful woman with light skin, grey eyes and long brown hair. You have tan skin and brown eyes like me, and long brown hair like your mother. Gabriella has curly black hair like me, grey eyes and light skin like your mother. Both of you look like the two of us, understand?"

"Yes, daddy. It's just isn't nice at school all the time. That's why I wanna be a teacher when I grow up." Henrietta replied.

"Why do you want to teach, Henrietta?"

"I like to learn, daddy. But I'm not able to learn right with pages missing from the books. If I were a teacher, all of my students' books would have all their pages."

"So you're gonna be a teacher when you grow up?"

"Yes! A music teacher!"

"Why do you want to teach music?"

"Because music makes brings people together and makes them happy!" Henrietta replied as she began to place syrup onto her biscuits as she continued conversing with her father. "When people be singing, I see that they all be singing together. Some of the albums you play have white and black people on the cover together and they seem to all get along. I wanna teach music because music isn't preja—peju—"

"The word is prejudiced, Henrietta," Benjamin interrupted as he spelled out the word to his daughter, gave her its definition again and continued speaking. "You're right, music isn't prejudiced. And you need to know that things will get better for you later on in life, too. And no matter what, don't you ever let them white folks, or anybody for that matter, tell you that they are better than you because that's not true. You hear me? It's not true. You are the smartest, most beautiful little girl in all the world and you can be whatever you want to be in life. If you want to teach music, then by all means Henrietta you go on and teach. You're making good grades and you are the smartest one in your class. Even with pages missing from your book. They have to cheat on you to beat you —and they are still losing. That says a lot about the person you are, baby girl."

Henrietta sat back in her chair and bit into her biscuit as she kicked her legs happily to and fro. Veronica heard the conversation from the nearby hallway and she smiled to herself; thanking God for the man in her life. Benjamin had given his daughter confidence to face the day and the time remaining leading up to his return. After breakfast, he took Henrietta to school, hugged her and told her to remember what they discussed earlier in the morning and he would see her soon. He then returned home, held Gabriella and rocked her to sleep as he sung into her little ears. Benjamin then made love to Veronica, took a bath and got dressed for work. As Benjamin walked towards the front door, he told Veronica what transpired between Henrietta and him earlier in the morning.

"I know," Veronica responded, "she asks me questions about it all the time. Whenever we go to the grocery store, she asks why nobody carries the bags to the cab, how come nobody bags our groceries? Why the white people are in one line and we are in another line at the bank? I get mad myself at times. I'm a thirty-eight year old married woman and they call me by my first name, while an eighteen-year old unmarried white girl gets called 'Miss'. The first time somebody speaks out, he or she gets labeled as a trouble-maker. Here it is 1957, and in this day and age—in *this* day age, my love—we still have to deal with ignorance and injustice—all the while being persecuted and ridiculed for who we are. For the color of our skin? Why is that so? It hurts me, Benjamin. I'm so glad I have you, Henrietta and Gabriella. Besides God and the congregation, the three of us are all we have in these god-awful times."

"You're right about that, my love. Henrietta says she wants to teach music someday. That's a beautiful dream to have." Benjamin responded as he smiled at his wife.

"I heard that conversation. Henrietta can't hold a tune in a bucket, but she picks up on melodies real quick." Veronica replied as she and Benjamin laughed together.

"You're lucky my little protector is not here to hear you say that about her, Misses Jenkins! Hey! I'm on vacation until the New Year after this week!"

"Oh my God! You tell a story!"

"No, really! I'll be back home tonight! I'll be home for Christmas Eve *and* Christmas, baby! I put in for it right before the start of summer. I was going to surprise you tonight, but after all that happened this morning, I thought I'd put a smile on that beautiful face of yours before I left."

"And that you did, lover. Come here." Veronica said as she

cupped her husband's face in her hands and kissed him passionately on the lips.

Veronica and her husband prayed together in the threshold of their front door before they kissed one another good-bye. The gleeful woman waved to her husband as his dark green Thunderbird backed out of their driveway and made its way down the block and out of sight. Veronica anxiously awaited her husband's return; hoping the day would go by as quickly as the weeks had done so many times before.

## CHAPTER 5

## WHERE'S DADDY

"Momma, it's nine 'o' clock! Put daddy's song on!" Henrietta yelled to her mother as she had done so many times before.

Nine 'o' clock had come quickly and Henrietta was overjoyed that her father was returning home after being gone only a day. Henrietta was out of school until after the New Year's holiday. She had to attend school for only one day of the week in order to take her quarterly exams. She was home just after lunch hour and had been anxiously awaiting her father's arrival. Having her father home during the entire duration of her holiday break was a Christmas gift Henrietta had never anticipated. Veronica walked into the living room and placed the needle onto the record player, cranked the phonograph, and Sam Cooke's melodic voice began to be heard through the speaker.

Veronica and her daughter happily danced the entire song of *You Send Me*, Benjamin's favorite song. Veronica never felt such joy. Having her husband home for Christmas had excited the woman beyond words. Benjamin usually had to work on holidays because the white men at the lumber yard made sure that they were all off in order to spend time with their families. This year, however, Benjamin had gotten ahead of the white staff, having put in the request months ahead of time.

Veronica danced slowly with Henrietta, her eyes closed and

her mouth displaying a proud smile of joy, anticipating her husband's arrival. It was something mother and daughter had done many times before and had enjoyed, so when the song ended, Veronica had no problem playing the song again at Henrietta's request. Mother and daughter danced the song again and Veronica played it a third time as Henrietta went and sat in the window in anticipation of seeing the dark green Thunderbird turn into the drive way.

Veronica was putting the finishing touches up on a special dinner this Monday night. She placed the oven-baked bar-b-cued short ribs next to the baked macaroni and cheese, and the scalloped potatoes next to the deep-fried catfish. The cheese biscuits were hot and fluffy and the crawfish ettoufe` appetizer was extra spicy, just the way Benjamin liked it. Dinner was all set. The time was approaching nine-thirty when Veronica had finished dressing Gabriella in her elf outfit and placed her in her playpen. Veronica knew Benjamin was running late; but she wasn't worried, besides, the extra time afforded her had enabled her to get her youngest daughter dressed and fed. She hoped the baby girl's outfit would be pleasing to her father when he got in.

By ten 'o' clock, Veronica had turned off the record player and was sitting next to Henrietta on the sofa holding Gabriella while she made small circles on Henrietta's legs with the fingertips of her right hand and sung *Silent Night* to her daughters. Veronica began tickling Gabriella's stomach and the baby began to giggle. She encouraged Henrietta to tickle her sister and sing along, but Henrietta was in neither a tickling nor singing mood because her father hadn't arrived home as of yet. Henrietta knew her father was late this day.

Veronica was beginning to get worried herself; but she was trying best she could to keep Henrietta calm. She looked at her eldest daughter, who seemed deeply concerned about the whereabouts of her father and asked her to place a pot of water on the stove and boil it.

"Your father will be extra tired when he gets in. He'll enjoy having a cup of hot coffee before dinner." she told Henrietta.

Henrietta rolled her eyes and sighed as she got up from the

couch and went into the kitchen and fulfilled her mother's request.

"Momma, where's daddy?" Henrietta asked through a soft inquisitive voice upon reentering the living room a few minutes later.

"He probably had to work late, or had a flat tire or something, baby. He'll be home soon." Veronica replied as she bounced Gabriella up and down on her knees and made funny faces towards the giggling baby.

"He never worked late or had a flat tire before, momma! I want my daddy!" Henrietta yelled before she ran into her bedroom, fell onto her bed and began crying.

"Your father will be home shortly, Henrietta!" Veronica yelled loudly.

Henrietta didn't respond. She remained in her room, crying in the darkness. Veronica could hear her daughter sobbing. She knew she had to do more to calm Henrietta so she decided to call Benjamin's employer and ask if anyone knew of his whereabouts. She was told that they knew for a fact that Benjamin had left work at exactly seven 'o' clock as he said he had a couple of gifts from Santa Claus to deliver to Henrietta. When Veronica hung up the phone, she had a sickening feeling in her stomach, one that told her that Benjamin would not be coming home this night.

When Veronica turned around, Henrietta was standing before her with a face full of tears. "What did they say?" Henrietta asked as she fumbled her hands together nervously. "What they said about daddy?"

"They said your father left at seven this evening."

"It's after ten, momma! Where's my daddy?" Henrietta asked desperately.

Veronica's eyes welled up. She honestly didn't know where her husband was at this time; but she couldn't tell Henrietta that fact. "Come on, Henrietta," she answered, "we'll stay right here on the sofa until he arrives. Everything will be just fine. Now, wipe those tears. You know your father doesn't like to see his daughters cry. Come on and sit. He'll be home. He'll be home," she ended in a confidant tone of voice.

Henrietta wiped her tears and sat on the couch. Veronica handed Gabriella to her and told her to rock her to sleep while she went and covered up the dinner dishes. When Veronica returned to the living room, she saw that both Henrietta and Gabriella were asleep. She placed Gabriella in her playpen and sat beside Henrietta and hugged her tightly and prayed that Benjamin was all right.

When Veronica awoke the next morning, which was Christmas Eve, she saw Henrietta sitting in the window sill crying. Veronica also noticed that Henrietta had knocked over her flower arrangement. Henrietta had never knocked over those flowers. Veronica would often warn her; but Henrietta was always careful not to touch them in the least. Veronica took the knocked over flower arrangement as an ominous sign of things to come.

She walked over and eased Henrietta from the window sill and sent her into the bathroom to clean herself up while she attended to Gabriella, who was crying at the top of her lungs. Christmas Eve for Veronica Jenkins, was spent making phone calls to Benjamin's employer and every police department and hospital in every town that lay between Hattiesburg, Mississippi and New Orleans, Louisiana, and giving Henrietta various tasks around the house to keep her mind off Benjamin.

As Christmas Eve drew to a close, there was still no word from Benjamin. Veronica knew she had to continue on, however, and she went about the family's preplanned holiday routine. She washed clothes and had Henrietta iron their clothes for church on Christmas Day. Mother and daughter then reviewed the scriptures that their pastor had given them the previous Sunday. Veronica and Henrietta were almost in tears as they reviewed the lesson together, both wondering what happened to Benjamin.

On Christmas Day, word had spread throughout the neighborhood that Benjamin had not returned home. During the sermon, the pastor said a heartfelt prayer on behalf of the Jenkins family. After the service, the parishioners did the best they could to comfort Veronica and Henrietta by offering words of comfort and encouragement. They also offered their services and assistance. Veronica was offered everything from free daycare to an automobile because everyone of the members knew Benjamin Jenkins was a strong, family-oriented, God-fearing man that once fought for his country during World War Two. Veronica, however, turned down every offer, except one: the automobile. She knew she could use the vehicle to drive to Hattiesburg to find out exactly what happened to her husband. Veronica was planning to retrace Benjamin's steps and maybe, just maybe, she would learn what happened to her husband.

Veronica explained to Henrietta that she and Gabriella would open their presents as soon as Santa arrives, which may take a few days.

"Christmas will be a little late this year, Henrietta. Can we leave the gifts under the tree for a few more days? Santa still has more gifts to bring." Veronica stated as she pulled the donated car into the family's driveway after church services were completed.

"Momma, I know daddy was Santa Claus. I'm not worried about opening my gifts. I'm not even worried about the bike I wanted. Are you waiting for daddy to get home before we open our presents?" Henrietta asked as she sat beside her mother in the passenger seat holding Gabriella in her arms.

Veronica wanted to cry at that moment. Henrietta was still optimistic; but her mother, unbeknownst to Henrietta, was preparing for the worse.

"Whether your father is here or not, just know that he loves you, Henrietta. You and Gabriella both. Will he be here before the day ends? I can't answer that honestly, baby. I just don't know." Veronica replied.

Henrietta looked out the passenger window of the car and just stared blankly for several seconds. "I'll take Gabriella inside now," she stated in a dejected manner before she opened the door.

Veronica eyed her eldest daughter as she exited the vehicle.

Henrietta had asked about the car and why it was given to the family when they had their own car, Henrietta's father's car. Veronica told Henrietta it was a gift. Henrietta had many a question about the changes in circumstances and Veronica was trying as best she could to ease Henrietta's anxiety. Veronica also knew her eldest daughter was trying as best she could to believe what she was being told; but she felt that Henrietta knew she was only being kept at bay.

Christmas Day was a day spent sleeping inside the Jenkins home. There wasn't much to do but worry; so to prevent the worry, Veronica and Henrietta, along with Gabriella, slept the whole day. Veronica got up later that night and she and Henrietta baked pecan cookies. They were in the kitchen moving about silently when Gabriella squirted into the room all gummed-up and slobbering and cackling. The four-month old baby had scooted across the living room floor on her belly from underneath the tree where Henrietta had placed her atop a blanket.

Veronica and Henrietta gasped and rushed over to the baby who was now raising her body up onto her knees. Gabriella was trying to crawl at four months. The happy baby had shifted Veronica and Henrietta's focus this night. They both lay on the carpeted living room floor and encouraged Gabriella to crawl. A little before three in the morning, four month old Gabriella Jenkins crawled for the first time, bringing joy to Veronica and Henrietta.

"I wish daddy was here to see this." Henrietta remarked as she used her mother's camera to take a picture of Gabriella on her hands and knees.

The family stayed up late into the night and went to bed just before sunrise. When they awoke in the afternoon, Veronica took her two daughters for a drive across the Louisiana country side in the same manner that Benjamin had done many times before on Saturday afternoons. Henrietta enjoyed the outing. She got to see dairy cows, chickens, goats and horses. A nice farmer even allowed Henrietta to pet his calves and gave her a pony ride this day. The family returned home refreshed; but still, that unanswered question, "Where's daddy?" had spilled forward from Henrietta's mouth towards her mother as she was being tucked in for the night.

Veronica had hoped Henrietta would not ask her about Benjamin again, but she knew she could only put it off for so long as Henrietta would not stop asking until she received a truthful answer.

"He's just not here right now, Henrietta." Veronica replied as she tucked Henrietta in.

"Did he leave us? Why would daddy leave us, momma? I thought he loved us. Why would he do this to us?"

Veronica began to get choked upon hearing Henrietta's questions. She knew Benjamin didn't leave his family. She turned and stared at the doorway as she choked back the tears and reflected on her daughter's questions. She grew to understand that Henrietta now believed that her father had left his family behind. Veronica had not the heart to tell Henrietta what she truly felt: that Benjamin was dead. She held back tears as she turned back to Henrietta and said, "He didn't leave us, Henrietta. Your father loved us. Remember that, okay? He loved us."

Veronica gasped under her breath after responding to Henrietta. She realized she had used the word 'love' in the past tense—as if Benjamin Jenkins would no longer be around. She hoped Henrietta hadn't made sense of her statement as she awaited her daughter's response.

"Well, when is he coming home, momma?" Henrietta asked lowly.

"I honestly don't know, Henrietta. But when he does, your father," Veronica responded through a fraudulent smile that was imperceptible to Henrietta, "your father, little girl, will have some serious explaining to do! I believe I'll have to put my belt to use on his hinny!"

Henrietta placed her hands over her lower face as she lay tucked in her bed, "You gonna whip my daddy?" she asked in a whisper.

Veronica smiled holding back tears once more because the

thought of whipping Benjamin, something she had seen done to black men when she was a child growing up in Vidalia, Georgia, was a thought Veronica dared not to phantom; but to ease Henrietta's anxiety, she continued with her act.

"Why, I may let you take a crack at Mister Jenkins' hinny when he arrives!"

"I can't whip my daddy!" Henrietta exclaimed through cracked chuckles and snorts.

"Neither can I, my sweet love. Neither can I. Now," Veronica said cheerily as she pulled the covers up to Henrietta's chin, "you have sleep to accomplish. And I have your sister, with her strong lungs to tend to, okay? Good news, Henrietta! Tomorrow, we'll celebrate Christmas! Mister Jenkins has kept us waiting long enough!"

"Okay momma! Give Gabriella a kiss for me!" Henrietta said as she turned on her side facing away from her mother.

"I promise. Goodnight, Henrietta." Veronica ended as she kissed Henrietta's cheek.

Veronica decided to go forth with Christmas the following day as she had found a thrift store earlier in the day that had a pink bike for sale. She secretly purchased the bike that afternoon and a church member brought it to the home shortly after Henrietta went to sleep. Henrietta told her mother she did not want a bike; but Veronica wanted to get Henrietta's mind off her missing father at least for a day or so. She believed Henrietta would be overjoyed to receive her bicycle as she had been telling her father ever since Thanksgiving that she wanted a bike for Christmas.

Henrietta awoke on Friday morning, December 27, 1957, to find a bicycle under the Christmas tree. She ran to the bike, stating that her father had bought it for her. Veronica smiled as she went and helped Henrietta take the bike down the stairs. Off and on throughout the day, Henrietta practiced learning to ride her bicycle. Veronica assisted whenever she wasn't inside with Gabriella; but several kids were around and they helped Henrietta to learn to ride her new bike. It took Henrietta only a couple of hours to learn to ride her new bicycle and she rode all day with the other kids in the neighborhood and returned home happily once it grew dark.

Veronica had fried chicken and made mash potatoes from scratch for her daughter and greeted her happily as she began to remove Henrietta's scarf and thick mittens. Henrietta was having a good day, and it got better when her mother reminded her that she had more gifts to open. Henrietta ate, then bathed; and as she sat in her pajamas along with Gabriella, who lay on the floor on a blanket beside them, she opened the two large boxes that her father had brought home the week before.

Henrietta was surprised to see that her father had indeed purchased the doll house that she wanted so badly. Veronica then opened her gifts. Henrietta snapped pictures of her mother holding up a brand new cream-colored cashmere coat with a matching pair of leather boots and a matching scarf and wool hat. Veronica smiled and cried at the same time, thinking of her wonderful husband as she made small circles with her fingertips upon the lovely scarf her man had purchased. Henrietta had the doll house she wanted along with the bike, but it was a bittersweet and belated Christmas for the Jenkins family, as their family head, their rock, Benjamin Jenkins, was still missing.

As Henrietta rode her bike slowly up and down the street on a cold Sunday morning, just two days after opening her gifts, she noticed a car carrying two white men slowly riding down her street. When the car stopped in front of her house, Henrietta hopped off the bike and ran inside to call her mother. Veronica came to the door with a sleeping Gabriella in tow, and asked what Henrietta was screaming about. When she saw the two white men approaching her stairs and flashing their FBI badges, Veronica leaned against the threshold and began to plead as her eyes watered. Gabriella began to stir awake as the two agents broke the news that Benjamin's car was found upside down in creek alongside a lonely stretch of highway, just below Hattiesburg, Mississippi.

"Where's my husband? Is he all right?" Veronica asked as her grey eyes began to display a look of worry and fear. Soon, tears began to flow, causing the distressed woman's vision to go blurry.

"Ma'am," the officer began to speak as he coughed lightly, "they found a body in the car and—"

Veronica shook her head from side to side. She nearly dropped Gabriella as she stood in the threshold of her home. "Please mister, not—not my husband. Tell me he's okay. Please. Tell me he's okay." Veronica whispered through her teary grey eyes as she stared at the men.

"I sincerely wish I could ma'am. We've identified the body in the car through a driver's license photo. It appears to be that of Benja—"

Veronica let go a heartfelt declaration of sorrow to God as she stared into the eyes of the agents. "Please, say it ain't so!" she yelled at the top of her lungs as she held Gabriella tightly in her arms, closed her eyes and slid to floor in the middle of her threshold. "God, please!" she cried aloud whilst shaking her head from side to side.

Henrietta heard the entire conversation and she, too, began to cry, calling out for her father. The two agents did the best they could to comfort Veronica and Henrietta, but it was to no avail. They then had to ask Veronica to identify her husband through a picture. They did so carefully, so as to not let Henrietta see the bloated remains of her deceased father. Veronica sobbed uncontrollably as she stared at the image, running her hand over the picture of her deceased husband's face.

*"He was my everything. Why'd they take him, Lord?"* Veronica asked silently as she squinted her eyes shut, gritted her teeth in a vain attempt to numb the pain and let the tears flow. Veronica's body heaved as she grimaced, trying unsuccessfully to absorb the pain coursing through her body, namely her heart.

The agents informed Veronica that it appeared that Benjamin had gotten drunk, fell asleep behind the wheel of his car and drove off into the creek where he drowned. Veronica knew her husband didn't drink and she adamantly notified the agents of that fact. She regained her composure and invited the agents into her home and offered them a seat on the couch. Veronica gave Gabriella to Henrietta and had them go into her bedroom and close the door. When Henrietta went in to the room, Veronica adamantly told the agents she believed someone had killed her husband.

The agents were under the same impression. They knew all-too-well that the Ku Klux Klan was very active in Mississippi. They had done their homework and had been investigating allegations of Klan activity at Benjamin's job; but without proof, the agents knew that proving murder would be an impossible task. One of the agents asked if Veronica knew of any conflict on Benjamin's job and she responded by telling the agents she knew many of the white men at lumber yard resented working under Benjamin, but they never really threatened the man. One man in particular, however, a Mister Henderson, who was a lead man at the lumber yard, had had a few disagreements with Benjamin in the past.

The agents took down notes; but it was their defeatist attitude towards the situation that gave Veronica the impression that much would not be done in the way of finding out what exactly happened to her husband. Many Black men were being lynched, shot, and beaten to death during this period of time and a great majority of the homicides were either ruled accidental, suicide, or left unsolved. Veronica believed her husband's case would fall into the realm of being an accidental death; but she was determined to find out the truth.

Thirty-eight year-old Veronica Jenkins buried her forty year-old husband Benjamin Jenkins in the family's church graveyard on New Year's Day of 1958. She then drove to Mississippi a week later to file a claim to collect the insurance policy Benjamin had purchased while he worked at the lumber yard.

Veronica stood before Mister Henderson, now the temporary supervisor, inside the small trailer that her husband once slept in and used as his office. She looked around at the small domicile, eying the bed her husband once slept in, feeling his presence. She looked at the small desk her husband

63

once sat behind, the typewriter he once used. An old pair of steel toe boots which Veronica knew to be Benjamin's work boots, were still neatly tucked away in a corner beside the small cot where the man spent many a night after a hard day's work.

Veronica stood before Mister Henderson, a husky, red-bearded white man, and pulled out her insurance policy; but Mister Henderson was already prepared. He'd made phone calls to the insurance company and mailed a report concerning Benjamin's manner of death. Mister Henderson handed Veronica a judgment and the woman was stunned to learn that since Benjamin was supposedly under the influence of alcohol at the time of his death, the life insurance policy was null and void. He then made Veronica an offer: he told her that he could free up cash if she was willing to do a favor or two for him and his buddies.

"What are you asking of me Mister Henderson?" Veronica asked, pretending to be unaware of the man's intent.

"You know what I'm talkin' 'bout. You can place your two daughters outside in the car, or you can have them stay if you want. You and I, I was thinking we can maybe discuss a payment plan. You get what you, which is the money from the policy; and I get what I want. And you know what I want." Mister Henderson said as he eyed Veronica and rubbed his crotch.

Veronica had seen Mister Henderson's gesture. She looked at his crotch and then stared him the eyes as she spat on the floor.

Mister Henderson chuckled. "Little girl," he then said. "I know you need that money to keep that lovely home of yours *and* to support your daughters. I'm willing to support your family if you allow me to—"

Veronica spat in Mister Henderson's face just as he reached his hand out to cup one of her breasts. The man raised his hand to slap Veronica and she kneed him in the groin.

Henrietta watched the scene unfold, growing frightful for the welfare of her mother. She held Gabriella in her arms close to her bosom as she watched her mother repeatedly pound her fists against a crouched over Mister Henderson's back until the man stood upright and stretched out his arm and slapped her mother with the back of his hand, knocking her back onto the cot.

Veronica got up again and charged the man but he was much stronger than she. Mister Henderson grabbed both of Veronica's wrists and shoved her back into the wall of the small office. She hit the wall and fell to her knees and lay on her left side as Mister Henderson started walking towards her, unbuckled his belt in the process.

"Don't hurt my momma!" Henrietta cried out as she ran and stood in between Veronica and Mister Henderson, stopping the man in his tracks. Tears ran from underneath Henrietta's glasses as she held on tightly to her little sister. "Don't hurt us, please." she cried.

Veronica regained her composure and gently moved Henrietta and Gabriella aside and stood up in front of Mister Henderson.

"You not a man, Mister Henderson. You're a monster. A *monster*! Does it make you feel good to take advantage of a woman right in front of her children? I always knew white folks in this lumber yard hated my husband—just because he was a Black man in a white man's position."

Mister Henderson slapped Veronica in the face again and she quickly whipped her neck around to present the other cheek.

Henrietta began to scream again.

"There's no need to fear Henrietta! He's not going to hurt us!" Veronica stated, her head facing away from her daughters and staring at her husband's steel toe boots.

Veronica stared at her husband's boots for several seconds. She thought of the wonderful memories she created with her husband and began to heave. Her face wrinkled and the tears flowed as she turned back to face Mister Henderson.

With tears running down her face, Veronica looked Mister

Henderson in the eyes and said, "For as long as I have breath in me, I will never sell out my *family*—or compromise my *dignity*! You're a lowlife! It may not happen this day, but one day you will pay for your treacherous act you merciless evildoer!" Veronica ended as she grabbed her children, shoved the man aside and stormed out of the office.

When Veronica left, Mister Henderson buckled his pants and poured himself a drink as he contemplated his next move. Within a year's time, Mister Henderson would become general manager of the lumberyard. The staff at the lumber yard would become entirely white as Mister Henderson had fired all of the black workers and hired an entirely white staff littered with members of the Ku Klux Klan.

Veronica completely believed that Mister Henderson was involved in her husband's death, but she just couldn't prove it. It pained the woman to know that the man was getting away with her husband's murder. Soon after Benjamin's death in December of 1957, Veronica and her daughters began to endure a hard life. The woman tried repeatedly to get the insurance company to accept her claim but they wouldn't budge. After weeks of trying, calling and talking to different agents on a daily basis, Veronica realized that the policy her husband had paid on up until his death would be of no value to his surviving family. The family's once tranquil and happy life had been abruptly shattered. Money had become scarce. Veronica obtained a job at a sugar refinery early in February of 1958 to help make ends meet, but money was always tight.

Mid-way through 1958, the Jenkins family had to give up their home when the bank foreclosed on it. Veronica had gotten behind on the mortgage four months in a row and the bank had no choice but to foreclose on the Jenkins' family home. Veronica knew she was going to lose the place, but she tried for as long as she could to hold on to it; but in the end, the bank won out. Veronica and her two daughters had to sleep in a homeless shelter for a week until she received her next paycheck. From there, Veronica rented a smaller two bedroom home about a mile and half from the home she once owned, but the good thing was that the home was nearby the sugar refinery where Veronica worked.

The family's new residence had very little furniture. The place wasn't kept that well either; the rent was affordable, however, and the home had working heat and hot water. Veronica was doing the best she could during this period of time. Benjamin had always been the bread-winner in the family; but with the man of the house now deceased, Veronica had to take the lead.

By 1959, Veronica, now age forty, was still barely scraping by, but the family always had a hot meal, and attended church regularly. Henrietta did well in school that year and Gabriella, oblivious to the state of the family, was happy and healthy. Veronica believed things would get better for her family, all she had to do was stay strong. She did just so; but when the sun went down, and bedtime came about, the pain and the reality of the situation would hit the forty year-old woman full-force.

Veronica cried herself to sleep nearly every night for almost two years after losing Benjamin; but she knew she had to remain strong because Henrietta and Gabriella needed her. Their total welfare and survival all hinged upon their mother. Veronica knew her kids, especially Henrietta, were looking to her for sustenance and she was determined not to let them down. It was also fair to say that without Henrietta and Gabriella, Veronica may have just given up, but for her children's sake, she pressed on.

Veronica Jenkins had a faith in God, and an inner strength within herself that she didn't fully understand at the time. She had endured the murder of her husband, and the loss of her home, but still found strength within herself to continue running the race of life. She would jump the hurdles placed before her and do what had to be done in order for the Jenkins family to survive. She supplied the family with clothing, food and shelter. The necessities of life were being supplied; but it still didn't ease the pain Veronica experienced night after night during the most trying time of her life. Plain and simple, Veronica sorely missed her husband, the only man she had ever known and loved.

Veronica also had to tolerate sexual harassment where she worked. She was a very beautiful woman; black and white men alike, knew she was struggling with two kids and had no husband and they eagerly tried to tempt her with money in return for sexual favors. Veronica had a lot of pride, though, and as far as she was concerned, she was still married to Benjamin, and even if she was interested in their gestures, Veronica had not the capacity within herself to offer her body for sexual favors. What kind of message would she be conveying to Henrietta?

Veronica turned down all offers—even though she could have used the money—if only to buy something extra for her daughters. Henrietta often asked her mother for a baby doll or a hula-hoop, and Gabriella's wooden blocks were so faded that the alphabets and numbers could not be seen clearly. Veronica could not afford even the cheapest of toys for her kids. She would redraw the numbers and letters on Gabriella's blocks and she and Henrietta would often sit and play 'steps', a game in which Veronica would draw a winding map with different instructions such as 'go back two spaces', 'play again', or 'move forward three spaces'. Henrietta enjoyed the times spent with her mother. The simplest things brought her the most joy.

Henrietta sometimes asked her mother about buying toys from the store and each time, Veronica would politely refuse to do so; never explaining why. The family rarely bought new items. Not even for birthdays and holidays. Christmas of 1958 came and went without any fanfare. There were no gifts under the tree for Veronica, Henrietta, nor Gabriella; but the family had a wonderful turkey dinner that year and played homemade games and sung Christmas Carols. Mid-way through 1959, Henrietta and Gabriella were beginning to outgrow their old clothes, but Veronica was unable to purchase new wardrobes for her kids. The family barely had clothes to wear, but Veronica, becoming an ever more resourceful woman, purchased a used sewing machine from the thrift store and purchased cheap linens and made her, Henrietta, and Gabriella new outfits from scratch. It was a skill she had never forgotten during the time she spent working voluntarily at the sewing factory which closed shortly before the end of World War Two. Later that year, Veronica had saved up enough money to buy her and her kids used coats from the Good Will for the upcoming winter.

Henrietta slowly grew to understand what was going on during that time. She watched her mother struggle. She heard Veronica crying in her bedroom at night. After a while, Henrietta simply stopped asking her mother for toys. She didn't want her mother to feel bad about not being able to buy her and Gabriella the things they wanted. They had what they *needed*, and for Henrietta, now age eleven, that was more than enough.

The men at Veronica's job steadily flirted with the woman but she relentlessly held on to her principles. By 1960, all Veronica ever did was work, pick up her kids from daycare and school and go home and prepare dinner. For the Jenkins family, home was a happy place. Henrietta and her mother talked a lot and listened to music. Two and a half year-old Gabriella was walking about clapping her hands often and had the prettiest grey eyes and the loveliest smile. For over two years, the Jenkins family lived a secluded life, rarely venturing out, except to go to the market and church.

The Jenkins family had suffered an injustice by losing their family head in December of 1957. They were poor in the year 1960—but they were alive—they were healthy—and they were strong. They would continue to press on and survive. The brick walls placed before them were tough, but the Jenkins family was even tougher. Veronica was slowly knocking down the obstacles that lay before she and her daughters, and for the down-trodden Jenkins family, the only way left to go was up.

## CHAPTER 6

## THE ACTIVIST

In September of 1960, Veronica Jenkins got a promotion at the sugar refinery where she was working. She was now a first shift supervisor in the packaging department. After a hard struggle, and by the grace of God, things were finally beginning to look up for Veronica and her two daughters. Veronica was so happy to receive the pay raise and better hours that she had decided to take both three-year old Gabriella, and twelve year-old Henrietta into town for dinner. The family got into the same run down Ford Thunderbird the church had given them nearly three years ago, and rode to a small diner on Tulane Avenue, near downtown New Orleans.

Veronica held Gabriella in her arms as Henrietta skipped playfully behind her mother. When they entered the restaurant, Veronica noticed a sign that said *Please Be Seated*. She took a seat in a booth with a window next to the sidewalk and grabbed a menu and began to read. Veronica waited for nearly ten minutes as she eyed the young white waitress who stood behind the counter talking on the telephone. She tried to get the lady's attention, but every time she did so, the waitress would turn her back to Veronica.

"Momma, I think I want to try the meatloaf. But I don't think it could ever be better than yours." Henrietta said softly.

"Just one minute, sugar," Veronica responded and turned her attention to the waitress. "Excuse me, miss, could we get some service, please?" she asked politely.

Just as Veronica asked her question, an elderly white couple walked into the restaurant and the waitress quickly hung up the phone, walked them to their seats and handed them each a menu. She placed the couple in the same section as Veronica and her kids and began talking to the couple in a friendly voice. Henrietta noticed what happened and she asked her mother why the lady didn't ask them what they wanted since they were there first.

Veronica ignored Henrietta's question as she got up from her seat and walked over to the petite freckle-faced young lady with an indignant look displayed upon her face. Veronica stood before the waitress and eyed her. "We were here first. You saw us *sitting* there and you purposely ignored us." she said matter-of-factly.

"If you can read, I suggest you look at the sign." the waitress said in an aggravated tone as she placed napkins before the couple.

Veronica looked over at another sign saw that it read *Whites Only*. She then looked around and noticed that besides her and her kids, the elderly white couple was the only other people in the diner. She turned back to the woman and placed her hands on her hips.

"You had me sit here all this time because of the color of my skin, little girl? You know what? It's folks like you that make life difficult for the decent people in this world. We came here to spend green money, just like these two people sitting right here!" she stated as she pointed at the white couple.

"Ohh lordy! Charlie, we got another one! She's about to start a sit-in in your building this evening." the waitress yelled aloud as she rolled her eyes and backed away from Veronica.

The elderly couple began to smile proudly as they waited to see the owner's reaction once he saw a trio of what they viewed as "niggers" sitting in the white section.

The man who owned the diner came out from the kitchen and asked the waitress what was the problem. She looked up at the husky 6' 6" two-hundred and seventy-five pound man as he held onto to a coffee jar, and then eyed Veronica, who was standing in front of her table as Henrietta sat inside the booth with Gabriella. Gabriella was standing on the red cushioned seat playfully tapping the white Formica table and laughing delightfully. She was in a happy place—totally oblivious to the events that were transpiring around her.

The man walked over to Veronica and stared into her face and was immediately struck by her beauty. He sincerely believed the woman and her kids posed no trouble so he personally sat her down and prepared to take an order. The waitress tried to take the white couple's order, but they abruptly got up and headed for the door, calling the owner a "nigger lover".

"You don't have to do this, Mister. I didn't mean to cause any trouble." Veronica said as she sat in the booth.

"Don't worry, ma'am. It's not the first time this has happened. This place used to be teeming with white folk. The first time a black man came into the establishment and I served him, white folks filed out of here by the boat load. Business has been real slow ever since. You don't mind do you?" the man asked as he sat across the table from Veronica and turned up two white mugs and poured the two of them a cup of coffee.

"No go right ahead." Veronica replied with a polite smile, intrigued by the man's uninhibited friendliness.

"Sugar?" the man asked as he poured.

"No. Cream is fine. Thank you, mister."

"My pleasure, ma'am. I'm Charles Santino." the man said, formally introducing himself after pouring the coffee. "Call me Charlie for short."

Before Veronica could reply, the jolly individual before her eyes sitting on the opposite side of the booth continued to speak. "Ever since I came home from Pearl Harbor, I have been so ashamed of my nation. I fought side by side with you people and the colored race is one of the most bravest and God-fearing group of people I know. The men I fought with gave their lives for this country. And this is how we repay them? It's sad. Terrible in fact! So I made a vow that when I left Mississippi and came to New Orleans, that I would treat everyone the same. This stupid Jim Crow law forces me to place that sign in the window. Today, it stops!"

Charlie got up from the table and removed the *Whites Only* sign and tossed it into the garbage.

The waitress, having heard Charlie's remarks, and bearing witness to his actions, grabbed her purse from behind the counter, threw on her sweater, and left the diner, stating that she "would rather quit than serve a nigger in the white section".

Charlie laughed as he stared out his front door, watching the waitress walk down the sidewalk telling every white person she passed what transpired inside the diner. Charlie then walked back over to his customer and smiled a wide smile, causing his cheeks to reveal their dimples. His curly, jet-black hair was matted to the top of his head and against the back of his neck. He quickly ran his huge hands through his hair, trying to neaten himself up as he asked if he could take the woman's order.

Veronica, realizing the man was a World War Two veteran, ignored his question and began to talk about her husband.

"My husband fought in the war, in the European Theater. His last mission was an escort mission to and from Blechammer, Poland. He was a member of the Tuskegee Airmen and one of the first black pilots to become a double ace pilot. He flew over one-hundred and thirty missions and was shot down once over the Black Alps. But he survived to fly several more missions before he returned home. The country doesn't recognize nor acknowledge his contribution—but he was indeed a hero." Veronica said proudly of her deceased husband as she smiled up at Charlie.

"Your husband fought in the war?" Charlie asked with amazement as he sat back down in his seat. "See, you know firsthand what I'm talking about! One hundred and thirty plus missions? That's just great! I know he fought hard to stay alive.

A lovely woman like yourself is more motivation than a man would ever need to stay alive." Charlie ended as he stirred his coffee and took a sip.

Veronica blushed. She had an inkling that Charlie was hitting on her and she was a little flattered; but for a black woman and a white man to so much as hold hands given the times, was just too taboo. Veronica quickly regained her composure, dismissing those taboo urges. She believed deep down inside that Charlie was indeed a fair man and a good man; but he was a white man. And Veronica was, in her eyes, still married to Benjamin. She then thought about what Charlie had said earlier, about being from Mississippi.

"What part of Mississippi are you from, Charlie?" she then asked.

"Grew up in Laurel. That's a small town about fifteen minutes north of Hattiesburg." Charlie responded. "Hey pretty little girl," he then said to Henrietta, "how would you like one of my famous root beer floats?" he asked with a wide smile.

"Yes, please. I never had one of those." Henrietta responded politely with a smile.

"Well, you're going to love this concoction!" Charlie responded as he got up from the booth and headed towards his counter.

"You familiar with the lumber yard there in Hattiesburg?" Veronica asked as she eyed Charlie behind his counter.

Charlie placed a scoop of vanilla ice cream into a thick, frosted mug and looked up at Veronica and smiled, "Familiar? Hell! I used to work there up until fifty-five! Held that job for ten years. The Klan started moving in, so I had to get out of that mess. Boy, I tell you some of the things those people—"

Charlie froze mid-sentence and watched as Veronica put her head down and started to cry, somewhat sobbing as Henrietta rubbed her back softly.

"What's wrong, ma'am?" Charlie asked as he emerged from behind the counter and placed the root beer float before the older of the two children, who began to sip eagerly.

Veronica regained her composure, got up from the table, grabbed Gabriella into her arms and shuffled Henrietta towards the front door.

"Momma, my soda!" Henrietta exclaimed as she reached for her root beer float.

"Leave it, Henrietta! We have to go now!"

Charlie was stunned. He was having a good conversation with his new customers; but things had suddenly changed.

"Ma'am!" He called out as he walked quickly and caught up to Veronica, who had her hand on the door handle. "Ma'am, you didn't even order your food! Your daughter hasn't even finished her float! Where're you goin'? Was it something I said?"

Veronica let go of the handle and slowly turned and faced Charlie. She told him she had to talk to him, but at a later date. "Come by anytime, Miss—Miss ..."

"Veronica. Veronica Jenkins."

Charlie raised his eyebrows in amazement. "Oh my God! Benjamin! Benjamin Jenkins! You're his wife? I never knew Benjamin was an old vet!" Charlie stated as he placed his hands on his hips and smiled proudly whilst looking towards the floor.

"Did you ever mention the time you spent in Pearl Harbor?" Veronica then asked.

Charlie looked at Veronica and dropped his smile. "No, no I didn't," he said somberly. "It was just an obligation I felt I had to fulfill to uphold the survival of our nation. You know, soldiers—the real ones? They never brag on the things they did when they fought. It was just something that a man had to do at a certain point in time in his life, Veronica. It was just a job. I guess that's why Benjamin never spoke of the days of old. The great ones never really do."

"I would love to talk to you about my husband, Mr. Charlie. I think maybe you can help me with a serious dilemma."

"Say when and where ma'am. For an old vet's wife, I'll do

76

anything."

"Here, tomorrow night after your diner closes." Veronica responded.

"Fine. I'll see you tomorrow, Misses Jenkins." Charlie responded gently as he stared Veronica in the eyes.

Veronica was preparing to leave once more when Charlie clapped his hands together and had her wait at the counter. He hurried into the kitchen and came back with a half of a honey-baked ham. Veronica refused, but Charlie insisted on giving the ham to Veronica and her family. Veronica thanked the man and the two agreed to meet the following night.

The following night, Veronica found herself walking towards the entrance of Charlie's diner wondering exactly what she was doing; but all the while she was hoping that she was making the right move for her husband's sake. She had brought along a .38 special revolver, a gun she had bought shortly after her husband's death. She was tired too; as she had been to work and then went home to tend to her two daughters and then had to gather all the notes she had accumulated during her fruitless investigation into her husband's death.

Veronica's grey eyes had a weary look as she carried the box down the sidewalk to Charlie's front door with Henrietta following close behind, toting Gabriella. Charlie was at the entrance to his diner awaiting Veronica's arrival. When he saw her approaching the entrance, he unlocked his door and walked and met Veronica halfway down the sidewalk and took the box from her arms and welcomed the family into the diner as he cleared a table and sat the box down. The first thing Veronica did was pull out a picture and showed it to Charlie.

"Do you know this man?" she asked.

"That's Mister Henderson," Charlie said. "He was heavy into the Klan. I mean, he just had a hatred towards *all* blacks. I remember some days he would come in bragging that he or one of his cronies had run a car off the road, or attacked a group of black people or some crazy stuff like that. Henderson and his gang got some kind of sick joy outta destroying people's lives. So, did Benjamin ever leave that place?"

"Mister Charlie, my husband was killed December 23, 1957. His car ran off the road into a creek. They claim he was drunk and he drowned."

"Wait a minute now. That doesn't make a bit of sense, Misses Jenkins." Charlie replied as he walked back and forth down the aisle in his all-white grease-stained chef's uniform. "The little bit I did know about Ben, I knew he wasn't a drinker. The man never touched the stuff! We gotta find out what really happened, Veronica. That's what you wanted to discuss with me, right? Me helping you out?"

"Yes. I mean, I was hoping you could. But how will we go about doing it? I can't get close to those people in Mississippi. I tried, but I can't get close enough to find out anything."

"You can't," Charlie said, then pointed his index finger towards himself, "but I can. An old ex-sailor, World War Two vet, with ties to Mississippi? Hell, I can fit right in, Veronica!"

"Maybe we should call the police." Veronica replied, unsure if Charlie could really help her in her endeavors.

"Are you kidding? Are you kidding? The police probably were in on it, Misses Jenkins! I'll go up there and see what I can find out for you. Once we know for sure, then we can go to the police. Don't say anything to no one until I go up there myself and see what I can find out. Deal?" Charlie asked as he extended his hand to shake Veronica's hand.

Veronica agreed. When she touched Charlie's hand, there was a spark between the two; but neither let on. The two then sat in the booth with Henrietta and Gabriella and ate bowls of gumbo and conversed about life in general until Veronica stated that she had to go as it was way past her kids' bedtime. Charlie secured his diner and followed Veronica home in his car, making sure she arrived, and entered her home safely.

Over the next few months, Veronica and Charlie would sit in her home going over every document that Veronica had collected since her husband died. People in the neighborhood wondered what a white man was doing in their neighborhood visiting a black woman—a black woman whose husband was supposedly killed by a white man. The union was indeed an odd one, but the two of them were a good team.

Charlie had taken a sincere interest in Veronica's plight. He thought the woman deserved better and Veronica in turn, felt safe and secure around Charlie. After a while, Charlie's visits became more social than business. The two would sit and talk for hours about everything from the time they were kids, up until the present and what the future may have in store for America.

The year of 1960 ended on a good note for the Jenkins family. Henrietta and Gabriella had finally gotten a Christmas, their first since their father died. Charlie was even nice enough to chip in and purchase the little girls some toys as well. He even bought Veronica a gift, a necklace with a locket that held a picture of both her daughters. Veronica, in turn, had gotten Charlie a bottle of cologne. In the year of 1960, the United States of America was a country heavily entrenched in racism, but on a small block in the Lower Ninth Ward section of New Orleans, Louisiana, a white man and a black woman were becoming dear friends.

## CHAPTER 7

## TABOO JUSTICE

On a cool morning in March of 1961, Veronica was loading her kids into her car to take them to school and daycare. She was in good spirits this morning because Charlie had informed her that he made contact with known klansmen from the lumber yard in Mississippi. She was just about to enter her car when two black males approached her.

"Misses Benjamin Jenkins!" the tall bearded man yelled aloud as his shorter counterpart walked beside him.

"How can I help you?" Veronica asked inquisitively as she eyed the two men, who were dressed in wool suits and wearing felt fedoras.

"Ma'am," the shorter man began to speak when the men grew nearer Veronica, "we don't agree with your relationship with this white man that's been parading through our neighborhood. He's been asking people questions about Benjamin and causing a stir. Now, we have people working to find out what happened to your husband, but they won't continue if you continue to associate with this man."

"You, 'have people'? Are you the police?" Veronica asked.

"No ma'am, we—"

Veronica cut the man's statement short by saying, "Well, I suggest you stay out of my business! You haven't done anything since 1957! And now you see someone else doing something you were afraid to do and you wanna try and stop it? Thank you gentlemen! But I don't need, nor do I want your help! It's too late to be brave! I have been brave long before you decided to lift a finger to find my husband's killers!"

The two men, who were part of an extremist Black movement, walked off in disgust and anger. Veronica watched them, her grey eyes hung low as she scoffed at the men and got into her car and quickly backed out of the driveway. When Veronica returned home from work with her kids, she saw that her house had been vandalized. Someone had spray painted TRAITOR all over the front, sides and back of her home. Veronica immediately grew angry. She walked and stood in the middle of the street, screaming at the top of her lungs for the perpetrator to show him or herself, but no one came forth. The neighbors merely stood on their porches and in their yards watching in silence. Veronica called them all cowards as she spat in the street and took her children inside. She then called Charlie and told him what happened. Charlie went and purchased a gallon of off-white paint and painted over the words and sat with Veronica inside her home as night fell.

Veronica had just tucked Henrietta in for the night, and Gabriella was already sound asleep. Charlie was disappointed that Veronica's own people would treat her this way. They sat at the table talking over a cup of coffee and listening to Sam Cooke's song, *(What A) Wonderful World.*

"You know," Charlie began to speak, "I believe that one day this country will eventually get it right."

"Get what right, Charlie?" Veronica asked as she blew steam from her coffee mug.

"That all people will be treated equally and have the freedom to live their life as they please without being mocked or persecuted for being a certain race. Our forefathers meant it to be that way. Truth is, this country was created for people of all races. *Greed* destroyed that dream, but eventually, they'll get it right." Charlie concluded as he smiled at Veronica.

"I believe that, Charlie. I really do. And I hope for it. At least for my children's sake." Veronica replied.

An awkward moment of silence ensued and the two stared

at one another before Veronica dropped her eyes and ran her hands across her navy blue all in one knee length dress in a vain attempt to knock out wrinkles that were not present.

Charlie slowly got up from the table and walked over to Veronica. The woman flushed as Charlie approached her. She looked at him longingly as he reached out and gently touched her face with the backside of his hand. She was so soft to Charlie. Veronica sunk her face into Charlie's hand and reached her hand out to touch his.

"It's been a long time, Mister Santino," Veronica said in a low tone as she closed her eyes and nuzzled her cheek into Charlie's comforting hand.

"You're so, so beautiful, Veronica. You deserve to be treated like the wonderful woman you are." Charlie stated as he bent down and pressed his lips to Veronica's.

The two kissed passionately for what seemed like an eternity, until Veronica pulled away from Charlie and stood up and hugged the man's neck. Charlie wrapped his arms around the woman's waist and pressed his nose to Veronica's neck and savored her naturally sweet aroma. Veronica hadn't felt the touch of a man since Benjamin was killed. It was something she longed for, to feel like a woman again, and on this night, Charlie was making Veronica feel like not just a woman, but a complete woman. In spite of her want, however, Veronica stepped away from Charlie, reluctant to go any further, but Charlie took charge and pulled her back towards him and grabbed her hand, turned, and guided Veronica to her own bedroom. She went willingly.

Once inside, Veronica began to slowly and nervously undress, but only half-way, as she was still somewhat apprehensive to go through with the act that her body so desired. Charlie, meanwhile, was in awe at the woman's gorgeous physique as she stood before him naked from the waist up. He stepped close and cupped Veronica's breasts and gently suckled on her hardening, light brown nipples. The woman moaned when she felt Charlie's warm mouth touch her skin. It had literally been years since Veronica had felt the touch of a man.

"Charlie, please." Veronica whispered.

The woman's voice was husky and filled with desire, but also emanated a hint of resistance.

Charlie removed his clothes and walked over to Veronica and began to undress her fully. She protested slightly, but assisted Charlie at the same time, slowly raising her legs one at a time to allow her panties to be removed. Veronica now stood naked in front of Charlie in complete vulnerability. She knew what she was about to do was forbidden in both the black and white community, but Veronica needed, and wanted, a man. Her body craved attention. Charlie was the nicest, strongest man she had met since Benjamin was killed.

Even though it was taboo at the time, the two would come together on this night as man and woman, not white and black. Charlie adored Veronica's body. He knelt down on his knees before Veronica, as she stood covering her breasts with her arms in a shy manner, and pressed his lips against her vagina and slowly slid his tongue back and forth over Veronica's glistening pink, and moistened outer lips. Veronica began to whimper and moan as she slowly moved her hands to the back of Charlie's head and held his face close to her sex. Soon, Charlie was easing his tongue inside of Veronica. She spread her legs slightly, allowing Charlie better excess to her achingly hot, love-starved pussy. Veronica's body didn't want Charlie to stop, but her mind was still in protest. She managed to gently push Charlie's head away from her pussy. She then looked down upon Charlie and stroked his curly black hair, pondering her body and heart's desire, versus that of her mind's resistance. Veronica was now plagued by a feeling of mixed emotions. Her mind was saying no, but her body was screaming a resounding yes.

Charlie looked into Veronica's hesitant grey eyes and sensed the woman's reluctance. Not wanting the flames of passion to be extinguished, Charlie stood and picked Veronica up into his arms and cradled her like that of a knight having rescued his damsel in distress. Veronica began to shed tears and shook her head from side to side as if to say "don't take me" as Charlie walked over to the bed and lay her down gently before he lay beside her.

Veronica teared up and closed her eyes as Charlie placed his rugged, callous-filled hands upon her face and wiped her tears. Veronica's hand then began to nervously slide down Charlie's body towards his mid-section where she found his hardened shaft, throbbing in want and anticipation. She hesitantly clutched Charlie's member and stroked it slowly, causing Charlie to moan in ecstasy and blow his warm breath into Veronica's ear.

In turn, Charlie's over-sized hand began to massage Veronica's moist outer lips, and she slowly spread her legs to allow him better access. When Charlie's thick index finger coaxed gently into Veronica's throbbing pussy, the woman's legs trembled and she cried out with pleasure. Veronica's mouth was agape and her eyes were wide open as she looked towards the ceiling and shook her head from side to side slowly with tears running down her cheeks. She soon began grounding her pelvis against Charlie's exploring finger as her cries took on a more sorrowful tone. Charlie didn't know it, but at that exact moment, Veronica was silently apologizing to Benjamin because she knew she was about to give herself over to another man who was not her husband for the first time in her life. She cried aloud and silently begged her husband's forgiveness as she grabbed Charlie's huge shoulders and pulled him on top of her wanting flesh.

Veronica let out a loud, pleading moan when Charlie entered her. It was a moan that Veronica believed had surely awakened Henrietta from her sleep; but at that moment, she didn't care, she needed fulfillment—and fulfillment is what she would receive.

Charlie gave Veronica three earth-shattering orgasms during their hour and a half love-making session. The woman cried, moaned, and threw her arms back into the feather pillows in total surrender as she called out to God and gave of herself to Charlie. Sweat rolled off their bodies. The sounds of flesh slapping flesh, proclamations of "yes", "please" "oh my God" and "take me" echoed throughout the home. Veronica screamed Charlie's name aloud during her final orgasm as the pleasure was that intense. The two climaxed together and Charlie drove his tongue deep into Veronica's mouth, bringing about another smaller orgasm. Veronica started to thank Charlie once they were done, but he quickly placed a finger over her lips and just held the woman close to his heart. Before the sun arose, Charlie cleaned himself up, got dressed, kissed Veronica good-bye and slipped out of her home and neighborhood.

It was only after Charlie Santino had left that Veronica began to feel remorse for giving herself over to the man. She had once vowed that she would never sleep with a white man. She now felt dirty, as if she had betrayed Benjamin by sleeping with a member of the race of people who had slaughtered him and destroyed their once happy existence. She jumped from the bed and ran to the shower and stood in there for almost an hour, trying to wash away the guilt.

Veronica hoped she hadn't made a fool of herself by giving in to Charlie. She wondered if the man was really going to help her; but she also couldn't deny the fact that she enjoyed the way she felt when she was around the man. She dropped her kids off at school and daycare, and went to work a troubled woman. She began having thoughts that she would never see Charlie again, and every time she did so, she felt sad. It was during those hours at work the day after she made love to Charlie, that Veronica realized that she had deep feelings for the man.

Veronica finished her shift and exited the sugar refinery to gather her kids. She walked slowly towards her car thinking of Charlie and was surprised to see him leaning up against her car. She walked over to him slowly and as Charlie went to hug her, Veronica stepped back and stretched out her hand. Charlie understood what Veronica was going through and he apologized for what happened the night before as he held onto the woman's hand tightly.

"I should've never done that Misses Jenkins. But I never felt about a woman the way I feel about you. I love—"

Veronica shushed Charlie and the two stared at one another as they held hands in the parking lot.

*"God, this is so wrong!"* Veronica thought to herself as she looked around at the mixed races of people in the parking lot.

Veronica was afraid to display her affections in public for fear of what people would say. She leaned into Charlie, looked beyond his stare and began to make small circles on the hood of her car with her finger tips; the circles becoming more prominent against the grit that covered the hood of her car. Veronica thought long and hard before she heaved, let out a flood of tears and wrapped her arms around Charlie's huge shoulders. The two kissed passionately in the middle of the parking lot, Veronica moaning into Charlie's mouth and shedding tears as employees at the refinery looked on in disbelief and disgust as the two kissed in broad daylight.

Veronica left her car at work and got into Charlie's car. The two picked up Veronica's children and went to Charlie's diner for dinner. For a brief period of time, Veronica felt like a woman again. Charlie made her feel good—in and out of bed. The two had become lovers. Off and on, for days at a time Charlie would stay in the Jenkins' home. Twelve year-old Henrietta had even gotten used to having Charlie around. Whenever he was there, Charlie would always help Henrietta with her homework and pique her brain in the same manner that Benjamin did when he was alive.

Charlie, however, knew that he could never take the place of Benjamin, and he didn't try to. He explained that to Veronica, stating that he wanted to make her an honest woman once more as he placed an engagement ring on her left hand. Veronica accepted, but delayed the marriage, telling Charlie to continue in the way he was going and, in due time, she would give him her hand in marriage.

"Veronica Jenkins-Santino does have a nice ring to it," she stated as she sat on the sofa next to the man, admiring the diamond ring and watching her two kids play with their baby dolls.

Henrietta heard the conversation and had witnessed Charlie on bended knee and she secretly grew happy at the thought of having Charlie as a father-figure in the house. Henrietta truly liked Charlie; he was strong, loving and caring, just like her father. Charlie grew excited at the thought of marrying Veronica. Having such a beautiful woman as his wife would make him the happiest man alive. Veronica was his world; he adored the woman and wanted nothing more than to prove his love to Veronica, and he set out to do so, in hopes of earning this beautiful woman's heart.

"I have to find out what happened to Benjamin, Veronica. I can't marry you until I do that." Charlie said as he sat beside Veronica on the couch.

"Charlie," Veronica said as she looked into his eyes, "my husband means everything to me and I'll always love him. It has taken me a while to get over his death. To be honest, I don't thin I will ever fully recover, but what we have is special and rare in this day and age. Don't you ever feel that you have to prove yourself to me in order to win me over, because my love, you've won me. You hear? You've won me. I just want to take it slow. You're the only man I've been with besides my husband, so of course it's going to take time. But don't think that I don't care for you. I do care. I care very much, Mister Santino."

Veronica was beginning to place the death of her husband behind her, but Charlie made an agreement within himself at the inception of he and Veronica's rapport that he would find out exactly what happened to Benjamin. It was an obligation Charlie felt he had to fulfill. The man would never feel right marrying Benjamin Jenkins' wife without fulfilling what he and Veronica had started. Besides, it was for that very reason, to solve Benjamin's murder, in which the two had become friends and eventual lovers.

At the end of March of 1961, Charlie drove up to Hattiesburg and pulled into the parking lot of the lumber yard. The lumber yard only had a skeleton crew working since it was a Saturday, but Charlie quickly found out that his old comrades hung out in an old wooden house that had been converted into a bar called *The Tavern* on the outskirts of town. Charlie waited until around 11P.M. and headed towards *The Tavern*.

Charlie walked into the establishment, which was filled with patrons and eyed the scene. This was a rowdy bunch. *The*

*Tavern* was filled with smoke that reddened Charlie's eyes. A bottle of liquor was on just about every wooden table and it seemed as if every white male had a beer or a shot of some brand of whiskey in his hand. The women were talking loud and being grabbed by the men on a whim for a quick dance or to be groped and kissed at random. Loud laughter emanated from both sex's mouths as well as the curse words. Charlie saw a few men he knew from the lumber yard sitting at the bar on the other side of the room and he began to part the crowd and make his way to the bar. He gently shoved patrons aside and shook a few hands as he walked through *The Tavern*. Ray Charles' song, *Georgia On My Mind* blared from the juke box as Charlie made his way to the bar and slapped an old friend on the back.

The man turned around quickly with a look of disdain, as if he was being bothered, but he quickly grew happy when he saw the towering figure standing before him.

"Oh shit! Charlie Santino! How you doing, you whop son-of-a-bitch?" the man yelled as he downed a shot of liquor and lit a cigarette and got up to shake Charlie's hand.

"I'm fine Casey. Just fine. I just earned my stripes tonight."

"Whatcha mean, good buddy?"

"What I mean is, I killed my first nigger tonight! Felt good too! Besides killing those slant eyes in the Pacific, the only thing that brought me more joy was to slay me a nigger! You wanna see the body?" Charlie yelled over the music and loud ruckus.

"Hell, yeah, I wanna see the body! Where's it at?"

"I got 'em strung up in the woods just south of Laurel. Bouta' light me a barn fire tonight! I want in! Tonight I've earned my stripes!" Charlie ended as he waved the bartender over and ordered a draft beer in a mug.

Casey danced around in his cowboy boots and took off his hat and waved it in the air. He then stood up on top his stool and yelled aloud, "I'm going have a grand ole time boys! Charlie done got me a nigger on a rope!"

The men and women in *The Tavern* went wild and erupted into cheers as Casey hopped from the stool, grabbed an overweight red-haired female companion along with another male companion and bought another fifth of whiskey in preparation for the celebration.

It hurt Charlie to see people behave this way, but he had to play along. He cheered as well; but he now had to figure out how he was going to incapacitate two full grown men and keep a heavy-set woman under control. He downed his beer quickly and the quartet exited *The Tavern*.

Charlie hopped into his pick-up with the heavy-set red head, and Casey riding shotgun. The other man, who Charlie later found out during the ride towards Laurel, was Mister Henderson's nephew named, Randolph, followed Charlie, Casey, and the heavy-set woman closely behind in his car.

The four headed up the road to Laurel and Charlie knew he had to make a move soon. He guzzled down some of the whiskey and passed the bottle to Casey. The medium built man guzzled the whiskey and grimaced as the liquor burned his chest. The red head then took a swallow and passed it back to Charlie. The three continued the routine until Charlie was just outside of Laurel where he exited the highway onto a dirt road lined with oak trees on either side, and prepared to make his move.

Charlie turned his headlights off, which allowed the full moon to illuminate the dirt road. The car behind him turned off its headlights as well. As soon as Randolph's headlights were no longer illuminating the cab of Charlie's truck, his right arm stretched out and flew swiftly past the red-head's face and his balled-up right fist struck Casey in the jaw, quickly knocking him unconscious.

The red-head looked at Charlie in a shocked manner. Charlie could see the whites of the woman's eyes through the darkness and he quickly placed his hand over the woman's mouth to prevent her from screaming. Charlie then stopped his truck and waited for Randolph to exit his car.

When Randolph walked over to Charlie's truck, he struck

the younger man in the head with the nearly empty bottle of whiskey and he fell onto the ground, dizzied by the blow. Charlie then got out of his truck, dragging the red-head with him. The female was in a state of shock as Charlie dragged her over to the driver's side of Randolph's Ford Fairlane and grabbed the keys from the steering wheel. Randolph was beginning to pull himself to his feet, so Charlie quickly dragged the woman to the back of the Ford, and shoved her into the trunk of the car and slammed it shut. He then ran and hit Randolph hard in the face, knocking him down again. Charlie then reached into the bed of his pick up, gathered a thick rope and tied Randolph to a tree. He checked on Casey when he was done and saw that he was still out cold. Charlie then began beating Randolph fiercely while asking him what he knew about a murder that took place in 1957.

"They had a lot of murders in fifty-seven!" the frightened young man said as he spat blood from his mouth.

"I'm talking about one in particular! A black man from the lumber yard! Drove a fifty-five T-bird! Got ran off the road and drowned in a creek in December of that year!"

Randolph, now frightened out of his mind, told Charlie that his uncle and two of his uncles' friends followed a man named Benjamin in December, just before Christmas, and forced him to pull over by using a police officer's strobe light. He continued on by telling Charlie they then beat the man and forced alcohol into his system which made him intoxicated. Randolph stated that his uncle and friends laughed at the man as he wobbled around in the woods in a drunken stupor before they beat him again and placed him inside his car and pushed the car into a creek with the man inside, unconscious, but not dead at the time.

"I wasn't with 'em Mister—but I know they killed that man because they bragged all that week after Christmas that my uncle had a new position at the lumber yard. That's all I know. Don't kill me sir, please." Randolph pleaded.

Charlie punched Randolph in the stomach once more and he gasped for air and coughed up more blood.

"You tell your sadistic friend over there when he comes through—Veronica—Jenkins—sends—her—regards!" Charlie spat the words in a broken sentence as he struck Randolph in the face five times, fracturing his cheek bones in the process.

Charlie knew Benjamin Jenkins was a good man; and to hear the manner in which he was taken away from his family had fueled such an immense anger within Charlie that it took all the man's inner strength not to kill Randolph and Casey. It was, however, easy for Charlie to kick ass that night and he did just so. He walked to his pick-up, slung Casey from the passenger seat and began kicking him about the head and chest repeatedly before he got into his truck and sped away, leaving a trial of dust behind as he approached the highway that lead through Hattiesburg, on his way back to New Orleans.

Before Charlie made it to the highway, Randolph had freed himself and struggled over to the trunk of the car. He released the woman and she helped Randolph and Casey into the car and sped back to *The Tavern*.

Charlie's arrival back to New Orleans was delayed because he had to stop at a gas station and repair a flat tire. His plan was also compromised when he tried to call his diner because the phone lines were down. Charlie eventually made his made way over to his diner, but he knew time was now of the essence. Before he left his diner, Charlie telephoned Veronica.

Veronica was still half-asleep when she answered her phone, "Hello? Hello? Who is this?"

"This is Charlie, Veronica! I'm on my way over there to pick up you and your kids! Get yourself and your kids together right now!"

"Charlie? Charlie, it's, it's after midnight! What's this all about? Where're we going at this hour?"

"No time to explain Veronica. Trust me please! I'm on my way!"

"Why? I can just take my car and leave now and meet you."

"Don't move Veronica! Benjamin's killers may be on their way to your home! Don't turn on any lights in your home! And please don't open the door for anyone! Understand? I'm on my way! Keep an eye out for my truck!"

Veronica told Charlie she understood and she immediately got up and tip-toed to Henrietta's room. She shook her daughter softly and told her to move quietly to her bedroom. Veronica and Henrietta huddled in her bedroom as she wrapped Gabriella in a blanket. The woman peeked out her window and noticed that the streets were asleep this cold night. She waited patiently until she saw headlights coming down her street. She figured it was Charlie, so she began to move towards her front door. She glanced out her bedroom window again to make sure, but she realized it wasn't Charlie's truck. She watched in horror as a group of hooded klansmen exited a Ford Fairlane, while others jumped from the back of an old pick up.

They were headed directly for Veronica's house. The woman began to panic when she realized what was about to transpire. She reached under her mattress, grabbed her gun and backed up against the wall, and squatted beneath the window with Gabriella secured tightly in her bosom. Henrietta clutched her mother and baby sister tightly in utter fear as a dozen klansmen formed a semi-circle in her front yard. They each held either a hand gun or a shotgun in one hand and a bottle with a rag hanging out of the top in the other. The men began yelling for Veronica to come outside. The neighbors on Veronica's block watched from their windows in terror as the klansmen stood in Veronica's yard and began lighting Molotov cocktails.

Veronica remained huddled on the floor with her two daughters and gripped the pistol tightly, preparing for the worse. She then heard a loud crashing sound coming from the back door of her home and she screamed aloud and aimed her gun at her bedroom door's entrance just as a white man, dressed in an all black silk suit and sporting a black fedora, rushed into her bedroom and reached out his hand.

"Misses Jenkins, come with me ma'am!" he said in hurried tone.

"We want that nigger bitch out here on the yard or we're going to burn this entire neighborhood down tonight!" a hooded klansmen yelled.

"Misses Jenkins, we have to go now! Please, ma'am! We're friends of Charlie!"

"Charlie!" Veronica said as she grabbed the man's hand and clutched Gabriella tightly as Henrietta followed close behind. "Where's Charlie?" she asked.

"He's outside waiting for you, ma'am." the man said as he was joined by two other men inside the hallway where they guided Veronica and her kids towards the living room.

As they entered the living room, the six were met with two Molotov cocktails. The first one shattered the living room window and flames encompassed the home's front exterior. The second Molotov cocktail went through the broken glass and exploded upon landing upon the carpet inside the living room. The fireball leapt from the carpet onto the lead man's clothing and he screamed aloud as he flailed about trying to extinguish the flames overtaking his body as Veronica and her daughters were ushered back into the hallway to avoid the flames. The lead man was quickly succumbed by the flames and he fell onto the living room floor, his body covered in flames and still flailing about as he pleaded for help. One of the men ran from the hallway and tried to cover his comrade but another fire bomb exploded inside Veronica's living room and spread rapidly across the window sill, the walls and furniture. The second man yelled aloud for the surviving four, ordering them to flee and they made a dash for the back door, narrowly avoiding the inferno and leaving the lead man's burning body behind as they escaped through the back door without harm. The second man would also die inside of Veronica's home while trying to rescue his comrade.

Charlie was anxiously waiting outside the burning home, holding a .357 magnum in his right hand and dressed in a black suit, black tie, white shirt, with a black trench coat and a black fedora. Veronica hugged Charlie tightly when she saw him. Charlie then guided Veronica and her kids to the rear of the house and onto the next block where a station wagon was waiting. He placed Veronica and her kids in the back seat, slammed the door shut and tapped the top of the car and the car quickly sped away. As the car sped away, Veronica looked back to see Charlie, and at least a half dozen other men firing their weapons. The gunfire crackled like thunder in the still cold air as Henrietta lay on the floor of the car clutching Gabriella, screaming in sheer terror. The driver of the station wagon fired a shotgun blast with his left hand as he tried to steer but the windshield shattered and he was shot in the neck by one of the klansmen. The driver dropped his weapon and let go of the steering wheel as he fell over onto the front seat and died.

The car veered onto the curb, heading directly towards a neighbor's home, but Veronica reached over the front seat and slammed the car into park when it rolled onto the sidewalk. As she was preparing to exit the car, Veronica quickly spotted two hooded klansmen running out into the open approaching the car from the right side of the neighbor's home. Veronica rearmed herself with her .38 special and immediately began firing her weapon out the driver's side window as she yelled aloud for Henrietta to lie still on the floor board of the car and cover Gabriella.

Henrietta had a death grip on her baby sister. She and Gabriella screamed at the top of their lungs as their mother exchanged gunfire with two the klansmen. Veronica emptied her gun just as bullets from the klansmen guns began penetrating the driver's side door. The passenger window shattered and the men continued firing, their bullets now hitting the interior of the car's dash and passenger side door. In one sweeping motion, and risking being struck by the gunmen, Veronica reached over into the front seat and grabbed the dead driver's shotgun and began to fire that weapon from the back window, her actions causing the men to search for cover. Veronica racked the shotgun again and fired once more, this time, one of the klansmen went down. The remaining klansman retreated behind the right side of Veronica's neighbor's home as gunfire continued to erupt in the night.

Veronica racked the gun again; but quickly realized she was out of bullets. She looked around, frightened, all the while hoping klansmen wouldn't approach the car once more; because if they did, she had no way of defending herself and her daughters. Gunfire could still be heard, but no one was in sight. Veronica was searching the front seat for more shotgun shells when she saw motion to her left. She looked in that direction and sighed a sigh of relief when she saw Charlie and his men emerge from the left side of the home and began making their way towards the station wagon.

Veronica saw movement to her right at that moment. She turned her head in that direction and gasped. Three more klansmen had emerged from the right side of the home. They were now impeding Charlie's progress by standing in between him and his comrades and the station wagon which held Veronica and her kids.

Both parties paused briefly and eyed one another. When one of the klansmen aimed his shotgun at the station wagon, Charlie and his men opened fire and another gun battle ensued. The klansman got off a blast, but Veronica had laid down on the back seat and shielded herself and her kids. The rear passenger window of the station wagon shattered and glass landed on Veronica's back as she screamed aloud right along with her kids.

Charlie and his men gunned the three men down and silence ensued. They seemed to be in the clear as the right side of the home was now devoid of klansmen.

Veronica slowly raised her head and looked around and waved Charlie onward from the backseat of the wagon when she saw no one was on the right side of the home.

"Hurry! Hurry Charlie!" Veronica screamed aloud from the backseat as Charlie and his men ran towards the station wagon.

Charlie and his men were fast approaching the station wagon until at least a half dozen more klansmen emerged from the left side of the home to Charlie's rear and opened fire once more. Charlie and his men turned around and returned fire upon the klansmen and another intense gun battle got underway.

It was was a scene that could only be compared to that of a military battlefield. Bodies were strewn about people's lawns and lying in the street. An orange hue, that of flames emanating from Veronica's home, was off in the distance. Men were screaming in pain, ducking behind bushes and trees, and some were even bold enough to stand out in the open and fire their weapon at this point. Charlie was right in the middle of the battle. As he stood in the middle of the street firing his weapon, he was struck in the stomach.

Veronica watched as Charlie dropped his weapon, clutched his mid-section and slowly sunk to his knees.

"Charlie! Charlie get up!" Veronica yelled through worried eyes and trembling lips as she watched from the back seat.

"Take the family and get the fuck outta here!" Charlie yelled as he fell to the ground, still clutching his stomach.

As Charlie's men exchanged gunfire with the klansmen again, one of Charlie's partners grabbed him and tried to pull him towards the station wagon where Veronica and her daughters waited, but the gunfire was growing more fierce. Veronica was lucky to dodge several bullets that hit the top portion of the back seat inside the station wagon. Charlie knew Veronica and her daughters' lives were at risk, so, forsaking that of his own, he ordered the man to leave him and his comrades at that moment.

"We can make it, Charlie! Run with me, brother!" the man pleaded.

"Take the family and get the fuck outta here! Go! Go! Go!" Charlie yelled as he lay on the ground clutching his stomach.

The man quickly ran to the station wagon, pulled the dead driver from the seat and jumped into the car and drove off, leaving Charlie behind. Charlie was down, and at least four more gunmen were still waging war with at least six hooded klansmen. Veronica pleaded for the man not to leave Charlie and the rest of the men, but the man had no choice. He had to save Veronica and her childrens' lives. He was simply obeying Charlie's orders. Veronica held her children tightly as the gunfire faded into the background. She cried aloud, screaming Charlie's name repeatedly as she watched his silhouette, and that of his comrades, and the klansmen, as well, fade into the distance.

Veronica was taken to a safe house in Baton Rouge, Louisiana and briefed on the events that had transpired. She learned that Charlie once worked for a civil rights activist group, authorized by J. Edgar Hoover, chief detective for the F.B.I., to investigate Klan activity. Charlie still had connections to the group and he used his influence to form a coalition to go after the klansmen in Mississippi. Charles Santino always had an intense hatred for wrong doing. By chance, he met Veronica Jenkins, a woman who suffered an injustice at the hands of the Ku Klux Klan.

Veronica's plight reinvigorated Charlie; and during the time he came to know her, Charlie fell in love with the woman. Charlie loved Veronica wholeheartedly, and he felt it was his destiny to bring to justice the men who murdered her husband. It was the only way he would feel right if he'd married Veronica. He drove to Mississippi and provoked the Klan, purposely stating Veronica's name, hoping the klansmen would retaliate. Charlie's plan had worked, but it was by no means the ending he had in mind.

Forty-five year-old Charles Santino died in the Lower Ninth Ward in the middle of the street. The shoot out was a fiery, bloody scene that left Charlie and four of his comrades dead, including the two victims that burned inside of Veronica's home, and two who were killed while trying to protect an injured Charlie.

Later, as the hoods of the dead klansmen were removed, it was discovered that Casey and Mister Henderson were among the five dead klansmen. Mister Henderson's nephew, Randolph, was captured along with six other surviving klansmen. Faced with life behind bars in a federal facility, and even death row at the hands of the federal government, the men all testified and confessed to over sixteen murders committed in southern Mississippi over a period of three years from 1954 to 1957, with Benjamin Jenkins' murder being the last.

Charlie perished in the gun battle, but Veronica would be forever grateful to the man who'd brought justice to her family and gave his life for a cause with which he, for what it's worth, had no solid connection or affiliation.

Charles Santino was awarded The Medal of Freedom by President John F. Kennedy shortly after his death. The Medal of Freedom is the highest award offered to civilians. Charlie was also given a hero's burial in Arlington, Virginia. Calling Charlie a martyr, the local and national news leapt on the story. Charlie Santino's actions would later spark a successful Civil Rights Movement in New Orleans. A park in the Lower Ninth Ward would later be named in honor the man.

Veronica and her kids, meanwhile, were once again on their own. Charlie's death wasn't as hard to take as Benjamin's death had been because even though she cared deeply for Charlie, Veronica had remained somewhat distant. She knew that she and Charlie would be the objects of ridicule and persecution; but she never figured Charlie would get killed.

Veronica had guarded her heart well. Another heartache would've broken her spirits; maybe to the point that she would have just given up on life once and for all had her heart been broken again—kids or no kids. Veronica put her heart and her daughters' well-being above all else, and by doing so, she saved herself a lot of unnecessary heartache and pain. As hard as it would be to go on without Charlie, Veronica would remain strong for her daughters' sake and look towards the future with optimism.

Veronica reflected on her life as she sat on the sofa in the living room of the safe house, clutching her two daughters, who slept peacefully in her arms. She smiled to herself and said a silent prayer. On this night, Veronica Jenkins had taken a vow of celibacy and would dedicate the remainder of her life to raising her daughters. She would take the things she learned from Benjamin and Charlie, face the world head on, and raise Henrietta and Gabriella to be as strong as they could be during these ever-changing times.

## CHAPTER 8

## YOU ARE A JENKINS

The remainder of Veronica's life would be spent raising her children, in church, and helping to fight in the cause for civil rights. She returned to New Orleans shortly after the shootout and rented a home on Kelerec Street in the Seventh Ward section. Veronica had become disheartened by the things that were transpiring during the turbulent sixties. War was on the horizon in Vietnam, and drugs were taking a toll on the black community. Veronica watched young men volunteer for service knowing they would be confronted with a nation of people, namely whites, that hated them, even though they were volunteering to serve their country. Many would come back home as either social-paths or heroin addicts that had become emotionally detached from the realities of life and highly disillusioned.

Still, Veronica pressed on. She became a board member in her church in November of 1961. That same month, a Cause worth fighting, in Veronica's eyes, had developed that she felt would honor her deceased husband and bring to life the last discussion Benjamin Jenkins ever had with his daughter Henrietta.

Integration had become law in New Orleans in November of 1961 when a six year-old black girl named Ruby Bridges was escorted onto the campus of William Frantz Elementary School, located in the Ninth Ward section of New Orleans, by local officials. Ruby faced death threats and white students' parents had excused their kids from class on that historic day. On that day, Ruby Bridges sat alone in class. Eventually some white students returned, but the white urban flight era had begun. The kids at the integrated schools, namely the black students, were still receiving out-dated text books with missing pages. Those things disheartened Veronica and the woman wanted to contribute to the Cause. She did so by advocating for new text books for all students since integration had become law.

Nearly a year later, after many petitions and protests, and with the aide of members from her church and local politicians' sympathy, Veronica had won the fight; and when Henrietta and Gabriella, who was to start kindergarten, started school, in 1962, every black child was receiving brand new text books thanks to Veronica Jenkins' efforts. Benjamin's vision was partially realized through his widow's actions.

Henrietta, now fourteen years-old, was proud of her mother. She remembered the last time she and her father ever spoke, when she expressed her concern over the heavily damaged text books she and the other black students were receiving. She knew her father would have been proud of her mother's efforts to change the school system's method of operation even more the she.

Henrietta entered her freshman year at McDonogh #35, one of the first predominately black high schools in New Orleans in the year of 1962. She was a proud fourteen year-old little girl. Henrietta was soon shocked, however, to learn that many of the students at the high school resented what her mother had done. They complained that they could no longer buy or smoke marijuana on school grounds because Veronica had forced the school officials to hire security guards. Many of the students could not appreciate the fact that Veronica was actually trying to keep them safe from racial threats and attacks which were all too common around McDonogh #35, G.W. Carver and John McDonogh, the only three predominately African-American local high schools at that point and time.

"You and your family ain't even from around here! Your righteous ass momma come from across the canal and fuck shit up for us!" a high school sophomore named Darlene said as she shoved Henrietta in the chest, knocking the books from her hands as she stood underneath the breezeway shortly before the start of classes.

Henrietta cherished her new books. Her mother was responsible for her receiving those new books. She thought about the sacrifices her mother made and she immediately began fighting back. She swung wildly at the tall, thick-boned, dark-skinned, Afro-wearing, big-eyed fifteen year-old, but as she did so, Henrietta's glasses fell off her face. As she scrambled to pick up her glasses to prevent them from getting damaged, Darlene got the best of Henrietta.

On just her second day of school, Henrietta had taken a beating from another teenager. Darlene hit Henrietta in the forehead leaving a hickey on the left side of her skull just as the fight was broken up. Henrietta grabbed her book bag and glasses and ran home from school home to her mother in a flood of tears.

"What on God's green earth happened to you, Henrietta?" Veronica asked as she stood in her living room staring at Henrietta as she stood before her crying.

Veronica had taken the week off to be home with her daughters, namely Gabriella, as it was her first year of school.

"I said what happened to you, Henrietta?" Veronica asked again as Henrietta stood before her crying heavily.

"This, this, this girl named Darlene knocked my books out my hand. I, I tried to defend myself like you taught me, but I lost my, my glasses!" Henrietta replied before she hid her face in her hands and heaved.

"You ran? Tell me you didn't run from that school, Henrietta!"

"I couldn't see mama!" Henrietta cried as she eyed her mother.

"Henrietta, how many times have I told you that you have to stand up for yourself? You lost more respect by running away than you would have ever gained by staying and fighting.

And no, you *were* able to see! Why did you run away from that fight child?" Veronica asked as she walked to the bathroom and grabbed a towel and wet it by placing a little alcohol onto it.

"I was scared!" Henrietta stated as she eyed her mother returning to the living room. "I was scared, momma! Everybody was cheering for Darlene to hit me! Nobody likes me in this part of the Seventh Ward! We should've stayed in the Lower Ninth Ward where daddy and Charlie was. If they were alive, they would—"

"They would tell you to get back down to that school and face your fears. You've been through worse, child, and you can get through this!" Veronica said as she opened her door and picked Henrietta's book bag off the floor and handed it to her.

Henrietta held her head down as she walked out of her mother's door. "Hold your head up proud, Henrietta! You are a Jenkins! Even when we're confronted with adversity and fear, Jenkins' always remain strong and face our fears head on! Understand? Don't you ever run from a fight again or else they'll always pick on you." Veronica remarked as she gently placed her hand on Henrietta's shoulder.

"I love you, momma," Henrietta said as she slid gently into her mother's arms, "it's just so hard without daddy."

"You've come this far without your father, baby. And you'll go even further so long as you don't give up. Your father wouldn't like that now, would he?" Veronica asked as she peered down into her daughter's pretty brown eyes.

Veronica brushed Henrietta's shoulder length brown hair from her face and rubbed her light-tanned, thin face adoringly as she dabbed the wet towel across Henrietta's forehead to cleanse her bruise. Henrietta grimaced at the slight burning sensation.

"I love you more than life itself, my child," Veronica continued, "and I want you to be strong. Momma won't always be around to encourage you like this. It's time for you to start fighting your own battles, Henrietta. Now, you go back to that school and show no fear when you walk past that girl. If she messes with you again, you take your glasses off this time, because it's the only pair you have. And then you beat the ever-loving shit out of her ass! Then pick your sister up from kindergarten and you two walk home from school like the two proud Jenkins' you both are and have dinner with your mother. If the school administrators have something to say about the matter, tell them I'll be there to talk to them myself." Veronica ended as Henrietta snickered into her mother's bosom.

Veronica had used a curse word for the first time ever in front of Henrietta. She wanted to reinforce what she was saying to her daughter that morning. Henrietta went back to school, and, during lunch, Darlene approached her again. This time, Henrietta took off her glasses and wailed on the sophomore until she pleaded for Henrietta to stop. Darlene now had a hickey on the left side of her forehead. Henrietta then rushed two of Darlene's friends and slapped them both as they ran off, leaving Darlene behind. Henrietta picked up her books and left the cafeteria with her head up in the air, smiling to herself, and no one, not even school officials, said a word to her.

Later, at the end of the school day, Darlene approached Henrietta again as she walked home with Gabriella. Gabriella was moving about playfully in front of her big sister, skipping and humming a church hymn as Darlene approached. When Henrietta caught sight of the older teen, she ran and grabbed Gabriella and pulled her little sister behind her.

Darlene approached Henrietta and congratulated her on her victory. "You won fair and square Henrietta." she said. "And I wanted to apologize for criticizing your momma. I know Misses Jenkins is only looking out for us. I was stupid to say those things. I'm sorry." Darlene concluded before she turned and walked off.

"Darlene!" Henrietta called out, causing Darlene to stop in her tracks and turn around. "You apologized to me and I accept. I'm still fairly new here in the neighborhood. Can you show me around?" Henrietta asked.

Darlene was really a nice girl, but she was easily influenced by her peers, Henrietta knew that to be a fact. She also knew that since she was big for her age, Darlene's so-called friends would often entice her to fight. What happened between Darlene and Henrietta earlier in the day was actually the result of two of those so-called friends enticing Darlene to fight Henrietta for their own enjoyment and Henrietta knew it all-too-well.

Darlene was flattered that a girl as nice as Henrietta would actually request her further presence. She believed at the outset that Henrietta would shun her; but when Henrietta showed kindness, Darlene was moved to show kindness in return. She apologized to Henrietta again telling her she was truly sorry.

"I hope we can be real friends, Henrietta. I'm tired of being a bully."

"You are not a bully, Darlene." Henrietta said as she smiled a friendly smile whilst tugging on Darlene's elbow. "Sometimes, people entice us into doing things we don't really want to do. I didn't want to fight you. That's why I ran at first. Besides the fact that you had me scared. But I'm more afraid of my mother than I am of you." Henrietta replied as she and Darlene laughed lightly.

"Believe me, I was just as scared. My size won me a lot of fights; but when you fought me back, I didn't know what to do, Henrietta! Nobody never fought me back! And when my friends ran off and left me, I was just as scared as you."

"Seems as if we were both afraid, but we can put that aside now, Darlene. This is my little sister, Gabriella."

"She's pretty." Darlene said in a low tone.

"Say thank you, Gabriella."

"Thank you, miss," five year-old Gabriella said softly as she peeked from behind her big sister and waved at Darlene coyly.

"Hey," Darlene then stated seriously, "my friends don't like you. I don't even know you that well but I listened to them and fought you anyway. I'm not like that. I actually liked what your mother did for us—even though most everybody else doesn't."

"Looks like you need to find some new friends, Darlene."

"Yeah, I know. Well, I would like to start with you, Henrietta. Call me Dee from here on." Darlene remarked as she extended her hand towards Henrietta and the two teens shook hands, becoming friends.

Henrietta then decided to invite Darlene to her home to meet her mother and get Veronica's opinion concerning her new friend. Veronica talked to both Darlene and Henrietta about the fight they had and after a while, she approved of Darlene and the three of them sat on the front porch and talked. Veronica shared some of the things she and her daughters experienced a few years back and Darlene became fascinated by Veronica's stories. Darlene also apologized to Veronica for calling her righteous. Veronica laughed at the teenager, saying she did what she had to do to protect and feed her children and if that branded her as righteous, then so be it.

"It seems like it's more than that, Misses Jenkins. You did a lot for your family and for us younger folk. A lot more people around here should have your courage. Yours too, Henrietta."

"We all do our part, Darlene. Some just do it better than others," Veronica responded. "What I did could've been done by anybody. There's a Martin Luther King Jr. in each and every one of us. You just have to believe in yourself. Inner strength is one of the most powerful forces a human being could ever possess; some of us fear it, some of us misuse it, and some of us come to have a healthy understanding of the power that lies within us. My situation would be the latter. You have that inner strength, too, Darlene. Only you don't see it as of yet. You made a smart decision to cut off ties with your so-called friends and that's a start. You are on your way. I think you and Henrietta will do just fine for yourselves in life." Veronica concluded as she got up from her stoop and walked into her home with Gabriella in tow, leaving Henrietta and Darlene alone to talk.

Henrietta and Darlene found out that they had a lot in common. The two became good friends for a while until Darlene graduated high school and left for college a year before Henrietta.

Hurricane Betsy struck the city of New Orleans in 1965 and

destroyed the Jenkins family home. The house was flooded nearly to the roof with water left behind by the hurricane. After surviving the hurricane and spending a night outside on the roof with her two daughters, which was a harrowing experience for Gabriella, Veronica used her insurance money to close the deal on a cozy two bedroom home in the Ninth Ward section of New Orleans on the corners of Benefit and Metropolitan streets, not too far from G.W. Carver High School.

The move to the upper Ninth Ward and the new neighborhood was a welcomed change for Henrietta, who would now be attending G.W. Carver. Henrietta had to often argue and squabble with various females at McDonogh #35 High School once Darlene had left. Her sophomore year was not a very good one as she was picked on because of the glasses she wore and her light-skinned complexion. Henrietta, however, quickly found G.W. Carver Senior High School to be a laid-back, free-spirited, close-knit environment. She thrived there, and she got plenty of attention from the boys, something she hadn't received in any shape, form, or fashion at her previous high school.

Henrietta was pleased with all the positive attention she was receiving during her junior year. She made friends at a rapid pace, but she was especially close to a studious classmate of hers named Marcel. Henrietta didn't like the athletic types, so when Marcel, who was on the school's debate team, and tops in Henrietta's Algebra II class, asked her to the junior prom, Henrietta graciously accepted. The two remained a couple up until Henrietta's senior year.

Marcel had brought up the question of sex to Henrietta a week before their senior prom and the eighteen year-old began to reflect on the sexual adventures that Darlene had shared with her during the time they were friends. Everyday leading up to the day of senior prom, Marcel would ask Henrietta, as they were leaving their music class, if she had thought about his question and did she have an answer.

"Baby, after school is done, you going away to college and so am I. We in love with one another, right?" Marcel asked two days before the prom.

Henrietta pondered Marcel's question concerning their being in love. She had feelings for Marcel, true enough, but she knew she wasn't in love. Henrietta had formed her own beliefs about what a man's love truly was, and real love in general, based on the things she had seen her mother go through early on. And what she and Marcel had, in Henrietta's eyes, was not real love, it more like infatuation or lust.

Love, to Henrietta, was powerful, protective and strong, like her father was towards her mother. Love was kind and considerate, like Charlie was towards her mother. Love was ever hopeful, full of pride and unbridled strength like Veronica was at all times. Those were the things Henrietta learned about love; but on the other end of the spectrum, Henrietta, up until this point in her life, had never been as curious as she was about sex as she was now.

Henrietta knew Marcel had more of an infatuation, and she wasn't in love with him either; even though he possessed some of the qualities Henrietta believed was the making of a good man. In spite of the fact that she wasn't in love with Marcel, Henrietta still wanted to know what it felt like to be made love to by a man; and Marcel was indeed pushing the right buttons in Henrietta's eyes. Henrietta secretly wanted to experiment with sex with Marcel; but she could not find it within herself to let that proclamation spill forth from her mouth. What would her mother think of her if she were to have sex so early in her life without being married?

"Let's just have us a nice time on Saturday. I'm not gonna answer that question, Marcel." she responded coyly after a brief moment of silence.

"By not answering the question, you have given your answer, Henrietta. Which is a resounding no." Marcel replied dejectedly as the two emerged from the small building which held their music class.

"By not answering, I *didn't* say no, Marcel." Henrietta replied as she turned and kissed Marcel on the lips under the breezeway just outside of the school's music room as students passed by, some whistling, and others yelling in mocked tone for the two to get a room. "Your bi-focals are fogging over, Mister Marcel." Henrietta joked as she turned and walked away, making sure to gyrate her hips in a seductive manner to further intrigue the young man.

Marcel removed his glasses and focused in on Henrietta's bottom which was wrapped in a tight fitting pair of bell-bottomed jeans that had no rear pockets. The eighteen year-old stared at Henrietta's firm, taut rear end, imagining what it felt like and how it would look in all of its naked glory.

"See you Saturday, baby." Marcel ended as he smiled to himself and watched as Henrietta walked down the long drive leading to the school's exit.

Henrietta knew Marcel was watching her as she walked calmly towards the exit. She looked back and saw Marcel still staring. *"He thinks I'm sexy!"* Henrietta exclaimed to herself as she exited the school's premises and ran and leaned up against the brick monument dedicated to George Washington Carver that was in front of the school, out of Marcel's sight.

Henrietta was tickled to high heaven that a member of the opposite sex was eagerly pursuing her and she found Marcel's attention more than flattering. Henrietta now had urges rising within herself and she knew very well what those urges were. Veronica explained sexuality to Henrietta early on and told her those urges were natural. Henrietta had those feelings before, but she never sought relief. On this day, however, Henrietta was eager to satisfy those urges.

She picked Gabriella up from the nearby elementary school and walked home at a rapid pace. Gabriella had to often run and catch up with Henrietta as her older sister had a stride upon her on this day in which eight year-old Gabriella had the hardest time keeping up with.

"Why we running, Henrietta?" Gabriella asked as she held on to her lunch box and school bag and jogged beside her sister.

"I have to use the bathroom, Gabriella! Come on now, keep up!" Henrietta answered as she and Gabriella walked pass numerous school students heading home.

Henrietta reached her mother's home and fumbled with the keys as she frantically tried to unlock the door. She was Hades hot, eager to satisfy the desire burning within. When she finally opened the door, Henrietta exhaled in relief. She knew she had two hours before Veronica arrived home, and after fixing Gabriella her after school snack, consisting of Cornflakes coated with sugar and sliced bananas with a glass of apple juice, Henrietta placed Gabriella in front of the TV and went into the bedroom and placed a chair under the door in order to block the entrance. Gabriella heard the moans, but she knew not what her sister was engaged in; she merely continued watching TV until she fell asleep.

Later that night, just after dinner was complete, Henrietta received a phone call from Marcel. The two talked for a while up to the point that Marcel related to Henrietta that he was allowed to use his father's car on prom night and invited Henrietta to go to the drive-in with him after the prom, an invitation in which Henrietta accepted without hesitation.

During the prom, Henrietta and Marcel danced and took pictures. Marcel couldn't keep his hands off Henrietta, but Henrietta, having realized that she was on the verge of losing her virginity, had grown shy. When the prom ended, Henrietta and Marcel rode to the drive-in on Airline Highway and parked in the back row where Marcel resumed his touching and feeling. Henrietta knew what Marcel wanted from her, but she was nervous and somewhat afraid. Each time Marcel tried to touch her, Henrietta, out of fear and anxiety, would start talking about the movie on the screen.

"I ain't worrying 'bout the movie Henrietta! You know why we came here, baby. We talked about this already. When you gon' get hip with the times, Henrietta?" Marcel asked, his slender 5' 9" dark-skinned frame reclining in the driver's seat of his father's '66 Caprice Classic, his hand gently stroking Henrietta's thigh, getting ever so closer to her sex.

"You keep trying to touch me there, Marcel, but I told you on the phone many times, I've never done nothing like this before and it makes me nervous." Henrietta announced over the *Temptation's* song *My Girl* as she shifted slightly and placed her hand on top of Marcel's to prevent him from going any further.

Eighteen year old Henrietta, dressed in a tight-fitting evergreen silk gown, wanted Marcel's affection, but she was too scared to let him touch her "there", for the simple fact that she'd never had sex before and she knew not what to do. Henrietta's body was burning though; she was just real nervous. She also wondered how many times Marcel had done this. The drive-in was packed with teenagers out on dates this muggy spring night in May of '66. No one seemed to be watching the movie *The Good, the Bad, and the Ugly* as it played on the drive-in screen. Marcel looked around the lot and saw numerous cars with fogged up windows rocking from side to side. He knew what was going on, and he wanted so badly to make love to Henrietta. He looked over at Henrietta and saw her looking out the window, away from him, patting her hands in her lap as she bobbed to the Temptations. She was so sexy to him—her pretty brown eyes, pert breasts, long brown hair and petite figure.

"You ever been kissed below the belt?" Marcel suddenly asked.

"Excuse me?" Henrietta said as she turned to face Marcel.

"Have you ever been kissed below the belt?"

"Ooohh!" Henrietta exclaimed as she began to fan herself.

Henrietta remembered a conversation she had with Darlene a couple of years ago. Darlene told Henrietta that whoever "busts the cherry" has to kiss her below the belt first. Marcel had offered to do that. Darlene told Henrietta how good it felt to have a tongue on her vagina; and now that the offer was on the table for Henrietta to take, she didn't want to refuse.

"I haven't. I heard about that—but I never did anything of the sort." Henrietta responded coyly.

"You wanna try?"

"If you want to, Marcel."

"Raise your dress up for me."

Henrietta rose slightly and pulled her dress above her waist. Marcel ogled over her smooth, creamy tan thighs. He reached out and ran his hand across her legs and up her belly which prompted Henrietta to moan softly.

"Let's get in the back seat so we can stretch out." Marcel said in a heated tone.

Henrietta was aroused as well. She wanted this experience all so badly. She and Marcel got into the back seat and Marcel laid her down gently. He slid Henrietta's panties off over her heels and looked into her eyes longingly. Both were breathing hard at that moment. As the heat of Marcel's breath grew nearer to Henrietta's sex, she had an immediate orgasm. Her body quivered as she grasped Marcel's head and pulled him into her aching womanhood. Marcel gave exquisite cunninglingus to Henrietta; and he wanted more. Henrietta kindly obliged by removing her shoes and dress as Marcel removed his trousers and rolled a condom onto his hardened member.

Henrietta Jenkins lost her virginity on prom night of her senior year of high school in 1966 in the back seat of a '66 Caprice Classic at the age of eighteen. She and Marcel never really went further in their relationship so as to talk marriage; but the two would often get together over the summer either to Henrietta's home, the drive-in, or Marcel's parents' home in order to relieve their urges as theirs had become a mutually agreed upon sex-based friendship and relationship.

Henrietta earned a scholarship to Louisiana Tech, in Monroe, Louisiana, about six hours north of New Orleans and moved on to college in September of '66 and majored in music, aiming to become a teacher. Her moving away left Gabriella and Veronica alone in their two bedroom home. Veronica had gotten her eldest daughter through high school and off to college and her attention now turned fully to her youngest daughter.

Gabriella, at age nine, was a little feistier than Henrietta, and Veronica knew that her youngest daughter would indeed be a little more difficult to raise; but the woman was up to tasks that lie ahead.

## CHAPTER 9

## A JOYFUL SORROW

The church choir sang joyously on a cool November morning in the autumn of '66. Gabriella, who had been leading the choir during various songs for over two years, sang Esther Ford's version of *Father, I Stretch My Hands To Thee*. The nine year-old, dressed in her blue and gold choir robe, rocked to and fro waving her tiny right hand into the air as she sang with her head bowed. The church patrons rocked in unison and shouted praise to the Lord as Gabriella stirred their spirits and heightened their love for the Man upstairs with her angelic voice. Veronica sat quietly on the front row, admiring her daughter from afar as she sang, her eyes filled with tears of joy. Never before had she heard such a beautiful voice. She thanked God that He had blessed her daughter with such a glorious voice so as to bring praise and glory to His Kingdom.

As Gabriella continued to sing, raising her head every now and then, revealing her gorgeous grey eyes, people began to approach the pulpit to seek forgiveness of their sins and dedicate themselves to the Lord. After the service was over, church-goers walked up to Veronica and congratulated her and Gabriella.

"I did nothing," Veronica stated to several parishioners, "my child is the one with the gift that has been given to her by the Most High."

Veronica knew Gabriella had a natural gift given to her, but she never over-praised Gabriella. She merely acknowledged her daughter's abilities. Gabriella in turn, was learning to become a humble person through Veronica's actions; but even at age nine, Gabriella knew her voice was special. Gabriella enjoyed the attention she was getting from her singing inside the church, but she wanted to do more than just sing in front of the pews. As she walked home with her mother, nine year-old Gabriella looked up at Veronica and stated her dream.

"Momma, I wanna be a singer when I grow up!"

"You can be anything you want to be, my dear child, anything. If singing is what you love to do, then go right ahead and sing." Veronica replied as she looked down upon her daughter proudly.

Gabriella smiled and released her mother's hand. She then began to sing *My Guy,* a song recorded by Mary Wells.

Veronica paused and asked, "Gabriella, when did you ever hear that song?"

"From you momma. You sing that song almost everyday." Gabriella said as she walked backwards whilst skipping, looking into her mother's eyes.

"I thought you wanted to sing church songs, young lady."

"I can't boogie like I want to in church, momma!" Gabriella answered as she turned to face the front of the sidewalk and slid into a sexy dance on the curb by placing her right hand behind her head and gyrating her hips slowly. "That's it right there, y'all!" Gabriella said happily as if she were talking to an audience.

"Hey, hey! Quit that! You are only nine years-old, little girl! I better never see you dance like that again!" Veronica said sternly, causing Gabriella to stop dancing and frown.

"Awww momma. Everybody do that dance. We dance like that in school all the time during recess. This is nineteen sixty-six! You need to get hip to the times, momma!"

Veronica couldn't help but chuckle to herself before she told Gabriella that she knew all of those dances and they were meant to be done by adults and not during recess by Gabriella and her classmates.

"Okay, momma." Gabriella said as she grabbed her mother's hand again.

Neither said anything as the two strolled down the side walk together, but Veronica was all-too-aware that Gabriella would still sneak into her room and do her little dance whenever she thought her mother was busy doing something else around the house.

Gabriella caught many a whipping doing those dance routines. By the time she was ten, Veronica had to often shout the petite little girl down to get her to comply with her wishes. Gabriella and her mother had a strong relationship, although the two were often at odds because Gabriella wanted so badly to be outside singing and dancing with her friends from school. Veronica knew what kids were doing in the streets and she didn't want Gabriella wasting her time with what she considered foolishness. The next few months went by smoothly, Gabriella was complying with her mother's wishes more and more; but she couldn't wait until she was old enough to venture outside on her own.

In early April of '68, Gabriella and her mother had just returned from the market on a warm spring evening and were now relaxing in the living room listening to Benjamin's old Sam Cooke album. It was one of the things Veronica managed to save from the flood besides a family portrait of her husband and two daughters, a picture of Charlie, and Benjamin's old flight jacket; items that were salvaged from the fire that ravaged their home the night Charlie was killed and had also survived Hurricane Betsy. The volume on the television was down as Gabriella sung Sam Cooke's song *Touch The Hem of His Garment* along with the album. Gabriella paused when a news flash came across the family's TV screen along with video footage of Dr. Martin Luther King Jr.

"Momma," Gabriella called out to Veronica, who was in the kitchen cooking dinner, "Dr. King is on TV again!"

Mother and daughter loved Dr. Martin Luther King Jr. They listened to his sermons often. Veronica was even planning a trip to Atlanta to visit the reverend's home church and hear him preach. Veronica walked into the living room smiling as Gabriella removed the needle from the turntable and turned the volume up on the TV. Mother and daughter were stunned to silence when they heard Walter Cronkite announce that Dr. King had been murdered in Memphis, Tennessee.

Gabriella stared at the TV in silence as tears began rolling down her thin face. Veronica sat on the sofa and wept aloud; her elbows resting on her knees as her head hung low. Gabriella hugged her mother's neck and asked why the man was killed.

"They didn't like his message, sweetie." Veronica said somberly as she kissed Gabriella's hand. "They, they just didn't like his message." she ended sorrowfully.

"Did the same people that killed daddy and your friend Charlie kill Doctor King?"

"What do you mean by 'the same people,' Gabriella?" Veronica asked as she looked into Gabriella's teary grey eyes.

"You know, momma—white people?"

Veronica looked back at the TV screen, which continued to show footage of Dr. King.

"I don't know, sugar." she replied. "There's a lot of bad people out there from all races. Good people, too, Gabriella. Your father was a good black man, and Charlie was a good white man. Good people exist—in all races—not just black and white. Remember that, baby." Veronica said, through her tears as she stared at video footage of Dr. King. "But I just can't imagine a black man killing another black man, especially one like Martin Luther King after all we as a people have been through." she ended.

Mother and daughter were saddened by the assassination of Dr. Martin Luther King Jr. and it propelled them ever deeper into their service to God.

Gabriella became an usher in July of '69, a month before her twelfth birthday. She and her mother were home celebrating the event that summer, along with Henrietta, who was home enjoying summer vacation from college before returning to finish her final semester before graduating.

As Veronica prepared dinner, Henrietta and Gabriella sat and chatted, catching up on old times and talking about the latest fashion, music and hairstyles. Veronica was enjoying quality time with her daughters when she suddenly felt a sharp pain in her side. The forty-nine year-old woman froze while standing over the stove. She couldn't move, but she was able to call out to her daughters just before she dropped the ladle she was using to stir the beef stew just as she collapsed onto the floor.

Henrietta and Gabriella rushed into the kitchen and saw that their mother was unconscious. Both girls carried their mother to the car and Henrietta drove to the emergency room at Charity Hospital in downtown New Orleans. Henrietta and Gabriella never left their mother's side. As she lay sedated in her hospital bed, Veronica no longer looked like the strong, vibrant, woman she once was. She had remained unconscious for two days. When Veronica finally opened her eyes, her daughters were the first thing she saw. She stretched her arms and hugged them tightly as the three wept together. The doctor came in a few minutes later with the prognosis and the family learned Veronica had lung cancer. Terminal lung cancer. The doctors could do nothing to stop the progression of the disease; they could only relieve the pain, and that would be only for a short while.

Henrietta transferred from Louisiana Tech to The University of New Orleans to finish her degree in music and tend to her mother with Gabriella's help. The sisters did the best they could to make their mother's life as comfortable as possible, but, just as the doctors had prophesied, Veronica's condition only grew worse. The woman was a fighter though, and even though she spent most of her days in utter pain, she continued as best she could to prepare her daughters for the inevitable. She never let on that she was preparing to leave the world, but the two sisters knew that day would soon come.

The sisters held on to their mother for as long as they could, and Veronica was determined to remain with her children for as long as possible. During the last few months of her life, Veronica spent nearly everyday in continuous pain. Knowing her days were numbered, she counseled her daughters daily, giving them advice; telling them to find a man that will love them for who they are and not just their bodies. Veronica demanded that Henrietta and Veronica make something of themselves.

"We've come too far to give up the race of life, children. Build a family for yourselves." Veronica would often state.

Veronica wanted to make sure her daughters could survive in a world that was rapidly changing as she knew that her time on earth with her children was short.

## CHAPTER 10

## MOTHER'S DAY

It was a warm and sunny Sunday spring morning, May 10, 1970. Henrietta, now twenty-two, and Gabriella, age twelve, went into the room to awaken their mother. Veronica slowly stirred awake and sat up in the bed. She was now very frail, but still, her grey eyes remained bright and optimistic.

"Happy Mother's Day!" Henrietta and Gabriella said in unison as they stood beside their mother's bed holding gifts and cards.

Henrietta had brought her mother a white straw hat for church and Gabriella had gotten her a pair of gold ear rings.

Veronica looked at the gifts and sat them aside.

"Thank you darlings. I'll wear them both today."

"Momma, why don't we all stay home today? It's Mother's Day and Henrietta's birthday, too. Me and Henrietta wanted to cook you a nice dinner." Gabriella stated softly as she and Henrietta stood beside the bed in their royal blue choir gowns.

"My word! Today *is* your birthday Henrietta! You're twenty-two years-old today! How do you feel?" Veronica asked as she tenderly grabbed Henrietta's hands.

"I feel fine, momma. For me it's just another day. Today we celebrate you because you're the best mother ever."

"Thank you. I'm, I'm sorry, Henrietta. I forgot today was

your birthday. I don't wanna—I hope I don't disappoint you today."

"Momma, you could never disappoint me. Ever, you hear? I love you always, momma." Henrietta said as she knelt down and hugged her mother.

Gabriella stood by watching her older sister and mother embrace and soon joined in.

"I bought Henrietta a pair of brown leather shoes, momma. She said she likes them, but I don't believe her." Gabriella said as she got up and grabbed a brush off her mother's dresser and began brushing Veronica's long brown hair that now had subtle streaks of grey running throughout.

"Why not?" Veronica asked as Henrietta shoved Gabriella's shoulders playfully.

Gabriella playfully tapped Henrietta's arm and resumed brushing her mother's hair and said, "Because every time we talk about the latest styles, Henrietta seldom talks about high heels. When she does, she always say they look tacky. So I bought her some tacky brown shoes just to see if she was gonna wear them. Are you going to wear your tacky brown shoes, Henrietta?" Gabriella asked through laughter.

Henrietta laughed lowly and said, "I will, but not today. They do not match my robe—so there!" she said as she poked her tongue at Gabriella.

"I'm so glad you two get along as friends and not just sisters. What you two have is special. Keep that intact, okay?"

"I ain't her friend!" Henrietta and Gabriella said simultaneously.

The two then began lightly tapping one another's arms as they laughed aloud.

"Say what you want, but you two love one another dearly."

"We do, momma. Henrietta the best sister ever. I love her." Gabriella said as she smiled proudly at Henrietta.

"Thank you, Gabriella. And no other sister on this planet could ever take your place." Henrietta said as she hugged

Gabriella tightly.

"Today is a blessed day," Veronica said as she rubbed Henrietta's back. "I want to see my babies perform in church. That will be the best Mother's Day gift ever. To see you two sing today." The woman said between coughs. "Help me up, Henrietta so I can get myself ready for the Lord." Veronica stated as she stretched out her weakened arms.

Henrietta and Gabriella helped their mother to the bathroom where they bathed and then dressed her. Veronica wore a light green pants suit, her new white hat and gold ear rings with white pumps and a white blouse.

"You know," Veronica said lowly as her daughters walked her towards the car, "spring is the beginning of new life. Birds hatch, flowers grow, and everything is reinvigorated. Spring is the start of a new life. Going meet the Lord today, yes I am. Going meet Him."

Henrietta, at that very moment, had a premonition. She foresaw what lay ahead and she began to shed silent tears as she and Gabriella helped their mother into the front seat of the family's car. Henrietta got behind the wheel and backed out the driveway. When she drove away from the home, Veronica began reminiscing about the day the girls' father was killed and the irony of how justice was served.

"Charlie was a good man. He earned his wings that night. Yes, he did." Veronica said as she rocked back and forth in the passenger seat.

Veronica then reached over and patted Henrietta's leg as her grey eyes lit up with joy. "I want you to know that I'm very proud of you." she said as she smiled and ran her fingers through Henrietta's hair. "You've graduated from college, and now you are about to become a music teacher. You fulfilled your dream, Henrietta. And Gabriella," Veronica continued, "you sing better than Aretha Franklin, Dianna Ross, and Tammi Terell all put together. You keep doing what you are doing. I've raised two beautiful daughters and I love you both very much. I wish your father was alive to see you two now."

Henrietta continued to let the tears flow as she and

Gabriella listened to their mother speak. "I sometimes wonder about grand kids. What they would look like, what type of people they'll grow up to be. I know you haven't Gabriella, but Henrietta, have you had intercourse yet? Or shall I say, lately?" Veronica asked as she blushed and looked straight ahead.

"Momma!" Henrietta said in a surprised tone as Gabriella snickered from the back seat of the car.

"Well have you? I'd like to know before I get to the church."

"Yes, mother, I have a friend, but there are no grand kids on the way."

"Marcel. His name was Marcel. That's not a question either, Henrietta." Veronica stated as she looked out the passenger window. "You had him in my home over the summer of sixty-six before you went away to college didn't you?" Veronica then asked as she looked towards Henrietta.

Henrietta managed to nod slightly. "I'm sorry, momma." she responded in a low, shy tone.

"Well, Charlie spent many a night in our home. I know you could hear us from time to time and you knew what was going on. That's only natural. It's nothing to be ashamed of, Henrietta."

"I thought you would be disappointed in me because I wasn't married."

"It took me a while to figure it out, but I caught on when I noticed you washing bed sheets every few days. I was a little disappointed I admit; but you were old enough at the time, and eventually, you grew wise enough to go elsewhere's. You, you were considerate of your sister towards the end."

"Thank you, momma. Again, I'm sorry. I never meant to hurt you or carry on in front of Gabriella."

"She used to give me Cornflakes with bananas in them." Gabriella stated lowly from the backseat as Henrietta and Veronica eyed one another and smiled.

Veronica then turned to Gabriella. "Do me a favor,

Gabriella."

"What momma?" Gabriella asked softly as she looked at her mother lovingly.

"Can you sing Get By With Help From My Friends? I just love Joe Cocker's version. I know I told you you are not supposed to sing those types of songs, but, a voice like yours is made to shine and shouldn't be held back. Let's celebrate today. Celebrate life and give thanks to the Lord. Can you and the choir sing it for me, baby?"

"It'll be the best you ever heard, momma." Gabriella said proudly.

"I'll make sure we all sing it for you, momma." Henrietta said as she wiped her eyes.

"Henrietta you can't hold a tune in a bucket. You can *teach* music, but God, you can't hold a note." Veronica said.

Gabriella burst into laughter as did Henrietta.

"Momma, that wasn't nice." Henrietta said as she rubbed her mother's leg.

"I know baby. I'm sorry, but I told your father that the last time I saw him alive and he said to me, he said to me, 'you lucky my little protector is not here to hear you say that'. Benjamin always said you were his little protector. Don't ever stop being that. Look after your baby sister, Henrietta."

"I promise, momma. I promise." Henrietta replied. "And I'll have a bucket on hand to help Gabriella out if she ever needs it." she ended as Veronica laughed aloud through nagging coughs.

"What's the bucket for, Henrietta?" Gabriella asked from the backseat.

Veronica and Henrietta laughed louder when they realized the joke had flown over Gabriella's head.

"Nothing sweetie," Veronica responded. "It's just a saying. When you can't sing, people sometimes say 'you can't carry a note in a bucket'. You, my child, you will never need a bucket, though." she ended as Gabriella smiled and leaned forward and kissed her mother's cheek.

The trio pulled into the church's parking lot and people greeted Veronica with hugs and kisses. "Blessed day today!" she said repeatedly as she walked slowly to the front row in the middle aisle, her daughters following close behind.

The girls sat on either side of their mother and held her hands tightly as they listened to the preacher's sermon from the front row.

"Life!" the preacher said the moment he stood up in the pulpit of the medium-sized white-brick church that contained three rows, each holding a dozen pews, "Life begins in the house of the Lord! We are put here on earth for a short time— but the Real Life begins when we enter into the House of the Lord. Today, let's reflect on our lives and gain the knowledge that leads to eternal life, for the real life is not here, it starts here on Earth but it doesn't end here does it brothers and sisters…John chapter three verse sixteen states…"

The preacher had concluded his sermon on "The Real Life" and called for the choir. Gabriella and Henrietta both kissed their mother and took the stage. There, they sang *Mount Zion*. The Lord's spirit flowed stronger than ever through the church that day. Gabriella and Henrietta eyed their mother, watching her wave her arms to and fro with her eyes closed. The choir rocked and clapped their hands in unison with the congregation throughout the song and silence encompassed the entirety of the church as parishioners awaited the next song. As they did so, Henrietta stepped away and instructed the band's guitarist and the drummer to play the chords and drum line to Joe Cocker's song as Gabriella prepared to take the lead.

"We have, we have a special request brothers and sisters," the reverend said as he stood before the congregation. "Sister Jenkins, on this day, wants us all to celebrate. How many of us have friends?" the reverend asked as he raised his hand in the air.

The entire congregation raised their hands as the reverend looked around the building. "Praise God. We all have, friends, yes we do, praise God. Can they help us get by?"

"Yes!"

"Sure can!"

"Umm, hmm!" the parishioners shouted aloud at random.

"Okay then, friends," the reverend said as he wiped his face with a silk handkerchief, "let us, let us get by with the help of our friends." he ended softly as an electric guitar began to play.

The crowd grew festive inside the church and the entire congregation stood and swayed to the guitarist's rendition of the song and the pounding of the drums as Gabriella walked before the choir. Gabriella had a versatile voice. She could sing in Soprano, Mezzo-Soprano, and Tenor. She was a very gifted child—but Joe Cocker had a raspy, Alto sort of voice, so Gabriella knew she would have to improvise. She decided to go Mezzo-Soprano as the opening words to the song were soft and gentle, just like the pitch she was going to use to sing to her mother. The drums soon stopped, the shouting and clapping subsided, and only the soft strings of the electric guitar could be heard. Gabriella looked towards her mother, and Veronica smiled.

With confidence, Gabriella eyed her mother and sung, *"What would you think if I sang you a tune...would you stand up and walk out on me? Lend me your ears and I'll sing you a song...I will try not to sing out of key...Oh I get by with a little from my friends..."*

The choir joined Gabriella in the chorus and before long, the entire congregation was singing the chorus. Gabriella could see her mother crying and she, too, began to cry again as she continued to sing the second verse. The guitar was on point, the drums were magnificent and the choir was in perfect unison.

Gabriella and the choir sung the chorus in unison and she began to wave her arms and really get into the song as Veronica sat in her seat with her head slightly bowed and her hands resting in her lap.

Henrietta noticed her mother looking as if she were about to go sleep, and, as Gabriella and the choir sung, she left the stage and ran to her mother's side and sat beside her as she placed an arm around her back and gently laid her head on her shoulder.

Gabriella was surprised by Henrietta's actions; but as she watched her mother resting her head on Henrietta's shoulder with her eyes closed, it suddenly dawned on Gabriella the reason why her mother wanted her to sing Joe Cocker's song: it was the song she wanted to 'Go Home' to.

The thought of her mother dying propelled Gabriella to sing harder and louder as she began to shed tears, now with the full understanding that her mother was going to pass away inside the church on this day. Gabriella had never sung so dramatically in her life. Her mother wanted her to sing to her and that is exactly what Gabriella did. She brought soul to the song, humming, leaning back every time she brought her voice to a crescendo and turning to face the choir a couple of times to keep them stirred.

*"Sing for my momma! Sing for my momma!"* Gabriella repeatedly told herself, all the while conveying that very same message to the choir and the entire congregation with her voice that had become all-so powerful.

Gabriella continued to sing, and she watched with watery eyes, as her mother and Henrietta hugged one another. She sung the last of the lyrics to the song to the top of her lungs as she jumped up and down in her choir robe with tears in her eyes as she watched her mother, who was slowly slipping into eternal sleep.

It would become the greatest song Gabriella had ever sung up to that point in her young life, and she sung that song to her mother as Veronica Jenkins sat upright dying a peaceful death in the arms of her oldest daughter.

Gabriella rushed from the stage as the choir continued to hum in order to join her sister and spend the last few moments with her mother. When she sat down, Veronica placed her free arm around Gabriella.

"Beautiful song. You were glorious. I love you, children," Veronica said just before her head slowly fell over onto

Henrietta's shoulder as if she had fallen asleep.

Veronica Jenkins died in the arms if her two beloved daughters on the front row of her church on May, 10, 1970, which was Mother's Day and also Henrietta's 22nd birthday, at the age of fifty.

Veronica had fulfilled her purpose on earth. She had received retribution for her husband and had raised her daughters to the point that they were able to fend for themselves. The woman was tired and ready to take on a new journey, a spiritual trek. Henrietta waved her hand in the air to signal the choir to stop humming, and the entire congregation gathered around the small family as the reverend prayed aloud for Veronica.

Henrietta knew by the way her mother was talking that she was going to die this day. Gabriella only caught on towards the end of her singing; but she was still able to sing to her mother under tremendous anxiety and pressure. Sadly, but in a joyful spiritual setting, with Henrietta leading the way, and with the aide of her little sister's angelic voice, the two sisters sent their mother 'Home'.

Veronica had a lovely funeral and was buried next to Benjamin in the church's cemetery; all the expenses were paid by the congregation. Much love and support went out to Gabriella and Henrietta in the spring of 1970.

Gabriella took her mother's death in stride. She would miss her mother dearly, but she knew she was in a better place and freed of her pain. The two sisters, while adjusting to having lost their mother at relatively young ages, now wondered what the next phase of their lives had in store for them. They both hoped they could carry on as Veronica wished, because at this particular point in time, Henrietta and Gabriella were the only two surviving members of the Jenkins family left on Earth. What the future holds remains to be seen.

## CHAPTER 11

## LOVE AT FIRST SIGHT

It was now August of 1970. A hot and sunny late summer day and thirteen year-old Gabriella's first day of high school. Having lost her mother only a couple of months ago at age twelve, Gabriella was still grieving the loss. She had moped around all summer, becoming somewhat of an introvert; but she grew a little excited when she received her school schedule in the mail a couple of weeks ago because she quickly learned that Henrietta was going to be her music teacher. Henrietta's class first on her schedule as well, and that brought even more delight to Gabriella. In spite of the good news, it was still an overall depressing summer for Gabriella. She couldn't wait to get to school so she could at least begin to get pass her mother's departure.

Twenty-two year-old Henrietta, still grieving as well, had encouraged Gabriella to get out of bed and get dressed for her first day of school by singing to her. She sung Sly and The Family Stones' song *Everyday People* as Gabriella sat up in her bed laughing, stating that her mother was right about her not being able to carry a tune in a bucket. Henrietta knew she had to get the depressed Gabriella out of her funk and she had succeeded by using the one thing that could make both she and Gabriella happy no matter the circumstances: music.

Henrietta had graduated from college two weeks before her mother died and she accepted a job teaching music at G.W. Carver Senior High School. She believed that by teaching at the same school that Gabriella attended, the two would remain in close contact and Gabriella wouldn't feel as if she had been abandoned. She, too, was happy to learn that Gabriella was going to be her student. The two sisters were very close and they leaned on one another for strength. It was fair to say that Henrietta needed Gabriella just as much as Gabriella needed Henrietta; but it was Henrietta who had to show strength at all times.

"Let me see how you look in those hip huggers, young lady!" Henrietta yelled to Gabriella from the bathroom.

Gabriella walked from her bedroom and stood in the doorway of the bathroom with her arms spread. Henrietta looked her little sister over, noticing that Gabriella, in honor of her mother, had on a nice fitting, light green pair of denim hip huggers and a white sleeveless shirt along with a white pair of clods. She wore her shiny black hair in a single ponytail that rested several inches below the base of her neck. Gabriella had lined her eyes with black eye shadow, but when she saw the disappointed look on her older sister's face, she grabbed a wet towel off the sink and wiped it off.

"You have the most beautiful pair grey eyes, Gabriella. Why you want to ruin your looks with that cheap make-up leaves me perplexed." Henrietta remarked as she touched up her hair in the mirror.

"I just want to look good my first day." Gabriella responded.

Twenty-two year-old Henrietta, dressed in a brown knee-length silk dress and the brown leather high heel shoes Gabriella had bought her for her birthday, slowly stepped back from the bathroom mirror and had Gabriella stand in front of her and look directly into the mirror as she set her hair brush down and removed her eye glasses and smiled into the mirror while looking at her younger sister.

"Look at that face," Henrietta said as she stood behind her little sister with her hands on either side of Gabriella's arms, "your coal black hair, slender grey eyes, and that pretty smile showing those pearly white teeth. You are beautiful everyday of your life, Gabriella. There is nothing you need to add to that gorgeous face, child. You could put on a few pounds because you are a little too narrow!" Henrietta ended as she ran her knuckles lightly across the top of Gabriella's skull.

"I see you finally wore them tacky brown shoes!" Gabriella said playfully before she slapped her sister on the arm and ran down the hall.

Henrietta gave chase and cornered her sister on the sofa and began tickling her something fierce until Gabriella begged her to stop. The two sisters then sat side by side and straightened themselves and went and sat at the kitchen table and said their prayers before they ate breakfast and loaded the last of Henrietta's supplies that she would need to teach her music class into their 1963 black two door Chevy Impala and made their way to the high school. Henrietta had her class set up nicely the week before, but she had bought a few last items that she felt would enhance her students' learning experience.

When the sisters arrived at the school, they saw teenagers walking onto the campus in masses. Gabriella was in awe over the number of people who were attending the high school her freshman year.

Henrietta's car traveled slowly up the driveway to the teachers' parking area and the two unloaded Henrietta's materials and began making their way to Henrietta's class. Both of their hands were filled with a cardboard box as they approached the double doors leading to the music room which was in a separate building from the school's main structure.

"Young man," Henrietta called out to a young, chubby lad with a huge Afro and a round, fat, face who was standing with another young, muscular black male just outside the double doors leading into the music class, "young man, could you please hold the door for us? Our hands are full!"

"That ain't my problem, lady," the round-faced lad, whose name was Alfred, said to the two sisters.

"Al! Man, you rude," the tan-skinned young man with a neatly tapered hair-cut and a small dimple in his chin said loudly.

The young man kindly opened the door and watched as Henrietta walked into the building. He then caught sight of Gabriella as she came into view and his heart nearly skipped a beat. She was the most beautiful girl he had ever seen.

The young man, dressed in a green short-sleeved silk shirt and white slacks, with a pair green eel-skin shoes on his feet, and a white B-bop canvas hat on his head, followed the two sisters into the music room, all the while eyeing Gabriella and smiling at her. Gabriella kindly returned the smile as she thought the young man was cute and was dressed real nice.

"You the new music teacher, huh, lady?" the fancy-dressed young man asked Henrietta.

"Well, yes, I am. How did you know?"

"Besides the fact that we in a music room and you just brought in a bunch of music note books and a microphone?" he asked sarcastically, causing Gabriella to laugh under her breath.

"Are you in this class, mister?"

"Yeah! You the new music teacher, huh lady?"

Gabriella quickly placed her hand over her mouth trying to conceal her laughter as she knew the boy was fooling with Henrietta.

"Just who are you, young man?" Henrietta asked as she sat her box down on her desk.

"My name is Samson. Samson Holland—but everybody calls me Sam."

"Well, Mister Sam, me and my little sister have a lot of work to do here, so I suggest you be moving along now." Henrietta said as she gently nudged Sam towards the door.

"Hey, wait a minute, miss! You messing up my shirt! That's silk you putting your hands on right there!"

"Silk, huh? Only players wear silk! Are you a player, Sam?"

"Shoot, lady! Sam Cooke wore silk! The Temptations wear

silk, and Marvin Gaye wears silk! All the good singers wear silk! No, I ain't a player. I just like music. That's why I was waiting in front of this here building because they said this where the new music class was. I got you for my first class, look." Sam said as he handed Henrietta his schedule.

Henrietta took Sam's schedule and saw that he was indeed scheduled to be in her first period class.

"Okay, Mister Sam, you're welcome to stay," Henrietta replied as Sam and Gabriella exchanged glances at one another, all the while smiling.

"Sam!" Henrietta shouted, causing the thirteen year old to whip his neck around quickly. "We have thirty minutes to get this class presentable for the rest of the pupils. Are you willing to help out?"

"Sure miss—umm, I didn't get your name, miss."

"I'm Henrietta Jenkins. And that giggling little girl that can't stop smiling at you is my little sister, Gabriella."

Sam had an immediate crush on Gabriella. She was so pretty to him. While they were unpacking Henrietta's belongings, Sam and Gabriella continued to smile at one another. Sam would continually pester Henrietta with his silly antics in order to make Gabriella laugh. Besides her sister, Sam was the first person who really made Gabriella laugh hard since her mother died. She felt she was making a new friend in her music class.

Henrietta noticed how Gabriella was responding to the questions that Sam asked her and she couldn't help but to feel as if Gabriella was making a new friend. Sam didn't get too personal—the two thirteen-year olds mainly talked about music. It was fair to say that the two sisters were warming up to Sam. When Henrietta plugged her new microphone into an old amplifier that was left in the classroom and walked away to tend to another part of the class, Sam noticed.

"Gabriella, watch this," Sam said as he picked up the microphone and turned on the amplifier. Sam began to sing the first verse of Sam Cooke's song, *A Change Is Gonna*

*Come...*"*I was born by the river...In a little tent...Ohhh and just like the river...I been running ever since...It's been a long...Long time coming but I know...A change gone come...*"

Sam Cooke was the sisters' father's favorite artist. They watched in gleeful joy as Sam tried as best he could to imitate Sam Cooke's voice, unknowingly bringing back memories to both Henrietta and Gabriella, especially Henrietta. He abruptly ended the song when his friend Alfred walked into the room and said, "Hey Sam, let's go to the four-corners!"

*The Four Corners* was where three long halls and the main staircase joined at one huge intersection in the school's main building on the second floor. Nearly everyone, especially the ladies, walked through *The Four Corners*. It was Sam and Alfred's first year in high school; but all the older kids in the neighborhood told the two boys that *The Four Corners* would be the spot to find a girlfriend, score drugs, even purchase a gun. Fights often broke out as *The Four Corners* was also a spot where gangsters hung out. It was a rowdy intersection, but it was the favorite hang out on the entire campus. Sam, however, didn't need to go to *The Four Corners* because he had his eyes set on one female in particular.

"Go on without me, Al. I'll catch up with you in second period," Sam replied to Alfred's request.

"Alright ya' jive turkey! You gone miss out on everything!" Alfred said as he walked out of Henrietta's classroom and joined another group of boys and made his way to the main building.

School kids were hustling about everywhere on this late summer morning in August of 1970. Gabriella stared out the window of the music class at the kids walking up the school's long driveway and filing into the main building. She looked at the smiling faces and the attire that some of the students were wearing, just to see if she fit in with her peers. Gabriella noticed that some kids, namely the females, wore bell-bottomed pants and tank tops like she, others, mainly the males, had on silk shirts and slacks just like Sam. Gabriella could easily discern the athletes as they wore their respective sport's t-shirt or jersey. Gabriella liked her high school. G.W.

Carver seemed like a pretty cool place down in the Ninth Ward. Horseplay abounded as the students, all seemingly in a festive mood, swirled about, laughing in groups and just hanging out on the huge campus and Gabriella was taking it all in. She watched Sam's friend Alfred disappear into the mass of people as he made his way to *The Four Corners*. It was fair to say that thirteen-year-old Gabriella Jenkins felt at home her first day of high school.

As the classroom bell rang, about twenty more students filed into Henrietta's classroom. As the seats were beginning to fill, Sam was at Henrietta's desk asking her if students would be allowed to sing in her class, and if so, how soon. As the two talked, the seats were getting taken so Sam started to find a seat. He wanted to sit next to Gabriella, but he noticed another young lad about to sit beside her. He then heard Gabriella say in a low-tone "somebody's sitting here."

Gabriella then looked over to Sam and smiled and he quickly slid in next to Gabriella and the two stared into one another eyes for a minute or two. Up close, Gabriella could see how smooth Sam's tan skin was. She adored his dark brown eyes and the way he wore his hair neatly trimmed. A thin mustache was beginning to appear and Gabriella thought that it was cute. Sam in turn, looked into Gabriella's lovely grey eyes and they nearly hypnotized him. Her hair was dark and wavy and he loved the small pouty lips and pearl white teeth she had on display. The two were entrenched in their own little world, admiring each other's beauty until Henrietta began to speak towards the class.

The two listened along with the rest of the pupils as Henrietta went over the schedule for the entire week. Henrietta informed her students of the fact that her first period class was a beginner's class. She told the students that they would have lectures most days and practice reading musical notes through the first half of the year.

"As you progress, you will be rescheduled to one of the advanced classes or an intermittent class if you need further instruction. The key to all of this, kids, is to pay attention and never be afraid to ask questions. There are no silly questions.

We are all here today because we love music right?"

A few of the kids answered yes in a low tone, but Henrietta didn't like the class's lack of enthusiasm.

"I said we are all hear because we love music right?" Henrietta asked again as she stood in the center of the middle row and extended her arms and looked around the class with a wide smile upon her face.

The class's unresponsiveness made Henrietta feel as if she was getting off to a bad start. She was preparing to introduce herself until Sam spoke aloud.

"You got that right, Miss Jenkins! We all love music right people?" Sam asked aloud as he stood up from his seat and looked around at the class.

A few kids answered more loudly.

"That ain't loud enough!" Sam said as he began to clap his hands. "This our new music teacher! Miss Henrietta Jenkins! She bought a lot of equipment for us and she deserve more than just a ho-hum answer! Come on!" Sam stated as he clapped louder, causing the other students, including Gabriella to laugh and clap their hands. "Welcome Miss Jenkins!" Sam ended as he sat down in his seat as the other students began clapping loudly and welcoming Henrietta.

"Thank you, Samson! Thank you all for the warm welcoming! And we will make this year—our first year together—the most exciting year ever! Thank you all again!" Henrietta stated as she went into her first lecture, which was centered around Beethoven and the many facets of the piano.

The class went by quickly—too quickly—and as the bell rung for the next class, Gabriella placed her head on her desk. She didn't tell Sam, but she was sad to have to leave him. Sam felt the same. He wanted to spend the entire day with this female whom he already adored.

The other students emptied the room and only Gabriella and Sam now remained behind. Henrietta walked over to the two, fully aware that they had a crush on one another and instructed them that they had to move on to their next class. They both sighed as they got up from their seats and looked at their schedules. Sam saw that after home room, he had an Algebra class. Gabriella saw that she had home room followed by a Physical Education class. The music class was the only class the two had together their entire day besides first lunch. As Gabriella grabbed her gym bag containing her gym uniform from under her desk, Sam walked over to Henrietta and told her that he thought Gabriella was pretty.

"That's why you flaunting your feathers and hanging all over my sister like a hound dog?"

"Lady, do I look like a proud peacock or a man named Elvis Presley?"

Henrietta burst into loud laughter as she walked away from Sam. She then turned around, placed her hands on her hips and asked Sam if he'd like to be Gabriella's friend. Sam answered a resounding yes and Henrietta invited him back to her class after school was over so he could keep Gabriella company while she finished up her paperwork.

"Can I walk your sister to class, Miss Jenkins?"

"Well, that's something you will have to ask her now, isn't it, Mister Sam?"

As Gabriella placed her bag on her shoulders and began walking from the room, Sam came up behind her and asked her if he could walk her to her next class. Gabriella smiled a wide smile and looked over to Henrietta for approval. Henrietta stood with her eye glasses low on her nose and her arms folded. There was a slight pause before she nodded "yes" and the two slowly headed towards the classroom exit. Sam took Gabriella's bags and held them for her; but before he disappeared out of sight, Henrietta told Sam to look after her sister.

"I won't let nobody fool with her, Miss Jenkins. I promise."

Gabriella and Sam walked to the gym holding hands their first day of school. They ate lunch together in the cafeteria, along with Sam's friend Alfred, and at the end of the day, the two sat in Henrietta's classroom and talked for an hour or so until Gabriella and Henrietta had to leave. Sam tried to get Gabriella to give him her phone number but Henrietta intervened, saying it was too soon.

Sam knew how to be patient, though, he saw Gabriella, on average, three times a day during school. Gradually, over the few months leading up to Christmas break, Samson Holland began to reveal things about himself to both sisters. He told them he resided not too far from where Henrietta and Gabriella resided. Sam lived with an older lady from another church named Miss Newsome, who'd adopted him. Samson's parents, according to Miss Newsome, were addicted to heroin and had been killed while trying to rob a bank somewhere in Alabama. Sam told the sisters he didn't remember his parents at all, nor did he know who they were. He also told the sisters that Miss Newsome had been his mother for as long as he could remember, and as far as he knew, he had no other family. The two sisters could somewhat relate to what Sam was going through and from time to time they would talk about their parents to Sam.

Over time, Henrietta had come to trust Sam because he had proven himself to be a trustworthy and honest individual and he sincerely respected the two sisters and made it a priority to look after Gabriella. Finally on New Year's Day in 1971, Gabriella was allowed to receive her first phone call from a boy.

Henrietta was there, snapping pictures to add to Gabriella's growing scrapbook about her school years. Gabriella widened her eyes as Henrietta stood in the kitchen talking to Sam on the phone. Henrietta got the message and left the kitchen so the two teens could have private time, or so they thought. Henrietta, like many a distrusting parent, hid behind the wall and eavesdropped on the two, listening for any taboo language. There was none; and that further endeared Henrietta towards Sam.

As the school year drew to a close, Sam, who was by now a very close friend to Gabriella, and thus also to Henrietta, started spending time at their home. Sam's adoptive mother, Miss Newsome, a white-haired, heavy-set sixty-one year-old church going woman, had met Henrietta a few times and the two discussed Sam and Gabriella's budding relationship. They both agreed that it was nice that the two got along so well and they promised to keep an eye on the two to make sure there was no 'hanky panky' going on. Henrietta had to admit that ever since Gabriella had met Sam, she was becoming more of an independent person. She was coming into her own being. She was ever proud of Gabriella and, over the summer of 1971, Henrietta, Gabriella and Sam, grew closer. It was fair to say that they were three people who had a fondness for one another. They were becoming a family so-to-speak.

# CHAPTER 12

## THE FOUR CORNER BRAWL

At the start of the school year in September of 1971, fourteen year-olds Sam and Gabriella had advanced so far in their music class that Henrietta had moved the two to her advanced music class which was normally reserved for seniors. Their music class was at the seventh period so the two would have class together, wait on Henrietta, and then go over to the sisters' house to do homework.

Sam had grown a few inches during the summer. He was now 5' 6" and weighed around one-hundred and thirty-five pounds. Gabriella was still short at 5' 3" and she weighed ninety-five pounds. The two hung out nearly everyday after school now.

The girls in the neighborhood were jealous of the fact that Sam, who was keenly handsome to them, had chosen Gabriella, the light-skinned, shy, sister with long, jet black hair, instead of one of the dark-skinned sisters that flooded the Ninth Ward. Sam proudly turned down many a girl's affection and wanted no other female. Gabriella, in his eyes, was the one for him.

Sam would walk through the crowded streets of the Ninth Ward from his home headed over to Henrietta's home, passing by drug dealers, fast women, and the like. He lived about six blocks from Gabriella's house and it often took him a while to make the short walk as he had to stop and speak to everyone he knew—and Sam knew many people. The females Sam's age, some older, would often flirt with him whenever they saw him walking to Gabriella's house; but Sam never responded to the numerous flirtations he received.

Before she died, Veronica knew that times were changing, but she would have never dreamed that her once humble, peaceful, quiet neighborhood had undergone such a serious transformation in such a brief period of time. The streets in the neighborhood, although each house had a driveway, were now lined with parked cars. A new sidewalk was put in on either side of the streets throughout the neighborhood. Stray dogs now patrolled the streets in search of food, and stray cats did their best to stay out of their way. There was a bar on just about every corner. Most were wooden two-story structures that sported boarded up windows on the top floor and a single black tinted door that was constantly being flung open by patrons hanging in and around these establishments. A lighted sign, usually Falstaff, Schlitz, or Pabst Blue Ribbon Beer, dangled from the structures just above their entrance. Music could be heard from inside these clubs, and Sam would often stop and hang out in front of the buildings whenever he heard a song he liked. Winos and junkies often panhandled in front of these places. Faster, older teens and young women looking to have a good time often hung out in these establishments. Sam came to know many of them; he was popular in the neighborhood. Samson Holland was known as "the cool young brother that got along with everybody".

Trash littered the ground, broken beer bottles were everywhere and old styrofoam plates filled with chicken bones, a favorite delicacy to the many wandering stray dogs, seemed to dot every section of Sam and Gabriella's neighborhood. The people in this small patch of real estate called the Ninth Ward were a tight-knit group of people. Everyone knew everyone. Although there were junkies, alcoholics and women of questionable reputation on nearly every block, they all respected one another. The '70's was a period of love. If it felt good, then "just do it, baby", that was the saying of the times. Everyone wanted to have a good time, and they did, but they were always respectful of themselves and each other when carrying on with their business.

Henrietta had watched the neighborhood undergo its sudden transformation. She wasn't pleased with everything she saw, but to Gabriella and her, the Ninth Ward was home. Everyone spoke to each other, and watched out for one another just the same. Although Henrietta didn't hang out in the streets, she was still respected. She was teaching the children of many of the older people in the neighborhood. Henrietta Jenkins was known as "the quiet lady with the glasses that teach music over at Carver".

Gabriella Jenkins was known as the "li'l feisty grey-eyed girl that argued and fought all the time".

Gabriella had to argue almost everyday during the summer of '71 and into the school year whenever a group of girls would harass her. They often called her a "mulato", a term used to identify a black person who bore a child bred by a white person, or vice-versa. Henrietta would often have to leave her home and walk to the corner or some other part of the neighborhood and separate Gabriella from a fight or argument and calm her younger sister down. Gabriella hated being called a "mulato", and she would firmly take a stand and reinforce the fact that both her parents were Black, so therefore, she was totally, and one-hundred percent Black.

During the 1971-72 school year, Sam and Gabriella shared a Biology class together during second period. The two hated Biology, so to pass the time, Gabriella would write poems to Sam and read them to him slowly as they sat in the back of the class. The teacher grew tired of the two making sweet-talk so she separated them. They then started to pass notes; but sometimes Gabriella would get caught when one of the jealous female teens would cut-off the passed note and turn it in to the teacher. Gabriella received many a detention for passing notes, but that didn't bother her in the least because she stayed after school everyday with Henrietta and Sam anyway. Whenever she received a detention, she would just sit in Henrietta's class just as she normally would do on a daily basis. Gabriella knew a lot of girls hated the fact that she was going with Sam, but she didn't care. She knew Sam wanted her and her only. Still, it didn't prevent other females from interfering in her and Sam's relationship.

Gabriella was forced into fisticuffs in Biology class one day just before Halloween of 1972 when a jealous girl by the name of Melanie grabbed a note from another student's hand that Gabriella had written to Sam. It wasn't the first time Melanie had intercepted a note that Gabriella had written, but on this day, Melanie would cross the line.

She took Gabriella's note, stood up and quickly read it aloud. *"My beloved Sam, you are my heart, my soul, my meaning for living. With you in my life I have found my purpose. If real love is for clowns, then I am a star in your circus. You inspire me to the peaks higher than the tallest mountains and my love runs deeper than the blue sea. Forever and ever, my one true love, you will always be."*

"Aww, that's sweeeet!" Melanie chirped as she burst into laughter and sat back in her seat.

Before the Biology teacher could address Melanie, Gabriella ran across the class and jumped on the girl and began wailing on her. Melanie tried to fight back from her seated position, but Gabriella had gotten the best of her. She knocked Melanie out of her seat and bloodied her nose, leaving her stunned on the classroom floor.

"This ain't over, bitch!" Melanie squealed as she looked at the blood on her hands.

"I ain't a bitch!" Gabriella answered angrily as she pushed Melanie's desk aside in an attempt to confront her again.

The teacher intervened and grabbed a hold of Gabriella and sent her to the office and called Henrietta.

"What on God's green Earth is going on in that class room, Gabriella?" Henrietta asked angrily as she entered the school's front office.

"Melanie always messing with me, Henrietta! She snatched a note that I had written. It wasn't even for her! It was for Sam and she took it and read it aloud! She mocked me in front of the whole class and called me a 'B'!"

Henrietta remembered when she and her old friend Darlene had gotten into a fight. It wasn't nearly the same scenario, however; Henrietta ran home her first fight. Gabriella, on the other hand, started the fight and by all reports, she whipped Melanie's behind. Henrietta told the Assistant Principal that she would keep Gabriella with her the rest of the class period and have a talk with Gabriella's Biology teacher at the end of the day to see if they could maybe have Gabriella and Melanie sit on the opposite sides of the class on the front row, thereby avoiding Gabriella getting suspended from school.

Henrietta then escorted Gabriella out of the office and down the hall where Henrietta told Gabriella she was wrong, but she wasn't upset with her. Henrietta knew of Gabriella's trouble with Melanie because she often complained to Henrietta concerning Melanie's jealousy.

"Did you break her nose?" Henrietta asked as the two sisters walked under the breezeway towards Henrietta's classroom.

"I don't think so. I hope not. I shouldna done that. I'm gonna apologize to Melanie when I see her."

"Why? You did nothing wrong. If anything, she should apologize to you for touching your personal belongings."

"I know. But I just feel bad about what I did."

"You'll get over it. She will too. And I'm willing to bet that she won't touch your items let alone mock you again." Henrietta stated just before she entered the music building.

About twenty-five minutes later, the period-ending bell rung and classes began letting out as Gabriella sat in music class with Henrietta. Sam, who was still in the Biology class, exited the room by himself. Melanie had been taken to the school's nurse and was purportedly sent home. Somehow, word of the fight had spread and everyone was gathering at *The Four Corners*.

Sam had run into Alfred in the hallway and the two were talking about the girls' fight. They weren't paying attention to the gathering crowd and the stares from the dozens of teenagers who packed the hall on the second floor. Just then, Harold, another one of Sam's friends, came to him in a rush.

"Some dudes waitin' on you at the four corners Sam!" he stated in a hurry.

"For what? Who?" Sam asked inquisitively.

"It's three of 'em. One say he Melanie boyfriend. I think the other two his cousins." the tall and slender fourteen year-old replied.

Sam, Alfred and Harold walked towards *The Four Corners*. At the same time, Gabriella was walking up the main staircase leading to the second floor. Gabriella noticed a lot of the teenage girls pointing at her as she slowly climbed the stairs. When she got to *The Four Corners*, she saw Sam, Alfred and approaching the intersection. As she walked towards them, the young man professing to be Melanie's boyfriend slapped Gabriella hard across the face.

Sam saw what happened and he immediately ran jumped on the teenager and began pounding his fists into the teenager's skull as Gabriella stumbled and fell onto the floor. The other two teens jumped on Sam, and Alfred jumped in to help his friend. People jumped in to help Melanie's boyfriend and other people jumped in to help Sam and Alfred. Harold had broken out and run from the fight that was quickly turning into an all out brawl.

Suddenly, amidst the fist pounding and cussing, a single gunshot rang out. Everybody broke and ran except the one person who had been shot. Sam and Alfred were running against the crowd trying to find Gabriella, but she was nowhere in sight. Sam looked to the floor as he fought his way through the crowd, and he soon caught sight of a white pair of bloody sneakers attached to a pair of light-skinned legs. Sam yelled Gabriella's name aloud as he grew stronger and powered his way through the crowd.

Sam called Gabriella's name loudly as he forced his way through the mass confusion. He made it through the crowd only to see Melanie lying on the ground. Melanie was convulsing as blood spewed from her nose and mouth. Her eyes were wide open and staring directly into her boyfriend's eyes. Melanie's boyfriend was kneeling beside her with a .38 snub nose in his hand stating over and over again to Melanie that he was sorry/

"I missed Sam! I tried to shoot Sam! Melanie!" he cried aloud.

Sam stared at Melanie as her body grew limp. He then looked around and saw no sign of Gabriella and grew anxious all over again.

"Sam! I got Gabriella with me! Let's go! Sam we gotta go, man!" Alfred yelled as he, Gabriella and Sam hurried off along with the rest of the crowd as security guards apprehended Melanie's boyfriend, handcuffed him and held him for the city police.

Gabriella, Sam and Alfred were running towards Henrietta's class room and they could clearly see Henrietta, who'd heard the gunshot, running towards them with her arms open crying aloud. Henrietta ran and met Gabriella halfway and Gabriella flung herself into her sister's arms.

"I thought I lost you!" Henrietta said as she cried. "I thought I lost you!"

"I'm all right, Henrietta. I'm all right." Gabriella said in a relieved tone of voice.

"Sam, you okay? You okay?" Henrietta asked as she clasped her hands to either side of Sam's face.

"I'm fine Henrietta. Gabriella you all right, baby?" Sam then asked.

"I'm okay Sam. I thought you was shot!" Gabriella cried as she went and hugged Sam, planting her face into his chest and heaving. "I don't wanna ever lose you!" Gabriella cried as she held Sam with death grip.

"Yea!" Alfred said out of breath and not wanting to be left out, "I'm, I'm all right too, y'all!"

Henrietta apologized to Alfred and hugged him.

Gabriella joined her sister and hugged Alfred as well.

"Alfred, thank you! I thought I lost Sam. Thank you for being there."

"It's cool, Gabriella. That's what friends do. We look out for another." Alfred ended as Henrietta reached for Sam and the four embraced in a heartfelt group hug.

Henrietta thanked God through prayer that her sister and friends were okay and she then learned through Sam that Melanie was shot and killed. It was a sad day on the campus G.W. Carver Senior High true enough, but Henrietta was also relieved that her baby sister was not injured or worse.

Melanie died on *The Four Corners*. Things had simply gotten out of control real quick and nearly everyone had blamed Melanie's boyfriend for what happened. There were often fights at *The Four Corners* but no one had ever fired a weapon. It was an unfortunate event that had transpired on this tragic day. Melanie's boyfriend was later sent to Angola Penitentiary for manslaughter. She lost her life over her own foolishness.

Eventually, things returned to normal at *The Four Corners* —whatever that may be; and as the weeks went by, the events surrounding that terrible day were put out of people's minds. *The Four Corners* still had a susceptibility towards violence, however; but an incident with Gabriella and Alfred just before Christmas break, would change the chaotic location's atmosphere forever.

## CHAPTER 13

## MAKING STRIDES

It was now close to Christmas break in 1971, and Sam and Gabriella were once again leaving Biology class. They both had to pass through *The Four Corners* and that was where a lot of danger often lurked. It seemed as if fights were becoming more frequent. As the two approached the hangout, Sam began yelling to his friends Alfred and Harold to get their attention. As he walked towards his friends, Sam held Gabriella's hand tightly. Fourteen year-old Gabriella could see girls eyeing her and pointing towards Sam and she started to grow tense. She hated *The Four Corners.*

Sam knew a lot of girls were green with envy and resented Gabriella, but he paid them no mind. The boys in the high school respected Sam a great deal, even though he was only fourteen. Gabriella wondered why the older boys never tried to disrespect him in front of her, the way they did other couples their age in school. She wondered about that for a while, but she couldn't deny that she always felt safe with Sam, so she never asked him that question. Gabriella didn't understand that Sam conducted himself as a young man on the streets, and in turn, he was treated like one wherever he went.

Sam and Gabriella were dressed alike this day. They both had on navy blue Lee jeans and navy blue and white button-up silk shirts. Gabriella wore a white pair of clods and a white safari styled fur hat. Sam had on a navy blue pair of suede Hush Puppies with a navy blue and white cow-hide belt and a navy blue fur safari-styled hat. Sam was a sharp dresser and he made sure that Gabriella often had clothes that matched his.

"You looking good, Sam! What's that you wearing boy, English Leather," a young teen asked sexily as she passed by the couple. "Man, you looking good."

She smiled at Sam and curled her lips up and rolled her eyes at Gabriella.

"Thanks Suzette, you know my girlfriend, Gabriella said the same thing not too long ago. You late, baby. Oh, don't my honey look good too?"

The girl turned her head and walked off as Alfred and Harold mocked her.

"Hey, what's going on lovebirds?" Alfred asked the two.

"Come on Sam, we going to the gym!" Harold said matter-of-factly as he combed out his Afro.

"No, you going to the gym. I'm trying to catch me a honey today!" Alfred quipped as he began humming a tune, trying to get a girl's attention.

"Man," replied Harold, "you been standing in that same spot trying to catch a girl and you ain't got one yet! You did it all last year and half of this year. You ain't never gonna get a girlfriend!"

"Yeah? Well you been right here with me the whole time and you ain't got a girlfriend neither, sucka! So there! We both losers!" Alfred remarked as he, along with Gabriella and Sam, burst into laughter.

Harold then grew serious, telling the three that he was a gangster and gangsters never lose.

"Man, you ran when the big brawl broke out not too long ago! Jive ass!" Alfred responded as he continued to sing to the females who strolled by.

"I knew the nigga had a gun!"

"Why you ain't tell us, brother?" Alfred asked.

"It's every gangster for himself when shit go down. That's

the rule, brother!" Harold responded.

"Man, you don't know the first thing about being a gangster." Sam said to Harold.

"And I suppose you do, lover boy?" Harold asked.

"It's a lot to being a gangster, Harold," Sam replied. "If it's not in you, it's not in you. Everybody can't be a gangster; but just because a person chooses not to be one, it doesn't mean that he, or she, doesn't have it in them. A family person will hurt or kill you just as quickly as a street gangster would. Remember, gangsters don't have nothin' to lose, so getting killed, or killing somebody would mean nothing. On the other hand, a family man has a lot to lose, his kids, his wife, his family, so he'd kill someone to protect his family—or he'll die trying. Two different men fighting for the same purpose—the survival of him and his family. Which one's the real gangster?"

Harold merely walked off mumbling something about how he was going to be a gangster someday soon.

"That's deep man!" Alfred chimed in. "I mean, you like the modern day Aritastata!"

"That's Aristotle." Gabriella said as she smiled and shook her head whilst correcting Alfred.

"Yea, that cat right there, Gabriella. Thanks. That's you, Sam." Alfred remarked as he burst into song and grabbed a young female's hand as she was walking by the trio.

Alfred began singing the lyrics to *Your Precious Love*, a song originally sung by Marvin Gaye and Tammi Terell. As Alfred sang, the girl, named April, paused and began smiling as she nodded her head slowly. Sam hugged Gabriella from behind and the two rocked together, enjoying Alfred's melodic crooning in the crowded school hall.

When it came time for Tammi Terell's vocals, Alfred began to fade out. Catching everyone by surprise, Gabriella, remembering what her mother had told her the day she died, turned to Sam and stared him directly in the eyes as she began to sing Tammi Terell's verse, mimicking the lady's verse to a tee. *"And now...I got a song to sing...Telling the world...About*

*the...Joy you bring...And you gave me...A reason for living...
And oooo you taught me...You taught me the meaning of
giving..."*

People in the school's huge intersection stopped and turned
to see who had the angel-like voice that sounded exactly like
Tammi Terell.

Sam shifted to the side and gave Gabriella the floor as a
huge crowd gathered around her and Alfred.

The two sang the chorus to song in unison. *"Heaven must
have sent you from above...Heaven must have sent your
precious love..."*

Alfred did the best he could with the remainder of the song
with what little talent he had; but Gabriella had blown the
crowd away with her vocals. Everyone that witnessed the
impromptu rendition applauded when Alfred and Gabriella
finished the song. Alfred knew the people were mostly
clapping for Gabriella, but he wasn't bothered at all as he had
gotten April's phone number and she allowed him to walk with
her to her class. Alfred winked at Gabriella as he grabbed
April's hand and the two disappeared into the crowd that was
flocking around Gabriella and Sam.

"Sam! We didn't know your girlfriend could sing like that,
man! Why you didn't tell us she could sing, boy?" an older teen
with a raspy voice, a huge Afro and dark brown skin named
Janice, who was a senior at the school asked him.

"I never knew anybody wanted to know."

"Yeah, man! Me, my friend Yvonne, and my cousin
Charmaine right here need a lead singer for a group we trying
to put together for the talent show!"

"You Miss Jenkins' sister right? You and Sam in seventh
period with me. My name is Charmaine." The other senior said
to Gabriella with wide eyes and a huge smile.

"I know you. You always humming from the back row. You
have a pleasant voice." Gabriella said as she shook
Charmaine's hand.

The tardy bell rung and the two senior students had to hurry off along with the rest of the students; but before she left, Janice wrote down her number and handed it to Gabriella.

"Look, ask your sister if you can be in the talent show at the end of January. If so, we can practice during the Christmas break. If we win, we get $250. Sam, you got a winner right here, man. Don't let him try and talk you out of it either, sister. You can sing, girl!" Janice stated.

"Right on! See you in seventh period, Gabriella!" Charmaine added as she gave a friendly wave to Gabriella and walked off with her cousin.

Sam and Gabriella, after repeated acts of pleading, finally convinced an apprehensive and uncooperative Henrietta to allow her to sing in the talent show within a couple of days. During Christmas break, Gabriella, Charmaine, Janice, and Janice's friend Yvonne, who attended a different high school, practiced at Henrietta's house almost everyday. Henrietta was leery at first, but as the weeks went on, she realized that Gabriella had made three more friends and she really enjoyed what she was doing. The three girls began hanging out a lot during and after school and that left a lot of free time for Sam, Alfred, and Harold to hang out together. At the end of the day, however, Sam would always find his way over to Gabriella's house to watch TV with his beau.

The night of the talent show arrived and the group who'd just performed before Gabriella and her friends were outstanding. The group of four males had just sung *Cloud Nine* by the Temptations. They had left the audience inside Carver's auditorium in an uproar, and the girls wondering if they could compete with their act by chiding them as they walked pass them in their lavish silk grey suits.

Henrietta was back stage with the girls helping them get ready. During that time, Charmaine grew extra nervous and started crying.

"They was real good! How we gonna go up against that?" Charmaine asked through her frightened tears as Henrietta straightened her hair.

Henrietta calmed Charmaine down and told her to close her

eyes and sing as if she were in the back row of her music class. Henrietta then asked Gabriella if she was okay.

"They were good—but me and my girls are way better." Gabriella said excitedly, her eyes wide as saucers as she looked longingly at the stage.

"Charmaine, come on now," Yvonne said softly. "We all a little, well, not Gabriella, but me and Janice a little nervous, too. We all in this together though, and if need be, we'll carry you. Try. That's all. Try." she ended as she grabbed Charmaine's hand, bringing comfort.

"That's right," Janice quipped. "Look who we got leading our group! Remember the first day we heard Gabriella sing? She got it, Charmaine! We gone win this thing!"

"Okay, y'all," Charmaine said. "I'm in! Let's do this!" she said with her eyes closed, something she would do throughout their rendition.

Gabriella, however, couldn't wait to get in front of the crowd. As a Dee-jay from the local radio station introduced the girls, who had titled themselves "The Sisters", the crowd grew quiet as the instrumental to *I Never Loved A Man*, originally recorded by Aretha Franklin, began to play.

Sam and Alfred stood up and began whistling as Harold remained planted in his seat. Janice, Charmaine and Yvonne, dressed in silk scarlet red knee-length dresses and wearing black knee-length leather boots stood on the stage side by side with their backs to the audience as the instrumental played, the three of them gently rocking from side to side and snapping their fingers in unison.

Gabriella, her hair pressed and slightly covering her thin face, was dressed the same as her girls. She stood before her three friends with her back to the audience as well and they all began to rock from side to side while snapping their fingers in unison. Just before the moment arrived for Gabriella to sing, she and her girls turned to the right, placed their hands on their hips and looked out into the audience.

When Gabriella leaned into the microphone and said, "*Your*

*a no good...heart-breaker...you're a liar...and you're a cheat..."* the crowd went wild. It was as if Aretha Franklin herself was standing on stage.

To see and hear this fourteen-year old, skinny, light-skinned girl sing Aretha's song with such heartfelt conviction and pure soul wowed the audience from the song's inception. They alternately went from applause to silence as the four girls held sway over the audience. They looked so womanly in their scarlet red dresses, and black knee-length boots and neatly permed hair. Young Gabriella sang with pure passion, and by the end of the song, she had Henrietta and many others stunned. Sam and Alfred were jumping up and down in the aisle and high-fiving one another, and the whole crowd gave the girls a standing ovation. Needless to say, "The Sisters" took home the two-hundred and fifty dollar cash prize and trophies for first place.

In the weeks following the talent show, *The Four Corners* was no longer a place used to score guns or drugs or even fight for that matter. It became a spot where people who loved music, and/or loved to sing, would meet and exchange albums, information, and often times, rehearse lyrics to songs they had written or were covering at some neighborhood club or talent show. The often chaotic gathering spot had ceased to exist; and the gangsters soon moved to an area behind the gym.

During that time, Gabriella grew to like *The Four Corners*. She never realized, until Sam pointed it out to her, that she was the reason the intersection had changed.

"It's for the better too, baby. Your voice really moves people." Sam said to her.

Gabriella and Sam had passed all their classes and the school year closed out with Gabriella singing the graduation song for the senior class. The fourteen-year old had definitely made waves in school that year. She hung out with Janice, Charmaine, and Yvonne a lot during the summer. She liked the girls, and although they were having sex and smoking marijuana, Janice and her girls never pressured Gabriella to do as they were doing. They never did anything around the young teen, either, and they often called her "little sister".

The girls were interested in music more than anything, and although Janice and her girls graduated that year, they remained friends with Gabriella. Janice and her girls sang in night clubs from time to time, and they said if ever Henrietta allowed her, Gabriella could definitely lead their group. Gabriella kept that in mind and was eager to start the school year to see what her junior year held in store.

## CHAPTER 14

### TELL ME NO LIES

"Hello, Sam! You ready for the new school year?" Henrietta asked Sam the first day of school as he walked through the front door of her home on a warm September morning in the year 1972.

"Yes ma'am, I am," Sam responded as he walked to the center of the room and gathered a huge box off the floor into his arms to load into her car.

Henrietta had asked Sam to help her and Gabriella bring new materials to her music class this first day of school. As Henrietta walked out of the door to unlock the car, Gabriella stepped out from her bedroom and ran up behind Sam and patted him on the rear end.

"Don't start nothing you can't finish, girl!"

"You right. I don't want to tease you." Gabriella said sexily as she nuzzled Sam's neck from behind with her lips and nose.

"You gone make me drop your sister box, Gabriella. Stop teasing me before I take charge today." Sam said as he paused in just inside the doorway.

"Take charge? You can't handle me Sam!"

"Look, just because you added another five or ten pounds or so over the summer and grew sexy don't mean I can't wrestle you down and take advantage of you."

"Do it Sam! Take me! Take me! Take me!" Gabriella said as she laughed aloud and walked past Sam. She then turned and gave him a sexy wink. Sam admired Gabriella's physique as she held the door open for him. When he got to the threshold, he paused in front of Gabriella and told her to reach into his shirt pocket. When Gabriella reached into Sam's pocket, she pulled out a box. Her eyes widened as she opened the box and saw a charm necklace that contained her sophomore picture.

"Sam, it's beautiful." Gabriella remarked lowly, almost mesmerized by the gift.

She then looked into Sam's eyes and placed her hand against his cheek and planted a soft kiss on his lips. Henrietta turned around and saw the two kissing and smiled as she stood beside her car watching the two. She then began searching for her camera inside the car's glove box. Sam and Gabriella leaned in to kiss one another again but they were distracted by a flash from Henrietta's camera.

"Ohh, look how cute!"

"Henrietta!" Gabriella yelled aloud.

"That was a moment in time. It was the first kiss you two ever had! Wait, it *was* the first kiss right?" Henrietta asked with a smirk on her face, purposely teasing the two teenagers.

"Henrietta, don't do that, please." Gabriella pleaded.

"Alright, I won't tease you any more, Gabriella; but I am going to put this picture in the scrapbook with the rest of you two's pictures."

The three loaded all of Henrietta's boxes into her car and made their way to the high school to get ready for the first day of school.

When they parked in the school's parking lot, they were greeted by Harold and Alfred and the two helped Sam, Gabriella, and Henrietta bring the boxes to her classroom.

"Man, I thought y'all was gonna meet me by Henrietta's house this morning." Sam said as the three walked behind the females.

160

"We was," Harold replied, "but we had to get that—"

Just then, Alfred kicked Harold on the leg to get him to stop talking. Sam looked around and gave Harold a cold stare just before the five of them entered the building. The three young males placed the boxes onto the floor and began to exit the classroom. Henrietta abruptly stopped them and asked them why they were leaving so soon as Gabriella turned and looked towards Sam with a worried look on her face, wondering what Sam was up to this morning.

Over the last two years, Sam had always remained in Henrietta's class until the school bell rung. Gabriella thought it was unusual for Sam to leave so early, especially since he was leaving with Harold. Gabriella knew Alfred was Sam's true friend, but she didn't like Harold all that well because she thought he was trouble.

"We going to the sandwich shop to grab a bite to eat. We'll bring y'all somethin' back if you want us to." Sam stated.

"That's nice of you Sam. I'd like a ham and cheese on toast if you don't mind." Henrietta answered as she unpacked her boxes.

Gabriella stared at Sam disappointedly because she knew Sam was telling a story. She walked over to him and pulled him into the hallway and asked him what he was really planning on doing.

"I'm going to the sandwich shop, Gabriella, just like I said."

"Sam, don't do this to me."

"Do what?"

"Lie!"

"I'm serious Gabriella, I'm going get a sandwich and I be right back!"

Gabriella hugged Sam tightly and looked into his eyes. "Tell me you're not going to end up like my father, found some where dead, alone, and helpless."

"Gabriella, you being ridiculous right now. I'm only going to the store."

Gabriella laid her head against Sam's chest and whispered lowly, "I love you."

"I couldn't hear what you said." Sam stated.

"I said I love you, Sam. Don't do this to me! Don't you ever lie to me again!" Gabriella remarked with tears running down her face as she ran back into Henrietta's classroom.

Henrietta came out into the hall as Sam stood alone and in shock at what Gabriella had told him. Alfred and Harold had witnessed the entire event unfold, and they were eagerly waiting to see what would transpire.

"What have you done to my sister?" Henrietta asked inquisitively.

"Nothing Henrietta! I told her I was going to the store and I'd be right back. That's it!"

"Well, she's in there crying her heart out mumbling something about you going behind the gym with Harold to hang with those gangsters back there!"

What Henrietta said hit Sam in the gut; he was wondering how Gabriella knew he was going behind the gym.

"Gabriella!" Sam called out as he walked back into the classroom. "I promise I'm not going to the gym today alright?" he said as he approached Gabriella. "I love you too, baby. And I won't ever lie to you. I promise." Sam said as he twirled the charm necklace that he had placed around Gabriella's neck earlier that morning.

Gabriella reached out and grabbed Sam's hand and they both held the necklace. Sam looked into Gabriella's pretty grey eyes and he realized how deeply the young teen felt for him. The two teenagers had a bond that was more than a physical attraction, it was spiritual. Gabriella understood that more than Sam.

Sam was all Gabriella ever needed, all she hoped and dreamed for. She wanted the two of them to grow old together and she worried, on this day, as she did on many occasions, that she would lose the love of her life.

"I be right back, baby. I promise."

Gabriella nodded her head and Sam told her that he would bring her a sandwich back.

Sam left the classroom and joined Alfred and Harold and the three walked under the school's breezeway towards the gym. When they got to the path that led off the school's grounds, Sam paused.

Alfred turned and smiled towards his friend as he knew what Sam was about to do.

"Let's go on to the gym, man!" Harold snapped towards Sam.

Sam looked to the ground and said, "Man, I can't go back —"

"You can't do what?" Harold snapped, cutting Sam off as he combed out his Afro. "We got a whole ounce of weed that niggas waiting on for us to sell to 'em behind the gym and you can't? Let's get this money, dude." he whispered lowly.

"Fool, you saw how Gabriella was actin'," Alfred said. "She know Sam like the back of her hand. If he go down to the gym, Gabriella gonna be right there to witness her old man sell a bag of weed. You know Henrietta and Gabriella wasn't raised like that."

"Man, Sam tripping behind a broad. What come first? Money or women brother?" Harold asked Sam.

"If you ever get a woman like Gabriella, which I doubt," Alfred chimed in, "you'd be doing the same thing Sam about to do. Man, look here," he then said as he pulled Sam to the side. "You know, April don't worry about what I do out here; I wish she did but she don't. Gabriella though, man, she care a lot about you, Sam, and that's a good thing. A *good thing*! Don't let the streets destroy the best thing in your life. Forget Harold! That's our brother, but he a knucklehead. There's dudes out here that's lining up waiting for the day you and Gabriella break up. People respect what you two have. You know what you about and you don't have nothing to prove to Harold. Go get breakfast for your family and me and Harold gonna handle this business this morning."

"I can't lie to her Al—I love her just that much," Sam said quietly.

"Hey brother, ain't nothing wrong with that. You *should* put her first. You took all your savings to buy this ounce for us, man, so, really, we owe you big time. You don't owe us a damn thing, Sam."

"I hear you, Al, but when we talked about it, all three of us agreed that we was gone be in this together. I feel like I should be out there with y'all."

"Sam, you put up the cash, let us work this first package. You ain't missing nothing not being back there. Be with Gabriella. You and Gabriella good together. Help her do that music, brother. You know that girl can can sing. Get that night club you been talkin' to me about. That's where you belong— with your lady—not out here trying to prove something. Make her happy and go fill her belly! Sucka!" Alfred concluded as he chuckled slightly.

"You a true friend, Al. They don't make 'em like you no more, brother." Sam stated as he shook Alfred's hand and the two parted ways.

Sam could hear Harold complaining about why Sam wasn't joining them behind the gym as he began walking towards the sandwich shop, but he paid him no mind. Alfred had spoken everything Sam was feeling and had solidified his decision to do right by Gabriella.

Sam, Alfred and Harold had agreed during the summer, while Sam worked with Miss Newsome's man-friend doing home repairs and was earning a good bit of money, that they would begin selling marijuana in school to their peers in order to earn extra money.

Sam and Alfred had entered the game with goals and aspirations. Sam wanted to open a nightclub someday, and Alfred wanted to own a car lot. While Sam and Alfred had goals, Harold wanted to sell drugs for the sake of selling drugs. He had no plans, no goals and no set time to exit the game. He was bent on selling drugs. To Harold, selling drugs gave him the right-of-passage into the gangster lifestyle. Sam and Alfred didn't view themselves as career gangsters, however; they were merely two fifteen-year olds who were trying to get a head start on life.

Sam went to the sandwich shop just off the school campus and purchased three ham and cheese sandwiches and brought them back to Henrietta's classroom. Gabriella was so glad that Sam had kept his promise. Sam now fully recognized what he had in Gabriella: a soul mate.

He made a promise to himself that he would never allow what he did on the streets to interfere in his and Gabriella's life because he didn't want to lose this young woman who loved him wholeheartedly. He also decided that he would earn the money he needed to invest in a night club and leave the drug game alone forever. Furthering his and Gabriella's life together at that moment on that day in September of 1972 became Sam's dream, motivation and ambition.

## CHAPTER 15

## COMPROMISING POSITIONS

Sam was standing behind the school's gym on a cold January afternoon in 1973 along with Alfred and Harold. All three were in possession of leather stachels that contained packets of marijuana. The three youngsters were selling the overstuffed envelopes of weed for ten dollars a bag. As various classmates bought their weed, they talked to Sam about the upcoming talent show. One senior asked if Gabriella was singing again this year, and when Sam nodded yes, the young man shook his head and proclaimed that everybody else had already lost before he walked off.

Sam, Harold and Alfred would usually sell a whole ounce of weed in two days; and on this day, they were going to sell out of their product entirely so they had to score another ounce to have something ready to sell for the weekend.

"Harold, you got in touch with Damon this morning and told him we need ta' cop another ounce today?" Sam asked as he leaned up against the side of the gym's steel wall.

"Yea, he said he gone be down about eight tonight." Harold responded as he made another sell.

"You better duck inside and grab a basketball bro, here come Gabriella," Alfred said to Sam as he eyed her walking towards the gym under the breezeway.

Sam quickly ran down the side of the gym and entered in

through the back door. He removed his black leather jacket and hurried onto the gym floor and patted his hands together to receive a basketball from one of the kids on the gym floor. Harold and Alfred slipped out of sight just as Gabriella approached the two main doors in front of the gym. Gabriella entered the building and saw Sam running down the basketball court. She ran onto the court and grabbed Sam from behind and jumped on his back. Sam began twirling around trying to get Gabriella off his back as she laughed hysterically while holding on tightly to Sam's neck with her right arm and waving an album in front of his face with her free hand.

"Gabriella, girl I can't play ball and hold you at the same time. Come on now, you getting heavy!" Sam exclaimed.

Gabriella hopped off Sam's back and stood in front of him. People on the basketball court began to approach Sam to tell him and Gabriella to clear the court. When they approached the two, they noticed Sam's cold stare. He looked at them as he stood in his black Lee jeans, white t-shirt, and white Converse sneakers if to say, *"Can't you see me and my ole lady talking right here?"* The group of males saw the look on Sam's face and they quickly turned and went to the other end of the court as Alfred and Harold approached the two.

"I love this song, Sam!" Gabriella said happily as she held out the album.

Gabriella had been trying to figure out a song to sing for the talent show. She had to sing alone this time because Janice and the rest of the girls couldn't sing with her because they had entered another talent show in City Park the night of Gabriella's high school talent show. Sam had been thinking of a song for Gabriella to sing as well; and earlier in the morning, he had come up with the perfect song: *Yes, I'm Ready.*

The song was originally recorded by Barbara Mason and Sam thought the piece had the most beautiful lyrics. It was a song that Gabriella could sing alone because Sam had the instrumental to it; he'd given the album version with the lyrics to Gabriella so she could listen to the song. When she listened to the lyrics during lunch in Henrietta's class room, Gabriella's heart grew warm. The lyrics perfectly reflected the way she felt about Sam.

*"Why I didn't think of this song? I love Barbara Mason!"* she thought to herself as she hurried out of the classroom to find Sam.

"I think I can cover this song Sam, you wanna come over tonight and listen to me rehearse it?" Gabriella asked as she climbed down off Sam's back.

Sam agreed, but he knew he also had to meet with Damon, his supplier, at eight P.M. And he began thinking of something that would allow him to be able to get away in time.

Later that night, as Sam listened to Gabriella rehearse the song, he noticed he had about an hour before he was to meet up with Damon. Gabriella's voice was getting tired so she decided to quit. Sam was relieved, as he knew he could now get away from Gabriella to meet up with his supplier. For months now, Sam had managed to keep his drug dealing out of Gabriella's sight. She had no clue as to what Sam was involved in, and no one ever told Gabriella what Sam was doing. Gabriella would not have believed them anyway. She had heard rumors of Sam fooling around with other girls, that he was a heroin addict like his parents, and even a thief; none of the rumors were true and Gabriella knew it.

Sam sat patiently chatting with Gabriella just as Henrietta came out of her bedroom and began setting plates for dinner. She asked Sam if he was staying and he told the sisters that he had to repair a broken elbow pipe on the sink in Miss Newsome's hall bathroom before she returned home from church. Henrietta and Gabriella insisted that Sam at least stay for dinner, Henrietta stating that it wouldn't take her and Gabriella but a few minutes to fry pork chops and mix the gravy and mash potatoes. Sam knew he had maybe forty-five minutes before he had to meet up with Damon, so he agreed to stay. He helped out by setting the table and making a picture of tea for dinner. At five minutes to eight, Sam excused himself from the table and told the girls he was headed home to fix Miss Newsome's sink. He adorned his ¾ length leather jacket, and grabbed his skull hat and kissed Gabriella on the lips before heading out the door.

Sam met Alfred and Harold on the corner and the three of them went and stood behind *Persia's*, the neighborhood bar about five blocks away from Gabriella's house and waited for Damon to arrive. The night air was cold and the three blew their breath into their hands to warm them up. After about a ten minute wait, the three teenagers saw a black on black 1971 Cadillac Coup de' Ville park on the street and a young man around nineteen-years old exited the car. He was dressed in a long, black leather trench coat and wore a black felt fedora hat. His slacks were neatly pressed and he had on a sharp pair of black and white alligator dress shoes. The older teen approached Sam and the boys and neither of them spoke a word. As the four of them stood in the dark alley behind the neighborhood bar staring at one another, the older teen turned and raised his right hand. The passenger door of the car opened and out stepped Damon. Damon was a 5'7" stocky-built two-hundred and fifteen pound twenty-two year old young man with permed and pressed hair and biceps the size of tank cannons. He'd played left tackle on his high school football team in the late sixties. Dressed more like a pimp than a drug dealer, he walked up the alley leading to the back of the bar and opened his bright red suede suit jacket and pulled out a .38 Saturday Night Special and aimed it at the three. They raised their hands and froze as Sam asked Damon what the play was.

"Me and my man Tate here being hearing rumors that niggas in this neighborhood switching over to a new supplier." Damon announced, as he stood in his red suede suit and white ostrich skin boots.

"That's worth shootin' somebody over?" Alfred asked.

"If I don't make the money, nobody will make the money."

"I don't deal with this new supplier you talking about, Damon," Sam stated as he and his friends slowly lowered their arms. "Believe me, if I was making a new connection, I would have told you personally. I never make waves when there's no need to. Whatever problem you having with the brothers down here, it shouldn't start with us. We been doing business for months and we never disrespected you. I think you owe it to us to put that gun away. Talk to me like a man and find out what's going on." Sam ended as he pulled his wool hat down over his ears.

"I already know what's going on down here." Damon remarked. "A new cat on the block named Taylor, a cat 'round the same age as y'all three done jumped in the game. Him and his big-booty ass bitch Joyce. Word on the street is that Taylor and Joyce set up shop in the Desire Project and they taking my customers away. Now, later on down the road, I might find myself at odds with Taylor and his people and it may force you three to choose a side in a war. Because it's coming, brothers. It's coming."

"Man, we not joining no side. The only thing that'll change from here forth would be the exchange point." Sam remarked matter-of-factly.

Damon turned to Tate and the two young men laughed heartily at the statement Sam made. Damon tucked the gun away in his suit slacks and then grew serious.

"You don't make the rules, Sam. I own this neighborhood! You do as I say or else!"

"I'm not asking to make the rules. If you stay making exchanges in this neighborhood, and this 'war' that you talking about breaks out and something happens to you or somebody out your crew, that could maybe, make me an enemy. Like I say, I'm not choosing sides—I'm just looking out for me and my boys' interests as well as yours in order to keep our connection smooth." Sam replied.

Damon had to admit that he liked what Sam was saying, but he didn't tell him. "By continuing to purchase Mary Jane from me, you know you already have chosen sides, cat. Taylor might not be so understanding if he decides to move in on your territory."

"I don't have no territory. I just hustle my school grounds. I might sell a bag or two here behind Persia's from time to time, nothing major. Look, Damon, we not a gang like you or this dude Taylor you talking about. We hustle from day to day at school and 'round the neighborhood mainly dealing with people our age. I don't know of this Taylor dude—and I'm really not concerned about him. That's you and his business. Now the four of us can still do business or we can go our separate ways, your choice. Just remember, we on the sidelines for whatever happen between you and Taylor."

"Cool, brother. I got no static with you. Just remember, if he tries anything, you can come to me."

"Nahh, man. We not even out there like that, Damon. Bloodshed can get a little messy."

"Tell me 'bout it, young blood. Alright, I'm gone take you on your word that you not involved with any of Taylor's activities. So, umm, let's do some business, gentlemen." Damon said as the marijuana was put on display.

"Acapulco Gold is what we have this go 'round, fellas." Tate said as he held the package out before Sam and his boys.

Sam, Alfred and Harold made the exchange with Damon and he walked back to his Cadillac with his henchman and pulled slowly away from the curb and down the street.

"Sam," Alfred said in a nervous voice, "you handled that shit! I thought we was dead! Damon cold-hearted, but you talked to 'em without fear! You didn't back down, Sam."

"Gangsters, at least the smart ones, are business men. Bloodshed can be costly, and it's mainly used as a last resort. I was able to talk to Damon because he smart. Some gangsters don't hold conferences though, and that's what worries me a little about this cat Taylor." Sam replied.

"Man, I woulda took that gun away from Damon, and shoved it up his ass!" Harold remarked as the three walked towards Alfred house to stash the weed.

"Man, you fulla shit!" Alfred remarked. "You ain't say nothin' the whole time Damon and Tate was out there and now you wanna talk brave."

"You ain't say nothin' either, sucka!"

"Sam had it under control. Besides that, I was scared shitless, but even so, I did ask a question and that counts for something."

"We all were scared, Alfred," Sam added.

"I wasn't!" Harold remarked.

"Then why you was wiping tears from your eyes when Damon and Tate walked off?" Alfred, inquired.

Sam just shook his head in amazement and laughed under his breath at Harold's ridiculous statement.

Alfred and Sam both knew Harold was all talk and no action; he was just a kid who wanted to be seen, so most times when ever Harold talked about being a gangster, Alfred would mock him. Harold was Sam and Alfred's friend though, besides, nobody else wanted to hang with him. Most people said he was trouble, including Gabriella. Alfred and Sam saw it different in the beginning, but now Harold was beginning to seriously annoy even him and Alfred.

"Man, the wind was in my eyes!" Harold remarked as the three paused in front of Alfred's front gate.

"You jive, ass!" Alfred answered as he took the package from Sam and welcomed him and Harold inside.

"You go ahead, bro. I need to head home and repair a sink for Miss Newsome.

"Aww man! You going back by Gabriella!" Harold said.

"Say Harold, what's the problem with you, me and Gabriella? You jealous?"

"No, I'm just saying if we gonna be gangsters we have to —"

"Harold, you just don't get it," Sam said in a disgusted manner as he cut Harold off. "You not a gangster! *We* not gangsters! Damon, and from what I just heard, Taylor, they are totally different breeds. We not nothing like those cats. Pay attention to what me and Alfred doing and you'll be all right. Stop playing hard brother, before you live to regret it!" Sam ended as he dapped Alfred and continued on up the sidewalk towards Miss Newsome's house.

When Sam let himself into Miss Newsome's home, he saw that she hadn't arrived home from church yet. He went to the

173

hall closet and grabbed his tool box and headed towards the bathroom. He opened the cabinet under the sink and applied a monkey wrench to the elbow joint and began to loosen the pipe. His plan was to loosen the pipe and let it drip a few times and then tighten it back. It was his way of convincing himself that he wasn't lying to Gabriella. Sam smiled to himself as he thought about the ingenious plan he had come up with. Miss Newsome would come home to find Sam working under the sink and would be able to confirm that he indeed did perform the task he set out to do if ever she were asked. He waited for about thirty minutes and when he saw Miss Newsome walking up the sidewalk, he ran into the bathroom and laid under the sink. When he heard Miss Newsome unlocking her door, he went to work. As he began tightening the pipe however, it burst for real. Luckily, there was no water in the pipes as Sam had turned the water valve off; but the pipe was broken and Sam really didn't know how to fix it.

Miss Newsome and Sam tried for almost two hours to repair the line but they couldn't. They had no running water in the bathroom and they couldn't take a bath this night. Sam made the decision to stay home from school the next day and wait on Miss Newsome's man-friend to come by and the two of them would repair the line together.

The next morning, Sam had awakened around eight A.M. to an empty house. He walked lazily into the bathroom and turned on the water to the sink. When the water didn't come on, he remembered what he had done the night before and went into the kitchen and boiled some water and poured it into the tub along with some cold water so he could take a bath. As he dried himself off and put on a pair of shorts and a white muscle tee shirt, he heard the door bell rang. He thought it was Miss Newsome's friend so he hurried to the door. Sam was surprised, however, to see Gabriella standing on the porch.

"Hey, Sam. You wasn't in class so I just came to see if you were okay," she said lovingly.

"Yea, I couldn't fix that pipe last night so I'm waiting for Miss Newsome's friend from church to come by and give me a hand. Sorry I didn't call. I got busy workin' on the sink."

"That's okay. I went straight to bed after I ate. What time he coming by?"

"He said eight-thirty or nine. Look that cold air biting. Come on in."

Gabriella walked into Miss Newsome's home and sat on the sofa as Sam went and straightened his bedroom up and then began to cook breakfast. Gabriella had the Barbara Mason album that Sam had given her and she noticed Miss Newsome had a turntable in her living room. She put the album on and began singing to Sam as he stood over the stove, boiling water to make a pot of grits. Gabriella stood in the center of the living room and sang warmly to Sam and he enjoyed every minute of it. He soon walked over to Gabriella and grabbed her by the waist and pulled her close to him. Gabriella, in turn, wrapped her arms around Sam's neck and sang into his ear, her angelic voice emanating smiles from Sam as he closed his eyes and sunk into Gabriella's soulful serenade.

"Hey, you know this the first time we ever been alone?" Sam whispered through closed eyes.

"Yea, this feel so good, Sam." Gabriella replied lowly as the two rocked in unison.

"I know, it's like we in our own home as husband and wife." Sam replied as he let his lips gently graze Gabriella's neck.

The two broke their embrace slightly and looked into one another's eyes without speaking a word. Gabriella looked deeply into Sam's eyes with a longing look displayed upon her face. Her heart was fluttering fiercely and she was beginning to get heated. She closed her eyes and continued to sing the lyrics to the song, which she felt in her heart, were right for the moment, "*I don't even... know how... to kiss your lips...at a moment like this...but I'm...going to learn...how to do...all the things you want me to...*"

Gabriella stopped singing at that moment and inched her face forward. Sam cupped her butt cheeks and watched as Gabriella tentatively pressed her lips to his. She jumped back when her lips touched Sam's and the two stared at one another longingly once more. Although they had kissed many times before, both Sam and Gabriella were feeling a deeper mixture of emotions this morning. Emotions they couldn't fully describe nor understand, but emotions neither wanted to go away anytime soon. They came together again slowly and embraced one another and drew their lips ever so slowly towards one another. This time they pressed their lips firmly together and shared a sexually arousing French kiss in Miss Newsome's living room. Gabriella removed her jacket, letting it drop to the floor, and pressed her body tightly into Sam's and the two stood for almost five minutes entwined in a kiss, a passionate kiss that had the two fifteen-year olds longing for more. Sam pulled Gabriella's clip and her long, jet black hair fell over her shoulders. Just as Sam reached around to grab Gabriella's rear end once more, he smelled smoke.

"The water!" Sam yelled as he released his hold on Gabriella and ran back to the kitchen.

The pot was smoking and red hot so Sam had to douse it with cold water, but he soaked his shirt as he did so. He apologized and walked past Gabriella to change into another shirt. As he pulled the crisp white tee shirt over his head, he saw Gabriella standing in his bedroom doorway. She had never been this far into Miss Newsome's home before. Gabriella was still aroused from the kiss the two had shared minutes before, and she told Sam how she was feeling.

"You wanna finish what we were doing in the living room?" Sam asked.

"If you want to." Gabriella responded as she leaned against the threshold of Sam's bedroom.

"Come over and sit on the bed." Sam responded as he sat down.

Gabriella sat down on the bed next to Sam and the two engaged in heavy kissing and soon began petting one another. Sam's hands ran all over Gabriella and she loved the feelings her body was producing. She clawed at Sam as she laid back on the bed and pulled Sam on top of her.

"You know what you doing, Gabriella?"

"Take me Sam. Take me! Take me! Take me!"

The two pressed their faces together and laughed heartily as Sam lay beside Gabriella and unbuckled her jeans. Gabriella stood up and slid them off and removed her shirt and bra. Sam admired her flat stomach and pert breasts. Her erect pink nipples were pointed straight forward. Sam removed his shirt and the two slid under the covers and began kissing and petting again, growing increasingly hot for one another. Gabriella moaned Sam's name and told him she wanted him to make love to her. Just as Sam reached to pull Gabriella's panties down, he heard the front door open and heard Miss Newsome's man-friend calling out for him. The two teens scurried out of the bed and picked up their clothes. Sam told Gabriella to hide under the bed as he slid on his shorts and shirt. He then shoved all of Gabriella's clothes under the bed and ran out the room and greeted the man.

"Well, I see you was unprepared for today's activity." the man said as he smiled at Sam.

"Yeah, man, I fell back to sleep boiling water for grits."

"You listening to Barbara Mason?"

"Oh, yeah, let me get that."

Sam had to distract the man as he kicked Gabriella's coat under the couch. He knew if the man found any evidence that Sam had someone in the house he would tell. He knew of Sam and Gabriella's "friendship" and he would promptly report to Miss Newsome that Sam and Gabriella were in her house alone. The lady would then tell Henrietta and the two teens would be in serious trouble. As Sam talked to the man, he started down the hall towards the bathroom. Sam had wanted to close his door but he didn't have time. He hoped Gabriella had remained out of sight. The man called out for Sam to give him a hand and Sam hurried down the hall.

As the two repaired the sink, Sam noticed movement coming from under his bed. The man had half his body under the sink so he couldn't see what was going on. Sam could see Gabriella wiggling under his bed. She still had her bra off and as she laid on her back under the bed, she looked sexily at

Sam. Sam licked his lips in hunger. The two were lusting for one another whilst the man worked on the sink. When Gabriella made a funny face, Sam smirked and made a funny face towards Gabriella and she let out a yelp of a laugh, causing the old man to slide out from the sink.

"What was that noise?"

"I had the hiccups." Sam stated as he pretended to hiccup.

The man looked around for a minute and got up and went into Sam's room. He looked in Sam's closet and saw no one. He then turned and looked under Sam's bed. When he did, Sam was prepared to speak, but the man merely got up off his knees and walked out of the room.

"Let's get this sink fixed, Sam. I have other jobs lined up."

Sam didn't know what happened. He looked under the bed himself and didn't see Gabriella; he looked in the closet and she wasn't there either. Sam looked around and wondered what the hell was going on and where was Gabriella. After an hour, the old man had the sink fixed, so he gathered his tools and left. When he did, Sam hurried back to the room. When he returned, he searched for Gabriella. He called out for her and Gabriella emerged from under a pile of clothes in the corner, laughing hysterically. Sam laughed himself as he fell on the floor next to Gabriella.

The two grew quiet as Sam twinkled Gabriella's charm necklace in his hands. They began kissing again as they lay on the carpeted floor. This time, Gabriella did take her panties off; and Sam and Gabriella gave each other of themselves. It was the first time for the both of them. They fell in love this day and professed a love for one another that the two of them knew would last a lifetime.

Gabriella sung at the school talent show and, once again, she took first place, winning the $250 prize. She sung the lyrics to *Yes, I'm Ready* with such conviction and heartfelt desire that the song could have been hers and hers alone. She had her eyes closed as she sang; reminiscing about the time she and Sam made love. She wanted to relive that moment over and over again with the love of her life. Sam felt the same way, and from time to time, the two of them would get together and experiment. Those times were far and few in between, however, because Henrietta and Miss Newsome kept a close eye on the two. They would have to cut class to be together sexually, and Gabriella really didn't like to do that. As school grew nearer to a close, however, the two knew they would have plenty of time to lie beside one another. And that they did.

CHAPTER 16

BLUE LIGHT BULBS, BEER AND WEED

The summer of 1973 was an intense and passionate period of time for Sam and Gabriella. They shared of themselves freely and as often as they could. Much of that depended on Henrietta's schedule; however, the young couple would get together whenever Henrietta had to go out of town to teachers' workshops or to purchase items for her music class.

Sam, Alfred and Harold were also making good money from selling weed. So much so that Sam had to take a full-time job with Ms. Newsome's man friend to hide his illegal activities from Henrietta and Gabriella. Sam constantly bought Gabriella new clothes and jewelry during the summer of '73. When Henrietta asked him how he could afford those items halfway through summer, Sam was able to tell her that he was working full-time with Miss Newsome's friend until school started back.

Gabriella had blossomed over the summer. She was gorgeous indeed; the envy of a great majority of women. A fine young woman she was. Gabriella had sprouted up to 5'8" and weighed around one-hundred and forty-five pounds. Her curvaceous body and pert, round rear end were the objects of desire to a great many men, both young and old. Sam made a good partner for her. He was as handsome as ever standing an even six feet and weighing around one-hundred and seventy-five pounds. The couple was adored by most, hated by a few, but respected by all. Gabriella was eagerly awaiting the start of the new school year, but she also wanted to party a little bit before summer's end.

Henrietta had thrown a nice party for Gabriella's 16th birthday the second week in August. Gabriella really enjoyed her "sweet sixteen" party. A lot of her friends from school were there and there was plenty of food and punch to drink, but the party ended at midnight with much protest from the teens. Gabriella thanked Henrietta sincerely, but she really felt she was becoming a young woman and she wanted more adult options in her life. Those options came during the last week of August.

"Gabriella, I'm on my way to the airport!" Henrietta said aloud. "You sure you don't wanna fly out to Dallas with me?" she asked as she walked and stood in the doorway of Gabriella's bedroom.

"No," Gabriella said, in between coughs as she lay in her bed on a Thursday night. "This summer cold got me real down. My throat hurts."

"You sure you gonna be okay? Let me check your temperature again." Henrietta said anxiously as she walked towards her sister.

"Henrietta, I'll be fine. You gonna miss your plane. And I need that new microphone for music class."

"Okay, sugar. Look, I got cold tablets on the counter, and fresh lemonade and honey in the refrigerator. You can call the school and ask for the nurse Ms. Adams if you need anything that's not in the house and—"

"Henrietta, you be back Sunday morning. Janice gone come and sit with me tomorrow and Saturday. I'll be fine." Gabriella remarked, cutting Henrietta's statement short.

"Okay, baby. Remember—"

"I know—not a house full of people. I never had anybody here none of the times you left this summer except for Janice, Henrietta."

"Alright, I'm leaving. Lock the door behind me," Henrietta announced as Gabriella got up from her bed and followed behind her lazily. "Nobody but Janice in my house, Gabriella!" Henrietta said as she walked out the door and hopped into her '63 Impala.

"I promise. I ain't gone let nobody in the house," Gabriella said lowly as she closed the door and watched Henrietta's car disappear down the street. "I promise I ain't gone let nobody in the house until I know for sure—until I know for sure—*for sure that you on your way to the airport!*" She then yelled aloud as she ran and grabbed the telephone to call Janice to let her know Henrietta had left for the weekend.

Gabriella had pretended to be sick this night so that she didn't arouse any suspicion from her older sister. She knew Henrietta wanted her to go to Dallas with her; but Gabriella had other plans. By pretending to be sick, the sixteen year-old got to stay home. She wanted to have fun with her friends one more time before school started—without supervision from Henrietta. About an hour later, Janice, Charmaine, and Yvonne made it over to Gabriella's house; each of them carried an overnight bag as they were going to stay with Gabriella until Saturday night. That way, the house would be clean when Henrietta returned Sunday morning.

Janice bounced through the door, holding her duffel bag and a case of beer with Yvonne following close behind. Charmaine followed with a blue light bulb, which she quickly placed in the living room bulb socket. The stereo was turned on, along with the light, and the girls began to dance.

"Paaaaaarty! Hey! Paaaaaarty! Hey!" they all shouted together as they danced in the middle of the living room floor.

The phone rang while the girls were dancing and everybody grew quiet as Gabriella turned down the music and answered the phone. Gabriella sighed in relief and told her friends it was Sam on the phone and Janice quickly went and turned the volume back up on The Isley Brothers' hit song *That Lady* while Gabriella invited Sam over.

When Sam arrived, nineteen year-old Janice, and eighteen year-olds, Charmaine and Yvonne, were sitting on Henrietta's front porch smoking a joint.

"Thanks for the weed earlier, Sam." Charmaine said in a low tone so Gabriella, who was inside fixing herself a sandwich, couldn't hear.

The girls mostly hung out on the front porch throughout the night. Janice, Charmaine, and Yvonne were the only ones to smoke weed and drink beer. Gabriella and Sam, meanwhile, were locked away in Gabriella's room up under the bed covers. Sam left Gabriella and her friends late in the night, but not before he and Gabriella made love repeatedly. The girls awoke the next morning with plans to prepare for another party once night fell.

Friday morning, afternoon and evening went by quickly. Gabriella and her friends spent the entire day doing each other's nails and hair and talking girl talk. Sam had gone to school, but he would return later, once he sold his package of weed. Gabriella had decided to style her hair into Mickey Mouse ears during the evening hours and her friends all agreed her new hair style was cute. She went and took a long bath and put on a tight fitting brown suede short set and matching sandals that Sam had bought her earlier in the year. Gabriella was now feeling all grown-up and when night fell, the girls were all dolled up.

"Man, we shoulda went ta' Persia's tonight!" Janice remarked as the four girls sat in the living room listening to music.

"Nah, if somethin' was to happen to Gabriella out there, Henrietta would never forgive us." Yvonne remarked.

"You right, sista' I'm trippin'," Janice responded. "Hey man, let's smoke some weed! I mean, we here to party right? Well, let's party shit!" Janice snapped as she turned up the stereo and began dancing as she lit a joint.

Gabriella, out of respect for Henrietta, ordered Janice onto the porch before she lit the joint. Charmaine and Yvonne followed, as did Gabriella. The three older teens, along with Gabriella, sat on the porch talking while listening to music. Sam, after learning the night before that Henrietta was out of town, had decided to walk back around the corner to

Gabriella's house. The girls greeted him happily as he walked into the yard. Janice, Charmaine, and Yvonne were passing the weed back and forth as they each sipped on a can of beer. Sam soon asked for a beer and Gabriella hopped up to get it for him. When she returned, Gabriella had not one, but two cans of beer. Everyone looked surprised as Gabriella pulled the tab back on the cold can of Schlitz and stared at the beer can.

"We supposed to be partying, right?" Gabriella asked cheerily as she gulped down a huge swallow of the beer.

Gabriella's face wrinkled and she gagged several times before she spat the beer out. The first taste of alcohol was distasteful to her palate.

"Hey! Hey! What the hell you doing with that beer, li'l sister?" Janice asked. "If you ain't gone drink it, give it here."

"No, I'm a drink it." Gabriella responded as she began to sip, instead of gulping the beverage. She nursed the twelve ounce can for nearly an hour, careful not to get drunk while slowly becoming accustomed to the taste.

Everyone was beginning to loosen up as the weed, beer, and music began to take effect on the group this hot muggy night. Janice and Charmaine had walked to the store and bought another case of Schlitz, and another bag of weed magically appeared, courtesy of Sam. Two hours later, the group had taken on a relaxed, calm demeanor as they sat out on the front porch. The radio was blaring a song titled *The World is a Ghetto* by the group War. Janice raised her hands into the air and bowed her head and snapped her fingers as the song seem to ring true of the times they were living in.

They were all feeling good as another group of teenagers passed in front of the house and spoke to Sam and the girls. The group of males continued down block and passed Alfred's house and saw Alfred sitting on his porch. Alfred asked the group if they had seen Sam.

"Did we see 'em?" one of the young men answered. "Man, Sam around there by Gabriella with three other females. He got all them fine honeys over there and ain't even invite a brother in!"

After hearing those remarks, Alfred immediately leapt from his porch and ran around the corner to Gabriella's house.

"Sam, why you ain't tell me y'all was havin' a party, brother?" Alfred asked happily as he walked into the yard. "I wanna party too, sucka! Let me get some kool-aid, man!"

Everyone on the porch burst into laughter at that moment. "Kool-aid? Who the fuck drinking kool-aid, chump?" Janice asked through loud laughter.

Alfred didn't realize what he had walked into. This was a party of a different caliber than he'd expected. It wasn't like Gabriella's "sweet sixteen" party. He jumped into his player mode once he caught on by calmly walking into the house and grabbing a beer from the refrigerator. He then joined the rest of the gang on the front porch. The group sat out and drink beer for another hour or so and then moved the party into Henrietta's living room once the mosquitoes became unbearable.

*Superstitious,* by Stevie Wonder, was now on the radio and the gang all danced in the center of the living room after sliding the coffee table into the hallway. The door bell rung while the group was dancing and the they all grew quiet. When Gabriella peeked out of the window, she saw Harold at the door.

"Oh lord, it's Harold." she remarked somberly as she pulled the door open.

Harold spoke to Gabriella and walked into the living room. He saw the blue light bulb and the beer cans on the floor and recognized what was going on; but still, he tried to act if he had bigger plans going on.

"Say, Alfred, you wanna go down and hang out by Persia's with me? They got a party going on down there and lotta fine honeys is in there brother!"

"*Persia's?*" Alfred yelled over the music as he danced with the group of females. "You scared ta' go in there without me and Sam! Anyway, the party right here, fool!" Alfred yelled as he grabbed Charmaine's short, petite brown-skinned frame and pulled her to him.

Charmaine's dark eyes lit up excitedly and she willingly returned Alfred's affection and ground her body against his as the two continued to dance. Janice, wearing a tight black mini skirt and a black sleeveless blouse, jumped behind Alfred and began grinding on his rear, her thick Afro bouncing up and down as she grooved to Stevie Wonder's hit song.

As Gabriella and Sam danced together, and Alfred partied with Janice and Charmaine, Yvonne, the voluptuous, bow-legged, dark-brown-skinned, 5'7" one-hundred and forty pound, D-cupped beauty queen walked over to Harold, grabbed his hand, and tried to pull him onto the floor. Harold pulled away and just sat on the sofa and watched the group as they partied on.

"Harold scared of girls, y'all!" Yvonne yelled over the music as she pulled a head-band onto her short jet-black hair and ran back and joined the group.

"Gabriella, go find some cards so we can play some spades!" Janice yelled over the music.

Gabriella walked off to Henrietta's room to find a deck of cards. She began searching Henrietta's dresser drawers and noticed all the sexy silk under garments her older sister wore. As she looked through her sister's most personal dresser drawer, Gabriella came across a thick piece of black rubber shaped like a penis. She held it her hands and sniggled when she realized Henrietta had a 'rubber thangy' stashed away in her drawer. She then noticed a set of beads on a string and she picked those up as well, wondering what they were used for. The alcohol had Gabriella buzzing and, against her better judgment, she took her sister's most personal items and brought them into the living room where she found Janice, Yvonne, and Charmaine sitting back on their heels in the center of the floor waiting to play a game of spades.

"You found the cards, Gabriella?" Janice asked.

"No, but I found this rubber thangy!" Gabriella said as she held up her sister's dildo. "Why Henrietta got this thing? What's it for?"

Janice and the other two girls burst into laughter as Sam and his friends looked on in shock. They couldn't believe Henrietta had "one of those".

"Sometimes, when ya' can't get no 'thangy' as you said, you gotta' do it yourself, Gabriella." Janice replied as she burst into laughter.

"How you do it yourself?"

"You mean you never rocked your little man in the boat?" Yvonne asked.

"Ohh, you mean masturbate. Nahh, I got Sam to rock my boat."

"I heard that!" Janice remarked. "Look like Henrietta like gettin' her boat rocked a lot; be it alone with a 'rubber thangy' or with a real thangy attached to a real man!" she concluded as she continued laughing.

Gabriella then showed the girls the beads on a string. "What you do with these beads? What are these?" she asked as she looked at the beads in a confused manner.

"Them Ben-Wa balls, Gabriella!" Charmaine said as she started to laugh. "Your sister is a freak!"

Gabriella was still perplexed by the beads. "Henrietta ain't a freak. These beads come from Mardi Gras or something." she said.

"I knew you was thinking that," Yvonne said through laughter. "Those ain't Mardi Gras beads, li'l sister. They rectum balls. You slide 'em all the way in your ass and you pull 'em out real fast right when you orgasm."

"In ya' ass and pull 'em out fast..." Gabriella questioned lowly to no one in particular as she held the beads up at eye level, still somewhat perplexed. Suddenly, it dawned on her. The 'rubber thangy' was in the shape of a penis, and the 'Mardi Gras' beads went inside...a...person's...Gabriella ran around in a circle a few times and threw the beads and the dildo down onto the floor and made a beeline for the bathroom to wash her hands.

"Yeah, you done touched your sister's ass balls and fake ding-a-ling!" Janice said as she lit up another joint. "Bring the damn cards when ya' come back you snoopin' little heifer! Ain't nobody tell your nosy behind to bring your sister's shit out here and put it on display! Say, who y'all think slidin' those beads in Henrietta's ass?" Janice then asked, causing Charmaine and Yvonne to laugh aloud. "Maybe she doin' it herself! No, I know! The brick mason teacher! They in the same building back there! She and dude used ta' eat lunch together all the time when we was seniors, remember?" she said quietly.

Charmaine and Yvonne were laughing to the top of their lungs now at Janice, who'd gotten on a roll from the buzz she had going. The three females had all caught the giggles and neither could stop laughing as they replayed the image of Gabriella running around in a circle throwing her sister's items on the floor.

"She, she...Ohhh! My stomach hurt!" Charmaine cried as she tried to put together a sentence and control her laughing. "Gabriella looked like a li'l woodchuck running around in a circle!" she finally blurted out as her hair fell down over her face.

"Then, and then, then she hauled ass to the bathroom! That shit was sooo—ow, ow! My stomach! That was some funny stuff right there, man!" Yvonne chimed in.

"Gotta wash that doo-doo off good, Gabriella!" Charmaine stated loudly and quickly, her face now covered in tears from laughing so hard.

"Gabriella, clean ya' pooh-pooh hands and bring the damn cards!" Janice snapped before she puffed on the joint real hard.

While sipping their beers, Sam, Alfred and Harold laughed along with the girls as they listened to them make fun of Gabriella.

"Maybe she putting Henrietta's beads in her own ass! What y'all think? Gabriella bring the damn cards and quit playing with your sister stuff! She gone bust yo' ass for touchin' her shit!" Janice yelled loudly over the music.

Gabriella came back with the cards a few minutes later and she, along with Janice, Charmaine, and Yvonne, started playing spades. Janice didn't notice that Yvonne had picked up the dildo and began playing behind her head with it. Everyone then began laughing at Janice. Janice thought she was still making everybody else laugh; not realizing the joke was on her. Janice, who was now high as a kite, ragged Gabriella continuously about finding Henrietta's stash as Yvonne waved the dildo over her head.

"So how you feel about discovering that dick, Gabriella?" Janice asked in a mockingly concerned tone as she dealt out the cards. "I mean, it's not often you come into contact with shit like Henrietta had stashed away, you know? You wanna talk about it? You okay?" she asked with a mocking sniggle as she arranged her cards in her hand.

"Janice, Janice, stop please!" Charmaine said as she waved her hands side to side as she heaved from laughing so hard.

"Alright, we gone move on now," Janice announced as she threw out the ace of hearts. "Can't believe that shit, though—Henrietta got a dildo and ass balls stashed away. Freaky-deaky, mutherfucka." Janice said under her breath.

"I gotta go pee!" Charmaine blurted out as she got up from the floor, no longer able to control herself.

Janice continued to smoke weed whilst they waited on Charmaine. The smoke was beginning to fill the air and everyone was starting to catch a contact high from the marijuana. Harold Melvin and Bluenotes' song, *If You Don't know Me By Now* came across the radio and Janice once again threw her hands in the air. When she did, she bumped Yvonne's hand and the dildo fell into her Afro.

"She got a dick on her head!" Sam blurted out as he started to laugh.

Everyone laughed at Janice as she removed the dildo from her bush. "Gimme this damn dick!" she snapped.

"You can't ask for a dick nicer than that Janice?" Yvonne asked as she laughed aloud.

"Y'all gone stop playin' with me about this damn dick!" Janice snapped as she held the dildo in her hands pointing it at the girls. "Harold, what you laughing at?" Janice then said as she stood up and walked over to Harold.

The sexy, nineteen year-old stood in front of Harold and then sat on his lap facing him.

Harold whimpered and pushed Janice off his lap.

"What's wrong, li'l boy? You, you scared of girls for real? Yvonne, I thought you was playing! This boy really scared of girls! How you gone claim ta' be a gangster and you scared of girls? Man, you a chump!" Janice snapped as she backed away and stared at Harold.

Everyone grew quiet awaiting Harold's reply. Sam and Alfred placed their hands onto their heads and sunk down in the sofa cushions and moaned in shock when Harold got up and walked quickly and quietly towards the front door without saying a word to Janice or anybody else.

Janice and the rest of the girls were shocked as well. Janice called out to Harold as he headed for the door. "Aww, man! I was thinking about giving you some nooky too, Harold! Harold? Man, I was just playing! Well, well go on then ole jive ass nigga!" Janice screamed as she slammed the door and locked it.

Janice knew exactly what she was doing. She knew she was a fine female, three years older Sam and his friends, including Harold, the purported gangster. Janice only wanted to expose Harold for what she felt he truly was on this very night, and she did.

"He talk all that gangsta shit, and he scared of pussy! Punk ass wanna-be gangster!" she ended as she rejoined her friends and continued to play cards.

As the party continued on, everyone was loaded to the max. Although Janice, Yvonne and Charmaine were the only ones to smoke weed again this night, the two joints they did smoke inside the home had given Gabriella, Sam and Alfred a good contact high. The blue light bulb was still on and the music continued to play. Everyone sat around quietly talking until *Papa Was a Rolling Stone,* by The Temptations, came on and the party heated up again. Everyone was feeling really good by the early morning hours. The mood was a relaxing, laid back type of atmosphere.

As Alfred sat next to Charmaine with his arm around the older teen, he asked to sleep with her. The petite eighteen year-old didn't want to disrespect Henrietta's house in that fashion, however; so she and Alfred merely kissed and petted one another that night. As the sun began to peek across the horizon, the mood was still mellow. A couple of hours earlier, Sam and Gabriella had gone to bed to fool around again.

Janice, Charmaine, Alfred and Yvonne had stayed up and talked and drank beer until the sun came up. When it did, Henrietta arrived home. She arrived home a day earlier than she had planned because she was worried about her little sister, whom she believed was sick in bed. As Janice, Charmaine, Yvonne and Alfred laughed aloud and drank beer, Henrietta unlocked her front door and entered her home and was stunned to anger. She yelled aloud at Janice, who was the oldest, "What the fuck is going on in my house?"

The teenagers scattered like roaches when the lights get turned on as Henrietta dropped the new microphone she held for Gabriella, kicked off her shoes, took off her glasses and began shoving the teenagers out of her house. They danced around the living room picking up shoes and duffel bags, half-full beer cans and albums as Henrietta swung, kicked, and shoved Alfred, Janice, Charmaine, and Yvonne out of her front door all the while cussing. Henrietta's brown eyes were full of anger, and her brown hair hung wildly over her face and shoulders as she stood in her front yard and yelled at Janice, Alfred, Charmaine, and Yvonne as the teens fled down the sidewalk, leaving behind a trail of dropped shirts, pants, full beer cans and mix-matched sneakers and high-heeled shoes.

Gabriella had heard the commotion from her bedroom and she began repeatedly shoving Sam, trying to get him to awaken so he could get dressed. Sam was so drunk off the beer, however, he wouldn't budge. Henrietta burst into Gabriella's room and caught her little sister, who was butt-naked, trying to shove Sam's naked, hung over body from her bed. Henrietta began to beat Gabriella with a leather strap until Gabriella cried and screamed at the top of her lungs. Sam had awakened by then and he, too, was whipped by Henrietta.

Sam could have easily overpowered Henrietta, but he knew he was in the wrong for what he had allowed and done inside of Henrietta's home. Henrietta went back and forth between the two teens, lashing them in a ferocious manner as she was deeply angered by what she had witnessed unfolding within the confines of her home. Gabriella thrashed about the room, her naked body receiving sting after sting from Henrietta's leather strap. Once Henrietta felt she had beaten some sense back into Gabriella, who was now full of red welts, and Sam, who stood silently and took his beating whilst covering his private parts, she ordered them to dress and come into the living room.

Once they were presentable, Gabriella, still crying, and an embarrassed Sam, pleaded for Henrietta not to tell Ms. Newsome what they had done. To do so would mean that Sam would not get to see Gabriella for a long, long time. They both knew Ms. Newsome would move him to another school and stop him from calling Gabriella. It was a thought too painful for either of them to bear.

"I've never seen anything like this my entire life!" Henrietta said as she flopped down onto her sofa, kicking aside empty beer cans. "To think I was actually *worried* about you, Gabriella! I feel like a damn fool!" Henrietta said angrily as she cried openly.

Sam and Gabriella walked towards Henrietta, and Gabriella knelt at her sister's knees and begged forgiveness while Sam sat in a wooden chair opposite Henrietta. Henrietta knew they were just a bunch of fun-loving teens, but she couldn't get over the fact that Gabriella had lied to her. Henrietta was deeply hurt by what her little sister had done. Gabriella promised to never lie to Henrietta again as she repeatedly begged for forgiveness.

Watching the two sisters, Sam realized that he, too, was living a lie by selling drugs behind the sisters' back. He promised himself he would stop soon, as things were beginning to spin out of control between he and Gabriella; the couple was simply getting involved in too much wrong-doing.

Henrietta sent Sam home and agreed not to tell Ms. Newsome as long as Sam didn't disrespect her home again by getting drunk and having sex with Gabriella. Sam promised her he wouldn't do those things again. He would tell Miss Newsome that he spent the night by Alfred's house, another lie he was not proud of in the least bit. Sam knew he had to change his ways as the lies and deceit were beginning to compound themselves.

After everything settled down, Gabriella cleaned the living room and her bedroom and went to sleep. Henrietta sat on the sofa for a nearly an hour until she calmed down. She then went into her room to gather clothes to take a shower. When she went to her drawer, she noticed the dildo and Ben-Wa balls were out of place. Henrietta had never used the items, they were gag gifts for a fellow colleague who was having a bachelorette party in a couple of weeks. She could only imagine what the teenagers were thinking when they discovered the items. She grew angry all over again as she pictured the teens making fun of her.

Henrietta walked back to Gabriella's room, attempting to confront her little sister again. She opened the door only to see Gabriella, with visible red welts on her arms and legs, lying peacefully across her bed sound asleep. Henrietta then looked upon the innocence in Gabriella's face as she slept soundly on her back; she was a picture of serenity at that moment and that image had softened Henrietta's heart. Henrietta knew her little sister was harmless at her core; she also knew Gabriella would hurt no one and merely wanted to have fun with her friends. She wasn't perfect by a long-shot, that Henrietta knew. Gabriella was sneaky, daring, and naively fun-loving to a point of conflict. With that aside, Henrietta knew at her core that Gabriella sincerely meant harm to no one. It was those heart-warming thoughts, and the calm innocence displayed by the sleeping Gabriella that kept Henrietta from pursuing the matter any further.

After all the chaos and ass-whipping that Henrietta had dished out, Gabriella was now resting peacefully. Henrietta stared lovingly at her little sister knowing full well that Gabriella deserved what she had gotten this day, but still, she smiled upon her little sister as she closed the door.

*"That little devil!"* Henrietta thought to herself. *"I think she got the point!"* she concluded as she shook her head from side to side, returning to her bedroom.

Henrietta began to realize that the kids could have been doing much worse. At least they were in her home and safe. They had enough sense not to hang out in the streets and run the risk of getting hurt or worse. They also hadn't brought over a lot of other kids, which could have caused even more problems. Only Sam and Gabriella were naked, which was good, in its own way as Henrietta thought real hard about some of the possible things that could have happened with a bunch of teens in a home all to themselves coupled with alcohol.

Henrietta loved her sister more than life itself, and she knew deep down inside that she was somewhat passive in her discipline of Gabriella, but she was doing as best she could to keep Gabriella in check and for the most part, Henrietta was successful. Still, some things would slip by the woman. Henrietta hadn't smelled the marijuana smoke so she had not a clue that drugs were being used; or she would have really flown off the handle and sent Gabriella to counseling for substance abuse. Henrietta knew she had taken it easy on Gabriella. She knew she should have punished her; but the moment had already passed, and besides, Gabriella seemed sincere in her apologies and Henrietta, no matter how hard she tried, could not stay mad at Gabriella for long. Telling herself she had done what was right, Henrietta reflected on the worst case scenario and was glad her sister was safe.

Henrietta quickly learned that Gabriella was a person who was unafraid to try something. It was a bold move for Gabriella to do what she had done inside of their home. Henrietta then smiled to herself as she went about gathering her clothes in preparation to take her bath. She reminisced about the times, during the summer no less, that she would sneak Marcel into her mother's home whilst Veronica was at work. Gabriella had done the same thing and took it a step further. Henrietta knew she could never have found the courage to invite her friends to Veronica's home and have a little party the way Gabriella had done. She wished she could have orchestrated a little get together like that when she was a teenager. *"I really should get out more."* she thought to herself as she stared into the mirror at her twenty-five year-old, 5'7" one-hundred and thirty-five pound figure.

Secretly, Henrietta admired Gabriella's boldness and found it within herself to forgive her little sister and her friends for the simple fact that she had done something similar when she was younger. She would never let on to the fact that she understood what Gabriella had done, however; after all, Henrietta wasn't meant to be one of Gabriella's girlfriends. She was there to protect and raise her younger sister properly. The task was becoming harder and harder for Henrietta, however, because the 1970s were a period of rapid change and growth for the next group of young adults, Gabriella's group, who were quickly coming up behind Henrietta Jenkins' peers and out-pacing them just as fast.

# CHAPTER 17

## TUMMY ACHES

Gabriella waited patiently for Sam as she sat inside Henrietta's class on the first day of school in 1973. It had been two weeks since the incident in Henrietta's home and all was back to normal. Sam, Alfred and Harold had arrived just before the bell rang and greeted the two sisters. Sam and Gabriella would have a shortened class schedule this year as they had passed all of their required courses. Alfred and Harold, on the other hand, had a full schedule and would have to remain in school the entire day in order to finish their required courses. The two of them would continue to sell weed behind the gym whilst Sam and Gabriella joined Charmaine, Janice, and Yvonne at *Persia's*, the neighborhood bar farthest from Henrietta's home.

*Persia's* was a medium-sized, dimly lit hole-in-the wall club owned by a laid-back, fifty-eight year-old grey-bearded slender man named Clyde. Clyde was a cool cat from back in the day. People loved his club because it had a nice sound system, and he served food. Clyde's kitchen served chicken plates and roast beef, ham and cheese, and hot sausage patty sandwiches on French bread, known as Po-boys, which was an asset that none of the other clubs in the neighborhood possessed.

When entering into *Persia's* front door, which was caty-corner facing the curb, a long bar was on the right and Clyde's small kitchen entrance was at the far end of the bar. The kitchen had a small grill, a deep fryer and a small deep freezer. The small grill pit was just big enough to keep the french fries warm, tender and fresh, and the fried chicken and Po-boy sandwiches hot and ready to serve.

The dance floor was directly in front of the entrance. Facing the front door, the stage sat behind the dance floor. To the left of the door were a few worn out chairs and tables where one could eat a meal. To the right of the stage was Clyde's office and a music room where a Dee-jay could spin albums that would blare out onto the dance floor. A long hall was on the left side of the stage and it led to the rest rooms.

Clyde opened his bar to teenagers during the day and allowed them to shoot pool, buy sodas, chicken plates and sandwiches, and play the juke box. He closed the bar at 6:30 and it reopened at 8 P.M., often with a guest Dee-jay on hand to spin albums. The night hours were supposed to be for adults only, but teens would still sneak into the club and buy food and drinks.

After the first week of school ended for Sam and Gabriella, they headed over to *Persia's* to meet up with Charmaine, Janice and Yvonne. When they got there, they saw Janice and company on stage singing to the instrumental version of *Will You Still Love Me Tomorrow*, which had been originally sung by The Shirelles.

Janice was on lead. She was holding her own, but her voice was a little too raspy for the song. Still, the girls were jamming, and held their audience's attention, some were even dancing to the rendition.

The three girls sang and danced in rhythm as the medium-sized group of teenagers in the bar cheered them on while Gabriella and Sam walked over to the bar and ordered two cream sodas. Just then, Charmaine began screaming Gabriella's name as she ran off the stage mid-song and grabbed Gabriella by the arm and led her back to the stage. The teens in the crowd surrounded the one-foot high stage and grew curious as the four girls drew into a huddle and talked amongst themselves. The teenagers in the club knew of Gabriella's singing ability and they were hoping that they would get to hear her sing this day.

"Okay," Yvonne said, "Janice, you got 'em warmed up, but now we got our entire group together."

Janice was elated, she'd been waiting on this day for a longtime. "Li'l sister, you ready to put on a show for these good people inside this club?" she asked excitedly.

"I been ready. My first time on stage in a club!" Gabriella said happily as she huddled with her friends.

"Okay," Janice remarked, "let's do, let's do the song we almost sung for our first talent show together. You brought that instrumental with you right, Charmaine?"

"Yeah, I got it! It's in the back with the rest of the albums." Charmaine replied. "Gabriella, you still remember the lyrics right?"

"I remember. I love that song, too, because it mentions our city."

"Okay," said Janice. "One line, facing the crowd, clapping to the beat—that's how we gone kick it off." she ended as she handed Gabriella the microphone.

Yvonne ran into the small room where the turntable was located and replaced The Shirelles instrumental with another instrumental and rejoined her girls on stage. The four females then lined up in a row and faced the audience and began to clap their hands in unison as the instrumental to *Dancin' in the Street*, as originally recorded by Martha Reeves and the Vandellas, began to play.

The audience began clapping in unison with the girls, and when Gabriella stepped forth and sung aloud, *"Calling out around the world...are you ready for a brand new beat..."* the die had been cast. The crowd had become enamored with her voice once again.

The girls had the bar rocking for almost three hours, taking breaks in between songs to enjoy free sodas courtesy of Clyde, as they sang songs by various female artists and groups from the sixties, including the Marvelettes' song, *Please Mr. Postman*, The Supremes' *You Can't Hurry Love*, and The

Crytsals' song, *Then He Kissed Me.*

Gabriella and her girls then wowed the audience when they began singing Jackie Wilson's song, *Higher and Higher*. Gabriella took it back to church on that song, but she was really singing her heart out to Sam, something she did on just about every song she'd sung since the day the two first met. Gabriella was singing with such force, her voice had spilled out into the street. She vivaciously danced around the stage, her hair matted to her sweaty head as Janice, Charmaine and Yvonne sung the chorus, *"Your love keeps on lifting me...Keeps...On...Lifting me..."*

As Janice and the girls sung the chorus, Gabriella sung to the top of her lungs, *"Higher and Higher...Your love...baby your love...Higher and Higher!"*

People hanging out in the neighborhood heard the powerful female voice shouting "Higher and Higher" and many of them walked into Clyde's bar to see who was jamming on stage. Before long, the bar was packed with scores of patrons, both young and old alike.

Clyde had never seen the bar so packed during this time of day, but he appreciated all the new business he was getting. Chicken plates and Po-boys flew out the kitchen at lightning speed and sodas sailed off the shelves. When the older patrons started asking Clyde where the beer and liquor was, he opened the bar early that Friday afternoon. The teenagers and adults partied together as Gabriella and her friends put on a show that left the entire neighborhood talking about Clyde's bar and the girls that were singing on stage, especially the young lead singer with the powerful voice that could cover just about every song imaginable.

Sam knew he had to pull Gabriella out of the bar before Henrietta arrived home because he knew she would raise Cain if she got hip to the fact that Gabriella was in a bar partying with adults who were smoking cigarettes and drinking alcohol. Gabriella reluctantly left with Sam amidst slight protests from club patrons. The two walked through the neighborhood hugging one another and laughing, Gabriella repeatedly telling Sam how much fun she had singing in the club.

"I never had so much fun in my life Sam! I can't wait to do that again! They loved us on Clyde's stage!"

"You mean you wanna go back to Persia's? All that cigarette smoke? All those grown people dancing and drinking and stuff? Henrietta would go crazy if she knew you was in Clyde's bar jammin' like that, Gabriella." Sam replied as he danced up the sidewalk in front of Gabriella, telling her how wonderful she looked on stage.

As Sam continued dancing, singing Jackie Wilson's song himself, Gabriella suddenly bent over and vomited right onto the sidewalk.

"Gabriella," Sam said as he rushed to her side, "baby, you, you okay?"

"I'm fine Sam. It must've been the cigarette smoke or something from the club. I'm fine now baby, I'm fine." Gabriella said as she up-righted herself.

Sam took Gabriella home and laid her down on the couch and went into the kitchen to warm her a bowl of soup to soothe her stomach. As Sam was heating up a can of chicken noodle soup for Gabriella, Janice knocked on the door, opened it and walked into Henrietta's home.

"Gabriella, they is going crazy down at Persia's, li'l sister! You have to come back and sing again! Let's do it tomorrow!"

"Henrietta will kill me if she found that out." Gabriella remarked as she sat up in preparation to eat her soup.

"Girl, you sixteen now, you can't stay under your sister forever. You been blessed with a gift. Tell her Sam." Janice replied as she stood in the middle of the living room, staring at Gabriella.

"You right, Janice, but Gabriella right, too. Henrietta not going for that one." Sam remarked as he sat the bowl of soup on the table and handed Gabriella a spoon and a napkin.

"Man," Janice said in frustration as she stomped her foot. "Alright then, li'l sister, you get out of school early, right?" she then asked.

"I do. Me and Sam both get out early. Why?" Gabriella asked.

"We can get together through the week and sing at the bar for a few hours and be done before Henrietta get home."

Gabriella looked over to Sam and they both cracked a smile. Janice smiled as well because she knew Sam and Gabriella were willing to go to the bar during the week. The following week, *Persia's* was once again packed. Monday was a little slow because people didn't know the girls were singing until the end of their show. The rest of the week, however, *Persia's* had standing room only.

On the Saturday following the girls' week of performances, people from all over the neighborhood had come to *Persia's* to see and hear the girl with the angel-like, powerful voice perform. When they realized that there wasn't going to be a show, a lot of the club-goers slowly began to file out of the bar. Clyde was beginning to realize that the girls had actually helped his business improve. In order for him to stay competitive, Clyde knew he had to have the girls sing on weekends during the night hours, which was his most profitable period.

As Janice and her girls sat at the bar waiting for Sam and Gabriella that following Monday afternoon, Clyde approached Janice and asked her about performing on weekends.

"We would love to Clyde, but Gabriella's big sister just won't allow it." Janice remarked as she sipped a bottle of Miller High Life.

"Tell that little girl that I'll pay each of you fifty dollars a week to perform three nights, Thursday, Friday and Saturday, from eight-thirty to midnight." the enthusiastic man announced.

Janice's eyes widened at Clyde's proposition. She eagerly told Sam and Gabriella what Clyde had offered the moment they entered the club and Gabriella jumped at the chance. Sam saw an opportunity for he and Gabriella also; so while the girls were on stage that afternoon singing, Sam approached Clyde and walked behind the bar counter and began serving drinks.

Clyde looked over at Sam and smiled in approval. After every sale Sam made, he handed the money to Clyde. When the rush was over, Clyde walked over to Sam and handed him a twenty dollar bill.

"Keep it, Clyde." Sam said as he walked from behind the bar.

"Are you serious, Sam? I know you, and you don't do nothing if you don't get paid for it." Clyde said as he rubbed his beard whilst staring at Sam.

"I can help you make this bar bigger and better if you give me the chance, man." Sam stated seriously as he cyed Clyde.

Clyde sat down on a stool behind his bar and poured himself a drink as he began to contemplate what Sam had just said to him. The fifty-eight year old man had been looking for someone to help him run the bar. Clyde even thought that, perhaps, that person would even take over someday. Sam was only sixteen, however, and Clyde was reluctant to go into business with such a young partner. Sam was of a different breed, however, and Clyde knew that to be a fact. He had known Sam since he was a younger lad, and he had watched Sam grow up in the neighborhood.

"You're going to have to earn this privilege, Sam," Clyde said, as he took off his dark tinted, big, round sunglasses and lit a cigarette. He leaned his back against his cash register and stared at Sam intently and said, "I just can't say yes, and then you start slacking up on me young blood."

"Give me a month, Clyde. Let me show you what I can do."

Clyde thought for a moment and cautiously nodded his head and extended his hand to shake Sam's hand in order to seal the deal.

Sam immediately began formulating a plan to gain favor with Clyde and become a partner with the man. Gabriella and the girls had just finished another set and they were taking a break before they went back onto the stage.

As the girls walked towards Clyde's office, Sam saw two opportunities to improve the club right away. First, he though the stage should be bigger and higher, about three feet off the ground. Second, since Clyde owned the vacant building next door, Sam could combine the two and make the entire bar twice as big. The girls could have their own private dressing room and there would be more room to eat and more room on the dance floor.

Gabriella and the girls were headed back to the stage and, just as they were about to leave Clyde's office, Gabriella bent at the waist and vomited onto the man's carpet. Janice and the girls sat Gabriella back down, but the sixteen-year old insisted that she always vomited around cigarette smoke. She told them she was fine and was ready to do the last three songs. The girls finished their performance and Gabriella headed home to rest after she cleaned Clyde's carpet in his office. Janice had to walk Gabriella home because Sam had stayed behind to go over plans with Clyde. He also had to meet with Alfred and Harold at *Persia's* later on in the evening.

Sam was eager to share his plans with his two friends. When they walked into the bar, the first thing Sam said was, "I'm about to be partners with Clyde, brothers!"

"Are you crazy? You don't know nothing about running a bar! Besides, you only sixteen, fool!" Harold snapped as he and Alfred walked up to the bar.

"This my exit out the drug game, Harold. You can keep your share and do whatever you want. Me myself, takin' my split and doin' something worthwhile with it. Something legal." Sam stated as the three friends sat at the bar sipping cream soda.

"We only been in for a year. You can't quit now!" Harold snapped.

"Had this opportunity not come up, I would've said you were right and continue on with the plan, but as luck would have it, all I needed was a year, brother. Like it or not, I'm out, Harold."

"That's cool, man." Alfred said whilst smiling proudly at Sam. "You about to live your dream, Sam. You got Gabriella singing in the club and getting paid and you about to be co-owner at sixteen. You doing exactly what we talked about that day under the breezeway on the first day of school back in '72. I'm happy for you, man. I made enough money, too. I think I'll buy a couple of old cars, fix 'em up and sell 'em. I'm gonna start doing something legal, too. I'm gone work towards my car lot." Alfred said with a huge smile on his round face.

"I see you got plans, too, brother." Sam stated as the two dapped.

"Yeah man. The drug game getting wicked, bro. They just robbing one another, shootin' each other, and don't nobody really have nothing to show for all the time they spend out there. We did it though, Sam—and we never got caught. Shit! We never even had to carry a weapon—and we made money in the process!" Alfred replied.

"Man, y'all two niggas is suckas!" Harold said aloud as he stood up from his bar stool.

Patrons turned to see what was going on when they heard Harold speaking. "Marijuana is what's gonna make us rich! Not no silly ass night club, not no fuckin' used car lot—and it damn sure won't be no bitch singin' on a stupid ass stage!"

Sam jumped from his bar stool and grabbed Harold around the neck and began to choke him.

"I'm sorry, I'm sorry!" Harold managed to speak through Sam's clutched hands before Alfred pulled the two apart.

Harold righted himself and said through gasped of breaths, "I'm, I'm sorry for sayin' that shit, Sam. I'm just, just mad it's over. We was having a good run, brother. We had the whole neighborhood buying from us, man! It's way more money to be got out there, cat!" Harold stated as he rested up against the bar, gasping for air.

Sam shook his head from side to side and said, "You wanna be a career drug dealer and a gangster, Harold—fine! You go and do that. We had a good run, true enough, but they got piranha's out there that'll eat your ass alive! So before we have ta' go to the gun-play, I'm going legit. I ain't going to the hospital or the morgue over some bullshit! Not a bagga' weed, not over some territory that don't belong to me, and not over tryin' to prove how hard I am! Don't make your choice and expect me to do the same. Just be your own man. I'm not the enemy, Harold, but I will be if you keep disrespectin' me and Gabriella and challenging my manhood, understand? Gangster!" Sam ended as he backed away from Harold and sat back down on his stool.

Clyde had heard what transpired between the three teens and he was impressed with Sam's state of mind. At that moment, Clyde made his mind up, to work with Sam and help bring him into the business.

The three sixteen-year olds went to Alfred's house and split $14,000 three ways. Sam got $6,000 and Harold and Alfred each got $4,000. When they finished splitting the money, Harold immediately got up and left. Sam and Alfred, however, sat in Alfred's room and talked about their future plans as they smoked a couple of joints and listened to Pink Floyd's album titled *The Dark Side of the Moon*, which featured the hit song *Money*. Both young men were excited about their futures by the time Sam left Alfred's home and made his way over to Gabriella's house. When he got there, Sam saw Janice, Yvonne and Charmaine in the bathroom with Gabriella, who was slumped over the toilet, vomiting again.

"You been throwing up all day, Gabriella. You need to go to the doctor. Sam, she really needs to go to the doctor," Janice repeated.

"I told you, Janice," Gabriella said as she cried, "that cigarette smoke makes me sick!"

"Li'l sister, we been from the bar for over five hours—and ain't nobody smokin' cigarettes around here," Janice stated as she patted her Afro back into shape and looked at Sam. "You two might not wanna believe or hear this, but I think Gabriella pregnant!"

## CHAPTER 18

### YOU'RE A BIG GIRL NOW

Thursday morning found Janice, Charmaine, Yvonne, Sam and Gabriella sitting in the free clinic located on the corners of Desire Street and Florida Avenue in the Ninth Ward awaiting the results from Gabriella's pregnancy test, which had been administered a couple of days earlier.

Gabriella was nervous and frightened. She knew Henrietta would be so disappointed in her, and she was also worried if she and Sam would be able to take care of a baby, and even more, she was wondering if Sam would even stick around if he learned she was pregnant. Gabriella feared that if her test came back positive, she would lose Sam forever. The doctor who'd administered Gabriella's test came into view from the hall leading to the labs and the five friends stood up. The doctor escorted Gabriella to his office and turned around and was startled to see the entire group in his office. He confirmed what Janice had already suspected: Gabriella was indeed pregnant.

Gabriella raised her hands to her face and leaned over into Sam's chest and wept lowly. Charmaine rubbed her back softly and Sam assured her that everything was going to be okay.

"She's in the early stages of her pregnancy." the doctor remarked. "There's still plenty of time for an abortion."

Gabriella raised her head from Sam's chest and told the

doctor plainly that she wasn't having an abortion.

"Ma'am, I know you are scared right now, but raising a baby on your own is tough now-a-days and—"

"She's not alone. The baby's father is right here, man. You think I actually wanna kill my child?" Sam replied angrily. "You think I'm a run out on Gabriella? I love my woman and I'll do whatever it takes to raise my child. Fuck an abortion!"

"There's no need for vulgarity sir. I'm sorry, Gabriella, I'm sorry to all of you. I didn't see a ring on Gabriella's finger, so I assumed the baby's father wasn't in the picture." the doctor replied in an apologetic tone.

"She's only sixteen, doctor. Both of them are sixteen," Yvonne remarked.

The doctor looked at Sam and then back at Gabriella and apologized again. He looked at Sam's muscular physique and Gabriella's well proportioned frame and had assumed the two were older than they were. He complemented Gabriella and Sam on their maturity and wished them the best of luck before giving Gabriella a prescription for prenatal vitamins.

The friends left the free clinic and began discussing ways to tell Henrietta that Gabriella was pregnant as they walked her home. Gabriella also had to sing at *Persia's* later on in the night so getting out of the house would pose yet another problem.

Gabriella, Sam, and Janice were sitting on the couch when Henrietta came home from work at about 6:30 P.M. She bounced through the door in a cheery mood. She had received her paycheck and had gotten an extensive raise this school year. Henrietta shared the news with the three and they congratulated her as she walked into the kitchen and began to prepare dinner.

Gabriella, dressed in a blue pair of bell-bottomed jeans and a black, tight-fitting blouse and black stacked shoes, clutched Sam and Janice's hands tightly then released them as she got up off the couch and walked into the kitchen.

"Henrietta," she said in a low tone, "I have something to tell you."

"When's the baby due, Gabriella?" Henrietta asked before she sighed and shook her head from side to side slowly.

Sam and Janice, as well as Gabriella, were surprised by Henrietta's remark.

"How'd you know?" Gabriella asked.

"Oh, let me see…I busted you two in bed not too long ago. Remember that day? Oh yea, the constant running to the bathroom and throwing up at all hours of the night. The widening hips. Ridiculous cravings. You haven't used any of your pads this month. What else?" Henrietta asked as she looked towards the ceiling in deep thought.

"Okay, okay, I get the picture." Gabriella responded lowly. "But I got a job so I can support the baby." she then said in an upbeat tone.

"What's he going to do?" Henrietta asked, peering over the top of her glasses, looking directly at Sam as she snapped beans in the kitchen sink.

"He has a job with me—at Persia's."

"*Persia's*? That hole in the wall bar on the corner about five blocks up the street? I know you are not working there!" Henrietta remarked as she turned to Gabriella and rested her hands against the sides of the sink.

Sam then got up from the couch and walked towards the kitchen. "I'm about to be part owner, Miss Jenkins, and—"

"At sixteen? How on God's green earth could you pull something like that off with just a part-time job, boy?" Henrietta shouted, cutting Sam's statements short.

"What difference does it make? It's done!"

Henrietta looked at Sam and Gabriella with a look of shock and disappointment. "This is ridiculous." she replied as she threw up her hands and shook her head from side to side in protest. "You both are talking nonsense! Sam get out of my house!" she ended angrily as she walked towards the front door.

"Miss Jenkins wait—" Janice started to chime in as she stood up from the couch.

"Shut up Janice! You get the hell out my house as well! If it wasn't for you, Gabriella wouldn't be in this shape! I'm not going to let a club-singing loose woman and a hoodlum destroy my sister!"

"I never influenced Gabriella to have sex with Sam, Ms. Jenkins. She made that decision on her own. And I ain't a loose woman!" Janice replied as she eyed Henrietta and placed her hands on her hips.

"It doesn't matter, she knew what you were doing out there. You didn't have to influence her by talking about it. And as far as that little drug dealing gangster over there, I'm gone have to —"

"I'm not a gangster, Henrietta!" Sam yelled aloud, cutting Henrietta off.

"Then what are you, Sam?" Henrietta asked as she stood in the living room eying Sam angrily. "Just what in the hell are you? A handyman? No! Because you lied about that! I know exactly what you are! You a sixteen-year old drug dealer! You stand there in those fancy silk slacks, the silk shirt and the brim hat, owning a *damn* bar? If that doesn't have drugs written on it my daddy didn't love me. *Leave!*"

"Did you ever see me sell drugs? You ever saw me selling or smoking anything?" Sam asked angrily as Gabriella stood at his side.

"Leave, Sam! Good-bye, Janice!" Henrietta reiterated as she did not care to hear, let alone answer Sam's questions of objectivity towards her accusations.

Janice headed for the door. Sam, however, was not willing to leave without stating his position. He believed Henrietta had no right to accuse him of something in which she had no proof, even if she was correct in her assumptions.

"Answer the question, Henrietta! Did you ever, *ever* see me sell or use drugs?" Sam asked loudly.

Henrietta was furious over the whole situation. The woman

wasn't foolish, and even though she had no proof, she refused to change her mind concerning Sam's lifestyle.

"It doesn't matter little man," she answered as she stood before Sam and pointed her finger directly at his face and continued to speak in a low matter-of-fact tone, "you hid that part of your life very well, Sam. But everything's out in the open now. You've been selling drugs, having sex with Gabriella—in my home no less—and now you and Janice want her to sing in a bar in order to make a profit?" Henrietta asked as she walked to her front door and held it open for Sam and Janice. "Please, you and Janice, please, just leave." she ended as tears began to well up in her eyes.

Sam had more to say, but the look in Henrietta's eyes let him know the woman could not be reasoned with at this point and time. He stared at Henrietta in dismay before he and Janice headed towards the door. Janice looked at Gabriella and told her she was sorry as she turned and headed out the door. Gabriella called out to her lover and her best friend and ran towards the two, but Henrietta blocked her by placing her hand before the threshold.

Gabriella, unable to leave the home, began professing her love for Sam as he walked down the stairs towards the front gate with Janice leading the way.

"Sam, I love you!" Gabriella cried out aloud. "She won't stop us! Sam! Janice!" she called out aloud as Sam and Janice walked out the front gate and Sam politely closed it before the two disappeared from sight.

Gabriella was heart-broken over the way she had been treated by her sister. She felt as if Henrietta was being unreasonable in her actions.

"Why you do that, Henrietta?" Gabriella asked through tears.

"After all I done for you, you go out and get pregnant for a hoodlum like Sam? You hang out in a sleazy bar with girls older than you that's doing God knows what, with God knows who and you wonder why? Momma would be so ashamed!" Henrietta stated as she wiped her eyes and closed the front door and turned to Gabriella.

"You don't know that!" Gabriella replied as she stood facing Henrietta, the two of them now only mere feet apart. "This is *1973*! Things not the same like it was when you was growing up!" Gabriella said as she sobbed heavily. "Maybe, maybe, momma would be proud that I have a job and friends— and a man that truly loves me—something you *never* had when she was alive!"

Henrietta raised her hand and slapped Gabriella across the face with so much force that she knocked Gabriella out of her stacked shoes as she stumbled across the living room, back into the kitchen. Gabriella caught herself in threshold and leaned up against the wall separating the living room from the kitchen in utter shock. She knew Henrietta had only once whipped her, the morning she was caught with Sam, and she had never raised her hands to her until this day. Gabriella covered her stomach, protecting her unborn child, all the while crying as Henrietta walked over and stood before her.

Henrietta was also crying as she pointed back at herself. "You are fine," Henrietta said through her tears, "I would never hurt your child, Gabriella. But what you have to understand is the fact that I gave up my *life*! *My life*! For *you*! And you insult me and your mother by saying that she would be proud of you and your whoring ways? No Gabriella! Veronica would *not* be proud of you because you 'have friends and a man that truly loves you'! Veronica would be proud of *me* for what I have done for *you*! Not for what you are doing right now!" Henrietta said as she sobbed heavily. "Why you hurt me, Gabriella? A baby? At sixteen?I'm so disappointed at the woman you're becoming, Gabriella! That's all, child. I'm hurt! Understand? I'm really hurt over this!" Henrietta concluded in a high-pitched voice as she ran to her room, closed the door, fell onto her bed and cried aloud.

Gabriella covered her face and sobbed heavily as she sunk to the floor, crawled into the living room, grabbed her shoes and got up and walked to her room, all the while sobbing and heaving as she went to prepare herself for her first night performance at *Persia's*.

"I'm sorry I hurt you, Henrietta!" she said through Henrietta's door as she turned and walked into her bedroom.

Gabriella was dressed inside an hour, her hair was flowing down her shoulders and she was wearing a mid-thigh-high beige, all in one silk dress with beige leather pumps. She walked down the hall towards the living room where she saw Henrietta sitting on the couch, crying as she sat on the sofa with her legs crossed holding a picture of Gabriella when she was twelve years-old. Gabriella walked over and knelt down on the floor beside Henrietta and placed her head in her older sister's lap and the two cried together as they stared at the picture. Henrietta reached out and hugged Gabriella's neck tightly, not wanting to let her go, literally and figuratively speaking.

Henrietta knew full well that Gabriella was laying a foundation for her future, and her life, which was hers to live. The young man Gabriella loved, Samson Holland, and the woman who was one of her best friends, Janice, were the two people that she had allowed into her life. *Her life. Gabriella's* life. They were *Gabriella's* friends. Henrietta knew she had to let Gabriella grow up; Sam and Janice, however, were causing Henrietta's little sister, her "baby", to grow up faster than Henrietta had anticipated or desired. She knew that once Gabriella walked out of that door, and entered *Persia's* on this night, she would be beginning a new phase of her life. It was hard for Henrietta to accept the fact that her little sister had grown up literally over night. Where had the time gone? It seemed like it was just yesterday when the two of them first walked onto the high school campus. Now, here it is, three years later, and her little sister has a job singing in a night club and a baby on the way.

"I'm sorry I hit you, baby." Henrietta said lowly, breaking the silence.

Gabriella wiped her tears and looked up to Henrietta meekly and said humbly, "I'm sorry I said what I said about your life, Henrietta. You raised me the same way momma would have and I thank you for that. I wouldn't know what to do if it wasn't for the things you taught me."

"I feel as if we're not close anymore. We were so close, baby. What happened to us?"

"We still are close. I just sing and hang with my friends, but this is always home, Henrietta."

"Yes it is. For as long as you need it to be, Gabriella. For as long as you want to be here."

The two sisters held one another in a loving embrace for a moment before Gabriella softly stated that she had to leave.

"You wanna walk me to the club?" Gabriella asked lowly, hoping her sister would at least try to understand what she and Sam were putting together.

"You know, for as long as we stayed in this neighborhood, I never been inside that place?" Henrietta remarked as she removed her hair from her face and wiped her eyes.

Gabriella got up and grabbed her twenty-five year old sister's hand and the two walked out of the house towards the night club. Just as Henrietta had helped Gabriella during her first year of high school, Gabriella, who was more familiar with the neighborhood, guided her older sister through the after dark neighborhood. The two sisters entered the club and saw that it was filled to capacity. Henrietta stared at all the people that mingled in the club. The woman was somewhat frightened, having never been around such a group of people. Henrietta considered club-goers to be a rowdy, rugged brand of people. Gabriella confidently led her sister through the club, however; stopping every few feet to hug a patron or two and to formally introduce her big sister.

Henrietta knew some of the patrons as her former students; some were still in her music class. To Henrietta's surprise and delight, everyone was nice. Gabriella finally made it to Clyde's office. She opened the door to find Charmaine, Janice and Yvonne rehearsing for their performance. Janice ran over to Gabriella and hugged her just as Henrietta came onto view. Charmaine backed away slowly, and then she and Yvonne exited the room leaving Henrietta, Gabriella and Janice alone in the office.

"I owe you an apology, Janice. I have to admit, even in my own house, I was out of line for talking to you that way. I just hate the fact that my baby sister is growing up." Henrietta said as she grew overly emotional and covered her lower face and stared at Gabriella.

"I understand, Miss Jenkins. Believe me, if I didn't think she was able to handle this scene, she wouldn't be here. Everybody loves Gabriella, though. She is awesome. Come on! Watch and see! It's gone be a groovy time, sister!"

Janice and Gabriella took Henrietta by the hand and guided her to the bar and sat her down and told Clyde to watch over her. Clyde chatted with Henrietta as he served patrons. When the lights went low, the crowd all turned toward the stage and anxiously waited for the girls. Gabriella appeared, along with Charmaine, Janice and Yvonne and the crowd applauded.

As the instrumental to *I'll Take You There* by the Staple Singers began, the girls dedicated the song to Henrietta. Gabriella began to sing a beautiful rendition of the song that had the crowd in a festive mood. Henrietta was enjoying the song thoroughly, she knew Gabriella was good, but she was surprised at how the crowd responded to her singing. Gabriella was a little bit different when she was on this stage. Henrietta could sense it, but couldn't put her finger on the difference between Gabriella's club performance, and the talent shows she'd performed in early on in high school. Her little sister was singing as Henrietta had never really heard her sing. This was not the way Gabriella sang in church when she was younger either, not exactly. Her sister knew how to please a crowd. She knew how to please *this* crowd. Henrietta was proud of her little sister.

As she enjoyed her sister's performance, a glass of vodka and orange juice was pressed against her elbow. Henrietta turned around to see Sam. She placed the glass on the bar's counter and hugged young Sam tightly and apologized. Sam apologized as well and the two sat and held hands and watched Gabriella and her friends perform. By the time the show was over, Gabriella had gained another fan. From that moment forward, Henrietta tried not to miss her sister perform. When she wasn't overloaded with school work, or had a meeting to attend, Henrietta was always at *Persia's.*

Henrietta became supportive of Gabriella's and Sam's vision; she supported them in every way she could. As the months went by, Sam made some improvements to the club and, in March of 1974, he became a partner of Clyde's. The bar was flourishing and Sam had drawn up the plans to expand the bar by the end of 1974. Earlier in the month of March, as Gabriella grew closer to her due date in April, Sam moved into Henrietta's home, allowing Miss Newsome to retire to Orlando, Florida.

Sam had placed a ring on Gabriella's hand and was planning to marry her on her 18$^{th}$ birthday day. Things were going really well for everyone, and on April 11th, 1974, at the tender age of sixteen, Gabriella Jenkins gave birth to a baby boy whom she named Benjamin, after her father. Gabriella gave her son Sam's last name, Holland, since she, too, was going to become a Holland in a little over a year's time.

Benjamin Holland was Sam and Gabriella's, and all of their friends' pride and joy. Janice was over to Henrietta's house everyday helping out with the baby. Alfred was a big help as well. When he wasn't working on his used vehicles, he would be at the house with Sam helping out while Gabriella rested. Benjamin had taken a lot of strength from Gabriella and she needed to rest to be able to finish school and begin to perform again.

During the summer after Sam, Gabriella, and Alfred had graduated high school, Henrietta stepped in and tended to the heavy-set, light-skinned, butterball baby boy. During that time, Alfred and Sam worked on the bar. Harold, who had dropped out of school in January five months before graduating, would join in, sometimes, when he wasn't doing "gangster shit" as he often liked to say.

By the end of 1974, Gabriella, now seventeen, was back at the club with renewed vigor and the club was bigger and better. Clyde could not be happier, as *Persia's* was in the process of transforming from a hole in the wall, to a respectable night club that featured a live act and a friendly atmosphere. The year 1974 closed out on a very high note for everyone, especially Sam and Gabriella.

# CHAPTER 19

## JOYCE AND TAYLOR

It was the summer of 1975 in mid-July, about a month before Gabriella's eighteenth birthday and wedding day. The sun was shining real bright this morning as Gabriella and Henrietta moved about on the porch playing with baby Benjamin, who was now over a year old. As Gabriella bounced her son up and down on her knee and made funny faces towards him, the baby giggled ecstatically.

Sam and Alfred were in the driveway placing a tune-up on a 1973 four-door Caprice classic. Sam had purchased the car from Alfred's small used car lot only a few days ago, and the two were putting the finishing touches on the car to get it road worthy as they were all planning an outing to Biloxi, Mississippi the upcoming weekend.

As Sam and Alfred, both now eighteen, worked on Sam's car, and while seventeen year-old Gabriella and twenty-seven year-old Henrietta entertained the baby, a little girl rode by on a bicycle with a small German shepherd following behind her as she passed Henrietta's home, which was on the corner of Metropolitan and Benefit Streets. The little girl and her dog crossed into the street and there was a loud screeching sound and then a thump. Sam and his family looked up to see a 1972 dark brown two door Caprice classic in the middle of the intersection, and two teenagers jumping from the car. The female, who was driving, got out screaming as the young man got out of the passenger side.

"Didn't I tell you slow this mutherfucka down, Joyce? Now you done killed some mutherfuckin' body!"

"I didn't hit the li'l girl! I hit the dog, ole stupid ass nigga!"

"I don't give a fuck! You still killed somebody!"

Joyce walked around to the front of the car just as Sam and his family made it to the intersection.

"She all right?" Sam asked worriedly.

"Yea, she fine," Joyce said of the little girl, who was crying as she knelt down in front of her dead dog, "the dog wasn't so lucky. Y'all know this little girl? What's your name, baby? Where you stay?" the dark-skinned thick-thighed woman asked the little girl.

"My name is Faye Sanders. I stay in the Desire project with my grandma." Faye answered as she sobbed, holding her head down.

"You a long way from home to be so young, Faye." Joyce replied. "You want us to take you home?"

"I want my dog!" Faye snapped.

"Sam, go grab a garbage bag so we can pick the dog up and bury it somewhere." Gabriella stated as she held baby Ben on her hips.

"Ohh, he so cute!" Joyce said as she reached out and touched Ben's hand. "Looka my baby in the backseat!" she added. "His name is Manuel Lawson Taylor after his daddy. We call him 'Manny' for short."

The two females chatted until Taylor, Alfred, and Sam had picked up the dog and buried it in an empty lot across the street from Henrietta's home.

"Hey, thanks for helping out brother." Taylor said to Alfred and Sam as the three walked back towards Taylor's car.

"No problem man, but look like that li'l girl gone be real mad about her dog." Sam stated.

Taylor suddenly stopped and looked Sam's six-foot frame over. "You used to sell weed with Harold a while back?"

"No, Harold sold weed with us!" Alfred stated angrily.

"Your name Al! Sam and Al? Man I been wanting to holler at y'all cats for the longest!"

"About what?" Sam asked.

"About Damon! He said he ran y'all out the game 'cause y'all wouldn't work for 'em. He tried ta' intimidate me with that lie man! Y'all own Persia's right? Man that's my plan—to go legit early."

"He goin' around telling people he ran us off?" Sam asked in shock.

"Aww, nah man, he just told that ta' me when we got into an argument one day. But I know what's up. It ain't nothin' for y'all ta' worry about. He trying ta' take over the neighborhood, but I been here in the Ninth Ward, and I ain't never gone let a nigga like Damon over take me, ya' dig?" Taylor said as he headed towards his car. "I'm gone have ta' come and check out your club, Sam. The whole neighborhood been talking. Look, if you ever need something, come holler at me. I be on Desire and Benefit everyday cat!"

"I'm cool right now. But thanks anyway Taylor. Watch Damon, though man."

"I know he a cold-hearted mutherfucka, Sam. But I'm too deep in this game ta' back down. I got a son ta' support you know? Not ta' mention Joyce big booty ass."

"Well I wish you all the luck brother, and stay safe." Sam concluded as Taylor shook Sam's and then Alfred's hands and jogged back over to his car.

Joyce had loaded Faye's bicycle into the trunk and she and Taylor were going to take Faye to the S.P.C.A. and buy her a new dog and then take her home. On this day in 1975, Joyce and Taylor became friends with Faye Sanders. They would take Faye everywhere and introduce her to people as their adopted daughter. Taylor and Sam never really got to know one another, they merely knew of one another and from time to time they would cross paths.

"You paying for this mutherfuckin' dog too Joyce! I didn't

kill the bitch, you did."

"Thanks for making me feel better you heartless son of a bitch!" Joyce stated as she went to get back into the driver's seat after placing Faye into the back seat of the car.

Sam and company walked back to their yard as they laughed at the young couple's arguing. Joyce and Taylor were a brash and explicit talking couple that controlled more than half of the weed that ran through the Ninth Ward. They were also funny to watch and listen to as they constantly argued about everything.

"Ohh, no," Taylor said as he snatched Joyce by her thick Afro and pulled her out of the driver's seat, "you done killed one soul today, I be damned if I watch you murder another one! Get your ass on the other side!"

Joyce stood up and slapped Taylor in the chest and Taylor grabbed her around the neck. As he choked Joyce, she kneed him in the groin and ran around to the passenger side of the car laughing. "I'm gone fuck you up when we get this li'l girl out the car you bitch you!" he growled as he crawled into the driver seat.

"Yea, yea, yea!" Joyce snapped as she lit a marijuana joint and passed it to Taylor just as the two sped off.

Later in the week, as Sam and Alfred were loading beach supplies into Sam's car, Harold came over to Henrietta's home.

"Man, we ain't seen you in weeks! Where you been, sucka?" Alfred said as he dapped Harold off.

"I been working, man."

"Oh, you got a job? That's good Harold. That's good." Sam stated.

"Yea, I got a li'l spot in the Desire project selling weed for Damon. Got two niggas under me and we makin' some serious money." Harold said excitedly.

Sam and Alfred looked at one another and shook their heads at the same time.

"What?" asked Harold.

"Man, you know Taylor working the whole Desire project. Now you gone go and start selling for Damon? When you know Damon and Taylor don't get along?" Sam remarked.

"Man, fuck Taylor! Damon the man, and before long, Taylor gone be working for me!"

"Harold, you don't know what you gettin' involved in cat!" Alfred said with a concerned voice. "Damon not to be messed up with, brother. You can't see he using you?"

"He right Harold," Sam added. "Taylor not a chump, and he not gone roll over easy. Damon might get his li'l war going on after all." Sam stated as he looked at Alfred before placing three folding chairs into the trunk of his car.

Alfred nodded in agreement with Sam adding that Harold was making a big mistake and he should leave Damon alone.

"Man, y'all bitches weak!" Harold stated.

Just then Sam turned and grabbed Harold and wrestled him to the ground. This time, Harold fought back. He managed to pull a gun from his waistband and he pointed it at the ground and fired one shot. The bullet hit the ground next to Sam's foot. Sam stepped back, looked at Harold in shock and charged him again. This time Harold aimed the gun at Sam's chest and cocked it.

Henrietta and Gabriella ran onto the porch to see what was going on. When they saw Harold aiming the gun at Sam, they began yelling at the two eighteen year-olds as they ran down the stairs. Alfred was standing beside Sam as Harold aimed the gun at the two with a wicked grin on his face.

"Harold don't shoot 'em! Please!" Gabriella shouted as baby Ben started crying.

"Gabriella! Henrietta! Stay on the porch! This men talkin' over here!"

"Yea, you tell them bitches ta' stay in they place!" Harold stated with a sly grin on his face.

Harold loved the feeling he was getting from frightening Gabriella and Henrietta. He loved the power and control he felt. He wanted so bad to be a gangster that he was willing to destroy his friendship with the only two young men that were truly his friends.

"Harold, I'm gone ask you one time ta' leave this mutherfuckin' yard and don't ever show your face around me and my family for as long as you live. If I see you around my family again, I'm gone kill you slowly, sucka!"

"You talk to me like that, and I got a gun in my hand Sam?" Harold asked in an aggravated manner.

"I don't care, man! I'm tired of your shit, Harold! You wanna be a gangster, go do it out there with Damon, Taylor and the rest of them. I'm asking you like a man not ta' bring your bullshit around my family."

Harold looked around at Gabriella and Henrietta and saw the two crying. He looked at Sam and Alfred, and the rest of the crowd that had gathered in the street to watch the scene unfold. He figured he had made a big enough scene to get people to notice him so he tucked the gun back into his waistband and walked out of Henrietta's yard with a smirk on his face.

"I'm gone be the man, Sam. You might own that bar, you might have a li'l money put back, but it's gangsters like me that's gone be around in the end. Before long you won't be able to open that bar without my permission. You gone wish you never stopped being my friend. You and that chubby mutherfucka standing next to you!"

Sam could see that Harold was not in his right frame of mind. Whatever Damon told Harold it seemed to be working as he was brainwashed into believing that he was really a top player in the Ninth Ward. To the real game players, however, Harold didn't even make a blip on the radar. Sam knew it, Alfred knew it, and so did everyone in the neighborhood— everyone except Harold. As Harold walked hurriedly down the block, scores of people ran up to Sam and Alfred asking were they okay. Gabriella and Henrietta rushed the two teens and Sam reached for his son and hugged him tightly.

After that day, no one found favor with Harold, he became

an outcast in the neighborhood, he started spending more time in the Desire project and that was beginning to agitate Taylor, it wouldn't be too long before they bumped heads. Sam and Gabriella's wedding day was just around the corner, however; and while Harold was busy digging his own grave, Sam and Gabriella were busy planning a wedding that all other weddings would be compared to for years to come.

CHAPTER 20

LET THE SUN NOT SET ON OUR LOVE

Sam and Gabriella were visiting New Orleans' City Park on a warm summer morning in August of '75, a week before Gabriella's 18th birthday and the couple's wedding day. The two of them, along with their one year old son Benjamin, Henrietta, Janice, Yvonne, and Charmaine, were walking through the Peristyle just before the sun had started to rise. The Peristyle, an open air pavilion with Ionic columns, was built in 1907 and is one of the oldest structures in the entire city. Lined with numerous columns reminiscent of Ancient Roman Architecture, and guarded by four huge concrete lions that protected the staircase leading down to the waters of Bayou Metairie, the Peristyle, in Gabriella's eyes, was the perfect place to have a wedding because of its grace and beauty.

Gabriella also liked the idea of having her wedding ceremony just as the sun was beginning to break over the horizon. She and Sam were there in the park timing the sun's rising and determining what time to begin their ceremony. It was 6:53 A.M. when the sun began to peek over the oak tress that were behind the huge white stone pavilion and illuminate the pristine structure's interior.

The Peristyle had a true Roman appeal to it; and Gabriella loved the oak trees that surrounded the stone structure and Bayou Metairie, with its hosts of ducks and geese, created the perfect back-drop to what was to be a very special day. Gabriella visioned in her mind, the Peristyle offering up a picturesque scene as the sun rose over the oak trees and letting it's light shine down upon her and her husband-to-be.

"Sam, it's beautiful, baby. Look like if we set it for 7:15, the sun'll be up and it'll be shining towards the front of the pavilion, right down the pathway."

"Yeah, yeah, I can dig that there, baby. This here building reminds me of the Ancient Roman days."

"It's similar, but it's actually a Greek design." Gabriella responded.

Most people have their weddings in the afternoon, but Gabriella wanted to be different. To her, the sun's rising on her wedding would symbolize the beginning of a new life, and a love that would always shine bright. Gabriella had worked hard to prepare for her special day and now it was on the horizon in clear view. She chose light green, and white as her wedding colors and was planning to sing *At Last* by Etta James to her husband as he walked towards her.

Together, Sam and Gabriella were planning a wedding that would leave the spectators in awe. They each went their separate ways that morning after satisfying themselves that they were ready to go ahead with their plans. The girls and baby Benjamin went to Henrietta's home to rehearse whilst Sam went to the race track to practice riding a white horse that he had leased from the race track. Sam had been practicing for the last month and he wanted to be sure he knew what he was doing when he rode the horse into the park and up to the pathway that led to the pavilion.

The night before the wedding found Gabriella inside her home with her friends. The bride-to-be was so nervous as she sat in front of a vanity while Janice polished her nails that she began to cry.

"What the hell wrong with you?" Janice asked as she cleaned Gabriella's nails with polish remover.

"What if Sam don't come tomorrow and leave me up there by myself?"

"What! Gabriella, if Sam don't show up tomorrow morning,

the sun ain't gone rise li'l sister. Sam loves you more than anything in the world. He'll be there, alright?"

"Alright." Gabriella said quietly.

Sam, meanwhile, was in a penthouse suite overlooking the downtown skyline on Canal Street with Alfred and Clyde. Gabriella had chosen Clyde to give her away the following morning; the old man was honored to escort the beautiful Gabriella down the aisle. The three men sat and drank a fifth of whiskey as they talked about life in general. Sam didn't want a bachelor party, he merely wanted a peaceful night with his two closest friends before the biggest day of his life.

The following morning, at around 5 A.M., eighteen year-old Gabriella was up getting dressed. She adorned her wedding dress, a beautiful white silk gown with specs of light green running throughout that flared out at the bottom. Her coal black hair was pressed against her face and curled beneath her chin. She wore white gloves that went up to her elbows and a light green tiara that had a diamond cut on it allowing it to sparkle in the morning sun. She wore little make-up as she was reminded by Henrietta that she was naturally beautiful and needed to do nothing more to enhance her beauty. Her grey eyes twinkled with joy as she stared at herself in the mirror. Her bride's maids, Janice, Charmaine, and Yvonne wore ¾ length, light green dresses and light green, full-length silk coats with white, five-inched heeled shoes. They each wore a white silk rose in their pressed hair. Henrietta, Gabriella's maid-of-honor, wore a light green, ¾ length dress with a white, full-length silk coat and white, five-inch heeled shoes. She had a white silk rose in her pressed brown hair.

While the ladies were putting the finishing touches on their outfits and make-up, Sam, Alfred and Clyde were getting dressed themselves. Sam was wearing a white tuxedo with a white silk shirt, light grey cummerbund and a pair of light green ostrich-skin shoes. Clyde and Alfred each wore light green tuxedos and white ostrich skin shoes to match the brides maids.

The three men exited the hotel and walked out onto Canal Street where they saw a horse and carriage waiting. Clyde climbed into the carriage and grabbed the reins on the seat and ordered the horses to begin trotting down the street as Sam and Alfred got into a white Rolls Royce and the chauffeur drove them to City Park.

As Gabriella and the girls scurried about the house, they heard a knock on the door. Henrietta opened the door to see Clyde standing on the porch.

"I'm here to escort the bride to the ceremony ma'am." Clyde said politely as he tipped his white top hat.

Henrietta smiled a wide smile as she admired Clyde's outfit.

"Gabriella, there's a handsome man at the door who would be honored to escort you to your husband." she said cheerily.

Gabriella grabbed her dress to raise it up off the floor and ran towards the living room. She hugged Clyde and the man then offered his arm. Gabriella wrapped her arms around his and the two walked towards the white and light-green carriage that awaited them at the end of the sidewalk. Clyde opened the door and Gabriella and her entourage slid into the carriage. It was 5:57 A.M. and the ride to City Park would take fifty minutes. Gabriella hoped that this day would go just the way she planned as she rode towards City Park.

Sam and Alfred had arrived at Delgado College in City Park at 6:10 A.M. The two young men exited the Rolls Royce and walked towards the horse trailer in the parking lot. Sam's trainer began to unlock the gates on the trailer and pull the white Arabian horse from its trailer.

"Here she is Sam. You've been riding her for over a month now, and she's ready to take you to your beautiful princess." the trainer remarked.

"Thanks, man. I hope I don't screw this up this morning."

"You gone be all right Sam. Go get that woman, man. The horse is here to serve you, brother," Alfred said in an attempt to encourage his friend, just before he hopped into the Rolls and was chauffeured to the Peristyle.

Sam waited in the parking lot until it was time to leave. Meanwhile, Gabriella was nearing the entrance to City Park in the horse drawn carriage. She and her party arrived at the pavilion at 6:47 A.M., and exited the carriage and stood before the pathway leading up to the pavilion. Gabriella wasn't really concerned whether any witnesses to her marriage would show, after all, she was marrying Sam, her true love. She was shocked and awed, however, by the masses of people that were showing up to witness the ceremony, which was quickly becoming an event that would have standing room only.

The sun began to peek over the horizon as Gabriella, escorted by Clyde, began to walk the pathway leading up to the stairs of the pavilion. As she did so, Janice, Charmaine, and Yvonne had taken their place underneath the canopy of the Peristyle with a live band and a choir. The choir wore lime green robes and white shoes, and the band players wore white tuxedos On Henrietta's cue, the band began to play and the choir began to sing *That's the Way of the World* by Earth Wind and Fire.

Gabriella slowly walked up the aisle as the singers sung and the band played on; people cheered, clapped and wiped tears from their eyes as the beautiful bride walked slowly towards the Peristyle. Gabriella began to cry as she stared at her friends in the pavilion, and the scores of people that were out at this early hour to witness the event. Most were patrons from Persia's, but their were many more people who'd attended high school with Gabriella and Sam on hand to watch the ceremony.

Janice was on lead this day, but she was joined frequently by Charmaine and Yvonne on lead and together, they created sweet harmony. Janice, Charmaine and Yvonne, was all smiles as they watched their friend make her way to the top and center of the Peristyle as they all sang in harmony, "*You will find...Peace of mind...Yea, if you look way down...In your heart and soul...Don't hesitate...'Cause the world seems cold...Stay young at heart...*"

Janice, Charmaine, Yvonne, and the choir sang as Gabriella approached the stairs leading up to the Peristyle and climbed them slowly. She then turned around to face the audience as the band played on and her girls sung loud and proud. Gabriella wondered where Sam was, as it was now 7:03A.M.

She hoped he would arrive on time as she sang her song.

After the group on the pavilion finished their song, the reverend walked and stood before Gabriella. He looked at his watch, then looked into Gabriella's eyes and said, "Not quite ready, yet."

Gabriella, and the reverend, along with everyone else, waited in silence for two minutes. Finally, as she looked down the long path leading to the pavilion, Gabriella noticed a white spot, far off in the distance, headed towards her with the sun now bright in the sky at her back. The reverend nodded to the band and the introduction to *At Last* began to play. Gabriella stretched out her left arm towards the pathway leading up to the stairs of the pavilion and the audience turned around to see Sam riding up the pathway on the white Arabian. The crowd cheered and clapped as Gabriella, in perfect tune with the violin, began to sing, *"At last...My love has come along...My lonely days are over...and life is like a song...."*

The horse trotted to the foot of the aisle leading to the pavilion and stood facing the sun. Sam stared at Gabriella from atop the horse as she continued to sing. He then dismounted his horse and walked slowly up the path towards his beautiful bride as the song approached its crescendo.

Alfred stood opposite Gabriella with Henrietta beside him and they watched with joyous eyes as Sam walked up the aisle like a knight in shining armor to claim his beloved princess. Gabriella concluded the song just as Sam took his place beside her and the two stared lovingly into one another's eyes as the reverend began to recite the vows of holy matrimony.

The reverend then asked for the ring, and Alfred reached into his pocket and pulled out a shining 1 ½ karat diamond ring and handed it to Sam to place on Gabriella's trembling hand. She was so nervous at that moment because her dream of being married to Sam was just seconds away.

When the ceremony was over, Gabriella, after throwing the bouquet, followed Sam down the aisle as rice was thrown on the top of their heads. Sam remounted the horse, and Gabriella climbed on behind him. She wrapped her arms around her husband's chest and Sam tapped the side of the horse and the two newlyweds rode off into the morning sun.

Sam and Gabriella's wedding day was an event for all to remember; it was talked about for months afterwards. The two eighteen year-olds had a classic ceremony and they celebrated with a reception at *Persia's* later that night and a honeymoon in Jamaica. They returned home in September of '75 eager to further the life that the two of them had created for themselves.

## CHAPTER 21

### HITTING BELOW THE BELT

I raised my head up from the table as Henrietta concluded her discussion with me and Yiska. My Aunt had shed a whole lot of light on the life of my grandparents, and the life my parents were living up until the time of my birth and a year or so afterwards. I was impressed by the intense love of family that my father had for my mother and I and also his friends, and I told Henrietta how I felt.

"Sam reminded me so much of your grandfather." she said to me. "That was one of the things I loved about him. We didn't see eye to eye many times when your father was younger, Ben, but I came to see that Sam was really a hard working, dedicated, faithful and loving man. Just like your grandfather. And Gabriella was the sweetest. Just the sweetest. She wouldn't hurt a soul." Henrietta said as she grabbed my hands and looked into my eyes and smiled.

I smiled back and touched Henrietta's face softly and she sunk her cheek into the palm of my hand and sighed pleasantly, a wide smile on her face as well.

Yiska patted me on the shoulder and smiled as he stood up from the table the table. "Miss Jenkins," he said as looked down on the two of us proudly, "it seems as if those two souls were meant to be together. It would have been an honor to know your family. I'm honored today, to have come to know of such a beautiful family. And I'm glad Benjamin is learning his family history, for without family, one is lost. You two still have each other and that is priceless. See you in the cafeteria, Ben." Yiska concluded as he walked slowly out of the waiting area.

People were beginning to leave now as visiting hours were coming to an end, but I wanted the day not to end.

"I need to know what else happened, Henrietta. I never heard these things about my parents. I want to know what all you know." I said eagerly.

"You will Ben, I promise. We've lost so much of our family history. So much of ourselves. Yiska's right—without family, one is lost." she said as her eyes began to well up. "Look at us. Here you are in jail with a life sentence and here I am—a fifty-seven year old woman with cancer. Neither of us never even had kids. Our family is coming to an end and it's all my fault. If I would have just been more patient with you, more caring, maybe you wouldn't be where you are. And maybe you would have kids to carry on for you. I did a horrible job raising you and I failed to protect Gabriella. For that I can never forgive myself."

"Don't say that Henrietta. If it wasn't for you my parents may have never met. I wouldn't be alive. And believe me, from the things you've related to me, my mother was an excellent woman. You did a wonderful job, and you can't give up hope concerning both of our situations. Maybe, maybe with God's grace and mercy we'll get back on track. I still have hope of getting out on appeal."

"I know, but look at the time we've lost! I'd give anything to relive the last ten years when we were all together as a family. I would do it all over again, just to relive those good times."

I realized that Henrietta was deeply affected by having to relive the events that would ultimately lead up to my parents' death. I told her she didn't have to talk about it anymore but she insisted on coming back the next day to pick up where she had left off. We talked a little while longer and had a laugh or two about Ms. Joyce and Taylor Senior.

I never knew my parents had ever made contact with Manny's parents before me and Manny met in 1989, yet we were literally feet from one another in1975. And I had never heard the story of how Ms. Joyce met Faye Sanders. I see clearly now that knowing your past can greatly impact your present situation and determine the decisions you make that will shape your future. If and when I get out I know exactly what I'm going to do—I'm going to live an upstanding, respectable life in dedication to my parents; it's what they wanted for me, I now know that.

My parents weren't criminals, drug addicts or neglectful. They truly loved one another and wanted the best for me out of life. I walked Henrietta to the front gate and hugged her tightly and she told me she would return bright and early the following morning. I then joined Yiska in the cafeteria and sat down to eat dinner. It was now after seven, a cold winter night in Colorado, but I knew the weather was nice in Phoenix, Arizona. I began wondering what Katrina was doing down in the desert at this particular time...

7:39 P.M. Phoenix, Arizona

Katrina walked down the long path in the airport's parking lot searching for her Bentley amongst the many cars on this warm January evening in Phoenix, Arizona. She found her car and placed her bags in the trunk and got behind the steering wheel to head home. As she backed out, she noticed a ticket on her windshield.

Katrina had had problems with airport security in the past, and today was no different. She would sometimes simply forget to place her parking permit in the windshield whenever she traveled, and for that reason, she would receive a parking ticket. She knew majority of the staff at the security office as they all ate at her restaurants and often used her catering services for luncheons. She drove up to the main gate and exited her vehicle and made her way to the security firm's main office. When she got there she saw a young man she knew, named Tre`.

Tre` was a good dude, hard-working and honest; a young man searching for love. Katrina thought he was cute. Tre` would constantly complain to Katrina about his love life and the two would talk from time to time about relationships. The conversation usually ended with Katrina remarking to the 5'10" one-hundred and seventy pound brown-skinned, braid-wearing twenty-three year-old that someday, the right woman would come along.

Tre` looked up from his desk and saw Katrina approaching him.

"Ohh nooo! Not again, Misses McMillan," he sighed.

"Yes, Tre`. I got my permit right here, and it's Miss Sanders not McMillan."

"Ohh! You got ridda homeboy?" Tre` asked as he took the permit from Katrina and began entering her data into his computer.

"No. Sorry." Katrina replied as she rested her elbows on the desk and smiled.

"Shit!" Tre` said jokingly as he processed and deleted Katrina's ticket from the computer records. "Look here, Miss Sanders, take this business card here, and if you ever have any more problems with your parking, give this number a call. Everybody here knows you don't have to sneak around the back to get in, so if this happens again, call us."

Katrina looked at the card and saw that it had the company's phone number on it along with Tre`'s name and cell phone number. Katrina looked back at Tre and smiled and told him he was trying to slip her his number on the sly.

Tre` smiled and said, "No, Miss Sanders, they give all of us those cards when we get hired. It's for people we consider our V.I.P.'s. And as of now, you are our V.I.P. You just call the next time you fly out and wait for the prompt, recite that pin number and all your charges are paid by the airport. As for as the other thing, if you know somebody, hit ya' boy up!" Tre` remarked as he cracked a smile and offered to buy Katrina a drink in the lounge as he was scheduled to go on break.

Katrina politely declined and took a rain check before she thanked Tre` and headed back to her car. She placed the card in her glove compartment and drove home. When she arrived at her mansion, she pulled into the C-shaped cobble stone driveway and exited her Bentley and walked up the marble stairs leading to the huge white stoned, four columned structure. She then noticed her husband's Escalade in the driveway beside her home to the left as she entered the key code. The door buzzed and popped open and Katrina sighed a sigh of relief, happy to be back in her own home as she had had a long day up in Boston.

As she made her way through the foyer, Katrina saw a letter from her son's nanny, Celeste, taped to her pecan wood and glass curio inside the foyer. She grabbed the letter and read it as she removed her sweater and boots. Celeste had notified Katrina of the fact that she had taken little Timothy to the pizza parlor.

*"She knows he has school tomorrow."* Katrina thought to herself as she walked into the kitchen and fixed herself a glass of champagne.

Katrina rested her back against the counter as she sipped her drink. She knew Timothy was in the house and if he was wearing his pager, it would have signified to him that someone entered the home. Katrina was waiting for Timothy to walk into the kitchen to greet her; but after several minutes, she gave up and walked into the living room and then entered the library to search for Timothy, whom she believed was unaware of her presence. Twice Katrina had caught Timothy by surprise when she returned from out of town. The first time he was on the phone talking to a female and trying to set up a date later in the night, telling her that he was going to tell Katrina that he was going to the club to chill with some of his teammates. The second time Timothy was in the shower. Katrina saw his blackberry on the bed and looked at the screen which had been left open. Katrina read the message in which Timothy was telling the person what a good time he had the week before. On both occasions, Katrina confronted Timothy and the two got into a physical altercation. Katrina was glad she didn't stumble upon another one of Timothy's adulterous scenarios. She told herself that she need not get into another argument with her husband. Katrina was sure Timothy didn't know she was in the home and she knew he was probably on the phone, or maybe online with one of his numerous mistresses. Katrina cared not to witness anymore of Timothy's careless philandering as it would only lead to more arguing and possible fisticuffs. Whatever Timothy was up to this night, if anything at all, Katrina decided to not let it bother her as she had had a good day and was making serious progress in her endeavor to free Ben.

She emerged from the library, topped off her glass of champagne in the kitchen and walked up the wide, marble spiral staircase and made a left turn and walked down the long hall past several bedrooms and the observation room and entered her office. She sat down at her desk and began opening mail that she had received the previous day. As she did so, Timothy entered her office.

"You can't let nobody know you made it in?" Timothy asked in a somewhat agitated tone as he walked over towards Katrina's huge cherry wood desk.

"I really didn't feel like walking all over this place to find you, Timothy." Katrina replied in a dejected manner as she rested her elbows atop her desk. Just the mere sight of Tim dampened Katrina's moods most times, and today was no different.

"Ohh, I see, I'm not important. Unlike your pet project you got going on!"

Timothy was a serious drain on Katrina's psyche. Just the mere sight of the man had taken all the happiness and energy Katrina had brought with her from her trip to Boston. She thought briefly about how depressed Timothy made her feel most times and closed her eyes briefly and let her nerves calm. She knew she should have been happy to see the man she married; but in all actuality, Katrina despised the figure that stood before her. She opened her eyes and picked up a letter opener and opened a piece of mail as she rocked back and forth in her chair and said, "I really don't feel like this tonight, Timothy. I'm tired and I have a lot of work to do. I gotta get Li'l Tim's stuff together for school and then go over this case to see if—"

"You know what Katrina? You spending more time trying to free Ben Holland than you ever do with me!"

"Well, if you were home more often, Tim, maybe I would spend time with you."

"Oh, so now it's my fault that I play in the NBA?" Timothy asked as he sat atop Katrina's desk.

"You never found condoms in any of my suitcases! And what I told you about sitting on top of my desk?"

"Forget your desk!" Timothy snapped as he stood up. "And as far as the condoms is concerned, maybe you used 'em all while you was visiting your charity case in Colorado!" he ended harshly as he knocked Katrina's mail off the desk.

"You only hope I was so you can justify your whoring ways!" Katrina responded, ignoring Timothy's gesture.

"Man, fuck this shit, I'm going to the club!" Timothy replied as he turned and headed for the door.

"Go ahead! You know you was going there anyway! You didn't have ta' pick a fight ta' leave this mutherfucka!" Katrina yelled as he got up and walked to the side of her desk and picked her mail up off the floor.

"What that nigga ever did for you Katrina? What he ever did besides manage to get you all shot up?" Timothy asked as he turned and faced Katrina.

"I told you what we been through when we first got together and you said you didn't care about that, but you always manage to bring it up." Katrina replied lowly as she back behind her desk and covered her face in shame.

Timothy knew how to get under Katrina's skin. Every time they argued, which was ninety percent of the time that he was home, Timothy would make it a point to bring up Katrina's past.

"Niggas like Ben Holland don't love nobody, Katrina! You need ta' wake up. If you wasn't rich, the nigga would have nothin' to do with you. Think about that while you spending thousands of dollars trying to free that loser!"

"Well that loser," Katrina said as she stood up behind her desk with tears in her eyes, "that loser helped support you and me. Remember when you were in college and couldn't even afford the lunch in the university cafeteria? Where you think the money came from Tim? How you think I opened those two restaurants? That loser you talking about did more for you and me than your entire family put together. We struggled in the beginning and now that we okay, you wanna act like you don't know what it's like to be without friends or family. Your parents are still alive. You never seen your best friends murdered one by one, all the people you love in the world gone. I'm all Ben has right now. And I be damn if I let you run me out of his life. That's my friend and I'll do what I can to see him come home again."

"If and when he get out, I give the poor bastard six months before he back in jail. Niggas like that don't change, Katrina. They can't change because it's in their nature. Waste your fuckin' money, but don't say I didn't warn you."

"You think you know people?" Katrina asked as she walked from behind her desk. "You been inside your whole life! You never even had a fight on the streets, but you talk all this shit like you the baddest mutherfucka around! You just a wanna-be!" Katrina said as she walked past Timothy and out of her office down the long hall leading to the stairs.

Timothy ran behind Katrina and grabbed her from behind. He turned her around to face him and he held Katrina over the balcony on the second floor of their mansion. Katrina looked at the long drop to the first floor and she was struck with fear.

"Timothy what ya' doing? You gone kill me!" she yelled with fear in her eyes.

"I should, bitch! I should kill your fuckin' ass right now! Make it look like an accident!" Timothy yelled as he shoved Katrina's body further over the railing.

Katrina's back was beginning to hurt from the pressure the six foot ten professional ball player was applying to her; she hadn't been this vulnerable since she was blasted in the stomach in '99. She was in fear for her life as she pleaded for

Tim to let her up. The twenty-five year old held Katrina in place while watching her scream at the top of her lungs in utter fear. Timothy then pulled Katrina away from the railing and flung her body up against the wall. She sank to her knees as her husband, who was much stronger than she, picked her up and held her around the neck with one hand and ripped off her business suit pants with the other.

"Put me down, mutherfucka!" Katrina said through clutched teeth and shortened breath.

"Fuck no! Bitches like you like it rough! All them so-called gangsters you was fuckin' in New Orleans—I bet they ain't do it like this huh, bitch?" Timothy said as he penetrated Katrina up against the wall.

Katrina grimaced as she struggled to free herself but Tim was just too strong. The young woman let her husband have his way with her body in order to end the experience. This situation was nothing new to Katrina. Timothy was an ill-mannered immature man-child that often felt he had to overpower her in order to keep her in line. The young man, sad to say, had an inferiority complex towards his wife, because he knew Katrina was a more worldlier person than he could ever hope to be; more over, he had come to despise the life Katrina had once lived and he came to view the woman who he once vowed to love, as an ignorant, malicious ghetto-bastard who somehow got lucky in life.

"Yea bitch! You just sit their and take this mutherfuckin' dick just like that! I like it when you do that shit there!" Timothy said as he humped away inside Katrina's sex. "Where them gangsters at now, bitch? They can't help your ass now!"

Katrina stared coldly at her husband's face, not making a sound as Timothy ejaculated into her vagina and let her drop to the floor; leaving her with tattered clothes and a bruised back.

"You happy now? Do feel like a man now, Tim?" Katrina asked lowly, pretending not to be affected by what had just transpired on the second floor of her mansion.

"I am the fuckin' man out here, bitch! I'm young, black, and rich! I can do whatever the fuck I wanna do understand? You ain't shit without me, Katrina! Look at you! You fat outta shape no good ghetto bitch! Scars all in your stomach looking like shredded wheat! The only thing good about you is the pussy, and I have ta' take that from your stankin' ass! If it wasn't for my son I would—"

Just then Celeste opened the door and in rushed Li'l Tim with a basketball in his arms.

"Daddy, where you at? I ate pizza today!"

Katrina got up and hurried herself to the bathroom in the master bedroom to get herself cleaned up before Celeste could figure out what had happened between her and Timothy. She sat on the toilet and cried; disheartened by her volatile relationship, wishing she was somewhere else. Katrina had just about given up on her marriage on this night. She had had enough. She sincerely longed for something better. As she sat on the toilet crying, Katrina thought of Ben as she regained her composure, trying without success to convince herself that the fight was her fault for insulting Timothy. Deep down inside, however, Katrina knew she was only lying to herself.

*"Hurry home Ben,"* she said to herself, *"I need you, baby."* she concluded with her thoughts before she entered the shower stall.

When Katrina finished showering, she saw that Timothy had already left the house and Li'l Timothy had just been put to bed by Celeste. The forty-nine year old Mexican woman from Juarez, Mexico, asked Katrina if she needed anything else before she turned in for the night.

"Yes," Katrina said softly, "could you please bring me a French vanilla latte downstairs to the gym in about ten minutes? I'm going say good night to my son."

Katrina walked to the opposite end of the hall and sat on her sleeping son's bed and kissed him good night. Li'l Tim stirred awake and turned and asked where was his father.

"He's going to take care of some business, baby." Katrina replied lowly.

"He was home all day and he didn't play ball with me like

he said he would, and now he's gone? He never plays with me, momma," the child said sadly.

"He'll be back in the morning to take you to school okay?" Katrina responded as her eyes welled up again.

"I want you to take me, mommy."

"Okay baby, but you have to go to sleep right away okay?" Katrina said as she tried to keep her composure.

Katrina knew if it wasn't for her son, she and Timothy would not be together. She knew all-too-well that the two of them were living a charade. Katrina and Tim would parade around town pretending to be the ideal couple in front of friends and associates, when in actuality, they were leading separate lives most times and they out-right abhorred one another behind closed doors. Katrina pulled the covers over her son and walked downstairs to the gym and met Celeste, who was holding her latte on a sterling silver tray. She thanked the elder lady and took a sip of the latte before hopping onto the treadmill and began running at a furious pace. Celeste had seen this routine before and her heart went out to her boss and friend.

"He's wrong you know?" Celeste said to Katrina as she stood beside the treadmill.

"Who's wrong?" Katrina asked as she ran furiously.

"Mister McMillan. You are the most beautiful female, Katrina. Don't let him degrade you."

Katrina stopped the treadmill and asked Celeste how she knew Timothy insulted her.

"At night, sometime I hear you two, and he is always wrong. If Ben is your friend, you do what your heart tells you. He has no right to insult your friends ma'am. Not to mention all the cheerleaders and strippers he fool around with." Celeste said as she looked away shyly from Katrina. "I notice you work out whenever you and your husband argue. I'm worried you're going to lose *too much* weight that way ma'am." Celeste said trying to ease the tension. "I hope I'm not out of line ma'am, but your son was so disappointed that his father didn't spend any time with him today. I had to try and cheer him up."

"You weren't out of line, Celeste. Thank you for doing what you id today. Li'l Tim is lucky to have a friend like you in his life. I'll see you in the morning ma'am." Katrina said before she took up running on her treadmill again.

The following morning, as Katrina lay asleep in her gym, having worked herself so hard that she was unable to climb the stairs, not to mention, her body still ached from the fight she had with Timothy, she felt something warm licking her hand. She jumped when she saw her chocolate Labrador retriever named Cocoa sitting beside her jumping from side to side and wagging her tail trying to get her attention as she lay on the carpeted floor. Her miniature Daschound, Atom tugged at her spandex as Li'l Tim laid beside her trying to shake her awake. Katrina looked over at her son and smiled and gave him a kiss on the cheek.

"Daddy didn't come home last night, mommy. I need you to take me to school."

"How many times do I have to tell you bratty boy, not to open the door by the pool to let the dogs in when an adult isn't around?"

"I know mommy, but they were barking and I just couldn't leave them outside alone."

"I guess you right, baby. Nobody likes to be alone." Katrina said as she stood up and cracked her back and guided her son down the long hallway leading to the kitchen.

Katrina smiled to herself as she watched her son run playfully down the long hallway with the two dogs gently tugging at his pajamas. She wished she had her camera at that moment so as to capture it in time.

Despite her troubled marriage, it was times like these that Katrina cherished in her home. She gave her son a life that others could only dream of giving to their children. It was hard for her to let go of the lifestyle she was living. When she got to the kitchen she saw that Celeste was up preparing breakfast, so she headed upstairs to get Timothy ready for school and began her day. As she did so, Katrina noticed it was 7:27A.M.

She immediately began to wonder what her friend Ben Holland was doing in Florence, Colorado.

## CHAPTER 22

### ONE DOWNED COMRAD

The sound of unhinging steel doors rang throughout the Colorado penitentiary as they slowly creaked open. I stepped out of my cell and looked to my left and saw Yiska step out of his cell, which was next to mine. I asked him how he slept as he walked towards me and he told me he had a dream about Henrietta. I chuckled and asked him what was the dream about, if he didn't mind sharing.

"Ah," the seventy-year old Indian smirked, "I dreamed I sat across from her eating scalloped potatoes and pot roast as we sipped sweet wine and listened to a classic rock song." he said as we began to walk towards the cafeteria.

"Yeah? What song was playing?" I asked.

"Fleetwood Mac's song, World Turning—my favorite—"

"I know," I said through a smile as I cut Yiska off, "you always talking about that song. It's a cool jam, but what you know about soul food, though, old timer?"

"You'd be surprised how much I know about the soul food. I used to run a restaurant inside the casino in Reno where I once worked, and my pot roast was *thee* meal, my son."

"Maybe you should ask Henrietta to bring you some of that good cookin' before she go back down south. You can pull some strings to make that happen right?"

"No. I mean I could, Ben—but I'd like the dream to stay just like it was. We were in the courtyard and a band was singing that song. I tell, ya' I would die a happy man if that were to ever happen. Enough of me and my preoccupations, Ben. Henrietta, Henrietta doesn't have time to fix a long laborious dinner for an old convict like myself. Someone whom she doesn't even know."

I soon picked up on the fact that Yis kept talking about Henrietta even as we sat and ate breakfast and then it dawned on me.

"You like my aunt, don't you?"

Yiska looked at me and smiled. "Henrietta is a very beautiful woman, Ben," he said happily, "but I'm in jail and Henrietta has far more important issues pressing her."

"She might could use a friend, though. I never seen my aunt with anybody."

"Maybe one day," Yiska replied, "but I think it would be rude to identify my feelings for Henrietta. She didn't come here looking for a friend—she came to tell her nephew the history of his parents. That is what is important here. Never mind me. Let's let Henrietta remain focused on the task at hand."

I realized Yiska was right. It was thoughtful of him to put his feelings aside to allow Henrietta to continue on without any distractions. Besides, Yiska might have upset her by making a pass at her. When the visitors began entering the prison at 8:30 A.M., Henrietta was among the first to enter the room. Yiska and I sat patiently as she approached our table smiling and sat down.

"How did you two young men sleep last night?" she asked in a perky mood.

I looked over to Yiska and saw him crack a smile and turn his head away.

"We slept fine Henrietta, yourself?" I responded with a chuckle as I thought about Yiska liking my aunt.

"Ohh, that hotel has the softest mattress and the most delightful buffet breakfast. I haven't had a breakfast that delightful in a long while." Henrietta replied as she reached into her purse and handed me a picture of my father and Alfred neatly dressed in bell bottomed suits and stack shoes.

I looked at the huge Afro on Alfred's head and chuckled at how chubby he was. I then took note of my father and became impressed over his physique. I admired his six foot muscular frame, his neatly trimmed mustache and tapered haircut along with his side burns and light-tan skin. My father looked sharp that day in his cream silk suit and gold bracelet and diamond wristwatch. I began to think that it was from him that I gained an intense liking for fine clothes and jewelery as he'd worn the best during his time, as did I.

Henrietta watched me stare at the picture for a moment and broke the silence.

"That picture was taken in September of 1976 in front of Persia's. Your father had just finished remodeling the kitchen in the club." she said to me. "The following week, Sam opened the kitchen and hired a cook and two waitresses. He and your mother were making good money by now; they even purchased a home in eastern New Orleans, a nice three bedroom brick house, but things weren't going so good for Harold."

"I remember that house. I had a few friends around there too, the short time I could remember. What happened to Harold?" I asked.

Henrietta sighed and began to elaborate on Harold as I closed my eyes and began to listen intently to her story as I imaged her words in my mind...


November 1976

"Yea, you tell that nigga Damon don't send no weed back in this project no mutherfuckin' more! Ya' here?" Taylor said as he punched Harold repeatedly in the face until he fell onto the ground on the corners of Benefit and Desire streets.

Two of Taylor's soldiers stood by watching as Taylor conducted business on Thanksgiving morning of '76. Joyce sat in the car parked across the street watching as she smoked a joint and rocked her son Manny as he lay on the front seat. The feud between Damon and Taylor was beginning to heat up as Damon was pushing more and more marijuana into the Desire project via Harold. On this cold November morning, Harold had severely overstepped his boundaries and entered Taylor's territory and Taylor reacted immediately. He knocked Harold unconscious and woke him up and made him strip off all his clothes. He then threw a bucket of sewer water on Harold and made him run down the side walk butt-naked and smelling like feces. People waiting at the bus stop laughed at Harold as he ran down the sidewalk and disappeared into an alley between two buildings. Taylor had also taken Harold's stash of weed and money and kept it for himself. Harold, meanwhile, had ran home and called Damon and told him what happened.

"Damn, that's cold-bloodied, Harold," the twenty-seven-year old gangster said as he held his hand over the receiver and laughed whole-heartedly, right along with four of his henchmen. "You alright man? I mean, you got some blankets and shit? It's cold out there brother! More importantly," Damon then said as he grew serious with Harold, "do you have my mutherfuckin' money and weed in your possession, nigga?"

"Man, he took everything." Harold quickly answered.

"Where your workers was when all this shit was going down?" Damon asked as he rubbed his beard.

"They ran!" Harold was actually lying on his soldiers to protect himself; they weren't even on the corner when Taylor approached Harold. Harold realized that Damon was getting pissed and he didn't want to face the gangster's wrath.

"They ran?" Damon asked in a shocked manner. "Now, I know Leroy and Teddy ain't no chumps. You wouldn't be lying to me would you, mutherfucka?"

"I'm tellin' you man, they saw Taylor driving up and they ran off. I think they went over by Sam aunt's house."

"What the fuck they doing over by Sam? He better not have nothin' to do with this shit! I told 'em a while back about Taylor and what I was gone do and he said he wasn't gonna get involved! I'm on my way down there and we gone have a talk with Sam and his aunt!"

Damon and his four soldiers went and picked up Harold and they all rode over to Henrietta's house. When they got there they saw Sam in the driveway loading a new stack of albums and a brand new microphone into his car. Sam saw Damon's car pull up in front of Henrietta's home and he knew something was about to go down. Gabriella was at the club checking in a delivery from the catering service, but Henrietta was home looking after baby Ben as it was the Thanksgiving holidays and school was closed for the week. Sam placed the albums and the microphone in the car and walked out the front gate and stood on the sidewalk as the six gangsters got out of Damon's Cadillac.

"Where Teddy and Leroy?" Harold asked as he walked up to Sam, doing his best to keep the rouse going.

Sam didn't answer Harold; he just began wailing on him and repeatedly telling Harold that he'd told him not to come in front of his family anymore. As Harold and Sam fought, two of Damon's soldiers jumped in just as Henrietta ran onto the porch screaming. A crowd was forming as the three men jumped on Sam. As the two soldiers punched Sam, Sam punched Harold until Harold broke out and ran. Damon pulled the two men off Sam just as Joyce pulled up in Taylor's Caprice loaded down with three of Taylor's soldiers.

Another car, a four door Delta 88 driven by Taylor, pulled up behind Joyce and that car held five more soldiers. Damon's soldiers began pulling out black steel revolvers and Sam pulled a revolver he had purchased the year before after Harold drew down on him. Damon jumped in between his soldiers and Sam, and told everybody with him to calm down once he realized he was out-numbered by Taylor.

"What the fuck you doing in my neighborhood, Damon?" Taylor asked as he stepped onto the sidewalk with all eight of his soldiers and Joyce following closely behind him and went and stood next to Sam.

"Sam hiding them two mutherfuckas that was with Harold this morning! And I want my money and weed back from you mutherfucka!" Damon stated angrily as he pointed at Taylor.

"Fuck that shit! That nigga Harold was on my turf by his self this mornin'! That was justified. Tell me you ain't never take shit from a nigga that was trespassin' on your grounds."

"I do the takin' Taylor! Nobody takes—*from me*! And if Teddy and Leroy don't come out that house, I'm gone fuck shit up this mornin' on Benefit and Metropolitan!" Damon stated in a furious manner as he wiped the spittle that dribbled from the corner of his mouth on the sleeve of his black leather trench coat.

"Nobody is in this house, young man!" Henrietta yelled from the front porch as she held baby Ben in her arms.

"Henrietta," Sam yelled back, "take my son inside and lock the door why we straighten this out."

"I'm not leaving Sam! These hoodlums not running me from off my own porch!"

"Just send Teddy and Leroy out and we won't have no problems!" Damon snapped loudly.

"Teddy and Leroy went ta' jail last night for auto theft! Or you ain't heard that from your main man Harold?" Taylor asked, changing the direction of the conversation.

Henrietta now stood in her yard a few feet from Sam, after placing baby Ben behind the screened-door to her house.

Damon began to look around and noticed that Harold was nowhere to be found. As Sam walked back into Henrietta's yard, Damon called out to him and everybody around.

"Stay right there Sam. Taylor don't make no sudden moves, we gone get to the bottom of this shit today."

Damon had his main man Tate run to the nearby corner store and make a phone call to the police station. When Tate returned, he informed Damon that Teddy and Leroy went to jail the night before for auto theft and were still in custody, just as Taylor had stated.

"Harold done made me look a fuckin' fool out here today." Damon whispered in a state of shock as he looked around at his soldiers.

"Harold just threw me in the cross," Sam said as he walked out the front gate. "He playin' both of y'all, and now he got me caught up some shit I'm not even involved with. That boy ain't for real and he causin' a lot of trouble on these streets." Sam remarked as he, Damon and Taylor stepped off to the side and began talking in low tones amongst themselves.

"You know, you right, Sam." Damon replied. "I got a thousand dollars for anybody that takes Harold out the game!"

"I'll do it!" Taylor stated. "This man own a club and he legit. He don't need ta' be involved in all this shit that's going down." he added, referring to Sam.

"You do that Taylor. You do that there and this li'l war that was about ta' kick off gone go away. I give you my word, brother. We gotta do it quick, though. Oh yea, your payment will be the stash and money you took from that mutherfucka, how much he had on him?" Damon asked.

"About sixty lids and two-hundred in cash. That's eight in total—but I want this nigga dead so bad, man, don't even worry about the other two hundred." Taylor replied lowly.

Damon and Taylor ended the war before it had ever started, all thanks to Harold. Sam walked off from the gangsters and they each went their separate ways. Henrietta watched the whole thing unfold and she was so thankful that Sam was still alive after witnessing so many gangsters welding so many guns in front of her door.

"Sam," she said as she hugged him tightly, 'I'm so glad you got out of that lifestyle. Harold is just foolish and he in way over his head. I'm glad you are a leader and not a follower." she ended as she and Sam went about their business.

Later that night, after finding a reliable baby sitter for baby Ben, Sam opened the club and it was thicker than ever. People were out celebrating Thanksgiving and they wanted to have a good time; and they all knew *Persia's* was the place to be. Gabriella and Sam delivered without fail. They had prepared a free turkey dinner for the first seventy-five patrons that wanted the dinner and had half-priced drinks the entire night. The dance floor was packed as music from the O'Jays, Marvin

Gaye, Earth, Wind and Fire and the like blared across the updated sound system that Sam had purchased during the summer. Alfred greeted people at the door and Henrietta, Gabriella, Charmaine, Janice and Yvonne, along with the wait staff, served the food to the patrons while Sam and Clyde worked the bar. Everybody was rocking and having a good time when Taylor and his eight henchmen, along with Joyce, walked into the club after paying admission.

People began to get uneasy as they eyed Taylor intently, hoping he wouldn't ruin the good time they were having. It was Taylor's first time inside *Persia's* and he was very impressed with the club. When Taylor and his clan sat down at a huge table and ordered a round of drinks, people began to go about their business until Damon stepped into the club and provided more uneasiness.

Damon and his four henchmen were dressed in silk suits and leather trench coats of assorted colors, some sporting fedoras, others sporting huge Afros. All of Damon's soldiers wore sleek gator shoes with sunshades covering their eyes. Damon paid the admission and walked into the huge room as people once again began to get weary. The gangster walked over to Taylor and everyone in the room stopped dancing. *Higher Ground* by Stevie Wonder blared across the speakers as Damon approached Taylor's table. The music played on as Taylor stood up and reached out and shook Damon's hand, officially ending the feud between the two gangsters. The crowd cheered, clapped and whistled as the two men and their respective crews sat down side by side and enjoyed a festive evening.

It was 11:30 P.M. when Gabriella, Charmaine, Janice, Yvonne, Alfred and Sam took to the stage and did a crowd-stirring performance of the Staple Singers' hit song *Let's Do It Again*. Henrietta had brought along the video camera that Gabriella had purchased and she had recorded the entire event. Gabriella and Sam then sung *Hope that We Can Be Together Soon*, originally sung by Sharon Paige and Harold Melvin and the Blue Notes. These two performances were a rare treat for the crowd because Alfred and Sam rarely took the stage, that was Gabriella and her girls' domain. The club parishioners jammed into the wee hours of the night before Sam and Gabriella closed the bar down at around 4 A.M.

The New Year came in and 1977 was business as usual for Sam and Gabriella, as well as for Taylor and Damon. Taylor had been searching for Harold for three months. He finally caught up with Harold at a bar in the Seventh Ward section of New Orleans. Harold thought he would be safe by hiding out in another part of the city, but that idea only worked for a limited amount of time because Harold was wanted deceased by two of the most powerful gangsters on the streets of New Orleans. It took a while, but Taylor finally tracked him down with the help of some friends he knew out of the Seventh Ward, having put the word out weeks earlier.

When Harold left the bar about two in morning and got into his white souped-up Chevy nova, he was unaware that he was being followed. He stopped at a red-light at the intersection of St. Bernard Avenue and Gentilly Boulevard and a two door Caprice classic pulled up alongside him on the passenger side. Harold was so drunk he didn't recognize the woman behind the wheel of the car as she waved at him through a sexy smile.

Harold smiled back and leaned over to roll down his window and asked the woman where she was going.

"I'm going home and get naked!" The woman replied.

"Can, baby, shay baby, can I's come?" Harold asked through slurred speech as he leaned across the front seat.

"Nahh man, you ain't gone be around to see that shit there!" The woman replied.

"What that supposed to mean?"

"It mean lights out mutherfucka!" a male voice suddenly said aloud.

Harold sat up and turned around and was greeted with a shotgun blast from Taylor that blew his head off completely. Taylor ran around to the passenger side of his Caprice and got into his car with Joyce and the two sped off from the scene. One of Taylor's soldiers, a husky nineteen year-old Afro wearing man named Kenneth, slid Harold's body onto the passenger side and drove the bloody car. He followed Taylor, Joyce, and another one of Taylor's soldiers to Damon's bar so Damon could get rid of the body; which was the agreed upon plan between the gangsters.

Damon, although he said the war between him and Taylor was over, still had it in for the young hustler. He wanted to take over the Desire project completely because there was just too much money for the greedy gangster to pass up. Damon hated the thought of the younger Taylor controlling the territory all by himself; and rather than compromise, Damon secretly reneged on the deal he and Taylor had cut in front of Henrietta's house and solidified inside of *Persia's*.

When he received the phone call from Taylor, letting him know he was on his way with Harold, Damon gathered his four henchmen and stood in the alley behind the bar he ran in the Third Ward and waited in silence. Damon was planning to kill Taylor and his henchmen once they brought Harold's body; and then he would dispose of all the corpses simultaneously and thus prevent a long drawn out war.

As Taylor and his crew pulled up behind the bar, Damon and his crew waited patiently with malice on their minds. The men all greeted one another as Joyce remained behind the steering wheel of the car she was driving. Damon looked into the passenger seat of the Chevy Nova and saw Harold's headless body and patted Taylor on the back.

"That's a good job. Damn good job. Y'all wanna come in for a drink?" Damon asked politely.

"Nah brother, I gotta get home to my son." Taylor answered.

"Alright then, we all squared away here young blood. Y'all be careful heading home. Hug that baby boy for me when ya' get in Taylor. Kenneth, be cool, brother." Damon stated, trying to loosen Taylor and his henchmen up a bit.

"You got it, brother." Taylor and Kenneth remarked simultaneously.

As Taylor and his crew turned to leave, Joyce, who was

watching everything, noticed Damon's henchmen going for their weapons. She screamed to Taylor, "Daddy, it's a hit! It's a hit!" as she jumped from behind the wheel of the car.

Taylor and his two henchmen grabbed their weapons and ducked behind the car that held Harold's body as Damon and his crew opened fire. The men were literally feet apart exchanging gunfire. Damon and his men hid behind the back wall of the bar and exchanged gunfire with Taylor and his men who were being pinned down behind the Nova.

Taylor called out towards Joyce as his main man Kenneth stood up and fired his weapon. Taylor tried to tell his friend to duck down but it was too late. He was struck in the forehead and fell dead in the middle of the alley.

Just then, Joyce stepped from behind the car and began firing a sub machine Uzi. Damon and his men had never heard, nor seen such fire power coming from one gun. They stopped firing their weapons and took cover behind the brick building.

Taylor's crew was the first crew of gangsters to introduce the streets of New Orleans to the overwhelming power of an automatic machine gun. Joyce continued firing the weapon as Damon and his men hid behind the building. When Joyce ran out of bullets, she began to load another clip, but she was having trouble releasing the empty clip because she was still learning how to use the powerful weapon. Damon, at that moment, saw an opportunity to gain the upper hand and he stepped out in the open to fire his revolver. When he did, he was again greeted with automatic gunfire, this time from Taylor and his remaining soldier as they had made it to the trunk of the car Joyce had driven and retrieved two more Uzis.

Joyce was able to remove the empty clip and she reloaded her Uzi and joined in and the three released an arsenal of awe striking fire power. Damon just couldn't handle the fire power Taylor and his crew were producing so he and his henchmen cut and ran. Taylor ran over and set the car that held Harold's body afire and the three survivors hopped in the car and sped away, leaving Kenneth's lifeless corpse on the ground in the alley.

That night, Damon had killed Taylor's main soldier and had sparked a huge war between the Uptown gangsters and the Downtown gangsters. By the end of May in the year 1977, Taylor had killed four of Damon's closest henchmen, the ones involved in the shootout the night he'd killed Harold. Twenty-eight year old Damon realized he didn't have enough man power, nor fire power to battle the younger, stronger Taylor, but he had other ways of beating Taylor's crew.

Damon was going to play the game raw by ratting. He tipped off the police, giving them the location to Taylor's home on the lakefront. A raid was launched and the authorities confiscated one-hundred pounds of marijuana from the attic in his home, thereby putting Taylor up on federal drug charges. Joyce took the fall as Taylor had escaped through a back bedroom window.

Taylor eventually called the police station and they made a promise that they were going to lock Joyce away for life and turn his son Manuel 'Manny' Lawson Taylor, Junior over the state if he didn't turn himself in. Taylor couldn't bear the thought of Joyce in jail and his son in a foster home, besides, he had money stashed away for his family. Taylor turned himself in the next morning and the police set Joyce and 'Manny' free.

Taylor received sixty years behind bars and Joyce had to move from her beautiful thirty-five hundred square foot home into the very project that she and Taylor once dominated. Damon finally took over the marijuana drug trade in the city, and, in spite of what he had done to Taylor, people enjoyed the period of peace that lasted into the eighties; but cocaine would soon hit the inner city and bring in a new era of violent crime.

Gabriella and Sam, meanwhile, had grown financially, relationship-wise and in popularity. By the early 1980's, Persia's was one of the most happening places in the city of New Orleans. Those four years, from 1977 to 1981 were some of the most satisfying times of Sam and Gabriella's lives. They enjoyed the life they were leading, and young Ben Holland flourished under his parents' loving care and guidance, but trouble was quickly approaching the horizon.

## CHAPTER 23

## TROUBLE ON THE HORIZON

Sam and Gabriella were inside *Persia's* sitting at the bar counter along with twenty-four year old Alfred reminiscing about their high school days on a warm spring afternoon in April of 1981. The year before, Sam had put a down payment on a new home for Henrietta, now thirty-three, in Ponchartrain Park, a middle-class subdivision a few miles from the Desire housing project. The Ninth Ward, especially in Henrietta's old neighborhood, as well as the Desire project, was becoming more of a violent part of the city and Sam felt that Henrietta was no longer safe in that part of the neighborhood so he moved her to a safer location.

"Sam, remember these pictures, baby?" Gabriella asked as she removed a couple of pictures from one of the family's photo albums and showed them to him.

Sam looked at the photo taken by Henrietta on the first day she had seen the two kissed and smiled. "I could never forget that day. The first time Henrietta ever saw us kiss. Remember that day with the sink and the water on the stove?" Sam then asked as he and Gabriella laughed lowly.

Sam then looked at the second photo, which was a photo of the two standing in Henrietta's class just after Gabriella told Sam she loved him.

"I haven"t seen these pictures in years, baby!" Sam exclaimed. "But you know what," he then asked.

"What?" Gabriella asked as she awaited Sam's reply.

"I feel the same today as I did back then, even deeper my love for you runs."

Gabriella melted into her husband's arms and kissed him passionately. Alfred began humming Here Comes the Bride which caused Gabriella to chuckle and tap his shoulder lightly before she sat back down and continued looking at the photos.

"Look at Alfred with that huge bush. Ohh, there's April. What happened to her, Al?" Gabriella then asked.

"She moved to New York the year after we first met. I never saw her again."

"Who you seeing now?" Gabriella inquired with a smirk on her face.

"You know me and Charmaine been dating for the last year." Alfred said as he smiled at Gabriella.

"I'm just making sure you still claiming my sister. That's all, man. She got you by two years, you know? So don't leave her when y'all get up in age," Gabriella said as she laughed and quickly handed Alfred the photo album just as Charmaine entered the bar.

"They're comin'!" Charmaine said in an excited tone.

"Time is going by real fast today! Sam come on before he sees us!" Gabriella stated through a wide smile.

"Hey, hey, don't forget to come out the dressing room either, y'all two lovebirds!" Alfred joked as he watched Sam and Gabriella walking briskly to the rear of the club.

A couple of minutes later, Henrietta walked through the front door of the club holding seven-year old Ben Holland's hand. Ben was dressed in a powder blue pant suit and white shoes. His full head of hair was neatly braided and hung just above his neck. The seven year-old looked around shyly at the huge empty room. He then looked towards the stage and saw his name on a banner with a large picture of him underneath.

He smiled and pointed at his picture.

"Who's that on that picture? Who's that?" Henrietta asked Ben, trying to get him excited.

"That's me, Auntie Etta! That's me!" Ben said happily as he jumped up and down, pointing to his picture.

Ben and Henrietta were walking towards the stage hand-in-hand when Sam and Gabriella, along with Ben's entire second grade class came out of the back singing *Happy Birthday*. Sam and Gabriella held a huge cake and sang along with the group as Henrietta guided Ben to the table directly in front of the stage.

Ben's eyes teemed with glee and astonishment as the crowd of forty or so people sang *Happy Birthday* to him. When the song ended, Ben blew out the candles and clapped right along with his parents, classmates and other adults who were in attendance. The lights were then turned on and a clown came onto the stage and performed for thirty minutes as Ben, his classmates, their parents and his family ate ice cream and cake. Young Ben Holland was having the time of his life and he grew even more excited when his mother sat down on the stage directly in front of his seat with a microphone in her hands.

Gabriella brushed her hair from her face and rocked to and fro as a band walked onto the stage and set up behind her. Her grey eyes lit up as she looked at her son lovingly. Henrietta sat on Ben's left with a new video camera to record the event. Alfred and Charmaine were on his right and Sam held him in his lap as the band began playing the instrumental to *Young Turk*, a song originally sung by Rod Stewart.

Gabriella did a soul-stirring rendition of the song along with Charmaine, Yvonne and Janice and dedicated it to her son and his classmates. As she sung the chorus, "*Young hearts be free tonight...Time is on your side...Don't let 'em push you around...Don't let 'em put you down...Don't ever let them change your, point of view...*" Gabriella held her son's hand tightly and pulled him onto the stage with her and her friends.

Ben's classmates ran and joined him and the kids danced with the women as they sung to them all. Gabriella loved her son dearly, and her rendition of the song reflected the love she had in her heart for Ben. The lady loved to sing to her only child; and she had moved the entire crowd with her version of the song as she dropped to her knees and hugged her son tightly.

"Happy Birthday, my handsome son! I love you!" Gabriella said through a wide smile and proud eyes as she hugged Ben tightly.

Four months later in August of 1981, a week before Gabriella's twenty-fourth birthday, Sam and Gabriella were in the front yard of their Eastern New Orleans home playing with Ben. Gabriella held a football in her arms as she ran around in a circle with Ben following close behind her. Sam was recording the entire event and he laughed aloud when Ben tackled his mother by the ankles. The two fell into the soft grass of their front yard and Ben took the ball from his mother's arms and spiked it into the grass next to her feet.

"Touch down! I'm the man around here!" Ben yelled as he jumped up and down.

Gabriella laughed loudly, enjoying the time she was spending with her son. She got up from the grass and took the camera from Sam and Sam began to wrestle with his son. As the two males wrestled in the yard, a furniture truck pulled up in front of their home.

"That is a huge truck right there. Look at that huge truck, Sam!" Gabriella said as she watched two husky black males in their late twenties exit the vehicle.

Sam began smiling to himself as Gabriella watched one of the men walk up the sidewalk. Gabriella looked confusedly at Sam as she handed him the camera and then turned back to the man approaching her front yard. The man held a clipboard in his hand as he approached Gabriella.

"Misses Sam Holland?" the man asked politely.

"Yes, that's me." Gabriella replied in a low tone, wondering why the truck had stopped in front of the family's home.

"We have a delivery for you, ma'am. A Steinway and Sons

baby grand piano with a Roland 808 keyboard..."

Gabriella placed her hand over her face and screamed in delight as the delivery man continued running off the items that she was to receive that day "... a stereo microphone, a Peavey amplifier..."

"Surprise, momma!" Ben yelled as he ran up and hugged his mother. "Just like you surprised me—me and daddy surprised you!"

Gabriella looked down at Ben and picked him up and twirled him around and thanked him; stating that it was indeed a surprise to her.

"You and your father are so special to me. I love you, Ben!" she professed as she sat Ben down and ran straight into Sam's arms, almost knocking the camera from her husband's hands. Gabriella kissed Sam passionately on the lips and fell into his lap. "God, I love this man!" she yelled aloud as the workers began unloading the musical instruments from the truck.

Sam guided the men into the house towards the spare bedroom he had cleared out specifically for Gabriella's musical instruments. The man had to sneak and remove the furniture from the room so he and his son could really surprise Gabriella. Sam had Ben help out by asking his mother to play football with him outside whilst he cleared the room. Gabriella figured out what her husband and son had done this day and she began to cry. Their thoughtfulness was so very special to her—far more special than the gifts she was receiving.

The delivery men sat up the equipment and left Gabriella, Sam, and Ben alone. Gabriella took to the instruments like a fish to water. She sang into the microphone as she played the piano and Sam recorded Gabriella as she sung *Easy*, originally recorded by *Lionel Richie*. Ben danced around in the studio as his mother sung to him. She ended the song and had Ben sit beside her on the piano bench and allowed him to press the keys on the piano. The family spent hours in the studio singing and dancing that afternoon.

*******

The same day Gabriella was enjoying her birthday gifts, Joyce was visiting Taylor in Angola State Penitentiary in Franklinton, Louisiana. Joyce looked like a disheartened and beat down woman as she walked into the visitor's room holding seven-year old Manny's hand, guiding the child towards his father.

Taylor stood up and Manny ran and jumped into his arms the moment he spotted his father upon entering the visiting room.

"Ohh, this my li'l man right here!" Taylor said as he gripped his son tightly.

"Daddy, I be cursing people out at home! They be tryna talk ta' momma but I be let 'nem niggas have it!" Manny said as he sat in chair beside his father.

"Yea, you keep doing that shit right there like that son! Lookout for ya' mother! How you been, baby?" Taylor asked Joyce compassionately.

The look in Joyce's eyes told Taylor that she was a troubled woman. He turned to his son and said, "Look here, Manny, I got ya' hamburger and fries! Go 'head and eat that and me and ya' momma gone talk some business."

"Okay, dad. When you comin' home?"

"That's what me and ya' mom gone talk about."

"Okay." Manny replied as he turned his attention to his burger and fries.

Taylor then looked at Joyce seriously as she grabbed his hands and looked into his eyes with sorrow.

"What's wrong, Joyce?"

"All the money we had saved," Joyce said as she looked away from Taylor and raised her hands to her face to hide her trembling lips.

"Baby, look at me and tell me what's going on."

Joyce looked back at Taylor and shook her head from side

to side. "Your appeal didn't go through. We have nothing left, baby. I don't know what I'm going to do from here. I have no money, no job, and, I, I can barely feed our child." she said through tears.

"Hey, that's not the Joyce I know. I know you ain't gone let this thing beat us, right? Forget about me, Joyce. I'll be all right up in here. You just do whatever you have to do to take care of my boy. You fought a good fight, baby, now it's time to move on and fight another battle."

"What about you? Without money, how can I get a lawyer to get you out?"

Taylor leaned forward and looked Joyce in the eyes. "Baby, I'm a be real about it—I'm gone be in this motherfuckin' joint for the rest of my days barring a miracle. But don't you stop living." Taylor said as he looked at his son who chomped down on his hamburger happily. "Forget about me. If I get out—I get out—but I need you to do right by my boy because you on the outside right now."

"I promise." Joyce said as she laid her head into Taylor's chest.

Joyce had never been so scared in her life. She held out hope for as long as she could that Taylor would return home soon, but that dream didn't come true. They both realized, on this day, that it would be years, decades, if ever they saw one another in the free world. They enjoyed the time spent together as a family, all-the-while knowing that Joyce would have to make decisions no longer with Taylor in mind, but with the survival of her son and herself being of the utmost importance.

Taylor was letting go of Joyce this day, and as bad as it hurt, he knew he couldn't keep her on a string. He knew his appeals were a long shot; so he was already prepared for the worst. As he and Joyce talked about her future, prisoners began whistling and laughing aloud at an inmate who was being paraded through the visitor's room dressed in a tight pair of cut off jeans and a halter top shirt. The five-foot ten bronze-skinned prisoner was wearing a wig and had tissue stuffed into his halter top to look like breasts.

The prisoner grew embarrassed upon hearing all the taunts and laughter and he abruptly turned and ran back towards the cells yelling, "my daddy can't see me like this!" The two prisoners following closely behind the transvestite turned him around and kicked him in the rear end.

"You gone show yo' fuckin' daddy what kind of bitch you is in this mutherfucka today!" one of the men yelled just before he slapped the prisoner in the face and shoved him towards the center of the room.

The prisoner screamed like a woman and tried to run out of the room as security guards wrestled the two prisoners with him to the ground.

"Old Man Tillman! Your son a bitch! That's my bitch. I fuck him in the ass every night! He a broad up in here! You bore a daughter Old Man Tillman! Manhattan ain't a gangster! I brought the bitch out that nigga the same night he got here! And when he get to the free world—he still gone be my bitch!" the prisoner yelled before he was dragged away into solitary confinement.

Manhattan's father walked away in shame as he yelled aloud that he was never coming to see his coward-of-a son again.

"Jesus Christ!" Joyce exclaimed as she held her hands over Manny's eyes. "What was that all about?" she asked Taylor.

"That dude name is Manhattan Tillman. He supposed to be this big bad pimp from New York. Come ta' find out, the nigga grew up in Kansas and was doing time for raping his step-daughter. She was only six. They don't take kindly to niggas like that up here. He done raped a few women in his day as well so I hear. He supposed to get out next year. His daddy came down to see 'em and those two cats right there decided to embarrass him in front of his daddy. They fuck Manhattan every night. Turned the nigga out. Got 'em wearing lipstick and panty hose and be trading his ass for cigarettes and marijuana, too. I can't feel sorry for 'em, though, any man that would harm a child or take advantage of a helpless woman deserves to be fucked over. Enough of that, let's go take some pictures before y'all leave this hell hole. How our daughter Faye doing these days?" Taylor asked Joyce as the two walked towards the photographer's area.

"That li'l girl is now sixteen with a new born baby." Joyce said matter-of-factly.

"Aww wow! Who the daddy?"

"This grown ass man from out of town named Eddie. Faye said she met him at a parade during Mardi Gras. He a hustler and all. Faye said when she told Eddie she was pregnant, he went to the store to get some ice cream to celebrate. She still waiting on that ice cream and celebration."

"Damn! Dude left her stuck out?"

"Not really. Word is, Eddie killed somebody on the way to the store that day and had to high tail it. He ran back up north somewhere after killing a dude outside the store. Faye on her own because Eddie on the run and is nowhere to be found. She don't even know her baby daddy's last name to track him down even if she did know where he at. She just, she just young and naive, Taylor. She has a cute baby girl, though. She named her Katrina, Katrina Sanders."

"I hope it work out for her and her baby. They got a lot of fucked up people out there in the world, and you right, baby, Faye is young and vulnerable." Taylor said just before he and his family sat to take a photo.

Joyce and Taylor spent the rest of the evening together, and before Joyce left, Taylor was able to bribe the security guards to allow him and Joyce to lock themselves in the bathroom for twenty minutes. The guards weren't going to watch Manny, so Joyce and Taylor had their son face the other way and cover his ears.

Manny smiled to himself; even though his ears were covered and he was facing the corner, he knew exactly what his parents were doing: they were having sex on the bathroom sink.

Taylor tried to get Joyce pregnant, but by the grace of God she didn't conceive. Joyce could barely afford to take care of

Manny and another child would have been nothing more than a major setback in the woman's life. Three months later, Taylor was moved to a federal penitentiary in Illinois. With the money low at home, Joyce had no way of visiting Taylor and the year closed out on a sad note for the woman.

Sam and Gabriella; however; had a glorious year. Gabriella had began writing songs and she and Sam had begun producing music to go with her lyrics. Gabriella had *Persia's* on fire when she began singing her own songs, and her friends, when they performed with her, had every last patron out of their seat and on the dance floor.

Although only a few miles apart, Joyce and Taylor, and Gabriella and Sam's worlds were so far apart that neither would ever come into contact with one another again. The two families hadn't spoken to one another since the night Taylor met Damon inside of *Persia's*.

After so much time, the two groups merely forgot about one another and life went on down in New Orleans, Louisiana—happy for most, sad for some, but optimistic for all. Unbeknownst to the Ninth Ward, where *Persia's* lay, however, trouble was on the horizon.

## CHAPTER 24

### AN UNKNOWN OCCURRENCE

Manhattan Tillman stepped off a greyhound bus in downtown New Orleans on April 27, 1982, having just been released from Angola State Penitentiary a day earlier. After spending six years of his life behind bars, he was happy to be a free man. A stranger to New Orleans, the now 27-year old, 5' 10" thin framed bronze-skinned man walked briskly through the bus station as people eyed him strangely. The reason being was because Manhattan Tillman was wearing a tight-fitting pair of red denim jeans and a white halter top with a pair of white pumps. It was clear to everyone that laid eyes on him that this was a man wearing a wig and lipstick and dressed in women's apparel.

Manhattan shamefully walked through the crowded bus station pass the people who mocked him openly and hurried to a taxi cab. The heavy set white cabbie turned around and did a double-take towards Manhattan when he jumped into the backseat.

"Where to?" the cabbie asked as he flicked his cigarette out the window and shook his head from side to side.

"Anywhere. I'm new in the city so wherever we go is fine with me."

"Well, I have a fare to pick up in the Ninth Ward. You ever

heard of that place?"

"Yes. I *have* heard of the Ninth Ward! My hus—this man I knew in prison was from there. Take me there, please, I'd like to see it with my own eyes. But before we go, I would like to get some new clothes." Manhattan remarked in a feminine voice, still unable to remove himself from the role he played in prison.

The cabbie drove Manhattan to a K-mart in the Ninth Ward and waited outside in the parking lot. Manhattan went in and purchased a black pair of men's jeans, a black and white striped knit shirt and a pair of plain white tennis shoes. When he came out of the store, he looked as normal as any other man who walked the streets.

"Care to share what happened?" the cabbie asked as he pulled out of the parking lot.

"Long story, white man," Manhattan replied, his voice now that of a masculine man. "Prison. Just came home from prison. I took my lumps and now it's over. I could never go back home to my father without something to prove to him that I'm still a man, though. He saw me dressed like that once while I was in prison and he never even came back to see me. Stopped answering my calls and cut off my commissary. I'm all alone in this world now."

"You from Louisiana?"

"No. I grew up in Kansas. I plan on returning home to my father someday. Hopefully, I can make him proud."

"Yeah," the cabbie replied, "seeing you looking like that behind bars may have disappointed him; but he'll come around. You should—"

"What the fuck you mean by 'looking like that', white man?" Manhattan spat aloud as he grabbed the cabbie around the neck from the backseat.

"Hey! Hey! Take it easy, man! I'm just making conversation!" the cabbie remarked in a panicked state as he held on to the steering wheel.

"Forget about the conversation! I don't wanna talk about

that shit no more! You know what it's like having some stranger rape your ass every night? Do you?" Manhattan asked as he held a tight grip on the cabbie's neck.

The cab began to swerve left and right as it headed down the busy two-lane street. People were blowing their horns and swerving to avoid the runaway cab.

The cabbie stopped the car in the Ninth Ward on the corners of Louisa Street and Higgins Boulevard and slammed the car into park. He then wrestled with Manhattan and broke free from his grip, got out of his taxi and opened the back door and grabbed Manhattan from the back seat. He shuffled Manhattan onto the sidewalk and threw him onto the concrete and then went into Manhattan's pockets and took all his money before he kicked him in the ass.

"You wanna act brave out here on these streets? You ain't nothin' but a jailhouse bitch! I know your kind, mister! You think you got something to prove to people for what happened behind bars! But you gone find what you looking for right here in this Ninth Ward if you ever try and do somethin' stupid! I felt sorry for your ass at first—but you probably got exactly what you deserved up there in the big house you lowlife mutherfucka!" the cabbie concluded as he walked back to his taxi, hopped in and sped off.

Manhattan picked himself up off the ground and began to wander around the Ninth Ward. It wasn't the first time he'd had his ass kicked; and when he was in prison, his ass had received much more harsher treatment. Quickly putting the beating behind him, something he'd learned to do the first night of his stay inside of Angola, Manhattan made his way into the Desire Project. While walking through the vast complex, he eyed many of the people who were out this sunny warm day, searching for someone vulnerable to set him right.

Manhattan needed money. The cabbie had taken every dollar he owned, nearly one-hundred dollars, and he was now penniless on the streets. The newly-released convict also wanted sex; and the only way he knew how to get those things, sad to say, was to take them by force. He walked around the Desire Project, blending in with the residents, yet remaining out of sight. When he entered a huge courtyard that contained a large swimming pool by the name of Betty Jean, Manhattan caught sight of a young teen sitting on her porch playing with her baby daughter amongst many other adults and kids that were out this day. He leaned up against the wall at the edge of the building and watched the young female intently as she got up and ran up and down the sidewalk, happily chasing her daughter. The young female had picked up her baby twice and carried her inside, and each time she returned, she was alone. Manhattan surmised that the young teen and her daughter were the only two people residing inside the project apartment that she and the little girl had entered and reemerged from on those two occasions. After spying upon the young female for a while, he'd made up in his mind that she would be able to supply him with the things he felt he needed and wanted.

Having formulated his plan, Manhattan went and hid in an abandoned apartment in the courtyard opposite from the teen. He entered the trash-littered, foul-smelling apartment and crouched beneath the living room window and spied upon the teen, watching as she entertained her little girl on the sidewalk across the courtyard. Manhattan rubbed his crotch as he eyed the youngster, admiring her round rear end and full-sized breasts. He could hardly contain himself as he looked at her smooth caramel skin and shiny jehri-curled hair. When she bent over to pick up her daughter, he caught a perfect view of the teen's ass. He could see the black on her butt cheeks, and it was all he could do to keep from unzipping his pants and stroking his erection until he ejaculated all over himself in a matter of seconds. He now had to have her for real. Satiated for the time being, Manhattan turned around and leaned against the wall and fell asleep on the gritty floor of the abandoned house amidst the cheerful screams and laughter emanating from the mouths of multitudes of kids that were playing in the huge grass-covered court yard.

Later that night, around 8 P.M., seventeen year-old Faye Sanders was gathering the things she needed to give her daughter a bath. Faye had just finished frying pork chops for herself and had fixed a pot of mashed potatoes and gravy for her one year-old daughter, Katrina Sanders. The naked one-year old ran up and down the hallway full of glee as her mother playfully chased her while singing *It's A small World*.

Faye's grandmother had passed away the year before, so she had merely started paying the rent after having the project apartment signed over to her. The young teen was going to school during the day, and supporting her daughter by working part time as a cashier at *Schwegmann's Giant Supermarket* in the evening. Life was hard, but Faye enjoyed everything she was doing, because everything she did, she did for her daughter. The two were in a world of their own, enjoying their life together, and having so much to look forward to in the future; but all the glorious things that lie ahead for mother and daughter would change with one simple knock.

Faye was bathing her daughter when she heard a soft tap at her back door. She shook the foam from her hands and got up and walked through the kitchen and unlocked her back door. She left the chain on and she cracked the door slightly to see who was knocking. The door wasn't ajar two inches when all of a sudden, it came crashing open. Someone had broken the chain and knocked Faye back into the kitchen sink. The young teen was frozen with fear as a slim bronze-skinned male figure entered her apartment and rushed her quickly and covered her mouth. Faye's eyes were as wide as saucers, and tears began to flow down her cheeks. She shook with fear as the stranger rushed her from the kitchen into the living room and forced her down onto the cold floor tiles. Faye worried about her daughter, at that moment, who was in the tub alone waiting her return. Faye was hoping Katrina would remain quiet and out of sight so as not to be seen by this beast of a man.

The stranger began to pry the tight fitting shorts from Faye's body and she protested by clinching her legs shut. The man threatened to kill her baby if she didn't cooperate. Faye then realized that she had been being watched by this stranger because he knew she had a child. The man held one hand over Faye's mouth and pounded his fist into her chest, causing her great pain and leaving the teen feeling as if she was going to die. She cried silently, praying that this monster wouldn't hurt her daughter.

Katrina remained seated in the tub playing with her rubber ducks and fluffy sponge, oblivious to the horrible events that were unfolding in her mother's living room. The man pulled out a knife and cut the shorts off Faye's body and ripped her panties off and proceeded to unbuckle his jeans.

"I'm gonna move my hand from your mouth. You scream, and I'll cut your tongue out before I slit your throat—and then I'll kill your baby girl! Now, you gone be quiet and take what I got ta' give ya'?" he asked as sweat beads trickled down the sides of his temples.

Faye nodded her head to say yes and the man slowly removed his hand, allowing Faye to let out a low yelp and beg him not to kill her.

"Say you want me to fuck you!"

Faye shook her head to say no, and Manhattan then put the knife inside her mouth and ordered her again. "Say it, bitch!" he commanded.

Faye muffled his request and Manhattan took the knife and placed it under her chin.

"Say it again." he commanded again as he sat on top of Faye's half naked body and unzipped his jeans.

Faye fulfilled his request a second time and Manhattan proceeded to mount the seventeen-year-old. She grimaced from his penetration but she soon was able to tolerate the pain. The man humped away on top of Faye as he held his hand over her mouth. She cried to herself, hoping that by giving herself to this man, she could save her life as well as that of daughter's. When Manhattan had completed himself inside of Faye, he rolled over onto her right side and attempted to kiss her, but Faye turned her head away from him.

"That's okay, bitch. I gave you what you wanted. Now I gotta get paid for my services."

"I didn't want nothin' from you. Just leave me alone." Faye cried as she rolled over onto her side into the fetal position, her back facing the stranger.

"You wanted it! You said you wanted it when I asked you!"

Faye cried incessantly at that moment, realizing that the man in her living room was a stark-raving lunatic. If she wanted to survive, Faye knew she had to play his game.

"I got money on my bedroom dresser. I can get it for you." she said in a cooperative tone.

"Yeah, we gone walk back there together and get my money." Manhattan replied as he removed his pants.

As the two walked down the hallway to Faye's bedroom, both of them naked from the waist down, Faye looked at her daughter. The one-year old was in a world of her own as she splashed the tub's water. Faye feared for her daughter's safety so she quickly walked past the child as she continued to splash the water and bubbles around as she sat inside the tub. Manhattan followed Faye into the bedroom where he grabbed the cash and food stamps off the dresser. He then asked the female if she wanted him to make love to her. The look on this man's face told Faye that she had better not say no. The man was now well into her home and had her backed up into a corner in her own bedroom. The lights were off inside the bedroom, but the light from the bathroom where Katrina was located had allowed Faye to see the coldness in this monster's eyes. Faye pictured herself being stabbed repeatedly just a few feet from her daughter and shook with fear. She took a chance and gave herself again, this time willingly to the beast that was invading her home. The frightened teen got on all fours and leaned forward, willfully inviting her attacker to violate her once more as she cried silently, all the while not knowing if she would survive this terrifying episode.

When Manhattan was done violating Faye anally, he began planting soft kisses on her neck and earlobes as he lay on top of her with his chest pressed firmly against her back. Faye trembled with fear and remained still as her attacker got up and walked out of the room without saying a word. Faye laid flat on her stomach crying to herself as the man whistled while putting his pants back on in the living room.

When she heard her back door close, Faye jumped up and ran into the kitchen and locked the door and shoved a chair underneath the door knob. She then hurried back Katrina and grabbed her from out of the tub and ran into Katrina's bedroom and curled up on the mattress in the fetal position as she held her daughter close to her heart and cried heavily.

Faye never told anyone about what happened that night; and since he'd gotten away with it once, the raping of Faye Sanders had set the wheels in motion for Manhattan Tillman to begin causing great turmoil in people's lives.

Faye, meanwhile, had become afraid to leave her home for extended periods of time. Eventually, she dropped out of high school and quit her job. To numb the pain, Faye began popping pills and drinking heavily. She later began holding drugs for various drug dealers to pay the rent. Her drug habit became worse in the months that followed, and it caused her to start neglecting and abusing her daughter and forfeiting her obligations; so much so, that she was put out of the apartment four months later.

Faye and her daughter then began to spend nights in the various drug houses inside the Desire projects. The room and board was paid for through sex on Faye's part. The once happy and attentive mother became a full-blown addict within a year's time and she began to regularly sell her body for drugs in order earn money and get by. During this period of time time, little Katrina Sanders endured hardships comparable to children that were living in a third world country.

Manhattan had wrecked what was once a promising life, future, and relationship for Faye and her daughter, Katrina. She became a broken spirit, all-too-ready to give up on life. Manhattan's reign of terror would not stop with Faye, either; and unbeknownst to the Ninth Ward at the time, there was now a sadistic serial rapist on the loose in late April of 1982. The man who was misused and lived his life as a woman in prison, came to the Ninth Ward that year with something to prove to himself—and that only set the table for heartache and pain for all those with whom he came into contact.

## CHAPTER 25

### SHE TOUCHED HIM

It was November of 1982 and *Persia's* was holding its yearly Thanksgiving bash this night. Patrons came from all over the city to participate in the annual event. The free turkey dinners were going fast and the drinks flowed freely. Deniece Williams' song, *It's Gonna Take A Miracle,* was blaring across the stereo as Manhattan walked slowly through the club holding his free turkey dinner and headed towards a table. Many couples were out on this night and a host of single men and women as well. Most of the men were dressed in silk leisure suits wearing fedoras and pointed-toed shoes, and the women were neatly dressed in knee-length dresses and the latest high-heeled boots and accessories and also sporting various hairstyles from Afros to braids. The men in the club that weren't dancing eyed the women carefully, trying to scope out the woman they each felt they would have the best chance to dance with before they made their move. The women were friendly and outgoing. They were sitting in groups at some of the tables vibing to the music and kindly offering their hand to take a spot on the dance floor with their respective dance partner.

Charmaine and Janice, meanwhile, were in the office getting dressed in preparation for tonight's performance when Janice produced a small packet of cocaine.

"You wanna do a line with me, Charmaine?"

"I told you I don't mess with drugs no more. And do you have to do that here in the club?"

Before Charmaine could get the words out of her mouth, Janice had snorted the cocaine into her system.

"Aww girl, stop being a party pooper. A li'l blow ain't never hurt nobody." Janice quipped as she wiped her nostrils free of the white powder.

"You better be careful with that stuff. I hear stories about people gettin' hooked on that powder. You got too much going for yourself to be caught up with drugs, Janice."

"I'm in control, sista. Drugs didn't beat you. We from the same blood and don't you forget it. I'm in control of things."

"I hope you right. I really hope you know what you doing, Janice." Charmaine concluded as the two cousins walked out of the office onto the club's dance floor.

A few minutes later, Manhattan having finished his dinner, got up from the table and walked over to the bar to purchase a drink. Upon his arrival, he saw Gabriella serving liquor behind the counter with Sam and Clyde and was immediately struck by Gabriella's beauty. The brown skirt she wore revealed her light-skinned, shapely calves. Her coal-black hair hung freely to her shoulders, and her grey eyes lit up the entire bar as she conversed and laughed with various customers while serving drinks.

"What can I get for you, mister?" Gabriella asked with a wide smile as she stood directly in front of Manhattan.

Manhattan was at a loss for words for a split-second, but he quickly regained his composure. "Let me have a seven and seven, young lady." he said calmly as he cleared his throat.

Gabriella mixed the man's drink and chatted briefly with him while doing so. "I never seen you in here before, man. You new to the neighborhood?" she asked through a bright smile as she slid ice into Manhattan's glass.

"Yeah, I just came down from New York a few months ago.

I decided I'd come out and enjoy the company of some beautiful women. I see that by coming to *this* night club I definitely made the right decision."

Gabriella blushed slightly as she slid Manhattan his drink and said, "If beautiful women are what you're looking for then Persia's is the place. Welcome."

Manhattan had gotten himself cleaned up during the six months or so that he was out on the streets. He had also taken a job as a cashier at a record store in downtown New Orleans. He was a good looking man who could easily charm a woman when he desired to do so. Manhattan, however, was a sadistic human being. He used his charm and good looks to lure women into *his* world—and there was nothing charming about the world in which Manhattan lived because this seemingly charming and caring individual had a propensity towards violence when it came to the opposite sex. He would brutally beat and rape the women who'd come to trust him before letting them go. The women were usually young and naive, like Faye, so many of his victims never mentioned, nor reported their attacks because they were either too ashamed, felt totally humiliated by the man, or a combination of both.

Faye was Manhattan's first victim. Since then, he'd beaten and raped five other women throughout the city. His desire to conquer the opposite sex stemmed from the abuse he himself received while in prison. The constant raping of Manhattan while behind bars had fueled his hatred of the opposite sex tremendously. He'd convinced himself that if it weren't for women, he would not have been treated like one in jail. Manhattan blamed all women, especially the beautiful ones, for his plight in life. He never realized that it was his own behavior, the raping of his young stepdaughter and other innocent young women, is what caused him to suffer so harshly behind bars. Now he was back on the streets doing the same thing that had put him behind bars once before; and he now had his eyes set on a new victim this time around. He told himself repeatedly that he was in love with the young woman who had just served him a drink and he was intent on being with her in his own special kind of way.

"Can you dance with me tonight, miss?" he asked Gabriella in a friendly voice when she walked passed him for a second time.

"Oh no," Gabriella quickly answered through a friendly smile. "I'm already taken. Besides, I wouldn't feel comfortable. Thanks for asking, though."

"Aww, come on, one friendly dance. I'm new in town and I don't have any friends yet. I just wanna dance that's all. No strings attached."

Gabriella had a tinge of uneasiness pass through her briefly. Manhattan was somewhat pushy in her eyes. She brushed her hair from her face and said, "Strings or no strings," as she pointed towards Sam, who was ringing up sales at the register, "my husband over there wouldn't—"

That's your husband right there?" Manhattan asked, cutting Gabriella's reply short as he hollered aloud and got Sam's attention.

Sam walked over to Gabriella and Manhattan and Manhattan introduced himself. Sam shook the man's and introduced himself and his wife and welcomed Manhattan to his club.

"Oh, you and your wife own this place?" Manhattan asked in surprise.

"You can say that," Sam replied as he hugged Gabriella. "Me and my wife been apart of this establishment since we were sixteen. Right baby?"

"Umm, hmm. Manhattan, is from New York, baby, and he's in town by himself. He asked me to dance with him, but I told him I was taken." Gabriella said as she laughed lowly.

Manhattan took offense at Gabriella. He felt the woman was mocking him. He didn't reveal his mounting angst, however; he merely smiled and said, "She's right. I was just asking the lady of the establishment if she'd do me the honor of having a quick dance with me tonight. With your approval of course."

"Nobody ever asked me that before," Sam said as he looked over to Gabriella whilst rubbing his chin. "But like my wife said, she's already taken—and she had no desire to dance with another man. There's plenty of women in here, brother, I guarantee you'll find that special one to dance with you."

"I know, but the best one's already taken. You're a lucky man, Sam. And Gabriella, it was a pleasure to meet you." Manhattan said as he extended his hand towards Gabriella.

"Thank you, Manhattan." Gabriella said as she shook Manhattan's hand lightly and smiled a beautiful smile before she and Sam walked away.

That one meaningless touch, coupled with that one innocent smile, instantly made Manhattan believe that Gabriella wanted him and he could now barely control himself. He wanted so desperately to reach across the counter and press his lips to Gabriella's smooth full lips, but he knew a move like that would only land him in a fight with Gabriella's husband, Sam. He knew he had to be more cunning in his endeavors to be with the woman.

While Manhattan was lusting after Gabriella, Janice came up to the bar snapping her fingers and bobbing to the music.

Janice still sported an Afro in 1982. Her fresh hairdo and low cut silk blouse, revealing some cleavage, quickly caught Manhattan's attention.

"Gabriella," Janice yelled over the music, "give me a vodka and orange juice and put it on my tab, sista! It's sad a woman has to buy her own drinks in this club with all these fine ass brothers in here tonight! We gone tear the club *down* tonight when we get up there, girlfriend!"

"You right about that, Janice," Gabriella said as she grabbed a fifth of Vodka from the bar counter, "we gone rock the boat...don't rock the boat baby..."

Gabriella and Janice began singing *Rock the Boat*, a song they were planning on singing tonight. Manhattan stared at the two women with a blank look on his face, his mind working overtime to conjure up a plan to be around Gabriella at all costs.

His thoughts were interrupted when Janice abruptly stop

singing and said, "You would think these brothers would recognize how much we put into our music when we perform. A drink is the least they could do for the entertainment we provide every week."

Manhattan now realized that Janice and Gabriella were good friends. After being shunned by Gabriella, he decided to move on to the next best thing with the hopes of gaining access to Gabriella. He pulled his wallet from the inside coat pocket of his royal blue silk leisure suit and slammed a couple of dollars onto the counter, bluntly saying that he wanted to pay for Janice's drink as he stared at Gabriella with a sly, sort of wicked grin.

Gabriella jumped back a little. She was startled by the force with which Manhattan slammed the money onto the bar counter; but only she seemed to notice that the slam was more out of disgust than a friendly gesture. Gabriella then had a strange feeling come over her, one that told her that Manhattan was not the person he was pretending to be.

"Thanks, man!" Janice exclaimed once she heard Manhattan's remark. "Come on honey," she then said as she grabbed his hand, pried him up from his bar and whisked him out onto the dance floor.

Gabriella watched the two dance for a minute until she was tapped on the rear end. She jumped, but was happy and relieved to see her husband standing behind her.

"Look like Manhattan got his dance, and Janice found herself a new friend in the process, huh, baby?" Sam asked as he stared at Janice and Manhattan.

"Yes. Janice needs a man in her life, but that one there?" Gabriella questioned.

"What about 'em?" Sam asked as he hugged his wife from behind and the two rocked in unison.

"I don't know Sam. It just seems as if he's a little too pushy to me." Gabriella replied as she rubbed her husband's arms and kissed his hands.

"He just came to have a good time that's all. The man new

in town looking for a woman. He just happened to push up on the prettiest woman in the world that happens to belong to the handsomest cat in New Orleans, though!" Sam quipped as he rubbed his sideburns and ran his fingers across his mustache.

Gabriella turned and smiled at Sam and the two laughed as they hugged and kissed one another behind the bar before they returned to their previous duties of serving customers their drinks.

Manhattan had watched the whole episode unfold as he slow-danced with Janice to the Isley Brothers' song, *For the Love of You.* He wished so badly that it was he instead of Sam who was hugging and kissing the beautiful young lady behind the bar. He couldn't take his eyes off Gabriella even if he wanted to do so. After watching Gabriella talk and brush up against Sam during the entire song as they worked the bar, Manhattan grew jealous and abruptly turned around and walked off, leaving Janice, who was really getting into him, alone on the dance floor.

"Hey! Hey man, where you going?" Janice yelled aloud to Manhattan, who never replied as he headed for the door. "Ain't this a bitch?" Janice said with her hands on her hips as she stood on the dance floor alone, watching Manhattan depart the premises. She then threw her arms into the air and walked back to the bar to get another drink. "I can't get no lovin'! A free drink and a half a dance is all I'm worth around here?" she asked herself as she took a seat at the bar and eyed Manhattan as he walked past Alfred and out of the club. "Shit! He was cute too! Ole crazy ass nigga!" she mumbled. "Gabriella, can I have my vodka and orange juice now, please, ma'am?" she then yelled aloud as she snapped her fingers and popped her neck.

## CHAPTER 26

### JANICE'S ADDICTION

Janice exited from the Mason Blanche department store on Canal Street in a hurry on a warm morning in March of '83. The twenty-six year old walked briskly towards an alley behind the store and met up with her cousin, Charmaine. She opened the passenger door and hopped into Charmaine' car and began looking around nervously.

"They not onto me, girl. Come on let's go." Janice said through her sniffles.

Charmaine had a worried look on face because she knew Janice was inside the store shoplifting. She watched from the driver's seat of her pristine 1980 two-door pink Cadillac coup Deville as Janice opened her over-sized purse and removed two men's silk shirts. She was planning on selling them to Damon and she was expecting Charmaine to take her to see the man.

Janice had finally succumb to the cocaine epidemic that was rapidly beginning to spread throughout the urban centers of America in the early eighties. Despite Charmaine's warnings only a five months ago, Janice had let her habit take complete control of her life. Charmaine had often pleaded with her cousin to get help, but Janice had been ignoring her pleas to go to the rehab clinic.

"Janice, you really need help!" Charmaine remarked as she watched her cousin smooth out the wrinkled silk shirts with her trembling hands.

"Help for what? I ain't hurtin' nobody, Charmaine. So I like ta' get a li'l high every now and then. I don't see the problem." Janice replied as she stared back at her cousin and scratched her neck and arms, in obvious need of a fix to Charmaine.

"This is the problem!" Charmaine yelled as she snatched the shirts from Janice's hands and showed them to her. "If you wasn't hooked on powder you wouldn't have to steal, Janice! You spend all the money you earn from Persia's on cocaine and now you have to steal in order to support your habit! And look at you—look at you sitting there shaking like some kind of dope fiend! What's gotten into you?" Charmaine asked as her eyes welled, her heart having become deeply saddened over Janice's state of being.

"Ain't nothin' wrong with me! I'm fine! I just need another toot that's all. I promise I'll stop soon, Charmaine."

"I don't believe you, Janice! If you were in control of things you wouldn't be stealing!" Charmaine yelled through tears.

"Well *you* give me the money and I'll take the shirts back inside! Besides, you act like you ain't never did a li'l tootin' in *your* life!" Janice replied in a mocking tone.

Charmaine widened her eyes and ogled her cousin and shook her head in disgust. Yes, Charmaine had snorted cocaine, but that was over a year ago. She and Janice had bought a bag of cocaine at the behest of Damon one night when they entered his club after being unable to find any marijuana within the city. Damon was the last stop they made, and wanting to get high, they bought a gram of cocaine from the man at a discount because he himself was out of marijuana. The two cousins liked the high that the powdered cocaine produced, so they dabbled lightly in the drug for a few months. Charmaine then realized that the drug was getting the best of her so she made a conscious decision not to use any kind of drugs ever again at the start of the '82 summer season.

Charmaine had quit cold-turkey. Janice, however, couldn't

stop herself; the cocaine had overcome her completely. Charmaine was feeling guilty about Janice's state of being. She felt that it was her fault that her cousin was now hooked on cocaine, and Janice, for a long time, never let the guilt that she knew Charmaine felt inside subside. Charmaine, however, decided to take a stand this day.

"You know what Janice? I can't do this no more." Charmaine said as she wiped her tears. "I been here four times with you and this ain't my style." she said as she started the engine of her Cadillac and asked Janice to exit her vehicle.

"I thought you was gone take me to score some blow, Charmaine!"

"I'm sorry Janice," Charmaine said sadly, "I can't support your deviance anymore. And I refuse keep feelin' sorry for you anymore. You're grown enough to make your own decisions in life and I see now that you know exactly what you're doing at this point and time. Until you get help, I can no longer take you anywhere. If you wanna get high, get high—just don't do it around me, sista. Now, please, leave. Just leave."

Janice looked straight ahead and nodded her head as she opened the door and got out of the car and stepped to the side. As Charmaine slowly pulled away, she looked in her rear-view mirror and could see Janice pointing her middle finger at her, and heard her say loud and clear, "I ain't your fuckin' sista' no more, bitch! Fuck you! Fuck you, Charmaine!"

Charmaine drove away disheartened. To hear Janice speak those words to her had cut deeply. She really wanted to help Janice; but Janice had to be willing to help herself. At this point and time in her life though, Janice was refusing to accept the fact that she had problem. She was in denial; and until she fully recognized that she was an addict, Janice could not be helped. That's what Charmaine thought about as she rode towards Gabriella's home in Eastern New Orleans.

Janice, meanwhile, now had to find a way to get uptown to score from Damon. She figured if she scored from Damon on the other side of town, she could hide her addiction, so she struck out walking down Canal Street in search of a way to get uptown.

As she walked down Canal Street, Janice passed a record shop and heard a voice call out her name. She looked around and saw Manhattan standing in front the store.

"Hey man!" Janice said excitedly as she ran up and hugged the man. "I ain't forgot about you! Your name Manhattan! I'm Janice remember? You still owe me a dance, sucka! Why you left so quick that night, man?"

Manhattan's mind began to work overtime again. Janice had just placed before him a sharp collection of statements and two questions that merited an answer. He knew Janice and Gabriella were close, and he had been thinking about Gabriella ever since he first saw her inside *Persia's* back in November of '82. He then made a conscious effort to use Janice to get next to Gabriella.

"I really don't why I left like that. I'm really sorry. I shoulda stayed, 'cause I really did want to get to know you better, you know? I guess I got nervous being in the presence of such a beautiful woman."

"Yeah, yeah, me too." Janice said as she began to rock back and forth as she fumbled her hands. "I mean, I was digging on you, man, and you just up and left." she concluded as she sniffed her nose repeatedly.

Manhattan quickly recognized all the signs that Janice was showing this morning. He knew the woman was an addict in need of a fix.

"Where you headed to, Janice?"

"Oh, well, you know, I'm just, I gotta go see a friend and pick up a package."

"Let me take you." Manhattan suggested as he went into his pocket and pulled out a set of car keys and extended his hands towards his brown 1979 Chevy Station Wagon.

"Man, you still at work!"

"My co-worker in there gone cover for me. I damn near own this record shop anyway. I'm thinking about buying a record shop myself someday. Anyway, where we going?" Manhattan asked as he nudged Janice towards his car.

Janice was somewhat unnerved by Manhattan's aggressiveness, but she wanted to score her cocaine more than anything. She brushed her nerves aside and got into the car with Manhattan and guided him uptown to the lounge where Damon hung out. As they rode, Janice asked Manhattan, "You mind if we stop and get a bag of cocaine? That's where I was really headed. Ain't no package."

"Cocaine," Manhattan asked as he eyed Janice. "Shoot! I think I'll grab me a bag myself! It's been a while since I had some cocaine. We can go to my place and have us a good time, baby. You wanna do that?"

Janice grew elated. She now had someone who shared her desire for cocaine; furthermore, the "somebody" was a man she had liked ever since she first met him several months ago. She grabbed Manhattan's free hand and the two rode into Damon's neighborhood, a rough part of uptown New Orleans known as the Third Ward.

Damon held down most of uptown, but he mainly operated out of the Calliope project; it was there, just outside the project outside a rundown lounge, called *The Beanstalk*, that Janice found Damon's red Cadillac parked out front near the entrance. Janice was relieved because she knew she was only moments away from scoring her fix.

The two went in and Janice spotted Damon in the back of the near-empty club that had just opened for business. Damon saw Janice walking his way and he waved her over to his table at the back of the lounge where Janice introduced Manhattan to Damon. Damon nodded quickly at Manhattan while Janice handed him the two silk shirts she had taken from the department store earlier. The drug dealer looked at the shirts and handed Janice a small packet containing a gram of cocaine upon his approval of the attire.

Manhattan wanted some cocaine for himself so he bought another gram from Damon. Damon made the two deals and hopped up from his seat to walk behind the bar and placed the cash into the register. Before Damon left his presence, Manhattan stopped him and handed him a five-dollar off coupon to the record store where he worked. Damon thanked Manhattan and tucked the coupon in his suit jacket and walked off.

Manhattan and Janice then left the club and rode to a corner store and purchased a fifth of Wild Irish Rose and a six pack of beer before they headed over to Manhattan's apartment in Gretna, Louisiana—about a twenty minute ride from uptown on the opposite side of the Mississippi River, known as the Westbank.

When they reached the apartment, Janice sat at the table and emptied her cocaine into a saucer and began to chop the cocaine into a fine powder with a razor blade she'd taken from her purse.

Manhattan smiled at her and walked slowly across the carpeted floor of the neatly kept, one bedroom apartment and sat at the table opposite Janice.

"What you know 'bout freebasin'?" Manhattan asked as he sat across from a fidgety Janice, who was heavily engrossed in the act of chopping her cocaine into a fine powder and separating the substance into neat thin lines in preparation to be snorted into her nostrils.

Freebasing was a method used to inject cocaine into one's system. A person would place a small amount of cocaine onto a spoon and hold it over a flame until it sizzled and melted into a liquid. From there, one could pull all of the liquid into a syringe, tie a rubber tube or some other form of rope around an arm, leg, or some other body part and then inject the liquid directly into his or her veins. This would result in an instant state of euphoria. The method was highly addictive and Manhattan was intent on introducing Janice to this potent method in order to gain control over the woman.

"I heard of it, but I never tried that before," Janice remarked just before she snorted the powder cocaine through her nose.

Manhattan sat at the table across from Janice, who was now eyeing him intently as he set up the paraphernalia to begin freebasing. Janice watched curiously as the drain from the cocaine she had snorted began to set in. What Manhattan was doing intrigued her because it looked as if it would make a person feel good. She watched as Manhattan injected the cocaine into his system and marveled at how quickly his high set in. Janice now wanted to feel what Manhattan was feeling. She grabbed the rubber tube from around Manhattan's arm and tightened it around her arm. Her fresh, virgin veins protruded like a mini garden hose as Manhattan prepared another dose to inject into her system. When he was done injecting the cocaine into her vein, Janice's eyes rolled to the back of her head and she leaned back in her chair in a euphoric state.

Janice was immediately hooked on the method. She looked around the room and everything seemed to be moving in slow motion. Manhattan said something to her, but his words were slurred. Janice thought she was imagining things when Manhattan, who now appeared to be completely naked, got up and walked towards her. Janice was staring at Manhattan in confusion, wondering what he was doing as he disappeared from sight. She tried to turn around and find his presence, but Manhattan shoved her head forward. The room was still spinning and it was hard for Janice to focus. She looked at the table and thought about snorting another line of cocaine but she was interrupted a few seconds later when she felt a belt being tied around her neck. Janice panicked and grabbed at the belt with both hands but Manhattan only tightened the belt tighter as she began to speak out in protest.

Manhattan then leaned down and kissed the nape of Janice's neck and whispered in her ear. "Don't be afraid, baby, you gone like this."

Manhattan then stood Janice up and leaned her over the kitchen table. The woman was trembling in fear. She had a belt tied tightly around her neck barely able to breath, the clothes on the floor told her that Manhattan was standing behind her naked. Janice really didn't want sex, she only wanted to get high. On top of that, Manhattan had never asked; he was taking Janice against her wishes at this moment and she was helpless to stop him.

"Manhattan, baby, baby please." Janice pleaded.

Janice's words of protest only fueled Manhattan's aggression. He tightened the belt and cut off Janice's air flow completely as he slid the chair out of the way and pulled her panties down over her hips and raised her skirt to reveal the woman's plump, dark-brown ass. Janice was about to pass out, but she grunted loudly through her clasped teeth when she felt Manhattan's dick sliding into her asshole. She tried desperately to breathe as the pain coursed through her body, but the tightened belt around her neck left her breathless. Manhattan soon loosened the belt and a rush of air suddenly filled Janice's lungs. She moaned aloud and sucked down oxygen as Manhattan anally penetrated her from behind. Seconds later, as Manhattan thrust into her with aggressive force, Janice felt as if she were about to float up to the ceiling. The cocaine was taking full affect; and it now had her submitting to what she now perceived to be innocuous actions emanating from Manhattan as the sex was beginning to arouse the cocaine-stimulated woman while taking her to new heights of sexual pleasure.

Janice looked over her shoulder towards Manhattan and moaned loudly as he ravaged her body. He then slowed his pace and placed a small dab of powder cocaine onto his middle finger and placed it in front of Janice's nose. She slowly snorted the powder just as Manhattan tightened the belt around her neck and obstructed her airflow once again. Janice gagged for air, and Manhattan released the belt and an immediate rush of oxygen and cocaine entered her system, producing an overwhelmingly stimulating high that left Janice wanting more of what Manhattan had to offer.

Completely lost in lust and a form of depravity that was surprising even to herself, Janice bent forward and rested her elbows on the table top and drove back onto Manhattan's phallus as she moaned aloud in heavenly bliss.

Manhattan grabbed Janice's hips and began stroking her furiously as the two moaned aloud in ecstasy. The sex that Janice was receiving, compounded with the high from the cocaine, and the belt being pulled tight and then loosened from her neck was driving her crazy with pleasure. She loved what Manhattan was doing to her and she only wanted more of this man.

Manhattan had pulled this routine off many times before, but the women never seemed to enjoy what he was doing. He always frightened them something awful by his actions, actions in which many of them perceived to be an act of attempted rape. Previously when Manhattan tried, the women were high on cocaine, but not to the point of where he'd taken Janice. This woman, much to Manhattan's delight, had a severe weakness, and he was planning to use her uncontrollable cocaine addiction to his advantage to the utmost degree.

A woman in her right mind would indeed be in fear for her life if a man had came up behind her and tied a belt around her neck and tried to anally assault her. The cocaine Janice had ingested, however, had heightened all of her senses and lowered her inhibitions at the same. She felt as if she was having the best sex she had ever had in her life with Manhattan. The two rocked in unison until Manhattan completed himself inside of Janice and walked back to the other side of the table to prepare another dose of cocaine for the two of them to freebase.

Janice and Manhattan spent the remainder of the day shooting cocaine, drinking liquor and having sex. She then spent the night with Manhattan, and during that time, she agreed to be his woman. She loved the way Manhattan treated her; and she now felt she had someone to call her own. Cocaine had a serious hold on Janice; the woman was no longer in the same frame of mind. Once, she had been happy and outgoing, but as the months went on, she became more and more irrational and isolated from her friends.

Janice kept up her appearances at *Persia's*, but it was becoming harder and harder to hide her addiction because she thought only about cocaine and Manhattan all the time. Singing was slowly beginning to take a back seat in her life; and before she could let it be known, Janice's addiction would cloud her judgment to the point of stupidity, and ultimately cause some of the people she had once held dear to her heart to lose their lives.

# CHAPTER 27

## PRELUDE TO THE SET UP

It was now the month of May in 1983 and Sam and Alfred were sitting in lounge chairs in Sam's driveway on a warm and humid evening talking about times past and reflecting on their lives as Sam watched his son ride his bicycle up and down the side walk in front of his home with another young boy who lived on the same block.

"Al, you happy with your life man?" Sam asked.

"Happy? Yeah, I'm happy. Sam. Me and Charmaine going strong. The car lot doing good. Life good right now. Why you ask me that, brother?" Alfred asked as he rolled a joint.

"You ever felt love so intense it hurt, man?"

Alfred looked over to Sam with a puzzled look on his face, "No. I can't say I have, Sam. As much as I love Charmaine, with her short, sexy self—I can't say I ever felt the way you feelin' right now. Where you going with this?"

"Last night," Sam replied as he reached down into a cooler and grabbed a can of beer, "last night, I just had this intense feelin' come over me. I can't describe it, except to say that I never felt an emotion like that. The way Gabriella looked at me, the way she touched me. I mean, the air was so thick with passion that we just, we just acted like pure animals with one another."

"Aww, Sam. You just had some hot, butt-naked ass sex that's all man!" Alfred said as he shoved Sam's shoulder and began laughing. "Me and Charmaine have hot sex all the time!"

"Al, I been knowing Gabriella for almost thirteen years. I been making love to this woman, and this woman alone, for over ten. I know every curve of her body. I know everything about my wife."

"And?" Alfred remarked as he lit up the joint.

"I guess I came about it wrong. The question I asked you, I mean. It was after the fact that I had that intense feeling. This woman is my life, man, and as a young man on my own, I have to deal with that li'l one there," Sam said, as he pointed to nine-year old Ben, "plus the one on the way. I hope the club continue on, man, because that's all I know. And if some—"

"Hey! Back up!" Alfred said with a wide grin. "What you mean, 'one on the way', Sam?"

"We found out last night, man." Sam stated proudly as he smiled back at Alfred. "Gabriella pregnant with our second child."

Alfred took a toke off the joint and passed it to Sam as he congratulated his friend. "That's what this all about? You just excited over your child, Sam. You had me worried there for a minute. I thought you was losing your gangster skills."

"Gangster," Sam remarked as he took a toke off the joint. "You know, all my life I been trying to avoid that label? But people just won't let that part of my life rest."

"Sam," Alfred said seriously, "look back to some of the things we did—sold drugs in school, you stood up to Damon, been shot at by Harold, and opened a bar—at sixteen mind you —from money that was made in the streets. Not to mention that classic wedding you and Gabriella pulled off. People still tryin' to copy what y'all two did up until this day, Sam. People respect what you did and how you did it, brother. Just because you never killed nobody, and never been locked up, that don't mean that the people on the streets don't see you as a gangster.

They see you as one of the smart ones, man. You wasn't out there like Damon and Taylor was—killing people and shit, going to jail and stuff like that, but still, you are what you are Sam. We were the best out there man, and people never forgot it. Harold wanted too much. He wanted to be noticed, but the real ones don't work like that, Sam. Like it or not, brother, you was a gangster. That was your life, once upon a time." Alfred ended as he reached down into the cooler and grabbed a cold beer.

Sam reflected on all that Alfred had said to him, but deep in his heart, he never felt as if he were a gangster, he knew he was involved in illegal activity that could have very well caused him his freedom or his life, but he never believed that he was a gangster. With that life behind him, Sam now had a family; and on this day, the life he once led was causing him conflict. Sam was worried that *Persia's* would fail. That he wouldn't be able to support Gabriella and his kids. Like any other man, Sam had fears, and his fears had overwhelmed him for a brief moment.

"Life has never been so good to one man in such a short period of time, Al. This day here, my life is complete, brother. I can't ask God for much more. I have all I need to get by, as Marvin and Tammi said, once upon a time."

Later that night, when *Persia's* opened, Sam, Gabriella, Alfred, Charmaine, Yvonne, and Janice all got together and sung *You're All I Need to Get By,* originally sung by Marvin Gaye and Tammi Terrell. The club rocked that night and everyone was thoroughly enjoying themselves.

Henrietta hadn't been to the club for several weeks but on this night, Gabriella had found a baby sitter for Ben, and Henrietta decided to step out. Henrietta got caught up at the hairdresser so she knew she had missed the performance; but she also knew there would be good music and good people inside the bar and she was eager to spend time with her sister.

Henrietta parked her brand new 1982 white four door Dynasty down the block from *Persia's* and walked through the darkness towards the club. As she crossed the street to enter *Persia's*, Henrietta was greeted by a strikingly handsome man.

His slender frame and smooth skin wowed the woman. The man introduced himself and offered to pay Henrietta's way into the club but she declined the offer as the two approached the front door. Henrietta hugged Alfred as she walked into the club and she quickly grabbed a table and looked around for her sister.

The man Henrietta had met briefly was about to approach her again, Henrietta saw him approaching and grew uneasy. This man seemed a little off to Henrietta and she really didn't like his presence. Henrietta was preparing to let the man know she wasn't interested as he walked her way, but he was cut off by Janice.

"Manhattan!" Janice yelled aloud. "I thought that was you! So you here to see your woman perform tonight?" Janice asked as she walked up and hugged Manhattan.

Henrietta looked on, feeling a little reluctance emanate from within her as Janice said to her, "Henrietta, this my new friend, Manhattan. He from New York!"

Janice had been talking off and on about Manhattan to her friends the past few months, but no one ever really paid her any attention. To them, it was Janice being Janice. She had many a man friend in times past, so they all figured Manhattan was just another one of her boyfriends. Had they paid closer attention, they may have seen the mental instability lying just under Manhattan's skin.

"Ohh, I remember you talking about him a while back," Henrietta replied. "So he's with you," she asked in a relieved manner, happy to know somebody else was willing to get acquainted with the odd-ball individual so she wouldn't have to set him straight on this night.

"Yes! He's with me, Henrietta. Come on, Manhattan," Janice said as she straightened her mini skirt, "let's go boogie!"

"I hope she only told you the good things about me, miss," Manhattan said with a smile, as he and Janice headed for the dance floor.

Henrietta laughed fraudulently as she shook Manhattan's hand.

"You kids have fun!" she yelled over the music.

When Janice and Manhattan left her eyesight, Henrietta dropped her smile shook her head slowly from side to side, wondering what rock had Janice found this bum underneath.

As Janice and Manhattan danced, Sam walked over to Henrietta's table, sat down and chatted with his sister-in-law.

"So who y'all told about the baby, Sam?" Henrietta asked.

"Alfred, Yvonne and Charmaine the only ones besides you who know. Gabriella wanna do a special show for Thanksgiving when she start showing and make it known that she's gonna be gone from the club scene for about a year or so. She really wants for her and the girls to start writing more songs of their own, you know? When she step away from the club, they gone start working on an album."

"That's wonderful, Sam. Gabriella can do so much with her voice. I wish all of you well."

About an hour later, everyone was out on the dance floor. Henrietta, Gabriella, and Sam danced together along with Charmaine and Alfred. Janice and Manhattan were right next to them as Hall and Oates' song *I Can't Go for That* blared across the huge club. Manhattan had been eying Gabriella all night, but Gabriella had never acknowledged him, an act which left Manhattan wondering why Gabriella didn't speak to him the whole while he was in the the club.

Truth was, Gabriella knew Manhattan was on the premises, but the reason she didn't acknowledge him was because she had no interest in becoming an acquaintance of Manhattan, even if he was Janice's so-called man. Gabriella simply despised the man because she felt he was not the charming individual he was portraying himself to be; she and Henrietta were unknowingly on the same page concerning Manhattan and his demeanor.

Undeterred by Gabriella's avoidance of him, Manhattan continued lusting after the woman. He eyed her closely over the music, convincing himself that Gabriella was only avoiding him so as not to arouse suspicion from her husband. Manhattan, in his own sick, twisted mind, had convinced himself that Gabriella wanted hers and his relationship to be a clandestine affair. He continued to dance with Janice, who was really getting into the song, as were the rest of the people on the dance floor; but the person Manhattan really wanted to be with was just a few feet out of his reach. He had to touch her. He wanted her to know that he knew she wanted to keep secret their budding relationship.

In an attempt to let the woman know he was aware of her desires, Manhattan began slowly shifting through the crowd towards Gabriella, Henrietta and Sam. Janice followed Manhattan's lead, and when he and Janice got nearer Gabriella, Manhattan began to slightly brush up on her with his back. Gabriella was really into the music, enjoying her sister and husband's company and didn't even think twice about the man brushing up against her because the dance floor was crowded and people were constantly brushing up against one another by accident. Gabriella's sincere inattentiveness was stirring Manhattan on even more so; it excited him so much that it provoked him to reach out and palm Gabriella's rear end.

"Don't you ever touch me like that!" Gabriella shouted as she turned around just in time to see Manhattan turn around and stare into her eyes.

Gabriella then grew scared and backed away towards her husband. This man, for some reason, frightened her, and he wasn't someone she wanted to know. Gabriella had never forgotten she and Manhattan's last encounter and the uncomfortable feeling she got then, and in spite of the time that had lapsed, Gabriella still wanted no part of what Manhattan had to offer—friendship or otherwise. "I don't want to be your friend," she told Manhattan to his face. "And the next time you touch—"

"What happened?" Sam asked as he cut Gabriella's remark short and quickly stepped in between her and Manhattan.

Patrons in the club began to clear the dance floor as Clyde turned down the music.

With Henrietta, Alfred and Charmaine now standing behind him, Sam stood face to face with Manhattan.

"What happened, Gabriella?" Sam asked.

"This man grabbed my behind! He was here sometime last year and I didn't like him then, and I don't like him now. Sam! He supposed to be Janice's friend, but I don't like him at all! And I don't want him back here inside of Persia's because he's trouble!"

"You wanna touch my wife? Go 'head and do it why I'm looking!" Sam told Manhattan as his nose flared and he began loosen his tie.

Alfred walked up behind Sam slowly and stared at Manhattan as he sized him up. Alfred knew of the man, but he never really thought nothing of Manhattan; but if Gabriella had reservations concerning his character, then Alfred would also have problems with Manhattan because Gabriella was not the one to treat people harshly unless she had a real good reason to do so.

"Everything okay here, Sam?" Alfred asked as he stood beside his friend.

"Yeah, we cool for now." Sam remarked as he turned to face Manhattan again. "I'm gone have to ask you to leave my club, Manhattan. If I see you in here again it's gone be trouble, brother. This woman taken—and if she wasn't taken—she don't want *you*! Understand?"

"She do want me, Sam! Your wife wanted me the first time she saw me! That's why I came back here, so we can finish what we started! Tell him, Gabriella! Tell him we belong together!" Manhattan said as he looked towards a stunned Gabriella and reached out to grab her hand.

Sam swung on Manhattan and Alfred jumped in as well. The two men began pounding Manhattan's face and body as patrons in the club began to scream and run for the door. Henrietta and Charmaine, who were soon joined by Yvonne and Clyde, tried desperately to break up the fight by grabbing hold of Sam and Alfred. At the same time, Janice was trying to pull Manhattan away from Sam and Alfred's punches.

When the men were separated, Sam, Gabriella, Henrietta, Alfred, Clyde, Charmaine, and Yvonne all stood together, and Janice and Manhattan stood opposite them. Janice was trying to console Manhattan as Sam and his friends grew dismayed.

"Janice!" Henrietta yelled in dismay. "Get over here and away from that lunatic!"

"He just drunk, Henrietta. I'm gone make sure he get home all right." Janice replied as she help Manhattan straighten his clothes.

"Fuck him!" Charmaine then yelled. "He tryna push up on Gabriella and you taking up for *him*?"

"Y'all don't understand! Charmaine, you got Alfred, and Sam got Gabriella! Yvonne doing her thing and what I got? Nothing! The first time I really like somebody, y'all wanna fight 'em! I'm not leaving without him!" Janice replied as she stood in front of Manhattan.

"Janice," Henrietta said softly, "you drunk right now. And it's obvious to everybody that you not thinking straight. This man is no good, you hear me? No good! This ain't you, Janice. What's going on with you, child?" Henrietta asked in a compassionate tone of voice.

Janice's addiction was blinding her thinking ability; any true friend in their right frame of mind would have had a serious conversation with her man friend if he had tried to approach one of her girlfriends in the manner in which Manhattan had stepped towards Gabriella and disrespected both her and Sam. Unable to think clearly, Janice was convinced that Manhattan was the man for her because he shared her interests, namely getting high. Had she revealed her addiction to her friends, whom she now considered "the goody-two shoe" type, she felt they would banish her. By not admitting her problem to her friends, however, Janice, in effect, was banishing herself.

Charmaine knew what the deal was concerning Janice, but she was reluctant to tell on this night; but she need not speak on it because everybody involved could clearly see that Janice was high off something more than liquor.

"Janice," Gabriella said to her friend. "Don't do this! You tripping right now, sista! We can—"

"I ain't your fuckin sista!" Janice snapped as she turned and faced Gabriella. "I'm the one who started your ass singin' in this mutherfuckin' club! And all I hear now is how good *Gabriella* is! 'Ohh, she got a nice voice'. Everybody notices you and only you! God dammit I started this shit!" Janice yelled aloud as she stomped the wooden dance floor.

Gabriella's eyes widened and she quickly realized that Janice was jealous of what she had going on in her life. Gabriella could deal with the jealousy—that ugly facet of life sometimes developed within friendships from time to time and could be worked out over time; what really hurt Gabriella, though, was when Janice said they were no longer sisters. Even though she understood the fact that Janice was high, the words still hurt Gabriella.

"All these years I been knowing you you never said anything like that to me, Janice," Gabriella said lowly as she stared her friend in the eyes. "Drugs can't be that powerful and I know you don't mean that. I want to help you, but I also have to look out for myself and the ones I love—including you. Janice, if you leave with this man tonight, so help me God, I'll never speak to you again for as long as he's in your life."

"We family, Janice." Charmaine then said to her cousin through tears. "We family. Come on, let's go get some help! Don't go out like this, please." she concluded as she reached out for Janice's hand.

Janice moved away from Charmaine and sank into Manhattan's arms. Manhattan smiled a wicked smile towards Sam and Alfred and the two men charged him again, but Janice moved back in front of Manhattan preventing the two men from attacking "her man" again.

"It's over for us," Janice snarled. "I don't want *nothing* to do with Persia's ever again! Me and Manhattan gone start our own life! We gonna build *us* something good! Better than what you and Sam could ever do!" Janice stated in an aggressive manner towards a disappointed Gabriella.

Manhattan and Janice walked out of *Persia's* hand in hand. Patrons of the club stood out on the sidewalk and in the middle of the street in silent bewilderment as they watched Janice and Manhattan walk down the moonlit street. They all knew Janice had been close to Gabriella and they were just as stunned as Gabriella to see Janice walking hand in hand with the man who tried to molest Gabriella inside the club. The crowd watched in silence as Gabriella wept for her friend in front of the club as Charmaine and Yvonne cursed Janice repeatedly for turning her back on friends and family.

Once the ruckus had settled down, the club reopened and Sam, Gabriella, Charmaine, Yvonne, Alfred, Clyde, and Henrietta sat at a table and discussed what had transpired. They all agreed that it would be better for business, and more importantly, better for Gabriella, that both Janice and Manhattan not be allowed back into the club until Janice omitted Manhattan from her life completely.

Manhattan had done exactly what he wanted to do: disrupt the friendship between Gabriella and Janice. Now he had an ally on his side who knew where the woman he lusted after resided. His obsession with Gabriella continued to fester and Janice willingly became his pawn. Manhattan kept Janice supplied with a steady supply of cocaine and encouraged her to repair the damaged relationship between her and her cousin Charmaine and Janice agreed so long as Manhattan remained at her side.

A couple of weeks after the fight, Manhattan, who was steadily spinning out of control, began to spy on Gabriella after Janice gave up the location of the woman's place of residence. He would trail Sam and Gabriella when they left the club and park down the street from their home in New Orleans East and just sit and watch the house. That had become his routine; he would leave three or four grams of cocaine with Janice to keep her sedated while he spied on Gabriella.

Manhattan was planning on having Gabriella the first chance he received. Gabriella, however, was never alone and that posed a problem for him. The sociopath wanted so badly to have this woman that he was willing to risk life and limb to have her all to his self. Manhattan's obsession with Gabriella, and his cocaine addiction had both gotten out of control. He would stalk Gabriella on a daily basis; snorting cocaine and sometimes masturbating as he sat in his car watching her go about her daily routine whenever she was home with her family. It pained him not to be able to touch her again; after one of his spying sessions in June of 1983, where he fantasized about completing himself inside of Gabriella, Manhattan had made up his mind to get what was rightfully his, in his eyes, at all costs as he drove slowly pass the Holland family's peaceful domicile.

# CHAPTER 28

## THE SET UP

It had been nearly a whole month since the incident in *Persia's*; it was now the last week of June, and the atmosphere inside the club was once again festive. The club was nearly filled to capacity this hot summer night and patrons were still lined up outside waiting to get in. Drinks flowed freely as the music blared throughout. Gabriella and Sam worked the bar along with Clyde, who was beginning to deal with health concerns, and was now ready to hand the club completely over to Sam within a year's time. Henrietta, Charmaine and Yvonne assisted the waitstaff with the waiting of tables as Alfred manned the door.

Alfred grimaced when he saw Janice approach the club. "Where you think you going, girl?" he asked in a harsh tone. "You know you not allowed in here!"

"You turnin' me away, Al?"

"You damn right! Get the hell up the street!"

As Janice walked away, another female, dressed in a tight mini skirt and high heels, walked up and paid her way into the club. Alfred admired the woman's physique as he counted her cover charge and placed it into the cash drawer. He admired her long shiny black hair and plump rear end. The woman entered and took the last available seat in a dark section of the club and was quickly approached by a waitress who asked her if she would like a drink and a menu.

"No menu. But can I have a seven and seven, please, ma'am?"

The waitress walked off to get the drink as *Backstabbers*, by The O'Jays, blared across the sound system. The waitress returned and the woman paid for the drink and sat and sipped her drink slowly, carefully eying Gabriella. Gabriella was in a world of her own as she entertained various patrons inside the club. The woman, meanwhile, sat at her table in obscurity. She reached into her purse and pulled out a cellophane bag and placed a small amount of powdered cocaine onto the table, leaned forward and snorted two lines of cocaine without being noticed. Once the drain kicked in, the woman entered into a state of euphoria. Her eyes glazed over and she got up to dance with patrons in the club. Men ogled over the slim bronze-skinned woman and offered to buy her drinks much to her delight, although she declined their offers. Once she realized she had the men in the club fooled, she went back to her seat and awaited the perfect time to strike.

Meanwhile, Janice had made her way back to the club after walking to another bar and having a beer all by her lonesome. She approached Alfred again and this time she begged and pleaded for Alfred to let her in the club. Alfred called Gabriella and Sam over to front door and the four of them talked.

"I told you," Gabriella remarked the moment she laid eyes upon Janice, "i told you not to show your face in front this club again!"

"Gabriella, I know I fucked up! But I heard y'all was singing Aretha Franklin tonight. That's the first song we ever sung together, remember? Just let me do that one song with y'all and I'm gone leave, I promise. Please, Gabriella?"

"Janice, it's best you leave from in front this door. Gabriella and no one else wants you around so long as you snortin' cocaine and dealin' with Manhattan." Sam said calmly.

"Good-bye, Janice. Go away before I call the police." Gabriella added.

"She your friend, Gabriella. She just wanna sing one song," a female patron waiting to get in the club said to Gabriella.

"She's a junky and refuses to get help because she's dealing with a sick pervert! I don't want her around here until she leaves Manhattan alone! If she's still here when I get back, I'm calling the police—friend or no friend!" Gabriella said before she walked backed into the club.

Sam politely asked Janice to leave and was on his way to check on Gabriella, but Janice called him back.

"Just walk with me to the corner, Sam. Let's talk for a minute, please?" she pleaded.

Sam walked with Janice down the sidewalk and listened as she began telling him she wanted to get help and was through dealing with Manhattan.

"Well, that's good. If you wanna get help, your friends will help you, Janice." Sam remarked as the two walked side by side at a slow pace.

"Thanks, Sam. Man, I made a big mistake and it's gone take a lot to repair the damage I done."

As Sam and Janice walked and talked, everyone else went back into the club and the festivities resumed. Gabriella was now in the dressing room alone, sitting behind the desk crying to herself as she was disheartened over the way she had to treat Janice. Gabriella meant what she said though, as long as Janice remained friends with Manhattan, and continued to use drugs, she would not associate with the woman; but as she reflected on the matter, Gabriella soon began to think that maybe she was a little too hard on Janice. Maybe letting her sing one song would be the beginning of a recovery, a turn-around for her longtime friend.

Gabriella was considering allowing Janice to enter the club when she heard the dressing room door open, close and then lock. She thought it was Sam, and she was prepared to tell him that Janice could sing one song; but when she looked up, she saw Manhattan standing in front of the closed and locked door. Manhattan had snuck into the club dressed as a woman early on and had finally cornered his intended victim when she was all alone.

Gabriella got up slowly from behind the desk and backed up against the wall behind the desk, her grey eyes now struck with fear. She brushed the hair back from in front of her face as she began to question Manhattan's motives.

"What do you want from me, you animal?" she yelled.

The music in the club was deafening, no one could hear Gabriella, nor were they aware of what was taking place inside the dressing room. Gabriella moved slowly into a corner as Manhattan walked towards her.

"Why you trembling, baby? I went through all this so we can be together tonight. I finally got you out from under your husband. Now we can be together—the way we were meant to be." Manhattan said calmly as he walked towards Gabriella, pulling up the black mini skirt he was wearing in order to reveal his hardening penis in the process.

Gabriella covered her lower face and screamed to the top of her lungs; but it was to no avail because the music in the club was just too loud. When Manhattan walked over and placed his hand around her waist, Gabriella leaned up against the wall and vomited onto the carpet. Repulsed beyond words, and determined to escape, the frightened woman began to swing wildly on the man, doing the best she could to defend herself as she called out for her husband.

Manhattan quickly covered Gabriella's mouth, threw her onto the desk facing away from him and raised her skirt and forcefully ripped off her panties. Gabriella tried to scream at that moment; but she could produce no sound as she was going into shock over the realization that she was about to be sexually violated. Manhattan began to mount the defenseless woman as she pleaded with him not to go through with the act he was about to perform. As he leaned over Gabriella's back, he placed a .38 revolver to her temple and ordered the woman not to speak anymore until he was ready for her to do so. He then leaned forward and placed his lips to Gabriella's ear and ordered her to tell him to make love to her.

Gabriella cried heavily. Tears were streaming down her face and landing on the wooden desk top. She just couldn't bring herself to say the words that Manhattan was asking of her.

"Say it bitch! Before I blow your brains all over this fucking desk!" Manhattan hissed angrily.

"Manhattan, please don't do this to me!" Gabriella cried lowly.

Hearing Gabriella call his name only fueled Manhattan's fire, as many of his rape victims had done. He demanded that Gabriella beg him to make love her as he placed the pistol up against her right eye socket. Gabriella threw up again, this time all over the desk as she reluctantly stated that she wanted Manhattan to have sex with her.

"I didn't say have sex. I wanna hear you say, 'make love to me, Manhattan'!"

Gabriella pleaded through tears for the torture to stop, but the person she considered to be a monster just wouldn't let up.

"Say it, Gabriella!" Manhattan commanded as he penetrated Gabriella from behind. "Tell me you want it, woman!"

Gabriella was broken; she gave in to Manhattan's wishes and blurted out through her tears, "I want it!"

"I knew you wanted me, baby!" Manhattan grunted as he ground into Gabriella.

Manhattan actually believed that Gabriella wanted him to make love to her; and in his sick and twisted mind, he did just so. Gabriella lay across the desk vomiting nonstop and grimacing in pain as Manhattan gripped her shoulders and pounded her from behind with lustful enthusiasm and unrelenting mercy. Gabriella's cries of protest were taken as moans of delight by Manhattan and he began to grip Gabriella's, breasts, stripping her bra from her body and leaving welts on her flesh.

This was a horrifying experience for Gabriella. Never had she known such fear, nor felt so much pain. She looked towards the doorway, hoping Sam would burst through and rescue her; but also, she feared that Sam would never forgive her if his eyes were to witness the event unfolding inside the dressing room. In great fear of losing her family, Gabriella turned and faced Manhattan and screamed aloud, "Please! Please, no!"

The tone in which Gabriella called out to him had driven Manhattan over the edge. He completed himself inside Gabriella and lay upon her back, planting soft kisses on her neck. Gabriella vomited again onto the desk as Manhattan slid out of her and rubbed her rear end tenderly. He then knelt down and kissed her cheeks before he tidied himself up and pranced out of the dressing room, stating to Gabriella that he would see her again.

"Alfred, you seen Gabriella?" Charmaine asked as she stood in the doorway watching Janice and Sam talk at the opposite end of the block.

"I think she went in the back. She probably had to get herself together after all that went down tonight."

"I'm going check on her and make sure she all right. Make sure Sam and Janice don't leave that corner, hear baby?" Charmaine concluded as she kissed Alfred and walked through the crowded club towards the dressing room.

As Charmaine approached the dressing room, Manhattan, still dressed as a woman, quickly passed her.

"Can I help you, miss?" Charmaine asked nicely, not recognizing Manhattan through the darkness of the club, coupled with the disguise he wore.

"Oh, I'm sorry, I was looking for your bathroom, ma'am."

"They on the other side of the stage you can't miss' em."

"Thank you, miss!" Manhattan stated in a feminine tone as he hurried down the hall and disappeared into the crowd.

When Charmaine opened the door to the dressing room, she gasped at the sight that lay before her eyes. Gabriella was slumped over the desk in a pool of her own vomit, the top portion of her outfit was hanging off her shoulders and she was naked from the waist down.

"Gabriella! Oh my God! Gabriella!" Charmaine yelled as she cried aloud and rushed to her friend's side.

Gabriella was unresponsive. She just lay face-down on the desk, her head turned away from Charmaine and her eyes wide open, gazing upon nothing.

Charmaine hugged Gabriella from the side and began screaming for help at the top of her lungs. The office door was now open, allowing several young men standing close by the stage to hear her screams. Two men peeked into the open door and one of the male patrons quickly closed it, turned away and began yelling for Sam, stating that Gabriella was in trouble.

It was total chaos as people began screaming for Sam whilst wondering exactly what'd happened to Gabriella. Alfred soon caught wind of the situation and hollered down the sidewalk.

"Sam!" Alfred called out loudly. "Sam! Something happened to Gabriella! Sam!"

Sam looked up the block and clearly heard Alfred yell aloud, "Gabriella in trouble!" and he quickly began a frantic run back towards *Persia's*. Janice, however, had taken off running in the opposite direction.

Manhattan made his way out of the club long before the chaos had started. He merely walked down the block unseen and turned the corner and disappeared from sight. He would rejoin Janice later that night.

When Sam entered the office, he saw his shaking wife huddled in a corner, in a state of total terror gripping Charmaine tightly and hiding her face in shame. Sam fell to his knees in front of Gabriella, and Gabriella, recognizing her husband, let go of Charmaine and hugged him tightly. She was covered in her own vomit. She was naked from the waist down, and had a foul odor emanating from her body. Gabriella cried on Sam's shoulder and begged his forgiveness. Sam, however, couldn't understand why his wife was asking his forgiveness, when in fact, he felt that *he* had let *her* down.

Gabriella held her wedding ring in front of Sam's face. "Still married?" she asked him through her tears.

"Baby, just don't speak," Sam said lovingly. "The ambulance is on the way and you're gonna be okay."

"You're not going to leave me?" Gabriella asked through closed eyes as she gripped her husband tightly. "I tried to stop him, Sam. I didn't want this to happen!" Gabriella screamed hysterically.

Sam could hold out no longer. He burst into tears at that moment, right along with Alfred, Henrietta, and Yvonne.

Charmaine, Sam and Henrietta, all huddled together with Gabriella as Alfred, Clyde and Yvonne escorted everyone out of the club to close it up for the night.

Henrietta's heart went out to her baby sister as she felt she had let Gabriella down by not protecting her when she needed her the most.

At the same time, Charmaine was devastated by what had happened. If she had been more attentive to Janice's coming around this night, she believed sincerely that she would have seen the play. Charmaine knew exactly what happened; and it all revolved around Janice and Manhattan.

Sam was grief-stricken. Family meant everything to the man, and when his family needed him most, he'd failed. He asked Henrietta to go get his son, and meet him at the hospital as he clutched his wife tightly and reassured her that he would always love her no matter what.

As Sam and Charmaine awaited the ambulance's arrival, Gabriella told them that it was the same man they had an argument with a month earlier—Manhattan. Sam felt like a fool; he actually believed that things had passed with Manhattan; but he now understood that the man was obsessed with his wife. Sam now had it it on his mind to find and deal with Manhattan personally.

Charmaine had an idea at the outset concerning what happened, and Gabriella's statements only confirmed her beliefs. She would share her thoughts afterwards, however, as top priority was getting Gabriella the proper care.

The medics took Gabriella to Charity hospital and ran

various STD tests on the woman and the police department also filed a report. It took a few days for the test results to come back, but after three days, Gabriella was released with a clean bill of health. She would require counseling for the trauma she suffered, and everyone showed their love and support by giving of their time and helping the family wherever needed. Sam, Henrietta, Charmaine, Alfred, and Yvonne, often accompanied Gabriella to the counseling sessions, which began a week after she was assaulted.

Gabriella's rape had deeply affected the entire community. Everyone's heart went out to Sam and his family. Everybody showed love and support—everyone except Janice. As Gabriella was slowly regaining her strength and confidence, Sam and his friends realized that they would have to hold court in the streets with Janice as the police had not a clue as to the whereabouts of Gabriella's attacker.

## CHAPTER 29

### GO ASK JANICE

Nearly two months after Gabriella's rape, Alfred and Sam were sitting in Sam's car in front of *Persia's* discussing Gabriella's situation. Gabriella hadn't been to the club since the night of her rape. She was at home with her son Ben, and her sister, who guarded her fiercely whenever Sam wasn't around. Gabriella had fully recovered physically from her traumatizing event; but the thought of returning to *Persia's* frightened her a great deal. She still loved to sing, so from time to time, Gabriella would sing outside of her home for the kids in the neighborhood. Slowly, she was healing from a mental aspect.

As Sam and Alfred sat and talked inside Sam's car, Charmaine walked up and tapped on the window. Sam unlocked the door and Charmaine jumped into the backseat. Charmaine was working with Alfred and Sam trying to find Janice. The three friends figured if they found Janice, they would find Manhattan. As Charmaine slid into the backseat, she sighed sadly. The woman had not a clue where Janice was hiding out. She had been searching for her cousin for weeks, but it was as if Janice had disappeared off the face of the earth —right along with Manhattan.

"Sam, I'm sorry. I don't know where this girl is. She may have left and went to New York with that crazy man. No one on the streets knows anything about those two fools."

"Hey Sam, what if we check uptown. Maybe Damon know somethin' about Manhattan," Alfred thought aloud.

"Damon!" Sam quipped as he frowned. "Man, I haven't talked to that man in years. I don't even know if he still alive or not."

"Alfred might be right," Charmaine added, being careful not to reveal that she knew Janice often scored from Damon, for fear of having her former cocaine addiction revealed. "It's obvious they not down here nowhere. If Manhattan not uptown, I don't think he nowhere in the city."

Sam begrudgingly rode uptown to Damon's old hangout, the rundown hole in the wall night club called *The Beanstalk*. Sam remembered the things that went down with Damon several years back and he really didn't like to be in the man's company because Damon often bred trouble. Still, finding Janice and Manhattan superseded all of Sam's apprehensions and doubts.

It was approaching late evening and the sun was beginning to set on a cool autumn night as the three walked up the sidewalk and approached the lounge and spoke to a few people they recognized as they stood in front of the club searching for Damon amongst the crowd. The trio recognized Damon's car and they figured he was inside so they entered the lounge to search for the man.

They found Damon at the back of the club with a slender, dark-skinned female sitting on his lap. Damon had put on a few pounds over the years. He sat in his chair looking like a cuddly black teddy bear as he rubbed the woman's legs softly while whispering into her ear. The woman giggled as she eyed the three friends approaching the table. Damon peered from around the slender woman and burst into laughter when he saw Sam approaching.

"Sam Holland! Funny seeing you here after all these years! How's life been treating you downtown, brother?"

"It's been good. Been good, Damon."

"What you need, brother? Some weed? Some blow? Smack? Buttons? I got it all, young blood! What's up, Al?

Lady you look familiar," Damon then said towards Charmaine.

"I'm sorry. You must have me confused with someone else," Charmaine said as she turned away from Damon. "Sam, I'll be outside by the car." Charmaine didn't want to be recognized by Damon at all; her former habit was something she was not proud of, and she wanted it to remain a secret for all times.

"We be out in a minute, baby," Alfred told Charmaine.

"Damon," Sam then said as he rested his hands on the table top, "we need some info, brother. Maybe you have what we looking for."

"Info? I look like the six 'o' clock news, man?"

"Damon," Sam replied lowly, "my wife was attacked by a sadistic cocaine addict. He still out here somewhere, and I'm hoping you can help us find him."

"Your wife? Somebody jumped on that sweet gal?" Damon said as he grew concerned and gently pushed the female off his lap and stood up. "Aww, man, I'm sorry for your troubles, Sam. Sit down and tell me what happened, brother."

Sam related the events that took place a couple of months back and told Damon that Janice was last seen with the man. He described the man to Damon and Damon leaned back in his chair, closed his eyes and thought for moment.

"I used to see Janice downtown at this record shop on occasion. I haven't been there in a couple of months or so, but I can give you the exact location where she used to hang out."

Sam and Alfred grew quiet as they waited for Damon to give them the information they so desired. Damon leaned forward in his chair and smiled at the two and Sam and Alfred quickly cut their eyes towards one another. They knew from past dealings that Damon was a very self-serving individual who wouldn't do anything without benefiting from the situation as well. That was years ago, however, but over that period of time, Damon still hadn't changed. Sam's brown eyes grew low as he rubbed his cleft chin and stared at Damon in anticipation of what the man would want. Damon began laughing as he recognized that the young men standing in front of him were on to his tactics.

"Hey brothers, I gotta get *somethin'* out the deal! Now, I feel your pain, but I got bills to pay. This is valuable information here! I promise I won't take a big slice out the pie."

"How much you talking, Damon?" Sam asked sternly.

"Okay, I'll be fair, man. Since I don't know for sure if Janice still downtown, how about you buy this half ounce of weed from me, cat?"

"Let's go, Sam!" Alfred interrupted harshly.

Sam was reluctant to leave; however, he needed to know what Damon knew.

"How much?" Sam asked.

"Fifty is what it go for, but when you couple that with this information, it's worth three times as much."

"You want us to pay a hundred and fifty dollars for a fifty dollar bag of weed, Damon?" Alfred whispered.

"It's not so much the weed—it's the information, young blood. I know this shit is important to all three of y'all. You can possibly end your search for the people that harmed Gabriella tonight. Help me help you, man!"

Damon leaned back into the chair and called the waitress over and ordered a pint of gin and a can of grapefruit juice. His thick jehri-curled hair shined in the fluorescent light that was emanating from the ceiling of the bar as he stood up to remove the leather jacket he was wearing. He sat back down and poured himself a drink as Sam and Alfred gathered what money they had on them and began counting out one-hundred and fifty dollars. Damon offered the two men a drink and they both declined.

"Alright, fellas," Damon said as he let out a sly smile, "Janice used to hang at New Age Record shop with some chump that used ta' work there; a kind of copper or a bronze-skinned fellow. Slim dude, good-looking brother named

Manhattan. Yeah, I tell ya' them two there—they could snort up a barrel of cocaine, man. I had many a good payday from those two."

Sam immediately slammed the money onto the table, left the weed behind, and he and Alfred began walking towards the exit. Damon laughed to himself as he placed the marijuana into his coat pocket and began counting the money given to him.

"Glad to help." he said in a low tone as he eyed the two walking briskly out the door. "Glad to help."

Sam sped towards Canal Street and pulled up in front of *New Age Record Store* and the three quickly exited the car and walked into the building. A female sales clerk greeted them and asked how could she help. Sam asked the clerk about a salesman named Manhattan who was working there and the woman cringed.

"God, I hope you not friends with that son-of-a-bitch!" the woman said with wide eyes. Her full-figured frame trembled behind the counter.

"Ma'am," Sam spoke softly, "this man hurt my wife and we looking for him to bring him to justice."

"Your wife? He hurt your wife? Ohh, God!"

"What?" Charmaine asked carefully. "What happened to you?"

"Nothin' happened to me—but Manhattan used to come to work braggin' about how he got this woman that used ta' work at a club downtown pregnant. He used ta' laugh and brag that the woman was married to another man but was carrying his baby. He tried to have sex with me in the stock room. He just a real creep and he scares me. I think he a raper man."

Sam wondered how Manhattan knew Gabriella was pregnant. He had only told four people: Yvonne, Alfred, Charmaine and Henrietta and he knew they didn't tell anyone. He was now under the assumption that Manhattan was stalking his family and spying on his wife.

"How the hell he know Gabriella pregnant, Sam?" Alfred asked.

"I don't know. I'll be sure to ask 'em before I kick his ass again." Sam replied.

"Mister, he don't work here no more. He left about a month ago with some lady, a dark-skinned chick with an Afro. They was staying across the river in Gretna, I believe. I have his last address right here."

The woman gave Sam Manhattan's address and the three hurried across the river into Gretna to see if they could finally catch up with him and Janice. Sam had every intent on delivering retribution for what the two had done to Gabriella. As they pulled into the driveway, Sam opened his glove compartment and retrieved his .38 revolver.

Alfred and Charmaine stared with wide eyes at Sam as he exited the car and hurried up the stairs towards Manhattan's apartment. Sam was bent on revenge. Alfred and Janice followed him up the stairs and the three now stood in front the door as Sam knocked repeatedly. No one answered and Sam knocked even harder. He soon started kicking the door, but still got no answer. Alfred and Charmaine backed away and watched Sam jump into the air and kick the door off its hinges.

The three friends were immediately hit with a foul odor that knocked the three of them back into the breezeway the moment the door was kicked open.

"What the fuck is that smell, man?" Alfred asked as he covered his nose with his shirt.

Charmaine was bent at the waist vomiting onto the wooden floor of the hallway, repulsed by the foul smell. Sam covered his mouth and nose with a handkerchief and slowly stepped into the dimly lit apartment. He walked through the ransacked kitchen and entered into the living room, holding the gun out in front of him as he did so, careful not to let himself get caught off guard.

The living room was completely empty, void of furniture, only the stained carpet was left behind. Sam noticed the apartment had two bedrooms. He turned and entered the hall and checked the first bedroom and found it empty. He went into the second bedroom and saw that it, too, was empty. The apartment was void of furniture but it had milk crates and newspapers strewn about. The carpeted floor was littered with small aluminum foil wrappers, and cellophane bags. Rats scurried about. There was feces in the hallway, along with used syringes all throughout the place.

Sam walked towards the bathroom and pushed the door open, and it was there that he found the source of the foul odor. There, dead in the bathroom, was Janice, her lifeless corpse sitting upright on the toilet with her eyes bulging out. There was dried up blood around Janice's mouth and she had a syringe sticking out of her arm. Sam backed into the hallway and covered his mouth as he knelt on one knee and stared at what was left of someone who had once been a friend.

Charmaine and Alfred entered the apartment and crept slowly through the kitchen into the hallway where they saw Sam kneeling on one knee and staring into the bathroom. When they got there, they both looked into the bathroom and saw Janice. They didn't know how long she had been dead, but the smell had them guessing that she had been dead for at least a week.

"Janice!" Charmaine screamed as she approached her cousin's body.

Charmaine gasped and fled back into the hallway when she saw a nest of cockroaches and smaller insects scurry out of Janice's mouth and scatter across her dead body. She screamed at the grisly sight and knelt next to Sam as Alfred closed the bathroom door to hide the scene.

When the police arrived and removed Janice's body, a manhunt got underway for Manhattan. APB's went out across the state of Louisiana, but the man would only continue to remain out of sight. Sam, Charmaine and Alfred went to Sam's home that night in a somber mood. In spite of what Janice had done, their heart went out to their deceased former friend. They broke the news to Gabriella and Henrietta and the two sisters were shocked over what they heard. They couldn't believe that Janice was dead. Gabriella's high school friend, the person who had encouraged her to use her voice for profit, the woman whom she once considered a sister, was now dead.

Gabriella was grief-stricken by the loss. As much as she hated what Janice had done, she never wanted to see the woman dead. Janice's funeral was met with mixed emotions. People hated her for setting Gabriella up, but they also were sad that she died such a horrible death and was found in such a gruesome manner.

In the end, everything led back to Manhattan. A wild man was on the loose and he only had more terror in store for Gabriella, and all the people involved in the woman's life as he continued on with his campaign of terror.

## CHAPTER 30

## THE TRUTH BEHIND BEN'S EVICTION

I opened my eyes slowly and stared at Henrietta as she grabbed a handkerchief from her purse to wipe her tears. The things she told me had left me speechless. I never knew the turmoil my mother, father, and their friends went through with this sadistic maniac of a man.

"You were always kept safe Ben." Henrietta said to me. "Your parents cared for you so much, they wanted to keep those ugly things away from you. That's why you never knew your mother was raped."

I asked Henrietta, just to affirm what she had told me, if my mother was pregnant at the time she was attacked and she told me she was.

"This man was so convinced that Gabriella was having his child, and he just wouldn't let her be, Benjamin."

"I remember my parents taking me to Biloxi Beach, not too long before they were killed. It's like one of the last good memories I could remember."

"They loved the beach, Ben." Henrietta said through a tearful smile. "You were too young to remember how often they went, but I'm glad you remember some of the times y'all shared together as a family. You really only have maybe four or five years of memories. You barely remember the club. A lot of things you have forgotten; but I hope I helped you remember some things."

"You did more than you could ever imagine, Henrietta. I love knowing the history of our family. My grandfather and grandmother were real strong people. That's where you and my mother got y'all strength. I think I have it too."

"You do Ben. But you have your father's strength as well. There's no denying it. Sam could be a real bull when he had to, and from what I know, you were a bull as well—only you went further. Not the route your parents had in mind by a long-shot —but I understand, son—and I don't judge you—nor do I hold you in contempt. Looking back, I wish Sam would have found Manhattan during the time he was looking for him. Everything would've ended differently. God, I wish your parents were here. They had your life mapped out, Ben. You shouldn't be here."

"I remember how happy my mother was. She always played with me, she sung to me almost everyday. I was a happy child. I had a wonderful childhood." I remarked as Henrietta clutched my hand tightly and smiled.

As she did so, I reminisced back to the day we were in Biloxi. I remember me standing in front of my mother as my father stood behind her hugging her while rubbing her belly. The three of us were watching the sun rise over the horizon of the Gulf of Mexico. We were such a happy family. We had so much to look forward to. Henrietta helped me to reconnect with memories long forgotten, but I was also angry at the loss we all suffered when my parents passed away.

"Whatever happened to Manhattan?" I then asked.

"After your parents and baby sister were killed, he just disappeared. I spent all of Gabriella and Sam's savings, mines also, trying to bring this man to justice, but he just vanished into thin air."

"I thought you spent my parents' money on yourself."

"Ben," Henrietta said as she grabbed my hand tightly and looked into my eyes with disbelief.

Before my aunt could speak any further, I knew right then and there that I was wrong in my assessment of what Henrietta had done to me back in March of 1989. She had that same loving look in her eyes the day we argued and I was thrown out of her house. I pressed my hands to my temples and said, "Henrietta, I'm sorry. I thought you was using my momma and daddy's money for yourself."

"I would never betray my sister, nor your father in that way. I told you, there were a lot of things I didn't do right, Benjamin. I remember the argument we had the day I threw you out of that house. I just couldn't bring myself to tell you I had failed in finding out who killed your parents and I could no longer support you. I spent every penny I had looking for that crazy man. I had a double mortgage on the house and was on the verge of losing it. A month after you left, the house was foreclosed. I moved to Washington D.C. to start a new life in education, but I failed in every way. I just couldn't get over losing Gabriella. I returned to New Orleans in ninety-two and took a job teaching music at the YMCA and watched from a distance as you took to the streets."

"You knew what I was doin'?"

"Yes. I wanted to reach out and talk to you, but I knew the person you had become. I was afraid to talk you. I remember how mad you were at me and I actually believed that you would hurt me. I'm such a coward, Ben. Gabriella and Sam lived life to the fullest. I never had the courage to do any of what they did. I watched them enjoy life as life slowly passed me by. I guess it's fair to say I lived vicariously through them. Their joy was my joy. You were my joy. I spent a lot of time with you. We were close once upon a time, and I hope we can be that way again."

"I always wanted a close relationship with you Henrietta. I wish you would've come to me earlier. I would've never done a thing to hurt you, no matter how mad I would've gotten, ya' dig? You my blood. The last of my blood and we need each other now more than ever." I said as I looked around at the concrete walls separating me from the free world. "I have a serious fight on my hands with these appeals, but if and when I

329

get out, I would like for us to reconnect."

"You two already have reconnected." Yiska intervened. "The few days Henrietta has spent here, Ben, has drawn you two together in ways never imagined. Just think—she flew all the way from Louisiana—drove through blustering snow all on her own—in order to see you and make amends. After years gone by, you two now sit face to face reliving Holland Family History. You two have laughed together, cried together, and reopened lost memories of days long gone. It can only get better for you two," he concluded as he smiled and excused himself from the table. "See you at dinner, son."

Henrietta and I sat for another hour or so talking about the last few months of my parents life and I shared with her one of the last happy memories I had of my mother and father…

*******

## Thanksgiving 1983

"Momma, can I have that spoon with the chocolate on it when you're finished," nine year-old Ben Holland asked his mother.

Gabriella stood over the stove in the kitchen of *Persia's* and smiled down at her son. "Yes son, when I'm done, you can lick the spoon clean. Just like the little puppy you have at home likes to lick your plate clean."

Gabriella had just bought her son a small Boston Terrier puppy in which he named Rollo after his favorite character on the comedy show *Sanford and Son*. Ben loved that little puppy, and he took it nearly everywhere he went.

"I ain't no puppy, momma!"

"I ain't?" Gabriella asked as she tied Ben's neck length black silky hair into a ponytail and placed a hair net on his head.

"I mean, I am not a puppy! And Rollo doesn't lick my plate!" Ben said as he corrected his speech.

"Mighty funny I saw him just last night with your plate. The one that had the steamed broccoli on it? The broccoli that you said tasted great?"

"I ate the broccoli the first time. But Daddy put another helping on the plate. He said I needed iron in my diet—I told him that was already an iron man. Anyway, Rollo needed the broccoli more than me because he's so little."

"We talked about that, me and your daddy. He said he did give you another helping, but you said you would eat it. So that means you told a story. Now, what will you do to make it up to me and your father before we really get mad and punish you from your friends?"

"Momma, you can't take Lubby out of my life! None of those girls can you take out of my life right now because I'm close to making Lubby mines!"

Gabriella laughed and said, "How do you know Lubby even wants you in her life, son?"

"The eyes, momma," Ben said as he pointed to his own brown eyes. "The eyes never lie. That's what my friend Calvin told me. He said that when a girl likes you, she will always smile and look you in the eyes."

Gabriella then put on a wide, beautiful smile and knelt down before her son. "What is my smile and eyes saying now, Ben?"

Ben knew his mother all-too-well. He knew she wasn't pleased over his feeding the broccoli to Rollo. "You're going to whip me if I give Rollo another plate of food that I don't want aren't you?" Ben answered seriously as he stared his mother in the eyes.

"Yes, little man. So let's not let that happen again. And now you know that mister Calvin doesn't know squat. He's still scared of Dominique from what I hear." Gabriella said as she stirred the cake batter and delved into her son's world of friends.

"That maybe true about Cal, but I ain't scared of Lubby, momma."

"She has you by three years, son. What are you goin' to do

with an older girl like Lubby?"

"I like the older women. They more set in their ways."

Gabriella laughed aloud and said, "You've been listening a little too hard to adult conversations, Benjamin."

While Ben and his mother were conversing, in walked Alfred holding a sack filled with four turkeys.

"What's up Gabriella? Hey Ben, come help me and your daddy unload these turkeys for Henrietta and Charmaine so they can fry 'em up for tonight."

Ben ran out the back door of the club just in time to see his father unloading turkeys from the backseat of the car.

"Son, let me see how strong you are!" Sam snapped as he handed nine year-old Ben four large turkeys.

Ben struggled with the turkeys, two in each hand, as his slim frame wobbled back towards the kitchen door of the club. Sam and Alfred laughed aloud at the young lad.

"I got five dollars say he don't make it to the kitchen with them turkeys, Sam!" Alfred remarked through loud laughter.

"You got a bet, brother! Come on, Ben!" Sam yelled as he backpedaled in front of his son cheering him on. "If you wanna earn that twenty dollar bill that Uncle Alfred got for ya' you gotta carry the turkeys all the way to the door without dropping 'em."

Young Ben's eyes grew wide after hearing his father and he struggled with all his might to make it to the door.

"Twenty dollars son!" Sam yelled as continued cheering his son on. "Twenty whole dollars!"

"I'm the iron man!" Ben yelled aloud as he dropped the turkeys and sat on the ground out of breath.

Alfred looked at Sam in surprise as Sam snickered back to him. "When I said I was giving Ben twenty dollars? The bet was five!"

"He needed a little motivation, brother! A bet is bet no matter how you win! Pay up, sucker!"

"Aww, Sam, you jived me, man! Ben wouldna never brought them turkeys that far for five dollars. That's low, man." Alfred said as he smiled at his friend.

"I know! You tried to get over on my son—but we just got over on you! Where our money?"

"Jivin'? Man this nineteen eighty-three and you still talk like that, Uncle Alfred? A bet is a bet. Pay up, sucker!" Ben remarked as he ran up and began to play fight with Alfred as Sam jumped in to help his son.

"Oh now y'all gone double team me, huh?" Alfred asked jokingly as he grabbed a turkey off the ground and began using it as a shield.

The three males played out in the cool crisp morning air, running up and down the alley behind the club play fighting. Ben was having the time of his life playing with his father and Alfred, something the three did on many occasions.

As the three continued playing, Charmaine came out of the back door of the club and looked down the alley and saw Sam and Ben getting the best of Alfred. She laughed at the fun they were having and wanted to join in so she ran to help her man. She ran up to the three males and stood next to Alfred and play fought with Ben as Sam and Alfred fought with one another.

Just then, Yvonne came out of the kitchen and saw what was transpiring. She ran to Sam's aid and wrestled with Charmaine, giving Ben a hand.

Meanwhile, Gabriella and Henrietta were in the kitchen wondering where the rest of the bunch was with the turkeys. Gabriella walked slowly towards the back door and out into the alley. She looked and saw the activity taking place in the alley and she walked slowly towards her husband. Gabriella was showing now, as she was seven months pregnant, so she took her time approaching the group. She stood beside Sam careful not to get knocked down and encouraged her husband by imitating his blows.

It didn't take long for thirty-five year-old Henrietta to come out of the kitchen to see what the delay was. When she saw what was happening, she walked briskly down the alley.

"Hey! Hey y'all knuckle heads! We got work to do down here and y'all out here having a back alley brawl?" Henrietta said, pretending to be serious.

The group stopped in their tracks breathing hard and laughing aloud. As Henrietta, dressed in a purple dress and black boots, approached, the group stared at her as they slowly grew silent.

"Y'all should be ashamed of yourselves! Got my nephew out here scrapping like the junkyard dog! And give me this turkey, Alfred!" Henrietta snapped as she snatched the turkey away from Alfred and stood in between the group and eyed them seriously. "And you," she then said as she turned to face Gabriella, "you nice and pregnant! You could get hurt out here with these hoodlums!"

Gabriella bowed her head in shame. She thought she had really upset her sister and she was truly mad at her, something she really didn't like to do to Henrietta. Just then Henrietta smiled at her younger sister and stated in a low tone as she slowly approached a crescendo and swung lightly on Charmaine with the turkey. "That's why I gotta help my li'l sister win this barroom brawl this mornin'! Come on suckas!" Henrietta joked as she began using the turkey as a shield and burst into laughter as the group began play fighting again.

The group played around for another five minutes and slowly walked back to the club. They were tired but happy. Ben, who was still full of energy, got the chocolate covered spoon as he sat on the counter and watched the adults prepare dinner for the patrons that were coming to the club that night.

The club opened and it was another successful Thanksgiving bash. Ben's parents had let him stay up with them on this night. It was the first time Ben was allowed to join his parents at the club. He helped his mother and father behind the bar by stacking glasses. He even had a huge glass of ginger ale all for himself. It made Ben feel all grown up to have a drink all to his own. Never had he had so much fun.

As the night wore on, it was getting close to Gabriella's

performance time. Patrons in the club watched with curiosity as the stage was being set for one of Gabriella's most memorable routines. The woman hadn't performed at *Persia's* since she was attacked inside the club back in June, but she wanted to assure her fans that she was not through with her career.

The stage was being set up with a baby blue piano, an electric organ, and a drum set. The piano and organ was set in an L-shape on the stage and a chair was placed behind the instruments. The drum set was to the left of the piano and organ if you were facing the stage.

Sam waited patiently outside the dressing room for Gabriella, Yvonne and Charmaine to finish adorning their attire. When they were done, they called Sam into the room. Sam walked in and saw his wife wearing a dark grey pair of Capri pants with a pair of white knee-length three-inched heeled leather boots and a white thin-wool sweater to hide her belly a little. Her hair was pulled back into a single ponytail, and she had on a pair of mirror tinted sunglasses. Yvonne and Charmaine were dressed the same, except they wore black sweaters and black boots with their grey Capris. The three women looked like certified rock stars in their outfits.

Sam was taken aback by Gabriella and her friends' appearance.

"Y'all three look gorgeous. Y'all gone really knock 'em dead tonight."

"Just like we always do, Sam." Charmaine answered.

Gabriella and Yvonne agreed and the group slowly began to walk towards the dance floor and climb the steps to the stage, Gabriella being aided by Charmaine and Sam.

Gabriella was to perform a solo act before her friends joined her on stage. As she sat down and took her seat, two guitar players took their place behind her, followed by the drummer. Gabriella said nothing as she adjusted her microphone and the lights went off in the club. People gasped at the darkness, but it was brief, as a white strobe light began to rotate in the center of the club.

Gabriella looked over to the photographer and the three camera operators she had rented for the event to signal she was ready, and they nodded and threw a thumbs up sign. Gabriella nodded towards Clyde and he turned the spotlight on the stage. The cameras began to roll, and the two guitar players began stringing the notes to *House of the Rising Sun*, originally sung by The Animals in 1964.

When the crowd recognized the tune they began making excited remarks.

"Go on, Gabriella!"

"Sing it, sister!"

"This gone be a bad performance, y'all!" people yelled aloud at random.

The two guitarists played on as Gabriella stared at the audience through her mirror tinted glasses and began to sing the lyrics.

*"There is, a house...in New Orleans..they call the rising sun...and it's been...the ruin...of many a poor boy...and God... I know...I'm one..."*

The audience clapped and cheered when Gabriella began to play the electric organ with her right hand, and baby piano with her left. She was putting her best effort forward this night in order to let everyone know just how much talent she truly possessed. Gabriella's voice grew louder as she continued.

*"My mother was a tailor...she sewed my new blue jeans...my father was a gambling man, down, in New Orleans..."*

The crowd was in awe over the performance. Gabriella's rendition of the song was soul-stirring. She added her own flavor to the ominous tune and really brought it to life in her own special way and voice. The crowd stood in stunned silence as Gabriella and her band played and sung one of the most intense versions of The Animals' song they'd ever heard performed live. When Gabriella and the guitarists were done, the crowd went crazy with applause and praise and begged for an encore.

Gabriella would deliver. She was joined by Charmaine and Yvonne, and the three of them sung one more song—*I'm On Your Side* by Angela Bofill.

Gabriella sat on stage in front of the baby blue piano and played the notes to the song as she, Charmaine, and Yvonne sung the chorus in tune with Gabriella. It was a beautiful rendition and some of the women in the crowd were in tears by the song's end.

After Gabriella concluded her two special performances, she began to say her good-byes to the club she had grown to love so dearly. The cameras continued to roll while Gabriella sat on stage behind her piano thanking the patrons for believing in her and her husband's dream as much as the two of them did. She then did a sort of impromptu farewell interview with the crowd as she strummed a few keys on the piano and answered various questions as she conversed with her friends, family and fans.

"We wouldn't even come here if it wasn't for you Gabriella," a female patron yelled aloud. "Nobody don't care about Sam!" She added as the crowd erupted into light laughter. "Just kidding Sam baby, we love y'all man." the female then stated as she raised her glass and tilted it towards Sam, who was standing behind the bar beside his son.

Sam smiled from behind the bar as Henrietta caught a snapshot of him, along with his son sitting on the counter beside him.

"And we love you too! All of y'all." Gabriella added.

"Gabriella, what ya' havin' a boy or a girl," another female patron asked.

"Ohh, I'm having a little girl! Sam wanted another son but it wasn't meant to be. We have Ben Holland, my handsome son over there with his daddy, and soon," Gabriella said as she clutched the microphone and looked down at her swollen belly, "soon we'll have a baby girl named Samantha Holland. It was as close to Sam's name as I could get and feel comfortable. Samantha Holland is my baby girl and I love her so." Gabriella said lovingly as she rubbed her belly.

Gabriella then got up from behind the piano and walked through the crowd and chatted with the patrons with Alfred following close behind. Everyone congratulated her as they left the club. They also told her to hurry back as they were looking forward to hearing her perform again.

Over the next two months Gabriella spent nearly every day with her son, Ben and they were closer than they'd ever been in life. Ben loved having his mother home every day when he came home from school, and he couldn't wait for the chance to finally hold his baby sister. Gabriella mostly hung around the house those two months eating and perfecting several songs she, Charmaine and Yvonne had written together.

Sam had set up a recording session, complete with professional producers from Atlantic Records and an audition in New York for a couple of A&R representatives on the Jive Record label in June of the following year. Gabriella, Yvonne, and Charmaine worked hard on the songs that the three women were writing together in hopes of gaining a record deal. Either way, Gabriella was scheduled to begin recording her first solo album in June of 1984, and that was more than enough to keep her satisfied, because she now had a chance to become a national recording artist.

Charmaine and Yvonne were so excited for their friend, they helped Gabriella with her lyrics on a daily basis; and they kept telling Gabriella how great she would sound once she got inside the recording booth in New York City. Gabriella had to constantly remind her friends that the three of them were going to New York to record once Samantha was born.

"We are a group. We should be thinking of a name for ourselves before we get to New York." Gabriella would say each and every time her girls congratulated her.

Yvonne and Charmaine really didn't care if they made it with Gabriella or not. In their eyes, if anyone deserved a chance at fame and fortune, it was Gabriella; and they were doing all they could to make sure that their friend would be ready to go to New York and show the world what talent she possessed.

# CHAPTER 31

## GETTING BACK IN FOCUS

I glanced over at Henrietta and she was smiling from ear to ear. She remembered those days all so well. We laughed heartily at the fun we had during my mother's pregnancy with Samantha.

"Your mother was an ambitious woman, Ben. By her middle-twenties, she had really become career driven; and your father and their friends was there every step of the way. Your parents took real good care of you and they loved you a great deal, son. Gabriella wasn't your average mother, you know? She had a lot going on in her life during her pregnancy with your sister, and she still found the time to make sure you had clean clothes, a hot meal and a warm bed. Your parents were very successful people, Ben. Someday, when you're released from this place, you will be, too. It's in your blood, son. It's a shame that bastard destroyed their dream. That singer, Alicia Keys, I think is her name—she reminds me so much of your mother. From her singing style, right down to her looks; only your mother had grey eyes. Gabriella played the piano superbly, and she could sing even better. Your mother was doing that twenty-five years before Miss Keys came on the scene. Gabriella would've been great back then, just as Alicia Keys is great today. He destroyed your parents dream and ruined your life. This should not be happening. I need to shut up, because I'm getting angry again." Henrietta said as she began to get down-hearted.

I could tell Henrietta was thinking about my mother. Emotions were running high at this point; I knew Henrietta was angry and sad, but I still had to ask her about the night my parents died.

"You really don't remember?"

"I somewhat do, but it's sort of vague. I have, like, flashes I can't quite put together. I was hoping you could tell me."

Henrietta related to me the events that transpired that night and I cried silently. God, it hurt me to hear what happened. I somewhat remember the events as Henrietta spoke, but something she said just didn't sit right with me.

Henrietta said my little sister burned in the fire and the authorities had only found a few bone fragments. I can't remember Samantha's face, not exactly. I do know she had light-tan skin and a small brown dot just under her left eye. Henrietta told me it was a beauty mark; that's the only way I remember a little bit of her features. As Henrietta continued to relate the story, I listened intently as she brought the last vestiges of my parents' life to a close. I must say I had mixed emotions about the history I had learned over the few days Henrietta spent with me. I was happy to learn how my father and mother had built a life for themselves; and I was glad to learn of the love they shared and the type of life they led. I was also sad over the way things had ended; angry at the tragedy. Still, in spite of all that I learned, something just didn't sit right with me about the night my parents died.

Henrietta decided to stay a couple of more days and we just talked about the present. She vowed to help out with my case as best she could so I gave her Katrina's phone number and told her to contact her and she could fill Henrietta in on how the case was going whenever she felt the desire to do so. The last day of Henrietta's visit, she, Yiska and I sat down and had a nice spiritual discussion. We prayed together and just before Henrietta left, she hugged me tightly. She then looked me in the eyes and told me she loved me. To hear that from Henrietta meant everything to me; I haven't heard those words from a blood relative in years, almost twenty-one years to be exact. I was moved to tears, I tell you. As hard a man as I was on the streets, those three words Henrietta said to me at that moment caused me to lose my composure completely. I broke down where we stood and I held her tightly.

Here I was, a grown man at thirty-one years of age, crying like a baby, and holding on to my aunt for dear life. All the love, all the memories of the happy life we once led had come back at that moment. I didn't want Henrietta to go. I looked into her brown eyes and told her I loved her and she promised to return in few months. She wiped the tears from my face with her handkerchief and then wiped away her own tears with that same handkerchief. Our family tears brought us together again.

"We must look like a couple of fools standing here, crying like this," she said as she started to laugh. "I missed you dearly, Ben. Can you ever forgive me for what I've done?"

"I had forgiven you a long time ago, Henrietta. You owe me nothing; just know you will always have a special place my heart, Auntie." I replied, causing Henrietta to blush.

"I haven't heard that since you were eleven years old. It sounds good to me."

"Well get used to it, because I plan on pestering the hell out of you to keep you in my life—Auntie!"

"Pester on Ben, pester on!" Henrietta said as she laughed and hugged me one more time. I was so glad to have my aunt back in my life.

Henrietta gave me her address and phone number and told me to call anytime. We knew we had to keep the lines of communication open to remain a solid, stable family—as small a family as we were. Henrietta hugged Yiska tightly and told him she looked forward to seeing him again. She thought Yiska was nice and she invited him to write and call her as well. Yiska's eyes lit up when he heard that. When Henrietta left, Yiska couldn't stop talking about her. I listened loosely as I sat in his cell. My mind was elsewhere, though; namely on the night my parents died.

In spite of what I learned, something about what Henrietta told me about the night my parents died just didn't sit right with me. Something was amiss. I couldn't put my finger on it though; eventually, the nightmares returned and I struggled for the next couple of months to remember what I had seen. Henrietta had taken me to the threshold; but it was up to me to put the pieces together and accurately recount what happened that night. My soul was once again tormented. I cried often, struggling with myself, pleading with God to help me, but it was all in vain. I just couldn't put it together.

After a while, my focus shifted to my appeal. The nightmares persisted, so I decided to write down everything I dreamt of each night I had a nightmare. It seemed to be working as, slowly, very slowly, the pieces were coming together. My main focus, however, had become my appeal. I could chase my memories on the outside. That was my reasoning.

Katrina had written me a letter and stated that she and Dante` O'Malley were scheduled to pay me a visit in April, which was now about a month away. She said good news was on the horizon. I looked forward to seeing my friend again. It had been a long time since we sat face to face and talked.

While wrestling with my repressed memories, I looked forward to meeting this lawyer. I felt good about that situation; Katrina would not fly all the way to Colorado to deliver a mediocre message. So what was on the horizon was huge, at least I hoped it would be. After reading Katrina's letter, I turned off my lamp and went to sleep thinking about her visit the following month.

## CHAPTER 32

### THE GANG'S ALL HERE

Dante` O'Malley had just hung up the phone with his paralegal assistant and immediately called Katrina at her home in Phoenix. Benjamin's court date was now set, and Dante` wanted to notify her personally. Ben also hadn't heard the news as of yet, and Dante` needed to discuss the case with him face to face. Dante` was hoping for an outright acquittal, but he believed sincerely that that would be a long shot. The esteemed counselor, however, knew for certain that he would be able to get the jury to find Ben guilty of a much lesser charge at worst. Dante` had so much good news to share with Katrina, he couldn't wait to get to Phoenix and tell her how much progress he had made with Ben's case. When Katrina answered, O'Malley told her that the subpoenas were all to be delivered that day to her friends in Atlanta and New Orleans.

"Did you call any of them to let them know what was going on?" he asked over the phone.

"I only called to confirm their addresses a few weeks back like I told you. I told them I was inviting them to Phoenix for a Ninth Ward reunion and I needed their addresses confirmed so I could mail invitations." Katrina stated as she smiled from behind her desk in her home office.

"Why didn't you tell them the truth, Katrina?" O'Malley asked in a frustrated tone.

"That is the truth, Dante`. When Ben gets out, we coming back here to Phoenix and celebrate his release."

"I'm glad you have all this faith in me, Katrina, but without your friends, we don't have a fighting—"

"Dante`, trust me." Katrina interjected. "I know these people. They would do anything for Ben Holland, just trust me. I haven't seen them in months and they haven't talked to nor have they seen Ben in years; but it doesn't matter, they'll do their part. This is just a friendly wake-up call. When they see my name in the subpoenas, my phone will start ringing off the hook. I'm just trying to retighten the bond we all once shared. I know what I'm doing, Dante`, don't worry. If neither of them call me, I'll call them and verify everything for you, okay?"

"Alright, Katrina. I know you know your friends better than I do. If circumstances change, however, give me a call, okay, young lady? I'll see you next month." Dante ended as he and Katrina ended their conversation.

After the call, Katrina exited her office to join her son and Celeste, who were in the kitchen. The three of them were going to make homemade pizza, Li'l Tim's favorite. As she fired up the brick oven in her gourmet kitchen, the flames quickly reminded Katrina of her old friend, Nonstop. He was a rapper from the Ninth Ward who now resided in Atlanta. The flames in the brick oven resembled Nonstop's current CD cover, *HOT ICE*. The popular rapper was currently on a nation-wide tour, and since he had no direct ties to what happened in New Orleans in '99, it wasn't necessary for him to cut his tour short and appear in Denver, Colorado on Ben's behalf.

Derrick and Torre`, however, were to play a crucial part in Ben's release. Katrina smiled when she thought of her old friends from back in the day. It had been a while since she had seen the two young men, and her girls back in New Orleans. As she cut bell peppers on the island counter, Katrina wondered what they all were doing this evening.

Atlanta

"Yeah? You gone take one hundred thousand dollars over a quarter of a million dollars? What school you went to mutherfucka so I know not ta' send my people there!" Derrick yelled into the speaker phone from behind his huge, black marble desk.

Derrick's business partner, Torre`, laughed as he stood beside him and listened to the call. Derrick Burkman and Torre` Spears were old friends of Ben Holland. The two of them, along with Jason Witherspoon, once ran a huge dope house in the Ninth Ward and were once under Ben Holland's command. After the crew was dismantled, Derrick and Torre` moved to Atlanta and started a record label with the money they made off the streets.

They formed *Dirty Deeds, LLC* and signed Nonstop to a record deal after he was dropped from Universal Records amid accusations that he was involved in a fight down in Daytona, Florida that left one person dead and another injured. Despite his troubles, Nonstop quickly became a hot rapper in the south and was propelling himself onto the national scene with Derrick and Torre` backing him through their label.

Derrick and Torre` also signed an R&B singer from Jacksonville, Florida, who was the label's current hottest artist and top earner, named Narshea (Narshay). *Dirty Deeds* was a success story—two local drug dealers who went on to become millionaires after grinding on the dirty streets of the south.

Although Derrick sold plenty of cocaine in his day, he never killed anyone, nor participated in any of Ben Holland's murders. Torre`, however, had gone on a hit with Ben Holland and had aided him in the murdering of a set of twins named Burtell and Jarell back in '99. *Dirty Deeds* lived up to its name. The two young men had indeed done some dirt back in the day, but when they started making legitimate money, Derrick and Torre` left the drug game alone completely. Their appetite for the streets remained solid, however; and a lot of the music *Dirty Deeds* produced often reflected the violent, fast-money-making lifestyle that Derrick and Torre` had once lived.

Derrick was trying to convince another rapper to sign to his label that evening, but the rumors swirling around *Dirty Deeds* frightened the young artist. Many people had come to believe some of the things that Nonstop, and several up and coming artists on the label rapped about on their songs because the rumors had Derrick and Torre` tied to the drug game back in New Orleans.

Whether the rumors were true or not, derrick didn't care. To him, it only added to the label's reputation and kept them in the headlines. Derrick hung up on the rapper, calling him a coward in the process.

An hour later, Derrick and Torre` were going over their itinerary for the following day. Derrick's six foot, two-hundred and twenty-five pound frame swayed back in forth in his leather chair, his ebony skin dripping sweat profusely as the a/c unit on the twenty-third floor of the forty-one story black tinted glass and steel structure was under repair.

"Man! It's hotter than baby piss in this mutherfucka! We paying all this money for this shit, and they got us sweating like some fuckin' slaves in here!"

"They tryna remind us that we still niggas!" Torre` answered as he sat on a leather couch in front of the desk, his tall lanky frame back and forth as he puffed on a huge blunt while listening to Nonstop's new CD.

As the two sat and talked, in walked Narshea. The five foot seven, one-hundred and forty pound diva was angry that someone had scheduled her for two publicity tour dates in the state of Oklahoma. She flung the door open and walked right up to Derrick's desk to state her case.

"How in the hell, or rather, who in the hell set me up for a fuckin' appearance in Oklahoma City, Oklahoma? Take me off that shit!"

"Whoa, whoa, mutherfucka! You don't just walk in here and give orders and shit! You go where we say you going!" Derrick announced as he revved back in his over-sized leather chair.

"Oklahoma, Derrick? Who in the fuck that's black goes to Oklahoma? I can do Dallas, Saint Louis, fuck it I'll even go to

Kansas City! But Oklahoma? Shit like that ain't even on my radar! That's fly-over-country, nigga! I don't do Okla—"

"Man, I thought I told security no fuckin' visitors!" Derrick said towards Torre` as the two began laughing.

"A visitor? A visitor? Nigga, I work here! I *am* Dirty Deeds! I want out this Oklahoma City shit, Derrick! I got better shit ta' do than—"

"Calm down, fuck!" Derrick yelled as he slapped the desk and took a toke of the blunt handed to him by Torre`. "It's late and you cranky and shit! You had your latte today? You need one?"

"A la—a latte? Nigga I don't want a mutherfuckin' latte! I want out of Oklahoma citay! How 'bout that one?"

"You get a lot of love out that way. It'll do you good to let some of your fans from the heart of the Midwest see you in the flesh. You can sign autographs and talk to 'em you know? See what they like and don't like. Maybe set up a couple of tour dates." Torre` interjected.

"Umm, who the fuck are you?" Narshea asked as she eyed Torre` disdainfully.

Narshea knew very well who Torre` was. The two actually had a thing for one another, but neither wanted to admit that fact. Everybody at the label knew that the truth of the matter was that neither Narshay nor Torre` wanted to be the first to concede their emotions—even if they really were attracted to one another.

"Y-y-y you know who the f-f-f-fuck I am, b-b-bitch! Don't tr-tr-try and—"

"Shut your stut-stut-stuttering ass the fuck up! " Narshea responded through laughter, cutting Torre off. Torre` still stuttered at times, but it mainly occurred when he was embarrassed or nervous. He had a speech therapist and now had more control over his speech impediment, but whenever he became nervous or embarrassed, he had no control over his speech.

"One of these d-d-days my foot g-g-gone go so far up your

ass that every time y-y-you blink you gone see this Lugz logo you horse-mouth m-mother—"

"You wish you can slide somethin' else up this round, jelly ass doncha? Ya' giraffe looking son of a—"

"Why don't you two just fuck and get it over with?" Wallace, the light-skinned, tall and slender thirty-six-year old Entertainment Lawyer for the record label asked as he closed the door behind him and walked towards Derrick's desk.

Wallace handed Derrick a subpoena and Derrick opened it as he continued to laugh and puff on the blunt. His smile dropped when he saw he was scheduled to appear at Ben Holland's retrial in Denver, Colorado the following month.

Torre` had gotten his and opened it as well.

"A m-m-murder trial?" Torre` stated lowly as he grew worried, thinking about some of the things he had done in the past. When he saw Ben's name, Torre` was not only nervous, he was terrified. He thought back to the day he helped Ben kill two people and thought, the same as Derrick at the out-set, that he had just received a subpoena. A subpoena it was, but as Torre` read further, he eased up.

"Ain't this a bitch? Ben gettin' out!" Derrick and Torre` exuberantly exclaimed as they smiled at one another.

"Let me call Katrina's ass so she can fill us in on this shit!" Derrick announced. "I wonder if anybody else got a subpoena." he added as he dialed Katrina's number.


New Orleans

"Hey, ya' nappy-headed bastard! I *told* you ta' sit your funky ass down didn't I?" JoAnne Clemmons yelled towards an eleven year-old child.

JoAnne was Oscar Henderson's old girlfriend. Oscar was killed inside the airport in '99 when Ben retaliated against the Lapiente` brothers.

Thirty-five year-old JoAnne had detention duty this day; it was a part of her job as a school teacher at Colten Middle

School in New Orleans' Ninth Ward that she despised.

"I hate this part of the job! I swear if I had a gun on me right now I'd blow my own muther—"

"Hmm, hmm," the school principal coughed aloud, getting JoAnne's attention as he stood in the door way holding an envelope.

JoAnne, realizing she had been heard, smiled and danced over to her boss. She snapped her fingers as she did so, trying to appease the man and make him believe she was in a good mood. He frowned intently as he handed JoAnne the envelope and walked off shaking his head. The woman thought she was fired. When she read the subpoena, however, she was subdued. She then cursed Katrina in silence as she grabbed her cell phone and dialed Katrina's number.

*"I wonder if anybody else got one of these."* JoAnne wondered as the phone rang.

Twenty four-old Alicia Mason was another friend of Ben's. She and her dead lover, a young woman named Tanaka Romaire, often partied with the Ben Holland Gang. Alicia was at the hospital back in '99, trying to convince Ben not to go after the person who had killed Ben's fiancée, Anastasia Gordon, and had almost killed Katrina.

Alicia had just finished a meeting with her district manager and was feeling good this day. She had been an assistant manager of a large department store for years, and she was just awarded a lead manager's position. She was now lead manager over the entire store in the Clearview Mall. She had just received a substantial raise that would help out tremendously because she had purchased a new home a couple of years earlier and was planning on remodeling her kitchen.

Alicia and an older black female, both dressed in professional business suits, were walking out of the office when Alicia was greeted by two sheriff's deputies. One of the men handed her a subpoena and Alicia immediately smiled at her district manager in embarrassment. It was an awkward situation to say the least, but after reading the letter, Alicia assured her boss that she wasn't in any trouble. The woman left after being reassured, and only then did Alicia whisper in a low, excited tone, "Ben coming home!"

She hurried to her office, grabbed her cell phone and dialed Katrina's number, eager to talk to her friend in order to get the full scoop. *"I wonder who else going to Colorado,"* she asked herself as Katrina's phone rang.

Dana Shelby was filling prescriptions in her parents' pharmacy when she noticed two Orleans Parish sheriff's deputies approaching the counter. Dana was an exceptionally smart female, having earned a double degree in pharmacy and biology. She now worked side by side with her parents in their family clinic located in the Ninth Ward, and she was set to inherit the store when her parents retired in five years. Dana signed for the subpoena, worried that she was now implicated in something her dead lover Jason Witherspoon had done in the past. She was relieved when she saw she was only scheduled to testify on behalf of Ben Holland.

It then dawned on Dana. *"Oh my god! He got a new trial? He might get out!"* she said to herself excitedly as she grabbed the telephone to call Katrina.

Thirty-one year-old Kantrell Luckett was inside her beauty salon in the Lower Ninth Ward braiding a patron's hair as she and a group of females listened to Nonstop's CD.

"Yeah, that's the shit right there, bitches! That nigga straight out da' fuckin' mighty nine, ya' heard me, hoes?" she asked aloud as she danced to the music while braiding her customer's hair.

Kantrell soon began talking about Ben and how he and his boys used to swing into her salon and buy everybody lunch as she listened to Nonstop spit rhymes.

"They don't make niggas like Dirty Red 'nem no mo', y'all! My niggas used to come through and comp all them hungry hoes from back in the day before they had they asses in the air over there at the Hyatt!"

"'Trell when the last time you talked to Ben?" a female asked aloud.

"I ain't heard from that nigga since the day of the shootout at the airport, but Katrina say he good. She got something working with that article she found in my drawer last year, but I ain't heard from her since."

Kantrell was telling the story of how she obtained the news article Katrina had found when two sheriff's deputies walked into her salon. Blunts went out, bottles of Hypnotic and Alize` was hidden and the talking ceased while Kantrell signed for the subpoena. Kantrell was scared shitless because she thought her rowdy shop was being closed down. She was relieved when she saw she only had to testify for Ben.

"Damn!" Kantrell said aloud once the deputies left. "I was just talking about Ben! That nigga gone live a *long* time, man! I *know* he 'bouta get out! Especially when I get my lying ass up there on the stand! Hand me my cell phone! I gotta call Katrina! I wonder where everybody at, man!"

After much worrying about their past lives when they were first handed the subpoenas, all of Ben Holland's friends began preparing themselves for the trip to Colorado.

Katrina knew what she was doing, she had indeed sparked a reunion of sorts as everybody had contacted one another and were looking forward to playing a role in aiding Ben Holland's return to the free world.

## CHAPTER 33

## I GOT YOUR BACK

Katrina sat in the office of her restaurant on a warm night in April. She had finished a hard day's work in the restaurant and was now going over the delivery schedule for the next week since she was going to be in Colorado. She had to make sure she left enough money in the petty cash so that her assistant manager, Priscilla Tyson, would have enough cash to cover the expenses. Katrina figured Priscilla would need at least three-thousand dollars in cash to keep the restaurant afloat whilst she was gone. The restaurant had made just under eleven-thousand dollars this day and Katrina began counting out the money she needed to place into the restaurant's safe. The rest she would tuck away in a safe at the condo she owned directly across from Bank One Ball Park in downtown Phoenix. Katrina rarely stayed at the place, but she bought it to use as a personal escape destination whenever she felt she needed to get away from her hectic home life back in Mesa. She had also been meaning to place some emergency money inside the condo and tonight, she was intent on doing just so. Katrina finished all of her business, grabbed her purse and a small satchel containing the cash and tucked her Glock .40 in her holster and exited the premises with her assistant manager.

As Katrina rode down the wide boulevard leading to the

condo, she thought about Ben and smiled to herself. Katrina was scheduled to meet Dante O'Malley at the airport in two hours and they would head out to see Ben in the morning. She was so happy to bring the good news to Ben that she couldn't contain her joy. She laughed aloud as she rode in her convertible Bentley with her stereo blaring *Slow Jam*, a hit song released by the rappers Twista, Kanye West, and singer/actor Jamie Foxx. Katrina let her hair down and let it flow in the warm spring air as she cruised through downtown Phoenix. She arrived at her condo within fifteen minutes, entered the key code and waited patiently for the gate to open. She then drove up the stoned driveway and exited her car, giving the valet a fifty dollar bill as he entered her Bentley to park it in its designated parking spot.

Katrina entered her lavish, white-carpeted, two bedroom condo and the first thing she did was begin to fill her over-sized Jacuzzi with warm water. She then exited the bathroom and walked past the Denmark glass dining room set and the plush Italian leather sofa set in the living room over to the brick wall above the fireplace and removed a medium sized exclusive oil painting of Tony Montana standing behind his desk with Manny Ribera holding M-16 rifles. There were stacks of money and bags of cocaine on the desk along with two AK-47's as well.

An old Chinese guy in one of the malls Katrina frequented had painted the picture from memory; he told her that his painting is his rendition of what the end of the movie *Scarface* should have featured—Scarface and Manny going all out to take down Sosa. The picture could only be described as "gangster" in Katrina's eyes and she was compelled to purchase it on the spot and it was a steal at only one-hundred dollars.

Katrina understood fully what the Chinese guy was saying, and she took it step further by applying the man's vision to her life. Katrina had felt for the longest that if Manny were alive at the time of the shootout during Lamont's funeral, things would've ended much differently for Ben. They may have eclipsed Damenga before things had gotten so far gone. Katrina stared at the painting for several seconds, picturing

Ben and Manny in the painting. She shook off her thoughts with a smile, mentally admiring the bad boys she once ran with as she opened the safe and placed her money inside before placing everything back in order. She then walked out onto the balcony overlooking downtown Phoenix as she sipped a small glass of cognac and waited for her tub to fill with water.

Katrina soon went back inside and undressed and sat down and slowly sunk into the jetting water and reached for the phone to call Celeste to check on her son, who she learned was in the gym with the dogs eating pizza and watching his father on TV. Remembering Tim had a big game, Katrina clicked on the TV on the wall at the foot of her tub situated over a garden in order to check on her husband to see how he was doing.

The Phoenix Suns were in a playoff race for the third seed in their conference. They were playing in Milwaukee against the Milwaukee Bucks this night and the game was nearly over. Katrina's husband was the best clutch shooter on the Suns' team; and with six seconds left on the clock, down by one, there was no doubt who was going to take the last shot for Phoenix.

Katrina watched attentively as the game resumed, watching the screen with hawk eyes as the Suns passed the ball to and fro.

"Get it to my husband!" Katrina yelled at the screen.

With four seconds left, the ball was passed to another player who dribbled once and passed the ball to Timothy with two seconds left on the clock.

"That's it right there! Come on, bitch don't you dare let me down!" Katrina yelled as she sat up in the tub.

Katrina wanted Timothy with the ball not so that he could hit the winning shot—she wanted him with the ball so he could be the reason the Phoenix Suns lost the game. That wish would not be granted, however; Timothy hit the winning shot at the buzzer and propelled the Suns into third place in the playoff race. His teammates rushed the floor and surrounded him, waving towels in the air and celebrating loudly on Milwaukee's home floor. When her husband walked off the court to be interviewed by ESPN, Katrina turned off the TV.

"That lucky mutherfucka! Dam!" she stated in a disgusted manner as she leaned back into the water and picked up her drink and took several deep swallows.

Katrina and Timothy's marriage was still a rocky one. They both secretly hoped for the other's demise. They each failed to realize that they were both perennial winners in life, however; their different backgrounds and upbringing was the reason they often clashed.

Katrina had lived a rough life on the streets, right alongside Ben Holland. When she started making money, the fear of being poor again was her driving ambition. For Timothy, it was his infatuation with the life that people in the streets often led. Timothy idolized drug dealers and rappers, and he imitated them at every chance. He wore the platinum chains, sported the tattoos and talked the lingo of the streets.

Katrina couldn't stand the fact that Timothy was pretending to be from the streets. She knew his whole story and she thought it was an insult to the people who had actually lived that life—people like her and the people she ran with, including Ben Holland. Katrina knew all-too-well that the street life was nothing to be proud of; and whereas she had removed herself from that terrible lifestyle and working hard to remain free of it, Timothy was drawn to the street life. For that reason and that reason alone, Katrina and Timothy could never see eye to eye. Katrina hated "fakes, frauds and phonies," and, in spite of the millions he was worth, Timothy, in Katrina's eyes, was all three.

Katrina reflected on those things as she dressed to head to the airport to meet O'Malley. She decided to partake of the condo's complimentary limousine service to pick up Dante as she wanted this meeting to be not only a comfortable rendezvous, but a powerful one as well. The more she grew, the more Katrina understood the power and wealth that she held at her young age. She loved being rich, and she handled herself and her money quite well considering her upbringing. Katrina was definitely a force to be reckoned with: strong, wealthy, and more ambitious than a great multitude of men in

America. A young, Black and driven woman, Katrina intimidated most men; and she rarely entertained the ones who could stand beside her and match her wits because she had no time for games.

One man, however, severely moved her: Ben Holland. In spite of coming into contact with handsome and available millionaires on a regular basis, Katrina had a special place in her heart for a former gangster who was penniless and locked behind bars. Ben Holland wasn't fraudulent like most men Katrina came into contact with, however, including her husband. Thinking how much she cared about a penniless convict when she could have any man she wanted, Katrina chuckled to herself as she headed out the door.

*"Gotta be love,"* Katrina thought to herself as she walked towards the elevator. *"Or I done lost my ever-lovin' mind doing this shit!"*

Katrina stepped off the elevator, walked out of the lobby and hopped into the limousine and met O'Malley promptly at 10:30 P.M. The two then headed back into downtown where Katrina had reservations at an exquisite late night French diner. As they sat inside the dimly lit fancy restaurant, the two sipped a thousand dollar bottle of vintage French wine while discussing the case.

"Katrina, we are in business!" O'Malley said happily before he sipped his wine. "What we have here is solid proof that that news article was indeed in the hands of Sherman Davis before he was killed. Anna's blood is all over that article also. With eyewitness testimony of the events that unfolded in front of the church that day back in '99, coupled with that one particular piece of evidence, we got a rock solid case that can garner freedom for Ben. We got 'em, Katrina! Baby, we got 'em by the balls! The Tenth Circuit has accepted the appeal on the grounds of new evidence and illegal police procedure. I filed for a speedy trial based on mitigating circumstances surrounding the conviction and that has been accepted also. Ben Holland's court date is set and we are ready to go to war, young lady!" Dante ended as he smiled and clutched Katrina's arm and shook it enthusiastically.

Katrina yelled aloud inside the crowded restaurant as customers looked on in surprise.

"Miss Sanders, is everything okay?" a waiter asked Katrina in earnest concern.

"Yes, yes, we are fine. Can you bring us another bottle of wine, please? And we are ready to order our entrées."

After enjoying calamari and scallop pasta, Katrina took O'Malley to her condo and the two slept in separate bedrooms before heading to the airport the next morning to fly into Denver, Colorado and make the two hour drive south to Florence.


### Florence, Colorado

It was about 1 P.M. when the guards came and got me from my cell, announcing that I had visitors. I turned off my radio and exited the cell and was greeted by Yiska. The two of us then headed towards the visiting room. When we got there, I was greeted with a huge hug and a soft kiss on the lips by Katrina. She then hugged Yiska, whom she had met on several of her previous visits.

Finally, I stood face to face with the man who held the fate of my life in his hands. I greeted him with a firm handshake and introduced him to Yiska before we all sat down. I was elated to hear the good news Dante` had given. Katrina was all smiles as O'Malley spoke about the circumstances surrounding my case. It seems as if she was more excited than I was. She grabbed my hand tightly and held on as O'Malley let it be known that I had received a new court date and my appeal to the Tenth Circuit had been upheld. I could barely contain my joy as I laughed and grabbed Katrina's hand tightly. I shook Dante's hand and thanked them both over and over again.

I knew of the Tenth Circuit. It consisted of six states, Utah, Oklahoma, Kansas, New Mexico, Colorado, and Wyoming. The Tenth Circuit mainly consisted of conservative judges that leaned towards the prosecution in any given case. I wasn't feeling too good about my chances of walking free; but I didn't let on. I only hoped that Dante` was fully capable of winning this case like he'd told me early on in the meeting. He said he never lost a case, but there's a first time for everything. I just hope he doesn't experience his first taste of defeat on my time, nor Katrina's dime.

"Mister Holland," O'Malley said, "what do you think of this opportunity that you have before you?"

"I'm a changed man, Mister O'Malley. Whether I walk free or not, my life will forever be guided by the love of family, and the friends, the true friends, who believe and know for a fact that I'm a good-hearted person." I said as I smiled at Katrina.

"I understand that, Mister Holland, but good-hearts don't register with judges. Especially conservative judges. We will be up against a conservative jury, prosecutor and judge. And all they will see is a convict. One with a bunch of gold teeth in his mouth. You need to get rid of those immediately. And regardless of the reasons behind the act, they will only see the person who *perpetrated* the act. They know nothing about your past, or that of your family. They will not care about any of those things either. If you are indeed changed, that will have to show in the court room. Your retrial is inevitable. I only ask that you prepare yourself for intense scrutiny from the federal prosecutor. Her name is Lisa Vanguard. I've brought along transcripts of several of her previous cases so you can read and review them and get a feel of the kind of person you will be dealing with. But again I tell you—get rid of the gold teeth."

I took O'Malley's words to heart and made a promise to remove the gold teeth and to study this prosecutor. I had to find out her angles, study her techniques. Whenever I would take the stand, I would be ready for this Lisa Vanguard person. We sat and talked for over three hours, going over the case, discussing the events that led up to that terrible day and before Katrina left, she and I had a heart to heart talk about my future.

"What do you plan on doing when you get out, Ben?"

"I hope to reconnect with Henrietta and strengthen that relationship. If she's still alive. I know she fighting with cancer right now, but if she still there, that's where I'm going, back to

New Orleans."

I noticed the sad expression on Katrina's face after I made those remarks. It was as if I had said something wrong. Something she didn't want to hear. I looked at her as I gently touched her cheek and she turned her down trodden head in my direction.

"Did I say something wrong?"

"No, no…Well, ain't no sense in pretending, Ben. Yes, you did say something wrong. I know you love your aunt and want to see her again, but I was hoping you would come to Phoenix. Where I am."

"What good would that do Katrina? You married and worth millions. What could I possibly offer you? If I come there, I would only mess your marriage up; you know that. Timothy hates me. For me to show up and all of a sudden start staying there, you would never have peace."

"I barely have peace now." she responded in a low voice as she looked to the floor. "The only time I'm happy is when he's away. I feel more joy when I *think* of you than when I actually *see* Timothy. Don't worry about messing my marriage up Ben, that's already done. You know what this is about, and if you don't, you'll figure it out—you're not stupid. But you need to know this, when I said I wanted you home, I meant with me. Whatever you decide to do though, man, just know that I got your back. Think about what I said, though, Ben." Katrina remarked lovingly as she kissed me fully on the mouth. "Think about us." she concluded as she patted my chest and walked off somewhat dejected.

I said my good-byes to O'Malley and walked slowly back to Yiska's cell. As he and I sat in his cell talking, I reflected on what Katrina had told me. Maybe Phoenix wouldn't be so bad. I could find work there, do something to earn money. I knew Katrina wanted to take care of me, but shit, I'm a grown man, and I don't want to be a burden on nobody. I know the newness of my release, if I were granted a new day at freedom, I know the newness would wear off and eventually, Katrina would grow to resent the fact that she was a young woman with money taking care of an older man with little or no money. True enough, I had made several million dollars on the street, but I'm broke now. I'm relying on Katrina and my aunt for support. The past was just that, the past.

Katrina came into contact with major players nearly every day of her life. I feel as if she's infatuated with the young Ben Holland, but that young man is long gone. I'm reformed, no longer a street hustler. That's who Katrina is in love with—at least, it's who I believe she's in love with. When she realizes the changes in me, I believe in my heart that she would come to resent me, but on the other hand, I would hate to ruin the love she has for me. Somehow, I got to figure out my position in life and play it right if and when I become a free man.

I received a formal letter a month later from the Tenth Circuit announcing my court date. It was now official—the wheels were set in motion for me to at least have a fighting chance to return to the free world. Me and Yiska celebrated that night with some homemade wine. My court date was set for the last week in July, and even though the nightmares persisted, I did all I could to learn about Lisa Vanguard, and prepare myself for a day of rejoicing—or a day of utter sorrow.

## CHAPTER 34

## A NEW DAY WITH OLD FRIENDS

The front of the court house in downtown Denver, Colorado was nearly void of people the latter part of July in 2005. Only two news reporters stood on the court room stairs awaiting the arrival of the key players who were scheduled to take part in this little publicized trial taking place in Federal Court.

"Ben Holland," the female reporter for a local news program said as she looked into her cameraman's lens, preparing a lead-in that would run on the evening news, "a man purportedly to be one of the south's most notorious drug kingpins, goes before the Tenth Circuit Court of Appeals today in hopes of earning an appeal for crimes he committed nearly six years ago. What makes this case so appealing, no pun intended, is that Mister Holland was caught on tape inside New Orleans' Louis Armstrong International Airport, gunning down a rival drug kingpin. It seems as if this should have been an open and shut case with no chance of reaching the appellate court, but it is a case purportedly entrenched in police corruption according to documents submitted to the court by Mister Holland's attorney. Mister Holland's entire appeal hinges upon the information that will be presented today by his lawyer, Dante` O'Malley, a prominent lawyer from Boston, Massachusetts."

As the reporter continued speaking, a black limousine

pulled up in front of the huge steps leading up to the court house and suddenly, a small group of a dozen or so people walked and stood in front of the huge grey-stoned structure. The small group of people were protesters. They stood on the sidewalk in front of the court room stairs holding signs that stated "Guilty as Charged", and "Victims Have Rights! Keep Killers out of Society!", and "Ben Holland is a Killer and a Drug Dealer!"

The crowd soon began to grow, and before long, there were three dozen protesters operating in a state of frenzy as Dante` O'Malley, along with Katrina Sanders, exited the limousine.

"Jesus," Dante` said lowly as he stared at the crowd.

"I thought this wasn't going to be a big deal, Dante`." Katrina said as she eyed the people holding the protest signs.

"It isn't, Katrina. Something tells me that Lisa Vanguard has set up this little fiasco to try and put Ben in a bad light."

"She's that savvy?"

"Yes she is. I told you that early on—this however—this has to be one of her most adroit acts to date." Dante` replied as he guided Katrina towards the courthouse.

The two were stopped on the stairs by the local female reporter wanting to ask them a few questions.

"Mister O'Malley! Mister O'Malley," the local news reporter called out as she clamored through the crowd, "Mister O'Malley, how do you feel representing a known killer and—"

"First of all, ma'am," O'Malley stated over the thunderous cries of protesters as he cut the reporter's question short, "this is a *retrial* case. So the question of whether someone's a murderer or not is still up in the air. Now, what I will say is that this case is leaning more towards the corruption of the judicial system that was put in place to protect its citizens, beginning with the local police department down in Memphis, Tennessee. Local police departments around the country have been manipulating their status in society for their own advantage while exploiting the innocent black youth of America's inner cities for years. That's all I have to say for now." O'Malley concluded as he hurried Katrina away from the cameraman and reporter before they had time to interview and film her.

As the crowd continued to grow that morning, two navy blue Lincoln Town Cars pulled up to the Federal Court House. The protesters cheered loudly when they saw the emblem of the United States Department of Justice on the car doors. Lisa Vanguard and her staff of seven aides exited the cars and stared at the crowd.

Laddy Norcross was the top F.B.I. Agent under Lisa. The thirty-five year-old Swedish man eyed the crowd with a smile and asked, "How'd I do, Lisa?"

"Hmm," Lisa responded with a wry smile. "Keep killers out of society? Ben Holland is a killer and drug dealer? Impressive, Laddy. Impressive."

"Thank you. I had to go down to a trailer park in Henderson and gather up these people. Everybody wanted a hundred dollars and a new outfit. I didn't think they all would show, though."

"Why not?"

"I paid them beforehand."

"I see. Let's not make that mistake again." Lisa said as she waved at the protesters.

"I figured most of them would come because of my backup plan; but this here really is impressive."

"What was the backup plan?"

"I told them the Democrat governor of Colorado, who many of these conservatives despise, was considering pardoning the man if the jury came back with a not guilty verdict."

"Hmm, you played politics, huh? I like the angle you've used, Mister Norcross. These people haven't a clue who Ben Holland is, but they're out there as if he'd murdered one of their own all because they hate the governor? Who has no power to pardon Mister Holland on this federal case? Classic, Laddy. Classic. They really should've paid attention in their American

Government class, you know?" Lisa said as she walked through the protesters, shaking some of their hands as she approached the stairs.

The local reporter, who'd been tipped off by Laddy, quickly caught up with Lisa Vanguard, the feisty forty-eight year old, red-headed woman from Baltimore, Maryland and asked, "Miss Vanguard, what are your views concerning this case? And how do you feel about your chances of keeping this convicted felon behind bars?"

"This entire case proves just how outrageously insane some portions the judiciary system has become." Lisa replied matter-of-factly as she removed her sun glasses. "Benjamin Holland was caught on tape, *murdering*, not one—but *two* human beings inside a busy airport in broad daylight! What else needs to be said? They sent me all the way out here from Washington, D.C. to keep a major drug dealer behind bars and that is what I will do. Mister Holland will not see daylight as long as Lisa Vanguard is prosecuting this case," the prosecutor ended before she turned and trotted up the stairs with her aides following close behind.

"How'd I do out there, Laddy?" Lisa asked as she removed her .9mm and walked through the metal detector.

"Great. The reporter will send us the footage and we'll edit it ourselves for this evening's news hour. Our boy Ben is going to have a contentious public to deal with if all goes well."

"Good! And when I win this trial, it'll look good for my run at Attorney General for the state of Maryland in a few years."

As the crowd continued protesting, several of them noticed four black females exiting an orange Dodge Neon and walking towards the court room. JoAnne, Dana, Kantrell and Alicia were fresh off a plane from New Orleans. They'd exited the rental car nervously and stared at the noisy, huge crowd looming in front of the court house. All heads soon turned towards the four women as they walked slowly towards the huge structure. No one knew who they were, but they figured they were involved with the trial that was taking place. The four women seemed to be out of their element amongst the protesters and flashing cameras.

"Got damn, it's a lot of mutherfuckas out here this morning!" JoAnne said to Kantrell, Dana, and Alicia as they continued walking at a slow pace across the wide boulevard towards the grey-stoned structure.

"You think they gone let Ben go?" Dana asked Kantrell.

"Shit, they better! The subpoena said they wanted my testimony to what happened that day and believe me bitch, my lyin' ass gone tell it all! Ben was justified in what he did that day!" Kantrell answered.

As the four women approached the stairs leading to the court rooms, they were approached by another reporter.

"Excuse me y'all," the man said politely, "are you friends of Ben Holland?"

"Yeah, yeah. I know 'em! So what's up, shaggy?" JoAnne responded.

"Shaggy?" the reporter asked as he smiled and eyed the four females. "Y'all from the Lower Ninth Ward?"

"I am," Kantrell replied happily. "Why?"

"Because, only true Ninth Ward Soldiers use the word shaggy. That's a down south thang. My name is Tavares Little, they used to call me T. Little back in the day."

"I know you, brer," Kantrell exclaimed. "You used to get haircuts at my salon."

"Kantrell's!" Tavares and Kantrell stated simultaneously whilst laughing aloud.

"Right, right," Tavares said. "Kantrell, I ain't gone lie, you used to have some fine ass women come through that camp."

"Still do. Still do. What you been up to, boy?"

"I'm a reporter for The Times Picayune back home now. My editor-in-chief had followed Ben's trial after the shootout at the airport and when he learned through contacts that he had a retrial, I got picked by him to travel here and do a report. I remember Ben and his boys used to come through on the weekends and buy everybody food. He was a good dude for the most part. How's he doing?" Tavares asked as he held out a microphone to record the conversation.

"He been okay," Kantrell replied. "I haven't talked to him in years, but our friend Katrina says he's well and optimistic."

"Do you think he should be set free?"

"Fuckin' right!" JoAnne responded as Tavares's photographer snapped pictures.

"And you miss?" Tavares asked, turning his attention to Dana.

"Of course, I wanna see him go free! What I'm supposed to say? No, let him stay in jail? That's my friend, brer. If you ain't grow up the way we did, you could never understand our life. But you did so you already know!" Dana responded in an aggravated tone as she, JoAnne and Kantrell walked up the stairs towards the huge courthouse doors.

"What about you, miss?" Tavares asked in a more compassionate tone towards Alicia.

"Shit, umm, my friend Ben wasted about six years of his life behind bars over some bullshit? Yeah he should go free! And today, the Ninth Ward gone settle the score with the crooked police!" Alicia replied and walked off.

"Boy I suck at this job!" Tavares told his photographer. "That interview was whack!"

The photographer aimed his camera towards the crowd, which was in a continuous state of flux. Protesters were everywhere and the photographer knew Tavares was searching for an exclusive concerning the case.

"It's not in vain, sir," the photographer said as he snapped photos of a black on black Hummer on thirty-two-inch chrome wheels gliding to a stop in front of the court house.

The people exited the ride and Tavares and his photographer made a beeline towards the group because they were recognizable figures.

Derrick Burkman and Torre` Spears walked briskly beside

their lawyer towards the courthouse stairs as their bodyguards shoved admiring protesters aside.

People in the crowd, including some of the protesters, flocked the rap entrepreneurs to get autographs and Tavares's photographer had snapped numerous photos. If ever Lisa ran her tape, Tavares would unknowingly have photos to contradict her reporter's story.

Torre's twenty-three-year old six-foot-four frame hovered above the crowd as he stopped and signed autographs. "That's right! That's right! Real niggas in the house!" Torre` said as he signed autographs. "Tell ya' daughters you was in the midst of a rich nigga today!"

Derrick had to remind Torre` that they weren't there to make friends; they were there on business. The two young men, along with their lawyer, Wallace, soon found themselves standing in front of Tavares, who had practically begged Derrick to allow him one question, telling him he used to hangout at Kantrell's.

"One question, brer." Derrick said as he tucked his hands into his jean pockets.

"What are two rap moguls doing at a little publicized trial in Denver, Colorado?"

Derrick looked over to Wallace and Wallace leaned in and whispered into his ear. Several seconds later, Derrick said, "We come here to Denver today to show love and support for a man who was wrongly convicted. It happens too often in our society."

"Okay," Tavares replied. "I didn't know Ben Holland had so many friends."

Derrick looked over to Wallace again and the lawyer whispered in his ear once more. Wallace told Derrick to say that he and Ben weren't friends, but merely passersby on the streets of New Orleans and since he was from his home city, he thought he'd at least show support.

"Nahh, I can't say that, brer, because it's not true." Derrick responded. "Look, man," he then said to Tavares, "there's a lot of things about Mister Holland that you and the world don't know. He's a good friend of mines, and he's affected many people's lives in a very positive way," Derrick concluded as he walked away from the reporter.

"Well said, Burkman. I have to remember those street codes that you live by, brother. I see my Yale School of Law Degree has its limitations after all."

"I understand all that shit, Wallace. You a helluva entertainment counselor, though, my nig and that's why you on our team." Derrick said lowly.

Just then, Torre` jumped in front of Tavares's photographer and demanded his picture be taken. He then yelled aloud, "And let me say, let me say—yeah!" as he jumped up and down in front of the camera, his platinum grill blinging in the morning sun. "That's a shot out to Li'l Jon and them Eastside Boys! We gotta a hot collab comin' out next month! And as far as them crooked ass cops in Memphis, we gone put our foot clean up inside they—" Torre` was immediately pulled from in front of the photographer by Wallace and shuffled inside the building.

All parties involved in the case were now inside the court room in separate chambers. They were each called separately into the courtroom shortly after the jury had been seated, and as they filed in, the "family reunion" began. Katrina first caught sight of JoAnne, Dana, Kantrell and Alicia, and she ran up to her old friends and hugged them tightly. It had been so long since she had seen them all. Tears flowed as the women huddled together.

When Derrick and Torre` walked into the court room, another outburst of joy ensued. The seven friends had reunited after years of leading their own lives. They had all gathered in Denver not for a reunion, though, but to attempt to solve a bigger issue. They all stood before their seats as Judge Gregory Bergstein entered the court room and took his seat behind the bench and the jury was then seated. As the trial was set to begin, Ben Holland's friends looked on and wondered where their friend was during this happy time.

## CHAPTER 35

### HALF TRUTHS

The bailiff stood in front of my holding cell, unlocked its doors, and escorted me towards the courtroom early that morning. I knew my old friends were scheduled to testify during the trial, but I wasn't prepared for what I saw and heard when I entered the courtroom: a huge roar along with a couple of camera flashes when I came into view.

I could see a large crowd of people whom I assumed were supporters of the prosecutor standing behind Lisa Vanguard on the left, and seven of my friends, including Katrina, cheering on my on the right behind Dante`. I reached into my suit pocket and grabbed a handkerchief and dabbed a few tears from my eyes. I was glad to see my old friends again, and when I smiled, I could see Kantrell pointing towards me as she covered her mouth.

Torre` ran his fingers across his grill, stretched out his arms and mimicked the words, *"what happened"*.

All my old friends, with the exception of Katrina, who was smiling proudly while flashing the 'okay' sign, were surprised to see that the ten gold teeth I once had in my upper mouth, had been removed.

Dana, JoAnne, Kantrell and Alicia all looked beautiful. I was glad to see they were okay. I had seen Derrick and Torre`

371

on TV from time to time and I knew they were fine. They pounded their hearts and threw up nine fingers, representing the Ninth Ward. The courtroom had to be silenced by the bailiffs as I was guided over to O'Malley's table and before long, the trial was underway.

As Lisa Vanguard recited her opening statements, I sat literally feet from my old friends. I couldn't help but peer over my shoulder and glance at them from time to time. They all smiled and I had this intense feeling of assuredness come over me at that moment—as if everything was going to be okay.

Miss Vanguard's opening statements lasted for over two hours and the court adjourned with Mister O'Malley barely speaking a word. Lisa pressed the judge to let Dante` give his opening statements, but the judge declined, stating that the court had a full docket that needed to be cleared on this day. Lisa wasn't happy with the judge's decision and Dante` told me it was because of the fact that Lisa knew the jurors may very well forget much of what she said over those two hours and he could start off fresh.

"It might not appear likely to you, Ben—but we're actually getting off to a good start." Dante` said happily.

I returned to my holding cell, ate dinner and eagerly awaited the next day.

The following morning, court resumed and for the first time, I saw Dante` O'Malley in action. When he was asked to make his opening statements, the man remained in his seat for several seconds. Dante` had not an inkling of nervousness. I liked that right away. I watched, me and my friends, and the entire courtroom watched as Dante` stood up and unbuttoned his snow white silk suit jacket and flattened his paisley tie. He grabbed a stack of papers as he walked from behind our table, placed his left hand into the left pocket of his silk slacks and strolled past the judge's bench and stood before the jury, resting his hand on the mahogany rail that ran across the front row. He then backed away as he stared at the entire jury as he held onto the papers.

"Yesterday," the man began to speak, "Miss Vanguard laid

out this elaborate time-line and synopsis of the life of a man whom she's never even met. In her synopsis, she indicated that Mister Holland was a drug lord, an extortioner, and a murderer. That is Miss Vanguard's *argument* and *opinion*—not a fact." Dante stated calmly. He then continued, saying, "For starters Benjamin Holland was never directly convicted of extortion. Look at his convictions." The peppered-haired lawyer stated as he handed copies of Ben's current conviction and sentencing to the jurors. "Nowhere is he charged with extortion. That's one way to discredit the prosecution's opening statements. She's told you half-truths from the very beginning. How can you be assured that everything else she says is true? You can't! But I have the truth! Ladies and gentlemen of the jury, this man, Mister Benjamin Holland, is not a cold-bloodied murderer as the prosecution alleged in her opening statements on yesterday. And this is not a narcotics nor an extortion trial. It is a murder retrial. The Memphis police department had a hit out on Benjamin Holland, in retaliation for Damenga Lapiente's sister being shot by one Sherman Davis, who also alleged that Benjamin Holland was supplying the city of New Orleans with enough cocaine to cover Mount Everest. Those allegations are not true! No drugs were never found in Mister Holland's possession—but he was charged with drug trafficking. The prosecution has no proof regarding her allegations. The courts have convicted Mister Holland under false pretenses and the defense will prove that here inside this court room to further discredit the prosecution. Also, the defense will prove beyond a reasonable doubt, that Mister Holland was justified in killing one Damenga Lapiente` and Alphonso Lapiente`, something that is not disputed by the defense. Was Mister Holland really justified in his actions? The emphatic truth to that question is yes. The defense says yes. In an act of blind rage, Mister Holland went after the man who factually destroyed his life, killed his fiancée, and nearly killed his childhood friend, Katrina Sanders. The video that will be presented by the prosecution only shows the act being committed, it doesn't show all of the emotions and underlying causes that led up to that event. I will show you that video in a different light." Dante` stated, then continued on with his presentation.

"Damenga Lapiente` was not a nice person in the least bit sense of the word. And Mister Holland was merely a pawn in a scheme perpetrated by one Sherman Davis, and various members of the Memphis police department, in an attempt to cover up their own mistakes. That scheme, ladies and gentlemen of the jury, that malicious, meticulously thought-out scheme ultimately led to death of Mister Holland's fiancée, Anastasia Gordon, and, in the end, it led Benjamin Holland, an unwilling participant in Damenga and Sherman's scheme, to commit murder by reason of what we call in today's society, Passion Provoked Manslaughter. Mister Holland had no connection to Damenga Lapiente`, the man whom he's accused of killing. The truth is that Sherman Davis lost an entire shipment of cocaine supplied to him by the Memphis police department, who was, in turn, working for this drug overlord from Houston, Texas. Miss Vanguard also alleges that Mister Holland was the one who took an entire shipment from Damenga in Memphis and killed three people in the process. The prosecution is wrong again. And I will not only tell you, I will *show* you that the prosecution is unable to prove her allegations. I can, however, *prove* that Sherman Davis orchestrated that home invasion and then tried to cover up the job by blaming Mister Holland when Damenga came looking for him. Sherman's fingerprints were found on a newspaper article describing those murders. That same article also contained the fingerprints of a known former Memphis vice squad cop. You may ask how this is relevant to why we are all here today? You see ladies and gentlemen, Mister Holland was convicted of a crime far more serious than the one he actually committed. And you all—each and every one of you upstanding citizens of the jury—you all have an opportunity to right a wrong. And I hope you will understand that fact and allow Mister Holland to once again be a free man." Dante` stated as he walked over and stood directly before the jury's foreman and made eye contact with with the middle-aged white woman.

Dante` then turned to the remaining jurors, three Hispanic males, an Asian woman, three white males, two black women, and a black male, and continued to speak. "Sherman Davis and this one ex-police officer had to have had contact outside of the jailhouse in Memphis in order for both prints to be on that newspaper. What kind of an association does a former vice squad cop have with a reputed drug dealer? I'll tell you. They were plotting how to set up Benjamin Holland to take the fall for their incompetence when they took an entire shipment of cocaine from a stash house Damenga had in the city of Memphis. Sherman's plan to rob that house would have worked; only he messed with the wrong drug dealer that morning. Davis grew terrified when he found out Damenga was in town looking for the person who had taken his drugs. Davis knew very well that Damenga would kill him. To save his own skin, he fingered Mister Holland as the person who had committed the crime. Damenga ordered the hit, and that ex-vice squad cop went along to make sure the job was done. How do I know? Because he was killed in front of the church in New Orleans. A gun was found clutched tightly in his dead corpse's hand, good people. Bullets fired from that former cop's gun match the ones removed from Anastasia Gordon's body. In a rage of fury, having seen his beloved bride-to-be blown to pieces over something he had nothing to do with caused a great rage inside Mister Holland. The evidence will speak for itself. I ask you today, as this trial proceeds, to keep in mind, what you would do, if the person you love more than life itself was killed before your very eyes?" O'Malley concluded as he stared at the jury for several seconds before he thanked them and turned and walked calmly back to the defense table.

## CHAPTER 36

### THEY LIED TRUTHFULLY

It was now the third day of the trial, and the court room was indeed beginning to heat up. Dana, JoAnne, and Alicia had already taken the stand and offered no help to Miss Vanguard during her cross-examination. The three women denied that they knew of my drug dealings, telling Lisa Vanguard that they never saw me sell drugs of any kind. They revealed nothing about any murder I or any of my friends ever committed. I have to admit I was worried that Dana, who was very straight-laced, would crack under Miss Vanguard's scrutiny but she stood solid. After spending almost twenty-five years in the Ninth Ward, and being involved with one of the hardest of my young hustlers, Jason Witherspoon, I should have known better to ever doubt Dana. Court recessed for lunch and I waited my turn to face Lisa Vanguard.

When court reconvened, O'Malley gave me a few last pointers on how to deal with the prosecutor. He told me that the key thing was not to lose my composure.

"She has an ace-in-the-hole—but I have a counteraction, my friend." O'Malley stated. "Remember, don't let her enrage you. Just stay calm and get through this last ditch effort on the part of this bitch, and we are home free. We're winning, young man. The court is buying what we selling," O'Malley whispered in my ear just before I was called to the stand.

As I walked towards the stand, I looked out into the crowd of people and saw all of my friends huddled together on one row directly behind O'Malley. Katrina moved her lips; she silently said she loved me. Torre` held up nine fingers and Derrick showed me a balled-up fist. I could clearly see the look of concern on the faces of Kantrell, Dana, JoAnne, and Alicia. Shit, they had nothing to fear; they had done their part—it was all on me now. I took my seat just as O'Malley deferred questioning me until the prosecutor was finished.

Miss Vanguard got up from her seat and walked quickly towards the center of the court room. For whatever reason, the woman was always angry. Maybe she felt she was wasting her time out here in Colorado, trying to keep a penniless drug dealer behind bars. Whatever the case, she began speaking in a loud harsh tone as she near-about ran towards the stand.

"Mister Holland, how well do you know Sherman Davis?"

"I knew of Sherman, he was an affiliate."

"An affiliate? Was he not a member of the notorious 'Ben Holland Gang'?" she asked me in a matter-of-fact tone of voice.

"We were not a gang, Miss Vanguard. We were just a group of friends that hung out together. The Ben Holland Gang was a name placed upon me and my friends by the newspaper back home."

"Okay. Well, 'back home', how well did you know Oscar Henderson?"

"Oscar was my right hand man."

"Your honor, the prosecution would like to admit DNA evidence from the crime scene in Memphis, Tennessee in which Oscar Henderson's DNA was taken from the nearly lifeless corpse of Carmella Lapiente`. It is the prosecution's accusation that Ben Holland, Oscar Henderson, Jermaine Duplessis and Manuel 'Manny' Lawson Taylor Junior entered Miss Lapiente's residence and proceeded to ransack her home, murder her friends and made off with eighteen kilograms of cocaine. That's why Damenga went after Mister Holland. Not because of some bad drug deal between Sherman Davis and the Memphis police department. That is a story that Mister O'Malley and his witnesses conjured up! Oscar was an under boss to Mister Holland, or as he said in his own words, his 'right hand man'. Benjamin Holland and Oscar Henderson never made a move without the other being involved! It stands as an absolute fact that Ben Holland was in that house the night this horrible crime was committed!"

"Objection your honor!" O'Malley yelled as he rose slowly from his seated position and then took on a calm and assuring demeanor as he began gesturing his hands while speaking. "The prosecution is basing *her* statements on statements made by the alleged mastermind of that incident, a Mister Sherman Davis, and she's moving towards pure speculation at this very moment. There's no evidence linking Mister Holland to the crime committed in Memphis. All the prosecution has proven is that *Oscar Henderson* was in that house at some point in time. Oscar is not on trial today. Furthermore, Mister Henderson is dead. So he can't give a testimony. The prosecution is headed towards speculation and false accusation. She has no evidence what so ever linking Mister Holland to the murders in Memphis. And I'd appreciate it if Miss Vanguard not berate, belittle, or mock this courtroom by calling my client and his friends liars. We didn't conjure up anything today. All we are trying to do is get to the truth here today, your Honor." Dante` stated as he straightened his suit jacket and sat back down.

The judge looked at Dante` then towards Lisa as he wrote a few notes down in his legal pad. He then looked towards the jury and said, "Sustained! The jury will forgo the prosecution's statements in reference to Mister Holland and Oscar Henderson committing an act of murder in Memphis, Tennessee. Miss Vanguard, as much as I hate to admit it, the defense is right. All you can prove as of now is the fact that Oscar Henderson, who's not on trial here mind you, was indeed inside the house in Memphis. Can you connect Mister Holland to that crime scene?" he asked as he peered over his thick bi-focal glasses.

Lisa had the tapes with Sherman admitting that Ben Holland and his cohorts had killed the men inside of Carmella's home, but Damenga's voice was on those tapes as well. If those tapes were played, Dante's accusation that Sherman and Damenga were working together would be upheld. The prosecutor also knew that Ben Holland had beaten Sherman when Ben found him wearing a wire in September of 1999. That recording, however, would only confirm that an assault was committed by Ben Holland against Sherman Davis. Lisa knew Ben could be released for time served on that particular charge based on Kantrell's statements, so that particular wire tap was useless. Lisa had the evidence—but Damenga's voice being on the tapes recorded in Memphis had spoiled her whole argument.

"Not exactly your honor. I have no solid proof." she stated angrily as she waited for the inevitable outcome.

"Then you need to drop the allegations concerning Mister Holland being in Memphis from your comments."

"Why did I know that shit was coming? No further questions for this guy." Lisa said as she looked back at her aides.

"Miss Vanguard, unless you wanna be held in contempt, I suggest you move along with your argument!" the judge said in a stern voice as he eyed Lisa angrily.

"Who really is the victim here?" Lisa asked rhetorically and towards no one.

"Excuse me?" The judge asked as he removed his glasses.

"No further questions, your Honor." Lisa ended as she walked back towards her table in frustration.

That was the last hurdle. I could see my friends smiling as they knew we had just smashed Miss Vanguard's attempt to connect me to the Memphis job. If she had done that, then the video she had shown earlier would be of no value to Dante`. The prosecution would have been able to justify Damenga's actions, and she would have also been able to charge me for the Memphis murders, thereby earning me a trip to death row. Dante` smashed Lisa's whole presentation this afternoon. Most lawyers, like the public defender I once had, would not have objected to Miss Vanguard's cross-examination; but by doing so, Dante` knew she could no longer attempt to connect me to Memphis. That simple objection leaned the scales heavily in my favor.

Dante` knew his shit I must say. Sometimes, it's not what's said in a trial, but what your lawyer prevents others from saying. The red-haired lady walked back to her seat in pure frustration because she knew the only connection she ever had to my being in Memphis, my dead friend Oscar, was silenced by the judge. She had nothing else to go on. O'Malley then nailed the coffin shut when he took center court. I sat at my table watching, as Katrina reached out and touched me on the shoulder. I grabbed her hand and kissed it softly as O'Malley hit a home run.

"The prosecution tried to convince the jury that Ben Holland stole nearly twenty kilograms of cocaine from a home in Memphis where three people were murdered and that's why Damenga Lapiente` went after him. I say otherwise. How and why do I know that? Because of this ladies and gentlemen." O'Malley stated as he held up a plastic bag in either hand. One held the newspaper article, and the other, a .357 magnum.

O'Malley then called Kantrell back to the stand. She approached the bench and quietly took her seat as the bailiff reminded her that she was still under oath. O'Malley walked over to her stand and asked her questions about my lifestyle. Kantrell told Dante` that she only knew me to come by the salon and buy lunch and just hang out with my boys while we got haircuts and the like and she never knew me to be a drug dealer, but I was known to fix cars for cash under the table, which was the claim all my friends that testified had told the the court. As far as the court was concerned, I was an unlicensed auto mechanic that had a large clientele.

"Did Sherman say anything about some trouble he was in just before he returned to Memphis?" Dante` asked.

"Yea, he said, well, I overheard him telling Ben he was in trouble because they had a war going on in Memphis and he needed a place to hide out because somebody was after him. Ben told him he couldn't help him because he wasn't into that sort of thing—but Sherman just kept hanging around the beauty salon pestering Ben. Finally, Ben put Sherman in a hotel but Sherman kept comin' 'round the salon telling me to tell Ben that somebody was after him."

"Did Sherman ever say who this 'somebody' was?"

"No, no, but a few days later, I got the article that you had earlier in the mail. I don't know why Sherman sent the article to me. Why he didn't just go to the police in Memphis and get help? I mean, that's what I woulda done if I knew somebody was tryna kill my black—if somebody was tryna kill me. After I read the article, I showed it to Ben at our friend Lamont funeral and Ben just kept it. That's how Anna's blood got on the paper, when them hit men shot up the church. We wasn't bothering nobody," Kantrell said as she began to cry a fake, highly believable cry, "and those hoodlums just came and shot up the place. They shot Anna in cold-blood and almost killed my friend, Katrina." she ended as tears rolled down her face.

"I'll tell you why Sherman didn't go to the police in Memphis ladies and gentlemen." O'Malley said loudly as he turned towards the jury. "It was because Sherman knew he had nowhere to turn. He knew the police were working for Damenga so help from Memphis's finest was not going to happen! You see, ladies and gentlemen of the jury, the police department failed an entire group of citizens. Their corrupt tactics caused innocent people to lose their lives—up to and including a four-year old little girl. Rather than take Sherman in and charge him with the murder of three people inside that house, they let him remain on the streets. Just, just threw the kid to the dogs! The police knew Sherman's finger prints were on that weapon. They had an airtight case for murder against Sherman and they could have brought him in and charged him." Dante` said as he stared at the jury and continued his argument.

"Whether Sherman killed those three people in that house in Memphis, and left Damenga's sister, Carmella near death is now irrelevant; but one thing is for sure—the police in Memphis were in a position to save Sherman and his family from the death grip of those brutal men he so greatly feared.

And, and you need to know this as well—because it proves just how violent these people were. Okay now, Carmella received two gunshots to the head, but she survived. You would think that after going through such a traumatic experience, one would make everything right in their life and follow the law. But no. Not Carmella Lapiente`. Where's Carmella Lapiente` today ladies and gentlemen? I'll tell you where she is. Carmella Lapiente` is now dead after being gunned down fifteen miles south of the U.S.-Mexico border. A tractor-trailer filled with ten tons, twenty thousand pounds of cocaine registered in her name, was found on the scene as well."

The jury could be heard sighing and gasping. Some shook their heads as Dante` continued. "You see, ladies and gentlemen, these weren't good, law-abiding citizens. Damenga and his family, and his associates were all ruthless murderers, and in the end, they met the same fate. When they went after Ben Holland, they were wrong. The man had nothing to do with what went on in Memphis. He was never even in the city. Remember," O'Malley said as he pointed towards the jury, "if it was your wife, your sister, your son or daughter, your mother or father—gunned down for no reason at all? What would *you* do if you *knew* who had harmed your loved ones? Society doesn't excuse vigilante justice. And I'm not asking for you all upstanding citizens to excuse what Mister Holland did—but I am asking for understanding. No one knows what he or she would do until faced with those hard issues. Ben did what we all know many feel in their hearts having been hit with such tragedy. Not the right decision, but the man was emotionally blinded having lost his future wife. To add fuel to the fire, Sherman was a pawn and a scared child caught in a web of corruption. The only way he thought *he* could escape death was by fingering a totally innocent person who was oblivious to the fate that was about to befall him and his family. Ben Holland is not a killer good people of the jury. The man merely reacted to a tragic event that played out before his eyes." O'Malley concluded.

As the video of the shooting inside the airport ran before the jury, Dante placed pictures of Anna's bloodied, lifeless corpse laying out on the stairs covered by white sheets in front of the jury along with her autopsy photos. Some of them turned their heads, unable to look at the gruesome images. A couple of the jurors wept. O'Malley also displayed a picture of Katrina as she lay fighting for life in the intensive care unit.

"You need to take a look at Sherman Davis again, jurors. There's your murderer. Your instigator. The path Sherman Davis decided to take put everyone's life in jeopardy. Ben is lucky to be alive, everyone who took the stand today is lucky to be alive because they were all standing outside of that church on that foreboding day when gunfire erupted. The airport shooting was the behavior of an innocent man, overcome with emotion and provoked beyond all rationale. It is not cold-bloodied murder. Benjamin Holland was provoked! Keep that in mind, ladies and gentlemen. Remember the testimony of the witnesses you heard today. Understand what Sherman did to Ben Holland and his friends. It was his prints found on that gun that matched the bullets pulled from Carmella's skull the night she was shot in Memphis! You need to take another look at Sherman Davis! He's the real culprit! And he brought trouble to Ben Holland's doorstep from over three-hundred miles away. Thank you ladies and gentlemen." Dante` ended lowly.

Sherman wasn't a bright dude. The guns we gave him to toss into the Mississippi River the night we raided Carmella Lapiente's home, he kept for himself. I'm guessing that he sold the rifles on the streets of Memphis and kept the .357 that Oscar used to shoot Carmella for himself. We wore leather gloves that night, me, Manny, Oscar and Jermaine. Sherman's finger prints were all over the gun Dante` had found in evidence down in Memphis; but the damning evidence was that the bullets from the gun matched the ones pulled from Carmella's skull and was found in Sherman's home when police removed he and his family's remains.

Even though me and my crew committed the murders, it was Sherman's prints on the gun. And it was found in his home. True enough, we were blaming a dead man for the crimes committed in Memphis, but Sherman had it coming. None of my crew ever ratted. When Sherman ratted to the Memphis police department, he basically sealed his own fate.

Dante` had used Sherman's death to twist the story around and put everything back on him and the Memphis police department. The man was a genius.

Dante` was indeed raising reasonable doubt. He then questioned me on the events that took place on the day of the shoot out in front of the church. I tell you, I had the jury in tears as I described the way Anna was gunned down in cold blood. O'Malley then recalled Dana, JoAnne, and Alicia back to the stand and they, too, moved the jury's heart when they related how distraught I was over Anna's death. The ultimate moment, however, belonged to Katrina.

Katrina told her whole life story, minus the murder she committed, up until the time she was blasted in the stomach that day.

"What was going through your mind as you lay on the steps of the church, fighting for your life Miss Sanders?" O'Malley asked in a compassionate tone.

Katrina let the tears flow as she spoke lowly, "I thought I was gonna die and never make it to college! I didn't know why that man shot me! And when I found out one of the men was an ex-policeman, I was even more shocked. Why would a police officer want to shoot us? We weren't bothering anybody. We knew nothing about what Sherman was up to in Memphis." Katrina said in the most innocent voice I ever heard.

If you know Katrina like I do, you could only describe the woman as beautiful but deadly. She seduced the crowd with her testimony. Their heart went out to her, I could tell. O'Malley then supplied the court with the evidence that linked Sherman to the ex-cop in Memphis, printed out cell phone calls and bank transfers from Sherman to the police department that matched the dead ex-officer's bank account. With that evidence, Dante` had thus removed all connections tying me to Memphis and had made a solid connection to Sherman conducting business with known officers. He rested his case under the belief that the jury would buy the story that I committed an act of murder in a blind rage called 'Passion Provoked Manslaughter', which carries a maximum of eight years.

Amongst O'Malley's half-truths, there was some fact. I *was* provoked by Damenga when I went after him. I was caught on tape, true enough; but Dante` had presented that tape in a different light. He kicked the prosecution's ass those few days in Colorado.

Lisa Vanguard declined cross-examination, but she called for a recess and a private meeting with Dante` and he accepted; and as we awaited Lisa's next move, everyone was on pins and needles, but we all felt good because Dante` told us that she was ready to possibly make a plea deal. Finally, after six hours of a closed door meeting with Lisa Vanguard, the trial was set to resume the following day with the jury announcing their verdict.

"It wasn't what I planned for Ben—this recess I mean—but trust me, we have a much better chance this way. I think we can work a deal with Lisa. I tried to get it done in court today, but we couldn't reach common ground."

"Common ground for what? You beat her!"

"I know, I know. But you have to understand federal law and the power a person in Lisa's position has. You can still be held in custody pending further investigation by the U.S. Department of Justice. Just, just hang in there with me." Dante said to me as he stood outside of my holding cell. "See you in court tomorrow, young man. Don't worry, Ben. I'm not going to let let you down." he concluded in a somewhat unsure tone as he walked away.

Dante` didn't seem so sure in what he was saying; neither was I; but Dante` was all I had left. I didn't eat and couldn't sleep. I knew this night would be one of the longest nights of my life. I just want this shit done and over with. I wanna go home, ya' dig?

## CHAPTER 37

### THE LANGUAGE OF MONEY

As court reconvened the following day and the jury took their seats, O'Malley had a nervous smile on his face. Me and my friends were worried sick because we thought the trial was all but over the day before; but everything now hinged on this decision. I was now nearing the end of the road. If I lost this case, I knew there would be only one appeal left: the Supreme Court, which left hope of me ever getting out in severe jeopardy. My heart pounded as the judge looked to the jury and asked if they had reached a verdict. When the foreman said they had, every one held their breath.

"How do you find the defendant?" the judge asked.

"In the case of the United States vs. Benjamin Holland," the foreman spoke loudly, "we find the defendant, Benjamin Holland—guilty!"

I leaned back in my chair in stunned silence as my friends broke down into moans and tears and the crowd behind the prosecution began to cheer in a roaring, deafening tone. The judge repeatedly rapped his gavel onto his desk to regain order. I looked at O'Malley and he now had a silly ass smirk on his face. I mean, here I was, condemned to life behind bars and Dante` was smiling at the events taking place. O'Malley's eyes were wide open and he was staring at the ceiling with his hands clasped behind his head as the judge announced that the jury had a further ruling. Everyone grew quiet as the foreman spoke.

"We find the defendant, Benjamin Holland, guilty of Passion Provoked Manslaughter. The jury recommends a sentence of eight years, but not more than five years and nine months with credit for time served. It is our belief that Benjamin Holland is indeed innocent of murder in the first degree and we request his immediate release from the Florence Federal Correctional Complex upon payment of a fine in the sum of four-hundred and seventy-five thousand dollars—payable to the U.S. Department of Justice and upon completion of the time remaining on his sentence which is twenty-two days. Failure to pay the fine within the allotted time will result in an eight year sentence, the maximum sentence allowed for the conviction of Passion Provoked Manslaughter, the charge hereby in which Benjamin Holland has been convicted and found guilty."

My friends erupted into a state of euphoria as I pumped my fist in the air wildly.

Dante` stood up and shook my hand. "This is what the recess was all about, Ben." he said lowly as he leaned over and whispered into my ear. "Sorry to make you sweat, but in this type of deal, I'm never at ease until the verdict is read. The deal was done last night outside of the court room between me and Lisa and she informed the jury this morning. Ask no questions about it, either. All I can say is Lisa has a bigger issue."

"What's that? It's concerning me?" I asked lowly.

"Not at all. It's all politics, Ben. The bitch is broke and wants to catch bigger fish in the Pacific North West. She could've pressed the issue further with your case, but let's just say the language of money is understood and respected by all. I knew if she lost, Lisa was going to try and take this thing all the way to the U.S. Supreme Court. That would've held you up on another appeal from the Justice Department if Lisa invoked her right to an appeal. You didn't need that so I made Miss Vanguard an offer she couldn't refuse." Dante` said with a smirk on his face.

I just stared at Dante` in wonderment. I guess he could read my face because he gave a little insight to what actually happened behind the scenes with him and Lisa.

"It helps to know your opponents' weaknesses, my friend. You know that move from being in the game, right? I know what Lisa's up to," Dante` said as he looked over to Lisa's table. "What she really wants is to take down this organized crime network presumably based in Seattle. But in order for her to engage in that undertaking she needed money because the Senate committee that approves her funds will not give her anymore grants. I studied her ass and found an angle that was too tempting to pass up. And that angle, my friend, persuaded her to not invoke her right to appeal."

"Sound like a bribe to me." I said lowly as I covered my lips and whispered into Dante`'s ear.

"You can call it what you want, my friend—but money is power—and some of your friends have both. You put that with my courtroom expertise, and the cage gets opened each and every time when I'm on the case. This is how I sometimes do business, Ben—and it works like pure science. To go home, all you have to do is pay the fine, but Derrick and Torre` took care of that for you already. You're going home, young man." Dante` said proudly as he patted my back and turned to shake my friends' hands.

"Now, hopefully we won't have to do business like this again, Mister Holland." Dante` then said to me with slight laughter.

"If I have to say so, we done man. I ain't going back to jail. I got too much to live for out there in the free world." I said as Katrina walked up and hugged me tightly.

I chatted with my friends for a few minutes and hugged them all and thanked them repeatedly for what they had done until the bailiffs came and broke up the love fest.

"See you next month, Ben!"

"Bye, Ben!"

"Love ya', dog!" They said at random as I was escorted

back to my cell where I waited for transport back to the penitentiary.

I now only had twenty-two days to serve and I would walk out of the federal penitentiary a free man with a new lease on life. Until then, I would converse with Henrietta daily. She was ecstatic to hear the news; her nephew was coming home! She couldn't make it to the trial because she was in LSU's research program undergoing treatment for her cancer, but I vowed to return to her once I was released.

With the trial behind me, and freedom close at hand, my mind was at ease. I now was able to focus more on the night my parents perished. I spent most days reading over the things I had written down from my nightmares. Slowly things were coming back to me. As I lay back in my bunk one night, almost two weeks after the trial, I closed my eyes and reflected back to the day my sister was born.

## CHAPTER 38

### THE BEGINNING OF THE END

Sam hurriedly grabbed a small suitcase containing a few of Gabriella's things as nine-year old Ben Holland poured water into Rollo's water dish. The dog pranced to and fro, copying the hurried pace of Sam as he quickly escorted his wife to their awaiting car.

"Ben! Hurry up, son! Your sister's ready to come into the world today and she ain't waitin'!" Sam yelled aloud to his son from the foyer.

Ben patted his tiny puppy and quickly ran out of the house. Breathing heavily, Gabriella sat in the front seat of the car this cold winter morning in January of 1984. The baby within the woman's womb was earnestly trying to make her way into the world.

As Gabriella held on to the dash board of the car, the baby gave her mother a hard kick.

"Whoa!" Gabriella shouted. "Sam, wait! Wait, baby! I,I have to lay down! Stop the car!"

"We almost to the hospital!"

"We at least ten minutes away! I have, I have to lay down Sam! This little girl is kickin' the hell out my belly!"

Sam swerved the car onto the shoulder of the interstate and

placed his wife onto the backseat of the four-door Lincoln town car and hurried his son into the front seat. Ben sat in the front seat happily making sounds like a police siren as his father sped towards Charity Hospital in downtown New Orleans. The family's car swerved in and out of traffic, its flashers blinking continuously as Sam cussed at motorists who were driving the speed limit the man wanted so desperately to exceed.

Gabriella lay on the back seat holding her belly.

"Hurry up, Sam! Samantha, hold on baby! Give momma, give momma a chance to make it to the hospital, my baby!" Gabriella talked to her child, trying to prevent the baby from arriving on the back seat of the car.

As Sam exited the interstate, the hospital directly ahead, he ran through two red lights. A police car followed him into the emergency drive way of the hospital and the officer got out preparing to write Sam a ticket. When he saw what was transpiring, the officer quickly assisted Sam by calling for a nurse. A gurney was rushed to the emergency room entrance and Sam and the officer, along with two nurses, lifted Gabriella onto the gurney and the woman was rushed off to the maternity ward, leaving Sam and Ben behind.

Henrietta, Charmaine, Yvonne and Alfred soon arrived at the hospital and they sat with Ben as Sam joined his wife in the delivery room to watch the arrival of his second child. Gabriella lay on the bed with her legs spread wide, clutching her husband's hands tightly. The woman's hair was matted against her face and she had turned a flush-red color as her sweaty body began to adjust itself in preparation for Samantha Holland's arrival.

Meanwhile, outside in the waiting room, Ben sat in a chair with pen and paper as he drew pictures of his little sister. He showed them to Henrietta and she complimented him on the pretty pictures he was drawing that morning. Charmaine and Yvonne, meanwhile, were fussing at the TV as they watched *The Price is Right*.

"Ain't that man from Florida?" Yvonne asked of a

contestant, as she talked to the TV. "What the hell he gone do with a set of skis, man?" she remarked as Charmaine started laughing. "For real, Charmaine! Skis? In Florida? Those skis going straight to the pawn shop!"

"Girl, he look like he wanna smack the you know what outta Bob Barker. Look at his face, he don't even want them skis!" Charmaine added as she laughed aloud.

Inside the delivery room, Sam, along with the three doctors and a nurse, were all in a frenzy as Gabriella began to push hard. The nurse gently placed her hand just inside of Gabriella's vagina and said calmly, "I can feel the baby's skull Misses Holland, just keep pushing for me."

Gabriella let out a loud scream and pushed really hard and the baby's head pushed forward and exited her vagina.

"Here is Samantha Holland. Hello, beautiful." the nurse whispered as she pulled lightly on the crying baby as Gabriella pushed.

The rest of the delivery came with ease as Samantha Holland was brought forth on January 28, 1984. Sam was so proud of his wife and overjoyed at the sight of his daughter. Samantha was a cute, pale-skinned baby girl. Not even an hour old, her head was already covered with matted, jet-black curly hair. She had grey eyes like her mother and a cute button nose and a tiny black dot just under her left eye. Gabriella thought her daughter's "beauty mark" would only enhance her identity as she grew older. The baby was plump and healthy and she looked like a living baby doll.

After the doctors cleaned Samantha, they presented her to her mother and father who proudly sat together and cooed at the newborn. When Gabriella began breast-feeding the child, Sam walked into the waiting room and announced that he was the proud father of a baby girl named Samantha Holland and his friends and son clapped loudly.

Two hours later, Sam Holland walked proudly in front of his family and friends towards the maternity ward. They stood behind a glass window as Gabriella waved at them. They all stared at the baby for several minutes before leaving as they knew Gabriella was tired; but Henrietta had stayed behind with Sam and Ben as they awaited Gabriella's release.

Gabriella's release was delayed by a day after she came down with a sudden fever, so Henrietta took Ben home the day before his mother's release whilst Sam stayed behind. Henrietta took Ben to his parents' home so they could check on his puppy and gather clean clothes. Ben remained with Henrietta and Charmaine inside Henrietta's home eagerly awaiting his mother's return the following day.

As they sat at the table playing cards, Henrietta mentioned that she wanted to record Gabriella's departure from the hospital, but she had left the video camera back at her sister's house.

"I'll go get it for you Henrietta." Charmaine stated as she grabbed her car keys and headed out towards New Orleans East to retrieve the video recorder.

As Charmaine drove, she listened to her radio and sang along to the music. Stevie Wonder's song *Isn't She Lovely* just happen to be playing on the radio and that brought Charmaine pure joy. She was so happy for Gabriella. Charmaine couldn't wait to hold baby Samantha; and she had every intention on spoiling the baby girl rotten. She smiled to herself as she thought about that prospect.

*"Gabriella gone be so mad at me for spoiling that baby!"* she thought to herself.

Charmaine never even noticed that she was being followed. As she made her way over to Gabriella's home, the car followed closely behind her. She pulled up to the custom built, three-bedroom, one story brick house, pranced happily up the drive way while humming Stevie Wonder's song and unlocked the door and entered the home. She didn't bother to lock the door as she was only going to be in the house for a minute or two. Charmaine walked into Gabriella's bedroom and opened the closet door and searched the shelf for the camera.

As she did so, she heard the front door of the home open and close. She stopped what she was doing and tip-toed towards the bedroom door and paused at its entrance. She looked down the hall and trembled in fear because she knew someone had entered the home, and the entrance had given her an uneasy feeling. Charmaine was scared to death as she peeked out into the hallway. She saw no one, so she decided to make a dash for the front door and exit the home. When she entered the living room, however, she saw Manhattan standing there, staring at a picture of Gabriella on the mantle above the fireplace.

For months Manhattan had disappeared from the face of the earth. Now he was back in New Orleans to claim what he thought was rightfully his.

"Hello there. I just got back in town and I was wondering what was going on with my child." he stated in a matter-of-fact tone.

Charmaine was stricken with fear; she dare not correct the man for fear he would hurt her. The woman was also puzzled as what to do in such a frighteningly perplexing situation. As Manhattan walked around the living room looking at all of the pictures of Gabriella, Charmaine stood frozen, watching the man walk about her friend's home in a carefree manner.

"Where are they?" Manhattan then asked Charmaine as he turned and looked at her with angry eyes.

"I don't know." Charmaine responded softly.

"I said, where are they?" Manhattan asked as he pulled out a .38 revolver and aimed it at Charmaine.

"Please, mister, I don't—"

"Don't fuckin' lie to me, bitch!" Manhattan yelled as Charmaine, out of fear, ran back down the hallway towards Gabriella's bed room.

Manhattan gave chase and caught Charmaine inside the bedroom before she could close the door and lock it and quickly pounced onto the woman's back. Charmaine dared not scream because Manhattan had placed the gun to her temple and ordered her to remain quiet.

"Now...where are they?"

"They at Charity Hospital!" Charmaine said through watery eyes.

Charmaine had never been so scared in all her life. She was relieved when Manhattan got up off her body and walked towards the threshold of the bedroom. She was again struck with fear, however, when Manhattan, having seeming to rethink the situation, paused and turned around and faced her, aiming the gun at her head. Charmaine covered her face as Manhattan walked back towards her, grabbed her by her jehri-curled hair and pressed the gun to her face. She screamed when Manhattan squeezed the trigger. The gun didn't fire, however, because Manhattan had the safety lock on. Charmaine was so afraid, she urinated on herself.

"I know where you live, bitch! I been following you for weeks. If you tell anybody you saw me, I'll do to you exactly what I done to your dope-fiend-assed cousin!" Manhattan announced as he proceeded to beat Charmaine about the head with the butt of the pistol until she lay on the floor unconscious.

Manhattan then proceeded to ransack Gabriella's home. He smashed her grand piano and destroyed her electric keyboard. He destroyed all of the family's furniture as well. The man was completely out of his mind. He then placed all of Gabriella's pictures into a pillow case, along with all of the trophies she had accumulated throughout the years. He smashed all of her albums and took the microphone Gabriella used to sing her songs. Every single item that bore a connection to, or had an image of Gabriella, was either destroyed, or loaded into his car. He then left the house, leaving Charmaine unconscious on the floor on her friend's bedroom floor.

The following morning, Henrietta had awakened, wondering what had happened to Charmaine as she had never returned with the video camera. It was almost time for Gabriella's release so Henrietta hurriedly got Ben dressed and headed to her sister's home to retrieve the camera and record her sister's arrival home with the baby. Henrietta was surprised to see Charmaine's car in front of the house.

Henrietta and Ben entered the home, and they both saw an

awful sight. The house was in shambles. Everything was destroyed or nearly destroyed. All of the family's pictures and videos were missing, there were holes punched into the wall and food from the refrigerator was strewn about. Henrietta clutched Ben's hands tightly as the two walked through the ruined home.

"What happened, Auntie?" Ben asked somberly.

"I don't know. baby. I don't know. Charmaine? Are you in here?" Henrietta called out as she and Ben tip-toed through the house. "I see her car outside, I wonder where she is." Henrietta stated as she walked down the hall towards the bedrooms.

Henrietta and Ben were startled when Ben's puppy ran out of Gabriella's room into the hallway. The puppy wallowed to and fro in front of the bedroom's entrance as the two approached. The puppy then darted back into the bed room and sat down next to Charmaine as Henrietta ran towards the woman.

"Charmaine! Charmaine! Oh my god!" Henrietta screamed as she pulled Ben from the room and raced to the telephone.

The telephones, however, were destroyed so Henrietta ran to a neighbor's home across the street and franticly begged them to call the police and an ambulance.

When the police and ambulance arrived, they took Charmaine, who was still alive, but in a comatose state, to the hospital. As the police conducted an investigation, Henrietta called the hospital to tell Sam and Gabriella what had transpired in their home. The couple had already left with their child, however, so Henrietta stood in front of the house with Ben awaiting their arrival. Alfred was at the hospital with Yvonne awaiting word of Charmaine's status along with the police, the two of them trying to piece together what happened the night before the same as everyone else.

When Sam and Gabriella arrived, Henrietta broke the news. They watched through saddened eyes as Gabriella walked towards the front doors, holding her newborn baby and looking at all the damage done to her once immaculate home as she entered the place. She eyed her cherished piano and keyboard and wept over the smashed instruments. Gabriella was even more disheartened when she realized all of her pictures , trophies and videos were taken.

"Who would do such a terrible thing, Sam?"

"I don't know, Gabriella. There were a few break-ins around here a couple of weeks ago. Maybe Charmaine can shed light on the situation."

The group all headed towards Oschner hospital in Kenner, Louisiana, just outside of Orleans parish and waited for Charmaine to come out of her coma. They waited until just before mid-night, but Charmaine never pulled through; doctors then told the family that it may be a few days before Charmaine reawakened.

Gabriella had to get Samantha to some place comfortable for the night so Henrietta quickly offered her place to her sister and brother-in-law until the insurance agency could come up with an estimate so they can began to refurbish their home. Gabriella and Sam first accepted Henrietta's hospitality, but they decided to spend the night at a hotel near the hospital so they could be close to Charmaine. Alfred and Yvonne stayed behind with Charmaine, and Henrietta headed home alone since she had to return to the high school in the morning.

When Sam and Gabriella opened the doors to their car, they were hit with a foul odor. They found Ben's puppy wagging its tail on the backseat and standing next to a small pile of feces.

"Son," yelled Sam. "what the hell is this dog doing inside my car? I told you not to bring him with us!"

"I didn't want to leave him in that house by his self. What if they came back?"

Sam understood his son's fear, but he reprimanded the young boy as he cleaned his car. Sam then found a small motel a few miles from the hospital that allowed pets and checked his family into the hotel.

As Gabriella and Sam settled in for the night, a dark brown station wagon was camped outside of their room. Manhattan watched intensely at the room that held the woman who he thought had bore his child just a few days ago.

Inside the room, Sam and Gabriella, along with Ben, played with baby Samantha as they all huddled together on the king-sized bed. After the baby's final feeding, the lights were turned off and Gabriella began to rock the baby to sleep. Ben lay across from his parents on a small cot with his puppy beside him as the family settled in for a night's rest.

## CHAPTER 39

### WHAT I NOW REMEMBER

As the day of my release grew closer, I was finally able to piece together the last moments of my parents' life. Finally, I could recall the events; and as I lay in my bed thinking of them, I recalled fully what happened to my mother and father the night they died. I reflected on the events that took place during the first couple of days of my sister's life and I replayed the final moments of my parents' last night on Earth—exactly the way I now remember them happening.

I remember lying asleep on my cot for what seemed like a couple of hours. Rollo had awakened me from my sleep by tugging on the blanket I was covered up with; that little dog loved to play no matter the time of day. I looked over at my parents, and saw that they were both still asleep as I waved the the tail end of blanket before a playful Rollo. Samantha lay in between my mother and father sleeping peacefully. I rarely heard my sister cry—never heard her voice ever. That's what I was thinking about as I noticed a figure standing outside of our motel room, which was on the first floor. The bed faced the window, and my cot was at the foot of the bed. Ignoring the silhouette outside our window and got up to use the bathroom, grabbing my puppy and carrying him with me in the process. It was while I was in the bathroom peeing that I heard a loud crashing sound and then a huge "whoosh" sound. I heard my mother scream as the room began to glow a bright orange. My father yelled aloud for me, but I quickly huddled inside of the tub, struck with fear as I began to smell the smoke and feel the heat of the fire that was spreading through our room.

I heard my father yell to my mother to grab Samantha.

"Wrap this blanket around you and the baby and run out the door!" he yelled as the fire blazed on. "Benjamin! Come on, son!" my father yelled towards me.

I jumped from the tub, inadvertently leaving my puppy behind, and ran into the bedroom just as my father swung the door open and motioned for me and my mother to run out the room. As we ran into the cold night air, I remembered I had left my puppy and I told my father so. While my father rushed in to retrieve my dog, I saw this man approach my mother as she stood in the parking lot facing the motel, holding onto Samantha, who was now crying. I stared up at my sister, listening to her wails and I remember thinking how loud she cried that night. I looked up at the man as he moved closer to my mother, who had her back facing the man. I thought he was coming to help, but that thought quickly vanished when the man turned my mother around and began beating her in the face with an object he held in his hands.

My mother screamed aloud as she fell to one knee, desperately trying to hold onto my sister. The baby wailed as the man slammed what I realized was a gun, into my mother's face over and over again. I ran back towards the burning room just as my father emerged with a small bag which held my puppy. My hysterical crying and frantic pointing alerted my father to the man fiercely beating my mother in the motel's parking lot.

"*Manhattan!*" my father yelled as he ran towards the man and dove on top of him, knocking him off my mother.

Screaming aloud as blood poured down her face, my mother now lay flat on her back with my sister on top of her body crying to the top of her lungs. As my father and the man fought, I ran to my mother and sat the bag containing my puppy beside me. My mother looked at me with a bloody, battered face and yelled for me to go get help. I didn't want to leave my mother, but she pleaded with me.

"Ben, go to the office," she said as blood ran down her temples and a portion of her bruised face. "Tell them to call the police! Take your sister and run. baby! *Run!*" she yelled aloud just as a gunshot crackled into the still, cold night's air.

We both looked up in and watched in horror. I saw my father sink slowly to the ground in front this man who was attacking us.

"*Sam! God no! Sam!*" my mother screamed as she lay on her back.

My father didn't respond, and as he lay on his stomach motionless. The man stood over him and shot him two more times in the back. I saw the back of my father's shirt rip open from the gunshots and I screamed in a high-pitched voice, calling out to my daddy.

My mother tried to hand me Samantha again, but I was just too afraid after seeing my father get shot. I scurried underneath a nearby car trembling uncontrollably with a face full of tears as the man approached my mother. I now could see him standing over my mother with the gun in his hand as she repeatedly begged for her life. The man ignored her pleas as he looked inside the small bag. I watched from underneath the car as a furiously barking Rollo was lifted into the air thrown into the inferno that was once our motel room.

My mother then let out a blood-curdling scream. "*No! No! Please, Manhattan! Manhattan, let Me go! Help!*" she screamed, as the man picked up my sister and then grabbed my mother's hand and pulled her up off the ground.

Manhattan was trying to pull my mother to his car, but she was putting up a serious struggle. My mother was dressed in only a brown teddy. She was bare foot and out in the cold with this beast who had murdered her husband and was now trying to kidnap her and my baby sister. She pulled away from the man just as I mustered up enough courage to crawl from underneath the car and go get help. As I started to run towards the office, I heard my mother scream aloud "*Benjamin! Oh, my God! Oh my God! He got our baby! He got Samantha!*

*Somebody help us! Help us!"*

My mother had broken free of the man and was running towards me, her eyes wide with fear, her face covered in blood, her body scratched and her nightgown dirtied and torn from fighting and lying on the cold concrete.

I now understand the fact that my mother was so afraid of this man that she had left her own daughter behind in an attempt to escape his wrath. I stood motionless as three more gunshots crackled in the cold night air. My mother then stood still for several seconds with her arms spread wide.

I watched through tears as my mother fell forward on her face just a few feet away from me. She lay motionless, her face flat to the ground as blood spurted from the back of her head. I crawled over to her and shook her body in an attempt to awaken her, but she wouldn't move. I sat crying over her body as this man approached me and pointed his weapon.

At that moment, I didn't care. I only awaited my fate. I knew my parents were dead, gunned down before my eyes and I wanted the nightmare to end. The man aimed his weapon at me as I looked him in the eyes. He squeezed the trigger but the gun didn't fire. I now know that the barrel was emptied when he unloaded three shots into my father, missed my mother twice and then landed a shot to the back of my mother's head. When the gun didn't fire, the man hurried off and I could now hear the faint sounds of sirens approaching. I watched as he ran back to his car and disappeared into the cold dark night with my baby sister crying in his lap.

I sat in between my mother and father's dead bodies as people came out of their rooms and were shocked to horror at the scene that was on display in front of their sleepy eyes: a young boy shocked to silence, unable to cry no more, having just witnessed the murder of his parents, whose lifeless corpses were sprawled out on the concrete in front of a burning motel room.

CHAPTER 40

THE AFTERMATH

The phone inside of Henrietta Jenkins' home rung at 2:45 on the morning of January 31, 1984. She slowly stirred from her sleep and answered the phone in an aggravated manner.

"Hello! Who is this at this hour?"

"Is this Henrietta Jenkins?" a male voice inquired.

Henrietta's heart dropped and she began to have a sickening feeling in her stomach. She got up as she slowly confirmed who she was and went and peeked inside of Gabriella's old bedroom. She then remembered that Gabriella and Sam spent the night at the motel in Kenner, Louisiana.

"This is an officer calling on behalf of the Kenner Police Department. Ma'am, there's been an accident."

"Are you sure it was just an accident? Tell me truth mister." Henrietta said slowly as tears began filling her eyes.

Clutching the phone tightly, Henrietta walked slowly from Gabriella's bedroom through the darkness of her home as she pleaded with the police officer on the other end of the line to tell her what happened. It was obvious that he was reluctant to speak over the phone. He repeatedly stated how sorry he was to Henrietta.

"We have a patrol car on the way to pick you up, Miss

Jenkins." the man said somberly.

"Where's my sister?" Henrietta asked as she heard a sudden knock on her door that caused her to jump slightly. She peeped through the peep-hole and saw two uniformed officers and slowly opened her door as the officers took off their hats and bowed their heads. With a face full of tears, Henrietta began shaking her head from side to side as she sunk to her knees in the threshold.

"No, no. God, No! Jesus, please! My sister! Not my little sister. Sweet Jesus, please! *God, please, no!*" Henrietta cried as the officers helped her up from the threshold and sat her on the sofa and explained to her that Gabriella and Samson had been murdered and they were prepared to take her to the crime scene so she could identify the bodies.

Henrietta asked about her nephew and newborn niece, and the officers told her Ben was in protective custody and they knew nothing of a new born baby. Henrietta was in stunned silence as she rode towards the crime scene wearing only a trench coat, her night gown and slippers. She looked out the window into the cold night in a daze as she rode in the back seat of the patrol car. She kept blinking her eyes, trying to wake up, but she just couldn't. The whole ride, Henrietta believed she was having a nightmare.

*"I'm dreaming. I'm dreaming. God, let me be dreaming so I can wake up soon."* Henrietta kept saying to herself.

The reality of the situation, however, was made known to Henrietta when the squad car pulled up to the crime scene and the horror was put on display before her teary eyes: Gabriella and Sam's bodies were still on the ground, covered with white, blood-stained sheets, while fire fighters sprayed water onto the burning motel in which Gabriella and Sam once occupied.

Henrietta went into a rage when she saw her sister's body on the ground that morning. When the officers opened the back door, Henrietta leapt from the back of the patrol car and ran towards her sister screaming Gabriella's name as she crossed under the crime scene tape and ran towards her sister. The closer she got, the weaker Henrietta grew. Her run had slowed to a snail's pace when she was only feet from Gabriella. Henrietta covered the lower half of her face and screamed a deafening scream as she stared at the two blood-stained sheet-clad bodies. She removed her glasses and brushed her hair from her face and closed her coat and stared into the clear, star-lit sky praying to God Almighty that she was having a nightmare and would soon awaken.

Henrietta continuously prayed to God that she was dreaming, but when she looked upon the corpse before her, Henrietta could see Gabriella's lifeless hand protruding from beneath the cloth covering her body. She recognized Gabriella's wedding band and knew right then and there that it was, indeed, her beloved little sister who lay on the ground and she was not dreaming. Henrietta dropped to her knees, cried for a few minutes, regained her composure and then slowly pulled the sheet back, only to see Gabriella's swollen, bruised and blood-stained face.

Gabriella's eyes were half-way opened as she lay dead on the cold concrete. She had such a sad expression on her lifeless face. Henrietta sighed deeply at the ghastly sight of her little sister's corpse lying on the ground.

"Gabriella, my child, look what he did to you. I'm sorry. I'm so sorry little sister. I didn't protect you when you needed me most." she whispered through her tears as she rocked back and forth in the cold, blowing wind.

Henrietta then stared at Sam's lifeless corpse as she placed her trembling hands on either side of her head and grabbed her hair as she knelt between her dead sister and brother-in-law and stared at them both as the pain and realization set in: Gabriella and Sam were dead—the victims of a terrible, terrible homicide and they weren't coming back.

In a flash, some of the most happy and memorable times, memories anointed and solidified through love, came flooding back on Henrietta: Gabriella's first day of high school when she first met Sam, her singing in the talent shows with her girlfriends, the sisters' disagreements, Gabriella's laugh, the birth of Benjamin, Gabriella's wedding day, *Persia's*, it all came back on Henrietta and painfully stabbed her in the heart like a blunt dagger.

Henrietta, reliving unforgettable memories of her beloved sister when she was alive, animated and blissful, clutched her stomach and leaned forward and heaved as she stared at her sister's dead body as her tears dripped onto the asphalt. She bowed her head to the cold concrete and screamed a loud, heart-broken, pain-filled scream that brought nearly every official to tears. There wasn't a dry eye out there this morning as Henrietta wept for her little sister and her brother-in-law and suddenly went into a hysterical fit, pounding the concrete as the pain grew unbearable. After seeing the horrible image of her beloved little sister's bloodied corpse, and realizing that Gabriella was no more, Henrietta, with memories of her sister's life running through her mind, convulsed uncontrollably and passed out in the middle of the parking lot laying beside Gabriella, her hand draped across her deceased sister's heart.

Henrietta was taken to the hospital and treated for hyperventilation, but she returned to the crime scene later that day and reported baby Samantha missing again as she tried to console her nephew Ben who cried uncontrollably and nonstop. People marveled at Henrietta's strength; they wondered how she, or any other person for that matter, could even function under such heart-aching, troubling times.

The lost of Ben Holland's parents affected Henrietta and Ben in the worst of ways; it just wasn't real to either of them. For weeks, Henrietta, still in a sorrowful trance, kept expecting to see her little sister every time she came home from school, and she had to constantly remind herself that Gabriella was not going to return anymore. That awareness caused her to cry at times—lots of times and she did her very best to hide her pain from her nephew, who was being torn apart emotionally himself during this period of time in his life.

Ben knew his parents were gone, but he couldn't understand fully what was transpiring, nor could he imagine why someone would do what they did to his mother and father. Henrietta knew exactly who was behind her sister and brother-in-law's death and she told the detectives everything she knew about the man she felt was responsible for her sister's death, but just like the death of her father, authorities had no solid evidence.

Even if the authorities caught up with Manhattan, it would be of little solace to Henrietta because the grief-stricken woman had a hole in her heart so big, a freight train could have driven through it and not touch either side. She missed her little sister something terrible and the only thing she wanted in life was for Gabriella to be alive again. Words could never convey the pain Henrietta Jenkins suffered upon losing her only sister, whom she loved more than life itself.

Nine year-old Ben Holland could never bring himself to talk about what he saw that night. All the police had to go on was testimony from witnesses who arrived on the scene after most of the tragic events had already unfolded. The morning of the fire, fire officials, fearing the worse, began searching the room for baby Samantha. Two days into the search, fire officials found small pieces of bone fragments inside the room where Gabriella and Sam were once tenants. No tests were run, as officials assumed that the baby had perished in the fire. Henrietta took the news hard. Besides having to bury her sister and brother-in-law, she also had to deal with the lost of her newborn niece.

Sam and Gabriella's death stunned the Ninth Ward. People could not believe that such a sweet, fun-loving couple that had brought smiles to literally hundreds of people throughout their young life, could be murdered in such cold-blood. The entire community was all riled up over the loss of baby Samantha as well, whom they never got to see. In commemoration of the three lost family members, a large procession was held inside *Persia's* the day of the couple's funeral.

Henrietta went to her sister's funeral a depressed woman. She was glad Veronica wasn't alive to have to bear the pain of losing her daughter, granddaughter and son-in-law. She sat at the funeral on the front row beside Alfred, and Yvonne, as Charmaine was still in a coma. She clutched her nephew Ben as the two of them wept during the opened- casket funeral. Ben hadn't spoken a word since that night. He sat on the front row of the funeral staring at his parents' caskets as he made small circles with his fingertips in the empty chair beside him.

After the funeral and during the weeks there following, Ben cried everyday all day. He would sometimes awaken from his sleep crying hysterically. Henrietta knew it was because of what he had seen. She took Ben to counseling, but still, he would never talk about what he saw; he was trying to block those terrible images from his mind. Eventually, he would succeed.

A few weeks after the murders, Charmaine awakened from her coma. When she heard what happened to Sam and Gabriella, Charmaine went into a deep depression. She lay in her hospital bed in a trance, devastated over what had happened to her friends and their daughter. Charmaine believed in her heart that if she had never gone to Gabriella's house that night to retrieve the camera, her friend would still be alive. She faulted herself for her friends' deaths and could not forgive herself for the pain she'd caused many people. She also grieved heavily over baby Samantha, having lived only a few days.

Charmaine checked herself out of the hospital that very day and filled her prescription for a bottle of pain killers that very morning. As Alfred worked his used car lot, and while Henrietta was instructing her music class, trying to restart her life without her beloved little sister, Charmaine sat in her mother's home, inside her bedroom, writing a long letter. She then took the entire bottle of pain killers.

Charmaine's mother returned home from work that night and discovered her dead daughter lying on her bed with her eyes wide open. Her mother saw the letter next to her in which Charmaine told what happened the night she encountered Manhattan. She also confessed that she was the one who had told Janice that Gabriella was pregnant. When Manhattan accosted her in Gabriella's home and asked about the baby he sincerely believed was his, Charmaine, out of fear, failed to correct Manhattan and it was for that reason, she felt responsible for the death of Gabriella and Sam and took her own life.

A few months after Sam and Gabriella's murder, Clyde, torn apart by the loss of Gabriella and Sam, two people he'd viewed as his own children, suffered a stroke and *Persia's* had to close down for good. Clyde died a month later and Sam and Gabriella's vision for *Persia's* had come to an abrupt end.

Even though it had been a few months since their deaths, Sam and Gabriella's presence was still felt in the community. People would walk pass the boarded up night club and just stare at the building, sometimes with wet eyes as they sadly shook their heads. It was now late spring and very warm outside, but without Gabriella, Sam, Charmaine, and the rest of the cast at *Persia's* around, the Ninth Ward still seemed cold because it had lost much of its liveliness and innocence. Gabriella and Sam, to put it plainly, were sorely missed in this part of the city.

Alfred couldn't bear losing all his friends. He sold his car lot and moved to New York City and rekindled a relationship with his high school sweet heart, April. Yvonne pursued a career in music. She moved to L.A. at the end of 1984 and became a successful song writer. People were moved over the depth of the woman's songs. Little did they know, Yvonne had suffered great losses in her life and that help fuel the woman's deep, thought-provoking lyrics.

Henrietta and Ben stayed behind in New Orleans, trying to live a normal life after suffering so much tragedy. It was hard, however, and the lost of Samson and Gabriella Holland eventually destroyed their lives. It would take years for the emotional scars to even begin to heal; and without his mother and father around to guide him through childhood, Ben Holland's life would take a turn for the worst five years later and end in a dreadful manner in September of 1999—but having learned all there was to know about his family, however, Ben's life, in August of 2005, had now come full circle.

## CHAPTER 41

### A NEW BEGINNING

I sat up in my cell crying to myself after reliving that tragic night and finally realizing that for over twenty years I've lived with the suppressed memories of my parents' murder. The next day, I related the nightmarish scenario to Yiska. I told him everything, except what I now knew about my sister. The Native American sat and wept with me and he helped ease the pain of my parents' homicide by reminding me of my upcoming release and that I had more to live for now than ever.

Little did Yiska know how right he was—because as he sat and talked, even he didn't know what I now knew. I announced to Yiska that God was setting me free to complete a new journey that had been a long time coming.

"What are you referring to, Ben?" he asked me inquisitively.

"I have a new mission, Yiska," I responded whilst smiling through my tears. "I now know my reason for being set free. God is setting me free to finish this journey. Henrietta told me all those things and I was able to put it all together. For a long time—I was in the dark—now I know the whole truth and it's up to me to make things right with my family."

"Ben, what are you saying, son?" Yiska asked again.

"Yiska," I said as I wiped the tears from my eyes and

smiled brightly. "My sister is still alive. Samantha still alive. She's with the man who killed my parents. When I'm released, I know what I'm gone do—I'm gone find the man who murdered my parents and bring my sister home."

To be continued…

Made in the USA
Middletown, DE
07 April 2021